The Double Image

Other books by Helen MacInnes

NOVELS

The Venetian Affair

Decision at Delphi

North from Rome

Pray for a Brave Heart

I and My True Love

Neither Five nor Three

Rest and Be Thankful

Friends and Lovers

Horizon

While Still We Live

Assignment in Brittany

Above Suspicion

PLAY

Home Is the Hunter

Harcourt, Brace & World, Inc., New York

Helen MacInnes

The Double Image

To the men who don't get medals

The Double Image

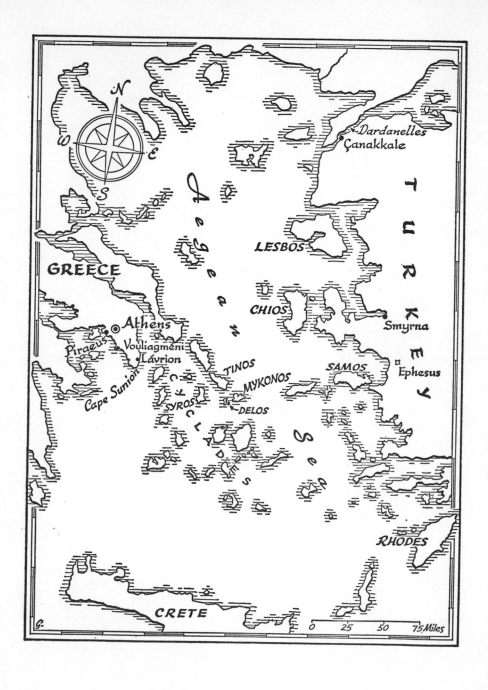

1

April in Paris, and a sprinkle of rain, a sudden whip of cool breeze, a graying sky to end the bright promise of the evening. John Craig decided that his saunter along the Boulevard Saint-Germain might come to a quick end any moment now, and began looking in earnest for a place of retreat.

He stretched his spine, bringing his height up to six feet, to let him look over the heads of the crowd and search for the café he wanted. His face, rugged in its features, was normally pleasant in expression, as if he were trying to soften the starker effect of a strong jaw and firm mouth. His eyes, under well-marked brows, were gray and alert; his neatly cut hair was dark and thick. He carried himself well, shoulders straight, waistline taut. He had the easy stride of an athlete; and yet, here again, he underplayed the effect by avoiding any flamboyance or overconfidence in his movements. An amiable young man, strangers thought when they met him, rather quiet on the whole. Later, they might change that opinion: he underplayed his real interests, too, as if he thought intellectual display was just another form of boasting, unnecessary if you were any good, embarrassing if you weren't. At this moment, the expression on his face was one of minor irritation. Damned fool, he told himself, to leave his raincoat back at the hotel.

The cafés were numerous along this stretch of the boulevard, some big and brassy, others dim and dreary, most of them with rows of little outside tables nudging the traffic on the broad sidewalk into a narrow stream. People hurried, either because of the time of day (half past five, a home to reach, friends to meet) or because of the threat of a soaking. Only one man, walking slowly toward Craig, seemed totally purposeless. He came to a halt, oblivious of the people behind, of their jostling and open annoyance as they maneuvered around him. Craig, his own path blocked by the bottleneck, drew aside to the curb and let three pretty girls regain their flouncing formation, then a stout woman pass with a bulging shopping bag and a bouquet of celery, then an old muttering man, then two young bearded men who had seized the chance to squeeze by, then—hey, enough of that! Craig stopped being polite and pushed on, glancing reprovingly at the day-dreamer who had started it all. Dreamer? No. The man's face was pale, worried, frightened. His fine dark eyes, deep set, stared unseeingly at Craig. And at that instant, Craig recognized the high broad brow, the long narrowing face, the prominent nose and vanishing hairline. "Why," he said in complete astonishment, "it's Professor Sussman—" and broke off, embarrassed. Sussman, at the sound of his name, at the friendly voice, had left his own world of dark thought. His eyes stopped staring blindly; now they were alive again, but puzzled, half-recognition dawning.

Craig wished he had just walked on and left the eminent Professor of Art and Archaeology formulating some new idea about Etruscan tombs right on a busy Paris street. "I took one of your courses at Columbia," he said awkwardly, "just the year before you left for Berkeley." He made a quick grab for Sussman's arm as the man's small thin body was shouldered aside, almost off the sidewalk.

Sussman was smiling, the old warmth back in his eyes. "I remember, I remember. Carr, isn't it?"

"Craig. John Craig."

Sussman's quick, rushing voice said impatiently, "Carr or Craig, I am still sorry I did not convince you to become an archaeologist. You had the proper questioning mind. Modern history, weren't you? See, I do remember!" His hand was tight, his voice suddenly intense.

Craig's embarrassment deepened. There was too much emotion here for his taste. He tried, politely, to disengage his hand from Sussman's grip. A strange city, taken at its most blaring and bustling hour, might bewilder an elderly scholar, but surely not to this point of despair. "There's the second rain warning. I think I'd better—"

"Have a drink with me. You have time?" Again there was that pleading urgency in Sussman's voice.

Craig nodded. He is the drowning man and I am the life belt, he thought. "If you don't mind retracing your steps, we might just manage to reach the Deux Magots before the rain really sets in. Actually, I was heading there when I—"

Professor Sussman looked back along the boulevard, shook his head. "Too busy, too noisy. I know of another place."

You do? wondered Craig. So you aren't lost in Paris? But he said nothing, found he was retracing *his* steps with Professor Sussman's arm guiding his elbow.

"Around the corner," Sussman directed. "I used to come here when I lived in Paris. That was in the days of my exile. Just before the war. In fact, it was the favorite café of the young intellectuals in the thirties." He stopped in surprise, perhaps even in dismay, as they saw a narrow faded awning stretched over two miserable rows of small zinc tables. The tables were empty except for one couple, a young bearded man and a girl in a belted coat, sitting in gloomy silence. "Oh, well," said Professor Sussman philosophically, "everything changes, nothing stays the same. Shall we sit outside, until the rain drives us in?"

That shouldn't be long, Craig thought wryly: the narrow awning over the sidewalk of this dingy little side street wouldn't give much protection. Sussman, anyway, seemed improved in spirits; he was almost back to normal, a little lost in thought, but with no more blank fear staring nakedly out of his face. He had chosen a chair that let him watch the boulevard some fifty feet away, which left Craig with a view of the narrow street curving down toward some thin bare trees faintly touched with green. Its buildings were old and grimy with city air, too unimportant to be scrubbed and polished like the grand monuments of the New Paris. Across the street was a small night club which might be interesting six hours from now, a dingy printing shop, a battered-looking school resting from its labors. But there was also a clear view of the girl who sat five tables away, and even if she was sad and her lips drooping and her large eyes only aware of the knucklehead opposite her—what else could you call a man who'd make a girl like that look so unhappy and, judging by the angry tilt of his jaw, meant to keep her that way?—she was still a very pleasant view indeed.

Craig settled back in his chair, ordered Scotch, was surprised to hear Professor Sussman echo that. (Strange how you could attend a year of a man's lectures, admire his books, stand in awe of his international reputation as a scholar, be amused by his mannerisms, be delighted by his praise and stimulated by his ideas, and still not know one real thing about his personal tastes or his private life.) Craig lit a cigarette, listened to the soft fall of rain on the awning above him, studied the view. She was talking, now, in a voice too low to be identified. Was she French? English? There was no doubt about her companion: he had just raised his voice sharply, "For Christ's sake—" The rest of the sentence was lost as he dropped his voice again.

Craig shook his head, half-smiled, looked at Professor Sussman for an acid comment. But the professor had been watching his own view —the corner of the boulevard, less busy now with people although the cars and buses still charged along its broad length like a herd of elephants stampeding from a forest fire. Strain had come back into Sussman's face, but he was in control of his emotions. "No, don't look round," he warned quickly, as Craig shifted his chair a little to let him see the boulevard, too. "He has gone," Sussman said softly. "He didn't see us." He was speaking almost to himself.

"Are you being followed?" Craig was incredulous enough to be blunt.

"I don't know. Perhaps. It could be likely."

"But why—"

"No matter now. He didn't see us. Let's talk about something more civilized. What are you doing in Paris? Are you working here, or visiting?"

"I'm on my way to the Mediterranean—Italy and Greece. Perhaps to Turkey, if the money holds out. I'd like to see Troy."

"So! Perhaps I converted you a little?" Sussman was pleased. "Let me see—it is five years since you were coming to my lectures—the First World War, that was your field. Or have I forgotten?"

No, the professor was completely right. But he can't be interested in me, Craig thought; he is really only trying to forget something else. All right, let's take it from there. This may not be the way I planned to spend my first evening in Paris, but it seems I'm stuck with it, and I might as well make the most of it. What would Sussman think of my idea for a book?

Sussman was remembering hard. "Yes, that was it! Blockade as a weapon of war. Did you finish your thesis on that?"

Craig nodded. He smiled at himself a little. "Never could find a more appealing title."

"We leave that to the historical novelists. And now you are traveling, and you will write a book?"

"If all goes well." He felt pleased, flattered. Old Sussman really did remember him and some of his little ambitions.

"On more blockades? No, no—I am not laughing. It is an important subject. Anything that can help to decide the outcome of any war is something to be treated most seriously." Sussman was speaking rapidly, with real interest, his own problem seemingly forgotten.

"I'm thinking not so much about the endings of war, now, as its beginnings. I've been doing some work on trade routes as motives for war."

"Beginning with the Trojan War?" Sussman was even smiling broadly. "So you did believe some of my theories—"

"Couldn't forget them," Craig admitted with a grin. He hadn't accepted all of them, but Sussman had certainly opened the doors of history wide.

"Then ancient historians have some use, even to young economists? And where will you end your book? Trade routes and colonies and coaling stations have had their eras. Of course, you might say that today the new control points for the extension of power are newspapers, radio, televis— Something wrong?"

"Nothing." Craig hoped his voice was nonchalant enough. Better, he decided quickly, to appear inattentive and stupid than have Sussman turn his head to look down the little street. "Just watching the rain, and wondering if it will clear before I have to leave." Just watching the rain and the narrow curve of street, and the man who had come walking slowly into view, then stopped, looking at the café, and stepped back into a doorway. "If I can't get a taxi over to the Tuileries, is there any short cut I could take? You know Paris well, don't you? This little street—where does it lead?" His suspicion was idiotic, he told himself, but he waited anxiously for the answer to his apparently innocent question.

"Back to the Boulevard Saint-Germain. It wanders around like so many little Paris streets." Sussman shook his head, looking at Craig's flannel suit. "Americans always think Europe in spring means sunshine and warm evenings." He himself was wearing heavy tweeds under his raincoat, even rubbers over his shoes.

"How long did you live in Paris?" The man in the doorway was lighting a cigarette. And what was abnormal about that, or even the fact that he waited in a doorway on a rain-soaked street? Craig tried to concentrate on his drink, to ignore the fact that the man could have been the same one who had worried Sussman. Idiotic, he told himself again.

"I left Germany in 1934. I went to Rome, then Athens. In 1936, I came here. I taught, and wrote my first articles, and married a French girl, and had two children. And then, in 1940—" Sussman threw up his hands. "Friends sheltered my wife and children, got them false names, false papers, saved them. There wasn't much that could be done to disguise me." He tapped his nose, smiling, but watching Craig closely. "I almost reached the Swiss border. I ended in Auschwitz. And that is why, my friend, I am in Europe. To bear witness. I have been in Frankfurt—"

"The trials?" Good God, no wonder Sussman had looked as if he had been visiting a mortuary. "That must have been a painful experience."

"It had to be done. I am one of the survivors of Auschwitz who could testify against a certain group of Nazis."

"And they pleaded they were only taking orders?" Craig asked in derision.

Sussman nodded. "Their plea was true. That is one of the grim aspects of that trial. Because the man who directed their operations, or at least the man who seemed to be in charge when I saw him at Auschwitz—" He paused, his eyes staring at the table. "That man is buried in the British sector of Berlin. I went there to see that grave." He closed his eyes. "His name was Heinrich Berg."

"Well, that's all over now. You've only to finish your visit to Paris and go back to California. How do you like Berkeley?" The man in the doorway was still there. Waiting for a friend? The rain had almost stopped.

Sussman's instant look of delight, almost child-like in its wonder, transformed his face. "We live on top of a hill. We have a view of the Bay, of the sunset over the Pacific. And in the garden—did you know you can have an orange fruit and blossom both on the same tree at the same time?"

Craig had to smile, too.

"And tulips bloom at the same time as roses!"

"I didn't know you were a gardener." And when did tulips usually bloom anyway?

"Oh, Marie is the gardener. I watch from my study, and give advice. I'm leaving Paris tomorrow. I'll be home by Friday."

Home . . . So the exile had found his refuge.

"I wouldn't have come to Paris, except Marie wanted me to visit her people, bring back a firsthand report. I shall have to invent a lot of nice things about them. I never liked them, and now they are more stupid and selfish than ever. It was fortunate I had the good sense to stay at a hotel. Families!" He shook his head over them. Then he noticed that Craig's interest had been slipping away. He gazed over his shoulder to look, too, at the table where the couple sat. "I don't think their talk has been so friendly as ours," he said. "Shaw was right: youth is much too good to be wasted on the young. And she is quite beauti—" He did not finish the word. His eyes dilated; he turned back to face Craig. From the doorway down the street, the man had stepped out and was walking toward the café.

"Shall we leave? Can I take you back to your hotel?" Craig suggested. The man was still some distance away, walking slowly.

"No. That would be an admission. . . . Besides, I must make sure I was not wrong when I saw him the first time."

"An admission of what?" Craig's concern grew as he noticed the return of fear in Sussman's eyes.

"That I have recognized him. If it is he. Perhaps it isn't." There was more self-encouragement than real hope in that phrase.

Or perhaps Sussman had been thinking too much about Auschwitz. "When did you first see this character?"

"On the Boulevard Saint-Germain. I was buying a paper. Suddenly, he stood beside me. He waited for me to look at him."

"*Waited?*" This is crazy, thought Craig. He looked at Sussman's long, intent face, uncomfortably, nervously.

"I don't think he saw my panic. I think—I hope I kept my face frozen. I walked away. And then, only a few minutes later, the shock really struck me." Sussman's voice was almost in a whisper now.

"But why?"

"Because I had just seen a dead man walking the streets of Paris."

The slow footsteps stopped. A chair scraped as the man sat down. He took off his hat, shook it free of raindrops, turned down the collar of his black coat. He was fairly tall, well fed and well exercised, somewhere around fifty, with a slight wave in his dark hair touched with gray at the temples and a calm, almost benign look on a remarkably handsome face. He ordered a vermouth cassis in quick and authentic French, and paid no attention at all either to the young couple or to Sussman and Craig. He could have been a lawyer or a diplomat or a business executive or—as things went nowadays—a leader of a large trade union. Successful and tactfully prosperous and, certainly at this moment, no threat to anyone. A man who had been caught in a heavy shower of rain, taken shelter, stopped at the nearest café for a drink just like a dozen other people—for there were others appearing in the little street, now that the rain had ended, and several were even heading toward the awning.

Craig relaxed. Everything was beginning to look more normal, even to the cheerful voices of two women who had just entered the café with two joking escorts, a bitter look following them through the doorway from the unhappy young man who was still arguing with his girl. Next came two more men, talking earnestly. Then a man with fair hair and a tightly belted trench coat, soaking wet. All these entered the café, too. "Things are looking up," Craig said. "I guess we got here too early."

Sussman was recovering. He even made an effort at normal conversation. "I've been thinking about your book," he said as if to excuse his silence. "It is a good subject, rich enough for five books. Perhaps you will do that? Now, I think I could help you a little. I still have friends in Italy and Greece who are working on archaeological sites. Some are historians, others are art experts. Would you like me to give you their names? I shall write them to let them know you may call on them."

"That would be very useful indeed. Thank you—"

"I thank you," Sussman said very softly. "Besides, scholarship is not much different from business or politics—the right connections are always necessary, and usually rewarding." He pulled out several letters from his jacket pocket, selected an envelope, took out a pencil and glasses. "Give me your address in Paris."

"Hotel Saint-Honoré. Rue de Castiglione." Craig watched his name and address being carefully written on the back of a business envelope.

"I shall think of the people who would be most interesting for you to meet," Sussman said as he put letters and pencil and glasses carefully back into their proper places, "and I shall mail you the list tomorrow, before I leave. When do you expect to be in Greece?"

"In a couple of weeks. I had the idea—"

"Excuse me," a voice said in French. "My watch seems to have stopped. I wonder if you could tell me the right time?" The man in the black coat was standing at Sussman's elbow.

It was Sussman, surprisingly, who recovered first. While Craig was still startled by the abrupt interruption, Sussman was taking out a heavy silver watch from an inside pocket. He studied it, looked up at the smiling, polite face looking down at him. "It is exactly twenty-two minutes past six."

"Thank you." The man was on his way, pulling down his hat as he began the short walk toward the boulevard.

"I didn't even notice him leave his table," Craig said, glancing toward it with amazement. In the doorway of the café, he saw the fair-haired man in the wet raincoat watching them. Or perhaps the man had been only gauging the weather, or expecting a friend, for he lit a cigarette as he moved back into the room. Sussman, his eyes on the Boulevard Saint-Germain, was quite silent.

"So it was the wrong man. You didn't know him."

Sussman said slowly, "On the contrary. That was Heinrich Berg."

"You are sure?"

"Quite sure."

"But it's twenty years since you saw him at Auschwitz."

"And thirty years since we were students at Munich University. And fifty-two years since we were born in the little town of Grünwald, not far from Munich. As young boys, we used to play together. Did you notice the twist on his left eyebrow—just a small thin scar, not too noticeable except when he is under tension? He got that from a piece of broken glass when we were climbing over a wall into an orchard. Oh yes, I was quite acceptable then: my father had won a medal in the First World War; my mother had plenty of food on the dinner table for my friends to eat. What astonishes you? That we lived so well? Or that Berg and I are the same age? Or that I remember the expression of his eyes when he was calculating how far he could push me? Clever blue eyes, giving nothing away, hiding his real thoughts,

11

looking so innocent. Yes, he has changed a lot. Once, he was very thin, very blond. But he has not changed in his eyes or in that little twist of the eyebrow where the hair never grew straight again. I know that man. The question is: did *he* learn that I know him?"

"You had me convinced that you didn't."

"Then I have to thank you again."

"For what?"

"For my recovery from shock." Sussman smiled in his relief. "Yes, I handled that quite well, I think. But it was typical. . . . The way he tried to force a recognition."

Craig felt a little uneasy. The incident had seemed insignificant, normal. He hadn't noticed any secret challenge in the stranger's face, or voice. "You are sure that he is Berg?"

"Positive."

"One of those who should be on trial?"

"Most definitely."

Craig, sensing the painful memories that the Frankfurt trials must have aroused in Sussman, said as tactfully as he knew how, "Couldn't it be possible that you might be—"

"Mistaken? No. He knew I was in Paris. He probably followed me from my hotel, chose the moment to confront me at the newspaper kiosk. He wasn't quite sure, he followed me again, and made me face him once more. You saw that part, at least."

"But how could he know you were in Paris or where—"

"It was no secret that I was coming to Paris," Sussman said angrily. "I was interviewed by a reporter in Frankfurt; I spoke of my plans quite naturally. Why not?"

Why not, indeed? "Well," said Craig slowly, uncertainly, "what are you going to do?" There might be a good deal of embarrassment for the professor if he couldn't bolster his assertions with some solid proof. Suspicions could become a neurosis, even a mania. They could destroy his work, all his career.

"I'm going back to my hotel and telephone the Embassy. If it is closed, I shall visit it tomorrow morning on my way to the airport. If I get no action there, I shall send a telegram to Frankfurt."

Craig was startled by all this unexpected efficiency. The old boy (not so old, if he was the same age as Berg—*if* that stranger had been Berg, *if* Berg were still alive and not six feet under Berlin soil) was not only aroused but determined.

"You are thinking it is all water under the bridge? That I am foolish to take action?"

"No, no. Not that, exactly. I just see you back at another trial in Frankfurt." Craig smiled to ease the small tension that had arisen between them.

"It would be worth it," Sussman said grimly. Then he smiled, too, rising to his feet, holding out his hand. "Water under the bridge flows on. There are other bridges, other people standing on them such as you and your generation, my friend. You think I should cling to the wreck of my bridge and not try to warn you of the hidden strength of that water?" He was shaking hands with great warmth. "Thank you again. Your moral support was all I needed, it seems."

"I'll walk part of the way with you. How far is your hotel?"

"Just a short block beyond the boulevard." He listened to the renewed patter of rain on the awning overhead, gestured to the splashing downpour on the street. "You stay here, I see."

"We'd better have another drink," Craig suggested. "It can't last long."

Sussman was buttoning his raincoat, pulling a small blue beret out from his pocket. "I'm prepared for it. Good luck, Craig. Write a fine book. Send me the proofs if you want an outside eye to read them." And he was off, stepping briskly up the street toward the bright boulevard.

As he stood watching Sussman's determined stride, Craig listened impatiently to the argument still coming from the bearded young man and his girl. Was this some new way of making love? Idiots, he thought, and turned away from the darkening street and the chill of the sidewalk to the warmly lit café. Another drink, even of that atrocious Scotch, would be welcome. He stepped quickly aside to avoid a collision with a man in a hurry—the fair-haired man in the damp raincoat, who was too busy looking up the street to notice Craig. Everyone's crazy except me, he thought in amusement, and I'm beginning to have some doubts about myself. For he was standing at the door, watching Sussman reach the boulevard, and behind him the man who had urgently remembered he had a train to catch. But the man's pace was more normal, now, and he started crossing the boulevard ahead of Sussman, who must have seen him and yet did not swerve or change direction. If Sussman paid no attention to this man, why should you? Craig asked himself: relax, fellow, relax.

He had his drink at the bar. The room was small, fairly clean, cosy enough, but sadly needing customers. It was just as well that Sussman hadn't come in here. The talk around the sparsely filled tables was uninspired, and even if French always gave an interesting flavor to the smallest remarks, they were still, when translated, just of the So-I-said-to-him and So-he-said-to-me variety. A large wooden Buddha was fixed up against one wall, smiling down at the tables through his coating of dust. Over the bar, above the bottles and new cheap chrome, hung a large yellowed lithograph of Socrates lifting his cup of hemlock in a farewell toast to his pupils. A little more of this cute irony, Craig thought, and it won't be this sickly tasting ice that makes me gag. He didn't finish his drink, but left in almost as great a hurry as the man in the wet raincoat.

The shower was tapering off. The awning dripped. Only the girl was sitting out there, now. She was sitting very still, hunched together, staring at the blackness of the night. How long has she been alone like this?

Craig hesitated under the awning's edge, glanced at her face. She was crying quite soundlessly. He looked away, but he didn't leave. His excuse could be that he was waiting for the last few splatters of rain to thin into nothing. But the silent crying troubled him. He hesitated, looked again. She seemed aware of nothing. She was trying to rise, stumbling against the corner of a chair. He caught her arm and steadied her. "Are you all right?"

She understood English, for she nodded. She drew her arm away, took a steadying breath, averted her face. The waiter, apologetic but insistent, called as he hurried out to them, "Mademoiselle, mademoiselle!"

Craig looked at the tab on her table, left under a saucer, completely forgotten in her man's Grand Exit. What does Sir Walter Raleigh do, he wondered now: pretend he has noticed nothing and stop embarrassing her? So Craig looked at the street, wet and shining, pulled up the collar of his jacket to protect his shirt from the last drops. She was fumbling with her purse. It dropped and scattered its contents. Sir Walter could at least bend his back and pick up the collection of small objects that bounced and rolled under the chairs. By the time she had paid the waiter, Craig had retrieved a compact, a lipstick, cigarette case and lighter.

"Anything else missing?"

First she shook her head, not looking at him. Then she said, in English, "Oh! My keys!" So he found them, too, after a little search. She was in control of herself by the time he had handed them over. She could face him for a moment, saying, "Thank you," before she stepped out into the street. Quite beautiful, Sussman had said, and the old boy had been right. Smooth black hair, pale fine skin, lips soft in color and in shape, dark eyes perhaps blue or gray. She drew the heavy collar of her sweater more closely around her neck, tightened the belt of her raincoat for warmth, shivered, and then started up toward the boulevard. Below the coat, her legs were slender, excellently shaped; her feet neat in high-heeled and very thin shoes.

He caught up with her near the corner. She hesitated there, as if the bright lights and the rush of traffic and the crowd of people, all purposeful, all knowing where they were going, had completely sapped the last remnants of decision. "If," he said as he stood beside her, "I'm lucky enough to get a cab, can I drop you somewhere?"

"No, thank you."

"If I'm lucky enough to get a cab, will you take it?"

She looked down at her purse, briefly, shook her head.

He remembered the bill she had given the waiter, not even bothering to wait for her change. Only a couple of francs, a few centimes left? As if to force the issue, he saw a taxi and signaled. Miraculously, it stopped.

"I'll give you a lift," he said firmly.

"No, thanks. I'll walk. Thank you." The quiet voice was less icy.

"On those wet streets, in these shoes? You're crazy." He held the door open. The driver looked round impatiently, firing off a staccato burst of short sharp syllables. "Get in," Craig told her. "I won't bite. I won't even bark." She stepped in.

"Now where?" he asked more gently. It would be just his luck if she lived out by the Champs-Elysées, or somewhere high on Montmartre. He would be late for Sue and George: a fine way for young brother to welcome them back from Moscow; a first meeting in almost four years and he wouldn't even have time to change his shirt and brush his hair. He glanced at his watch, but—he hoped—not too noticeably. "Where do I drop you?"

"Rue Bonaparte at the Quai Malaquais."

"That's no detour at all. Right on my way." And somehow, he was sorry about that.

She sat very still, head up, eyes front, her arms tightly folded as if to warm her body. He didn't press her for an exact address. He didn't ask her name, or where she lived in the United States. He kept his promise, and did not talk at all. He had a feeling she was very close to a second bout of tears. When he helped her out of the taxi, he only said, "I'd recommend two aspirin and a hot toddy."

She tried to smile, gave him her hand. "I hope I didn't make you late. I—" She turned away quickly, cutting her good-bye short. He watched her for a brief moment, and then got back into the cab.

Blue eyes. Of that, he was sure now. And a pity, a pity about everything. He hoped she'd have better luck with her next young man. Or perhaps tomorrow night she'd be sitting at another café table taking another emotional beating. Sussman, echoing Shaw, had been right: youth was far too good to be wasted on the young. Of course, Sussman probably included him among the oblivious; thirty-two would seem almost juvenile to Sussman. Good God, he thought suddenly, Sussman was just about my age when he was caught by the Gestapo. A cold finger touched his spine. If I had been he, would I have made as good a showing with my next twenty years? Some generations really got the sharp-toothed end of the stick.

He put these thoughts aside as they crossed the Seine. They were hardly good preparation for a family reunion. So he concentrated on the buildings rising around him, scrubbed back to the color they had been centuries ago. Calculated lights outlined their proportions, discovered their detail, added drama and grace to their solid strength. Trees along the winding river were covering bare arms with bright spring dresses. And above the rooftops, above the glow of a large city, high overhead in a clearing sky, there were the first stars shining into view. Paris in April. This was how it should be.

2

When a man was thirty minutes late for a party, he might as well take ten more and arrive in a clean shirt—especially when he was armed with a bottle of Piper-Heidsieck, 1955, to launch his apologies. The Farradays were at the Meurice, probably because that was the place most diplomats seemed to drift into. Fortunately, it was only a short distance from Craig's hotel, although a long way in price and style. But as his brother-in-law explained once the exuberant welcome eased off, he was celebrating hard, and Sue deserved a suite no less, and in any case it was only for one night, and even a press attaché who didn't rate this splendor could damned well dip into his own pocket for that length of time.

Craig had never heard so much rush of self-explanation from George. He was a lot thinner and looked more than his thirty-eight years. Sue, on the other hand, had put on some weight, cut her fair hair short and bushed it straight. Not pregnant, John Craig decided, glancing at her thickened hip line; just an excess of solid-silhouette food, and not enough exercise. That accounted also for the loss of color in her face. Her lipstick was much too dark and vivid, a remembrance of days past. It was the shadows under her eyes that really troubled him, along with the worry creases on her brow. But she was still as quick and sensitive as ever, still with her sense of humor. For she was laughing in the old way, pulling down the skirt of her dress from its wrinkles around the waist, guessing his thoughts correctly, saying, "George is the lucky one. When he worries, he loses weight. All I do is eat and eat. And sit brooding. Don't be so alarmed, John. I'll soon get rid of this." She smacked her waistline lightly, threw her arms wide. "I'm free, I'm free, I'm free! Oh, it's wonderful, wonderful. Wonderful to see you, wonderful to talk my head off, wonderful to go where I want when I want, wonderful—" She broke off, almost in tears. "John, you look exactly the same, and thank God for that." She gave him a very intense hug: he had always been her favorite brother.

Craig patted her shoulder, ruffled her hair, and looked over her head at George. "What was that you said about one night?" he asked, trying to get emotions calmed down. "I thought you were planning to be here for a week." And that's why I had planned two weeks in Paris, he thought ruefully: one week for family, one week to recover and see the town on my own.

"We're leaving tomorrow for Washington. Say, you got this champagne iced!"

"Four hours, courtesy of the barman at my hotel." And a nice-sized tip.

"Then it's just right for drinking. Sue, get some glasses—sure, these will do, over on the table."

Craig noticed that a little dining table, places for three, flowers, candles and all, had been set up near the window of the sitting room.

"We thought we'd have supper here, easier for talking, less waste of time," George said. "And we are having a few friends drop in here afterward. Just some men who have been stationed at one time or another in Moscow."

"They belong to the I-Was-There Club," Sue said cheerfully. She had quite recovered. She noticed the expression on her brother's face. "I'm sorry, John; we had to see them tonight—but you know how it is. There really is quite a bond between men who have lived through the same tensions—"

"A bond of curiosity," George said dryly. "They want to hear the latest inside gossip and informed guesses."

"Veterans of Foreign Peace?" Craig suggested.

"They'd never have forgiven us if we had slipped through Paris without seeing them," Sue went on. She had a habit of overexplaining out of sheer politeness.

"That doesn't surprise me," Craig assured her.

"But you look so astonished."

"Well, after all—one night in Paris!" And that really did amaze him. There must be some kind of emergency, he thought. "Why, you only got here a couple of hours ago."

"And we very nearly didn't," Sue burst out.

Craig stared.

George said quickly, "Now let's not exaggerate. We'd have got here eventually." He looked at the astounded Craig, gave a thin smile. "We were almost detained." His hand was steady as he poured the champagne and offered a glass to Craig.

Almost detained? Craig regained his breath. He raised the glass. "Then here's to your safe arrival!" He noticed that both drank to that without one smile. He tried to make a joke of it and lighten the heavy moment. "Don't tell me you were doing some cloak-and-daggering."

"Haven't the training, or the stamina. But that's the label Moscow wanted to pin on me."

"Don't you see," Sue said impatiently, "so many of their embassies are engaged in active espionage that every now and again they have to polish up their public image? So they tarnish ours."

"Now, Sue," Craig said, "we do have spies floating around. You know that."

"And that makes us just as bad as them? So there are no good ones and bad ones, and we are all equally to blame? Oh, John! Leave that kind of talk to the neutralists who want to justify their evasions!"

"Darling," George said quickly, "have some more champagne. We said we wouldn't talk about this, remember?"

"I think we'd better," Sue said determinedly, "or else we'll leave John thinking his sister is filled with prejudices instead of experiences. Dear John, I'm still me—just a lot older, a little wiser and much sadder. Come on, choose a Louis Fifteenth chair, and listen to George before you start judging me." She sat down, tried to relax, act normally. "George was arrested four days ago," she said.

"What?" Craig almost spilled his champagne over the blue-and-gold rug. He sat down, carefully, on a yellow satin sofa, placed his glass safely on a smoked-glass table top, lit a cigarette. "Ready and waiting," he said.

George Farraday chose to pace slowly around the room as he talked. He, too, had abandoned his glass for a cigarette. He tried to keep his voice light, as if to play down his memories. "Oh, it wasn't much. I was released in five hours. And I have to thank Sue for that."

"Wasn't much!" That was Sue, indignant. "Why, they hadn't even notified the Embassy that they had picked you up."

"That couldn't have been very pleasant," Craig said.

"No," Farraday admitted. "I kept thinking of Barghoorn, the Yale professor who got arrested last November. Not one of us knew about it for a couple of weeks. He wasn't guilty of a damned thing, either. That's one thing you've got to remember, John. When we detain a Russian or satellite citizen in the United States, we have an honest case against him. We have real evidence. The Russians invent evidence. So that is a big difference between them and us. Apart from all that good-ones and bad-ones talk, and God knows there are plenty of both groups in every country, there are some very big differences indeed between us and them." He looked at his brother-in-law, waiting.

There was no argument in Craig's eyes, simply curiosity.

"All right," Farraday went on, "then I can tell you what happened." He stopped at the mantelpiece to drain his glass and set it back on the marble top. "I had been having lunch with one of our visiting newsmen. I left him, and got onto a bus to get home. The bus was crowded. I was standing halfway down the aisle. A woman who had followed me onto the bus was standing beside me. Suddenly she whispered, in English, 'Mail this to my daughter in America for me. Please!' And she shoved an envelope into my hand. Now my arm was down by my side, just like this, and as she looked away I opened my hand and let the letter drop on the floor. No one noticed that. It was lost under the feet as I pushed toward the door, anywhere to get away from that letter. Almost at once, the bus stopped. And strange, strange—a black car was waiting just ahead of it. Two men got onto the bus, knew me at once, hustled me off. I made a bit of a protest. No one moved, no one did anything. The men strong-armed me into the car. I was taken to headquarters and charged with receiving secret information from one of my 'agents' who had already confessed. They were annoyed a little—" George paused to savor his understatement —"when they didn't find the envelope in any of my pockets. However, they found it in the bus, and then charged I had got rid of the 'evidence' when I saw I was about to be arrested. It could have been nasty. I kept demanding to get in touch with our Embassy but no one seemed to listen."

"Could they do that?" Craig was horrified.

"As long as the Embassy wasn't asking about me, they weren't worrying about protocol."

"Then how—"

"Sue. Your sister has brains; did you ever appreciate that?" George was smiling broadly, now, ready to tell the more pleasant part of his story. "She had been wary for the last few weeks, expected something to happen to someone at the Embassy—"

"I was only remembering their usual tit-for-tat diplomacy," Sue broke in, disclaiming any sixth sense. "After all, we had recently arrested some spies of theirs, and they would be looking for someone to hold as a future exchange if he hadn't diplomatic immunity—"

"But George *has* that," Craig interrupted.

"Let me finish, my bright young brother! Someone as an exchange if he hadn't diplomatic immunity, *or* someone with diplomatic immunity whom they could boot out of the country in disgrace. Get it now?"

"I get it. And were you booted out?"

Farraday said, "I just scraped through, there: no envelope on me, and the Embassy taking a very firm line. If you act fast enough, you can assert your rights."

"Well, congratulations to the Embassy!"

"The minute Sue told them I must be in trouble, they moved."

Sue? Craig looked at her in amazement. Old scatterbrained, happy-go-lucky, pink-bespectacled Sue?

"As I said, she had been expecting something. She had talked me into promising to telephone her every hour on the hour, no matter where I was. And a damned fool I felt keeping that promise. So, when three o'clock came that afternoon and no phone call, she got in touch with the Embassy, told them where I had lunched and with whom, told them she'd give me until four o'clock and if no call came from me by that time, she was pressing every panic button in sight. However, they took charge. We didn't even make the newspapers, thank God."

"She certainly deserves a suite at the Meurice," Craig conceded. He rose and went over to Sue, and kissed the tip of her nose. "That's for you, bright eyes. You can dine out for six months on that story."

"No, no. I keep my little lips tightly buttoned, even in Washington. There's always some goony bird who'll believe that if George was arrested, there must be a real reason and it's possible he was a spy; dear me, the Russians would never behave that way if he were not, now would they?"

"Let's finish the champagne," George said. "There will be more arriving with dinner any minute now."

"Cue to drop all interest in your story? But as family, George, and I hope not as a goony bird"—Craig shook his head over his sister's slang, as out-of-date as her lipstick—"why did the NKVD choose you? Or is it now the MVD? Or KGV? Never could keep those initials straight."

"Smart to change them," Sue said with one of her old light laughs. "Rouses hope way back in our minds that the secret police changes its nature along with its name. But security remains security, whether it's KGV or any other title. And one thing that's maintained is 'No ideological coexistence.' That's why they didn't like George."

George said briefly, "I just kept trying to persuade them to let a free flow of newspapers and magazines come in from the West. We can buy their newspapers in Times Square; why not our newspapers on sale in Moscow?"

"And they won't allow it?"

George shook his head. "Some of our representatives at that cultural-exchange meeting in Moscow, last January, pressed this point. All they got was a bang on the table and an angry 'There is no ideological coexistence possible!' I've had the same treatment twice. Really ends all conversation. As one of my British chums said, 'If that's final, what price peaceful coexistence?' Which, of course, is the sixty-four-dollar question." He fell silent, frowning. Then he forced a pretty good smile. "Where's that dinner, blast it? I'm hungry. What did you order, Sue?"

"What you used to like: oysters, *langoustes* and some Sancerre nicely chilled, *tournedos* with insertions of *pâté Strasbourg* and a Nuits-Saint-Georges, asparagus with drawn butter, followed by a little Brie just properly flowing, and brandied cherries straight from the flames."

"We'll be eating hamburger for the next three weeks." But his warning was decorated with a large and happy smile.

"We're celebrating," she said firmly, and laughed. She got up, and danced around the room. "Wonderful, wonderful night!" The waiter, whose well-trained knock had been lost in Sue's improvised singing, recovered his well-trained face after the initial shock of entry. Dinner was served.

And now there were only the pleasant things to be discussed: the comic things that had happened in Moscow, the kindly people, the family at home (Father Craig still being sought for advice by the old patients in his little town in Ohio; a country doctor never could retire, it seemed), and all the nephews and nieces scattered around the country (three brand new since Sue had last seen her four other brothers). Then there were John's plans to be talked over. Sue was relieved, tactfully, that her youngest brother had at last made up his mind what he wanted to do with his life. George was still enough of an old newspaperman to have some practical reservations.

"I suppose," he said, "this book will be read by five hundred people instead of five hundred thousand? In a way, that's a pity. You can write, John."

Sue said, "But they will be the most important five hundred."

"I guess so," George conceded. It had been an excellent dinner. "In fact, he'll probably end up in Washington as one of those whiz-bang economic historians telling all the rest of us what to do."

John Craig was amused, shook his head. There were some plans you couldn't formulate, not at this early stage of the game. It took a long time to build up any reputation, any standing in his world. He thought of Professor Sussman. There had been some pretty hideous and violent interruptions in Sussman's life, of course, but he was now becoming a "world authority" in his field. A heady phrase, world authority . . .

"A nice racket, anyway. You can choose where you want to travel," George said amiably. "Before you start writing a book, you say, 'Now let's see: what places do I want to visit?' And then you get hold of a map, and start planning your chapters. Back in my young days, there weren't so many foundations willing to give traveling fellowships for a tour through the Greek Islands. It's the splurge in culture."

"High time there was an explosion in that, too," Sue said. She was watching John. He had always had too many interests, spread his talents too widely, but now he was concentrating. She hoped it wasn't too narrowly. She remembered the slight family panic, some ten years ago, when a talent scout had offered John a test in Hollywood. "And to think you might have become one of those television stars with a long, lean look and a quizzical expression in your quiet gray eyes," she murmured. She studied him with approval. "You haven't altered, did I tell you? How nice that some people don't change much! Reassuring, somehow. But what are you thinking about, John?" It certainly wasn't about college dramatics, or weekend skiing parties, or all the girls he hadn't married.

"Actually, I was thinking of a professor I met today; bumped into him on the Boulevard Saint-Germain." He noticed the solemn polite silence settling on both their faces, and decided to startle them out of their incipient boredom. "He was on his way home to Berkeley from the Frankfurt trials. He had been giving evidence on Auschwitz. A strange mixed-up world, isn't it? He is an archaeologist."

"A cruel mixed-up world," Sue said softly. "That must have been a frightful experience, remembering all those hideous details."

"I'd like to have met him," George said, definitely interested. "A pity we aren't staying longer. What's his name?"

"Sussman. He's leaving tomorrow anyway. You might meet him on the plane. His flight leaves at noon."

"Must be hitchhiking, courtesy of army or air force," George decided. "We leave by regular flight in the evening. What was his impression of the trials? The Germans really do mean business?"

"He didn't talk so much about the trials—"

"Is archaeology as engrossing as all that?" George asked, astounded. "My God, those scholars—"

"He had his worries. He was sure he had just seen one of the important Nazis walking free on the streets of Paris."

"Well, that could be. There are several quiet ones who escaped in the general collapse."

"But this one is dead. At least, he has a grave, tombstone and all, in Berlin."

"Dead, and alive? Are you sure Professor Sussman hadn't been under too much strain?"

Craig didn't answer.

"That can happen, you know. When I got off the plane today I kept looking at every face, wondering who was friend or foe. Nerve ends rubbed just a little bit too raw. That's all."

Sue said, "If your professor really did see a war criminal, he'd better report it. Don't you think?"

"He was going to telephone the Embassy here."

"Poor old Embassy," George said. "It gets every traveling citizen's troubles."

"But where else can a citizen go? When we're up against something unexpected, what can we do? We don't know the proper channels."

George admitted that, with pursed lips and a shrug of his shoulders. "Oh, well, anyway, I think he'd have done better to get in touch with Frankfurt."

"He will do that if necessary."

"He really believes his story?"

"He's completely convinced."

"And you?"

Craig was saved by the ring of a telephone from the embarrassment of openly admitting his doubts. He had believed, and then he had retreated from that belief. All those details about being followed, tracked down from Frankfurt . . . Sussman had only been guessing; how could he have known? Yes, it had been the details that had stopped Craig believing. And yet, and yet . . . Why else would he have mentioned Sussman at all to George and Sue if he didn't deep down, somewhere inside his mind, believe part of the story?

George said from the telephone, "They are on their way. Let's get rid of that table, Sue. And where's the coffee? Perhaps we should order brandy, too."

"Scotch," Sue corrected. "They don't sip. They drink. Who's arriving first?"

"Bob and Ed. Val is on their heels, they say."

Sue, amid the flurry of waiters and table removal, of coffee tray brought in, of orders for extra ice and soda, briefed her brother. Bob Bradley was now with NATO; he had been with the State Department, for a short time; stationed in Moscow when they first arrived there. Ed Wilshot was a newsman, who also had been in Moscow then. Val Sutherland was another reporter, who had taken Wilshot's place after he had been asked to leave, and was now in transit to another post. Then there would be Tom O'Malley, an Australian journalist; and Joe Antonini, who had been one of the experts in tracking down all the hidden microphones that had recently been discovered in the U.S. Embassy in Moscow.

It was, thought John Craig, going to be a merry, merry evening for everyone except him. He had that stranger-at-the-reunion feeling even now as Farraday greeted the first arrivals. The Old Boys' Club, most definitely. Sue seemed to know what he was thinking. "You won't be the only one who hasn't been to Moscow," she told him gently. "Frank Rosenfeld is going to drop in. He's a businessman—refrigeration—used to be in charge of his firm's office in Saigon when George was a reporter there. Goodness, that's over ten years ago, when Viet Nam was still Indochina! Then Rosie was moved to the head office in Paris, and George was transferred to the Embassy here, so they got together again. He's not really very bright about the things that matter—"

"Snob," he told her.

"I mean, he's inclined to repeat this morning's editorial as his views on the world situation. But he's very sweet and helpful. About finding you an apartment, or a hotel at short notice. You know. . . ."

"He sounds as if he needed someone to be nice to him in this setup. Me?" He grinned widely, and pushed her off to welcome the rest of her guests. They were all here except the businessman. None of them looked as if they needed any help at all in feeling right at home. They were introduced to him, gave him a warm handshake and an appraising look, friendly enough; made a brief attempt at general remarks; and then grouped together talking their heads off. Once the questions they were firing at George Farraday were answered, or fended off (no mention, Craig noted, of the arrest), and the general talk of Moscow had simmered down, there might be some reasonable conversation.

Craig settled himself near the window, where Sue joined him tactfully. She wasn't much needed either, at this moment. She talked and he watched. It was interesting, in a way, to place character by voice, manner and face. It was dangerous, too, of course: the mildest-mannered man could turn out to be a roaring lion; the bellowing bull could be a braying donkey. And what do they think I am? he wondered with some amusement. A little frog puffed up in his own puddle of scholarship? Someone who was putting his brains and energies, such as they were, into tracking down facts that would never make tomorrow's headlines? And yet, the past was prologue.

The last guest arrived, and the tight group around the fireplace broke their close formation. He wasn't known to any of them, for

George was making careful introductions all around. He was a heavy-set, dark-haired man in a quiet dark gray suit, slightly formal in manner, almost solemn, although—as George made a few jokes—his grave politeness could ease into a beaming smile. They were talking as old friends do; no serious discussion about world-shaking problems there. The others drifted away, once the phrase ". . . sales conferences all week . . ." dropped like a dud bomb into the room's sudden silence. "Frank!" Sue called delightedly, and her sweet and helpful businessman started toward her with hands outstretched. His grip was strong, Craig noticed when his turn came to have his hand pumped. His smile divided his face into two camps: below, was a rounded jaw line, a full underlip, a chin with a marked cleft; above, was a sharp nose, clever brown eyes, a remarkable brow. He'd probably sell a lot of refrigerators, Craig decided. But what the hell do I talk to him about? The question was answered by Rosenfeld (after a warmly expressed welcome to Paris) wandering away toward Bradley and Antonini. Craig repressed a wry smile, caught Sue's worried eyes for a second, then looked around the blue-and-gold sitting room. There were more interesting prospects, tonight, than a slightly strayed scholar.

She went into action. "I'll get you another drink, John."

"No," he said quickly. "I'm all right." But his protest didn't stop her. He knew what would come next, and wished he was a couple of miles away, walking along the Boulevard Saint-Germain to have that drink at a crummy little bar. What was that girl with the blue eyes and smooth dark hair doing now?

Sue was saying, "Don't you men ever get tired standing around talking? It really is more comfortable to sit. We have plenty of chairs. George, help me." So the wide circle was formed, men sitting down around Craig in silence. Now what? he wondered. He thought he might try a question to start them off again; they were looking at him with polite expectancy. What about something wild like When will Stalin become an okay word again? Or, How many agents have the Russians infiltrated into NATO?

But Sue rushed on, most charmingly. "John was telling us about a very odd thing that happened to him today. He met one of his old professors who insisted that he had just seen a Nazi walking the streets of Paris. A supposedly *dead* Nazi—one who should have been on trial at Frankfurt!"

Oh no, thought Craig, not all that story to be told again to all those disbelieving faces!

"Did you get his name?" O'Malley, the tall Australian, asked. He had a thin face, a permanently tanned complexion which contrasted with his thick crown of white hair. He was the oldest man in this room; the others were in their thirties or forties, while he was at least around fifty. His manner was sharp, but his eyes were friendly.

"Berg," Craig said. "Heinrich Berg."

"What was his particular specialty?" Bradley, the representative from NATO, wanted to know in his calm quiet way. "Shoveling gassed corpses into ovens?"

"I have no idea."

"Your friend didn't tell you?" Bradley raised his eyebrows just a little. Everything he did would be just a little; he was much too well mannered to let emotion distort his handsome face. It wasn't just the neatly tailored tweed suit and the casual way it was worn that made Craig think Bradley was probably one of those intelligent civilians who had found a useful niche for their talents in NATO's vast organization. He had a diffident way, almost self-effacing, pleasantly modest, combined with the attentive eye of the natural diplomat. Even his indiscretions would be calculated.

"No, he didn't."

"But he can't go around pointing out someone on the streets of Paris, saying, 'There's a war criminal!' Now, can he?"

"No," Craig agreed with a smile.

Sue rushed in. "John, don't be so resistant. We're all interested. This professor—what's his name?"

"Sussman."

"He was a prisoner in Auschwitz, wasn't he? He had just been testifying at Frankfurt. So he could know what he was talking about, couldn't he?" She looked around the circle of polite faces.

"Perhaps. Perhaps not," O'Malley said slowly. "I covered some of the opening trials at Frankfurt last year. There were a lot of emotions aroused—horror, fear, bitterness, shame. And a lot of wild talk, including accusations."

"And denials," someone said.

"Fewer than you think," O'Malley asserted. "Give them credit for having the trials at all. That's more than the East Germans have done.

My God, when I think of the Nazis *they*'ve got as ministers of culture, agriculture, trade and supply. What about them, Val?"

"You're the expert on the Nazis," Sutherland said agreeably. "You tell me."

"Well, they've got Reichelet, and Merkel, and—" O'Malley stopped, noticing Sue's look of resignation. He turned back to Craig. "Look, Sussman's story is worth listening to. Where can I find him?"

"I don't know that, either. I just met him walking along the boulevard—"

"Accidentally?" Bradley asked. "I mean, you aren't an old friend of his?" Someone, his voice implied, you really know?

"Nothing like that. Haven't seen him since I took one of his classes at Columbia back in 1959. He's a remarkably sane and sensible man. Today, of course, he was upset. He was sure this Heinrich Berg—" He stopped. How could he explain Sussman's fears without making him seem ridiculous to a batch of strangers who had never known him? "Oh, well," he said, "I gave him a drink to cheer him up, and then he left. He's going back to Berkeley tomorrow."

"What does he teach?" This was Rosenfeld's only contribution to the conversation. But Craig was thankful for it.

"Art and archaeology."

That did it. Interest evaporated. Talk began about travel. O'Malley was trying to be sent to Rhodes; Sutherland was on his way to Viet Nam. (Rosenfeld didn't even bat an eyelash, far less talk about his experiences there, Craig noted, and George Farraday simply said, "I bet it isn't much changed since I was in Saigon. Rumor and suspicion and back-parlor plots. Just don't listen to too many Buddhists, Val. And make sure they really *are* Buddhists before you listen.") The morose Ed Wilshot poured himself another drink and mumbled something about taking three weeks off the chain and heading south for some sunshine. Joe Antonini, the hidden-microphone expert, was tight-lipped about his next assignment and turned that question neatly aside by saying to Bradley, "Hey, Bob, let me finish that story I was telling you. The day before I was leaving Moscow, I was hit by a car. Fortunately, I jumped in time. Just a scrape on my leg and a bruise on my shoulder. They took me to the hospital, very efficient, very polite, wanted to make sure there were no serious injuries. But once I was over the first shock, I felt fine. And I started using my head again. So I balked at the hospital door, made my good-byes, and struggled free from their help. It was like one of those old Keystone comedies—everyone gesticulating wildly, no one listening to anyone else. I ran for twenty yards, then turned and yelled, 'See, I'm all right! I just proved it. Thank you and good-bye.' "

"They slipped up there," Bradley said with a laugh.

"In more ways than one. If they wanted to inject truth serum into someone, and find out how many hidden microphones we had put out of commission, then I was the wrong man. I was only a very junior member of our team."

"I thought the number was published," O'Malley said. "Well over a hundred, weren't there? Or was that a careful underestimation?"

Craig was startled by the calm way they were talking about matters that would have roused loud headlines only a few years ago. He was still more startled when the full meaning of O'Malley's remark hit him. Was Soviet interest not so much in the number of microphones discovered in the Embassy's walls and ceilings, but in the few that had been discovered and left in position? Or in any which possibly had not yet been found? The difference between the answers to those two important questions would be vital for the assessment of any information gathered by the Soviet monitors.

"You look shocked," Bradley murmured. "Or is it difficult to swallow our little stories?"

It wasn't shock so much as surprise over Antonini's cool detachment. There he was now, telling of a light bulb discovered in a lady's bedroom that had transmitted everything from a sigh to a rustled nightgown, as if he had forgotten the threat of a forced stay in a Moscow hospital.

"Sue," Bradley went on, "I don't think your brother approves of our talk."

"Your brother," Craig assured her worried face, "hasn't a thought left in his head except that of bed, and sleep. It has been a long day." At least he had concealed his annoyance. Damn Bradley's eyes, did he think historians only studied the soft, sweet side of history? We don't shock so easily, he thought as he smiled all around and began shaking hands.

Bradley said, "Time for me, too. Can I give you a lift? You won't find a taxi at this hour."

"Oh, I'm close by, practically within running distance."

"Where are you staying?"

"The Saint-Honoré."

"I'll get in touch. We could have dinner some evening when I get into town. By the way, would you like me to take any steps about Professor Sussman's problem? I know some people in Frankfurt."

"That might do no harm."

"But not much good?"

Craig shrugged his shoulders. If he were Bradley, he'd take the necessary steps and risk looking foolish if Berg's body was found in Berg's grave. But that was for Bradley to decide.

"The trials always stir up a lot of ghosts from the past," Bradley said. "If I were Sussman, I suppose I'd suffer from delusions, too." So Bradley had decided. And he ought to know about such things, Craig thought as he hid his disappointment and made for the door. Sue and George were there. He found himself promising to come to breakfast next morning—they both had a very full day ahead of them before they left for New York. Breakfast, even with one eye open, was the only hour left for a family farewell.

"And," Sue added to her hug and kiss, "heaven knows when we'll see you again. We may be en route to Burma or Greenland by the time you get back to New York."

So breakfast it would be, promptly at nine. And after that, he thought more cheerfully, I'll be free; free to do what I want to do, to go where I want to go, and all in my own sweet time. Rosenfeld, standing behind him to make his own good-bye, was saying that it had been a wonderful party, a wonderful evening. A nice, simple-minded soul, Craig decided, and possibly a successful businessman, too.

Out in the cool, quiet street, there was only the sound of his footsteps ringing out rather more briskly than he actually felt. His sense of depression wouldn't leave him. He blamed it on the wasted evening. What else did you call a party where the men he had met would soon forget his face, even his name? Sue Farraday's young brother; that would be the fading memory, dimly recalled if he ever saw any of them again.

But he was wrong: in two places far removed from the Meurice, he was under serious discussion in Paris that night. One was a studio, high over a garage; the other, an unused dressing room behind the stage of a smart girl-show.

The garage was halfway down a most respectable street, part of an old building sandwiched between two new apartment houses. Soon the improvers would have their way; the old building would be torn down, replaced with a square block of unimaginative concrete and rows of mass-produced windows for decoration. It would be ten stories high to match its neighbors, and the last remnant of Toulouse-Lautrec in this district would be swept out with the plinth and plaster. Meanwhile, the garage was a useful place to have the car washed, a tire changed, a slow puncture repaired; something quiet and noiseless so as not to offend the status-conscious incomers.

Androuet, its owner, was an obliging fellow. He even sold gasoline by the can, the usual pumps being out of the question, and reserved some of his floor space, stretching far out behind the old building, for a few of his best customers. There they could park their cars overnight, or when they were away for weekends and didn't need them. There was even room for the light pickup truck which belonged to his only customer living in this building—the man who had rented the two old studios on the top floor for his antique furniture business. He was young, but he paid his rent regularly and didn't give any noisy parties to annoy the two old women, or the retired butcher and his wife, who rented the flats below him. Between them and the garage lay the overcrowded rooms of Androuet and his enormous family, and Androuet's only complaint about the top-floor tenant was that he had clients who would too often come blundering through the garage looking for the wooden stairway that led to the floors above. Others knew their way, didn't interrupt his work. And others, again, probably out-of-town dealers, stayed overnight. But without dealers and clients, there would be no regular rent: Androuet's complaints died away completely on the first day of each month.

He was waiting, now, one of the garage doors half open, for one of his customers to park his car. That would be the last tonight; he could close up and get to bed, and his oldest boy could take care of the early-morning business. It was past midnight, he noted, but he waited doggedly for Monsieur Rosenfeld to appear. And if M. Rosenfeld again protested that there was no need to have kept the garage open for him, that he could have left his car out in the street for one night, then Androuet must have a quick answer ready. He studied that problem as he stood at the door and looked down the street toward the well-lighted avenue—brakes were good, battery had been recharged last week, tires checked only yesterday, so what now? But there was M. Rosenfeld's gray Renault, making a left turn into the street. Androuet pushed the door wide, still debating his problem.

M. Rosenfeld wasn't in a talkative mood tonight. He drove the Renault into its own small parking place at the back of the garage, leaving the entrance clear for any other car in the morning. Not that he needed to bother. M. Rosenfeld was usually out first as well as last in. But Androuet admired neatness just as he liked earning some extra cash, so he was friendly and voluble in spite of his tired face and sore feet. "You must be missing the wife and kids, Monsieur Rosenfeld," he said, noting the time again on the big wall clock. Seven minutes past twelve, exact. "When do you expect them back from America?"

"In two or three weeks. Sorry I kept you up. Tomorrow, you'd better leave the door unlocked. I can push it aside myself."

"With all these crooks around nowadays? No, no, Monsieur Rosenfeld." Androuet's thin, earnest lips meant what they said. "We can't take chances like that. Besides, it was better to bring the car in here tonight. I've noticed the indicator for the last couple of days. It's not working properly. I'll get the boy to look it over in the morning. When do you want the car tomorrow?"

"Eight. Eight-thirty." Rosenfeld halted at the big door. "And you might get him to do a complete overhaul on the wiring. Something's wrong with the taillights. Good night, Androuet."

Androuet watched him go. It never ceased to cause him a little wonder, a little resentment, that an American could speak French just as accurately as he did. He forgot all that, however, as he locked the big door, then pulled a little book from his cash drawer and entered carefully under the date of Thursday, 16th April: *Arrived 12:07* A.M. *Unaccompanied.* He put his small record safely back in its locked compartment, switched off the one meager light, climbed the wooden stairs to his wife and twelve children. She would grumble at being disturbed so late, but five hundred new francs were good pay for a little overtime. As for the man who had made the bargain with him, two weeks ago—he was a detective hired by Madame Rosenfeld, to keep an eye on a lonely husband. It was an explanation Androuet easily accepted: his vision of life was always focused between two sheets of a bed.

Rosenfeld entered his apartment, switched on the lights in the living room. He threw aside his hat and raincoat, and walked slowly over to the window. Casually, he closed the long curtains, turned on some music, and settled down to wait for ten minutes. Then he entered his bedroom, switched on its lights, drew its heavy curtains as he unfastened his tie. After that, he moved quickly, turning off lights and music in the living room to show anyone who might be watching the windows that he was now going to bed. He put on a black raincoat, French in style and fabric, slipped his feet into black tight-fitting slippers, and checked his pockets for small flashlight and keys. Entering the bedroom again, he locked that door securely. From a drawer, he drew out a small tape recorder and, as he put it down at the side of his bed, started its play back. Gentle sounds of soporific music filled the rose-pink room. He left the small bed-table lamp glowing, but switched off the bright ceiling lights.

He paused at the bathroom door. Nice picture of a man reading in bed, he hoped. Soon, the music would end, and the sound of a man's deep breathing would be played; and then, as the table lamp on its automatic control blacked out, the sounds would change to a mixed variety of masculine snores. The boys who thought up that tape had a nice sense of humor as well as of timing. He gave a last glance at Milly's bed: yes, he missed her and the kids, all right. Tonight, though, he was glad they were safely out of this, three thousand miles away. He was suffering from an attack of premonitions, and that was something he had learned to take seriously. In his job, you had to develop a kind of built-in radar all your own.

With his hooded flashlight, and his two master keys ready, he began his journey. Quickly he passed through the bathroom, locked its door behind him. Quickly along the carpeted corridor, with the children's empty rooms staring blankly after him. Quickly through the small kitchen, out by its service door, into the back hall with its stone floor and garbage cans. Eight silent paces and he was at the service entrance of another apartment. He had every right to enter it. It was his.

He had leased it under another name, for a bachelor who only wanted a very small *pied-à-terre* in Paris. (The bachelor even made an appearance, now and again, whenever it seemed necessary.) The place was basically furnished and looked as heartless as that sounded. But even if it had no stretch of front windows, or no view of the rear courtyard, its position was good: it lay along the side wall of the apartment house, right up against the four-story building of Androuet's garage. And the chief asset was its bathroom window, standard in size, easily negotiated. It looked out over the flat crest of Androuet's roof.

Rosenfeld locked and bolted the bathroom door, swung open the bathroom window, stepped up on the toilet seat, climbed over the window sill, and was on the stretch of flat roof. A clutter of tipsy chimney pots, poking their ancient heads through the blue slate tiles, protected him from any watcher across the street. Eleven quiet paces toward the back of the building and he had reached the small attic door that had once let chimney sweeps and roof repairers get to work. He had a key for that, too. The inside ladder was short, thank God; that always seemed the worst part of this little journey. He lowered himself carefully.

He was now on the top landing of the old house, blocked off from the staircase by a very solid door so that this small area had become a private hall for the two studio doors. He stood in the darkness, by the ladder's bottom rung, and took out his flashlight again. The door that led into the front studio had an elegant sign in sixteenth-century cursive, no less, YVES DUCLOS, FURNITURE REPAIRS, ANTIQUES BOUGHT AND SOLD, BY APPOINTMENT ONLY. But it was to the other studio, at the back of the building, that Rosenfeld turned. He pressed the button beside the door. There was no sound of ringing. Instead, a small flashing light would now be signaling inside Duclos' living quarters. Duclos must have been waiting for it. The door opened at once. Rosenfeld stepped inside, glancing at his watch. Four and a half minutes, all told, since he had stood in his bedroom. Not bad, he thought, for a man in his forties. And five pounds overweight, too, he added, just to cut down his vanity.

Duclos said, "Don't worry about being late. I knew you were at the Farraday party." He spoke English fluently, without any trace of French accent. He was in his mid-thirties, of medium height and weight, with the dark hair, bright blue eyes and fresh complexion of a true Celt. He had brought some Breton touches into this large room, too, with a tier of heavy box beds blocking the fireplace completely (he distrusted chimneys), faded red linen covering every inch of the giant windows, heavy candlesticks on a long table (he also distrusted electric light bulbs in places where talk might be serious), a couple of carved wooden screens to give some tactful privacy as well as to break up the vast floor space. "How did it go?"

"Always good to see them." Rosenfeld was keeping his voice low as he took off his coat and threw it on the nearest chair. There were two men sitting behind the screen that lay farthest from the window. He could see their shapes through the latticework, but the candlelight wasn't strong enough to let them be identified. He nodded his head in their direction, cocked an eyebrow.

"Got in from Berlin today," Duclos murmured. "I told you this meeting was urgent."

Rosenfeld thought of Androuet. "When did they get here?" he asked, frowning.

"I picked them up this afternoon near Versailles, where I was buying a couple of chairs at an auction. They came here, inside the truck. No one saw them."

"What about Androuet?"

"Is he causing trouble?"

"No, but he's watching my times of arrival and departure. Someone is curious about me. You've had no signs?"

Duclos shook his head. "Androuet didn't see them, anyway. I drew him out of the garage by pretending to notice something interesting on the street, and then wandering out to have a look at it. He followed me like a lamb."

"I hope it was a good excuse, something that will stand up in Androuet's afterthoughts."

"It was a very handsome woman. Don't worry. My guests were out of the truck and upstairs before he stopped thinking of hips. I even got his help to carry the chairs upstairs to the landing."

It was possibly all right, Rosenfeld thought. Duclos had a lot of panache to disguise his essential caution. His chief, Bernard, over at the Sûreté, wouldn't have selected him to work on this special job of co-operation with the Americans if he wasn't one of his most careful, as well as diplomatic, operatives.

"Don't worry," Duclos repeated softly. "I'll watch Androuet from now on. How did they hook him? Women, or money?"

"I don't know if he is hooked yet. Probably just accepting a hefty bribe, and finding reasons to excuse himself."

"That's always the first step in being hooked," Duclos said, and he was right. It was one of the first steps, anyway, Rosenfeld thought, and—his warning about Androuet given and taken—he began walking toward the screen. Duclos caught his arm gently, and asked again, "How did the Farraday party go? I know who was there. Was Antonini questioned?"

Okay, okay, Rosenfeld thought: he co-operates with me and I co-operate with him. That's Bernard's bright idea, and it has been a good one so far. "Only in a general chitchat kind of way. He dodged giving any serious answers."

"Did no one show special interest in him?"

"No approaches that I saw, except normal friendly ones."

"Yet we had information that a Communist agent was going to be at that party tonight."

Rosenfeld halted completely. "Are you serious?"

"Never more serious."

"Any name?"

"No. But there was a photograph of the man. Our agent was bringing it to us yesterday morning. A truck smashed his small car to pieces."

Rosenfeld glanced over at the screen.

"Tell me. Quickly."

"He was following one of their couriers, saw him make a drop in the Bois de Boulogne at eight in the morning. He decided to stay around and see who would pick up the message. That's generally a long wait. So he took a chance, walked past the seat where the courier had sat and found an old pencil stub lying on the ground."

"Did he examine it?"

"Yes, he knew what to do. He pulled out the false lead to check if there was the usual roll of microfilm inside. Instead, there was a thin roll of paper with very small writing."

"What?" This was wrong, this was all wrong. . . .

"It read: *Get invitation for Farraday party tonight. Call us six o'clock further instructions.* He replaced it, sealed it with the lead, dropped it where he had found it. Then he waited almost two hours behind some trees, until a man stopped at the seat, picked up the pencil, and strolled off. He just had time to photograph the man—one shot caught him full face."

"How tall?" The French agent must have made some contact with the Sûreté before he was killed, Rosenfeld guessed, or else Duclos wouldn't know so much.

"Height was difficult to estimate accurately. Around average, perhaps a little over. He stooped, carried himself badly. Clever? Also, he wore a shapeless coat. So his weight and build were impossible to judge at that distance."

"Not six foot three, with white hair, deeply tanned complexion?"

"Nothing like that. Nothing particularly noticeable."

That eliminated Tom O'Malley, the Australian, from the Meurice gathering. "Then he was an American," Rosenfeld said. He sighed.

"Our agent got back to his car, and radiophoned us from there. He decided to bring in the photograph rather than try to follow the American. Ten minutes later, our man was dead."

"What about the camera?" A brutal question, but needed.

"Lifted from his pocket before we got to him."

They knew what they wanted, Rosenfeld thought. They must have seen him use it, probably were watching him ever since he picked up the pencil stub. Time enough, in those two hours, to sound an alert and be ready to act. It was the American they were protecting, not the simple little message. Yet it still baffled him, or, rather, the manner of delivery puzzled him. The Communists used such pencils, but only for some really important message, microfilmed, lengthy, usually filled with items about highly secret matters.

Duclos was saying, "The truck was stolen, of course. The driver and his helper vanished after they lifted the camera. There was a terrific uproar, complete traffic jam, shrieking women, crowds of people. If we hadn't received the radio report, we might have thought they were only two hijackers who panicked after an accident and ran. That is what we were supposed to think, I'm sure. And that's how we gave it out to the press."

Rosenfeld was still thinking about the pencil stub. "It's all wrong— using a valuable drop for a simple message like that. They could have telephoned him quite safely if that was all they had to say. D'you think—is it possible that they had no other way of contacting him that day, no way of instructing him to get an invitation to the Farraday party?"

"Just as we," suggested Duclos, "couldn't reach you before the party began to warn you who might be there?"

"Wednesday was my day off the chain this week," Rosenfeld said lightly. "I didn't expect business to pick up so—" He paused.

"Perhaps it was the American's day off, too?" Duclos asked thoughtfully. "We might begin from there."

Rosenfeld nodded. His lips tightened as he recalled the faces of the men he had met less than three hours ago. His eyes narrowed. He felt, as he always did when he found an American involved in such work, just a little sick.

Duclos probably suffered from French traitors in the same way, for he said tactfully, "Perhaps he didn't go to the party. The action today might have scared them off. His instructions could have been changed on that six o'clock call, you know."

That could be. Sue Farraday had mentioned three guests who had to beg off at the last minute. Poor Sue . . . she had been happy about reaching Paris, getting away from mystery and threat. And a man had died because of her little party, and what more would come of it? Rosenfeld decided he had better find out the names of the three missing guests. His feeling of sickness increased.

A cheerful voice said, "Haven't you chaps finished your local gossip? Hello, Rosie! Come in and join our little séance. We need help with an obstreperous ghost." The Englishman had risen and was standing at one side of the screen. He laughed with real pleasure as he saw the astonishment on Rosenfeld's face. "Rosie!" he said again, coming forward with his light step, his hand outstretched.

"Chris Holland!"

"Three years, isn't it? Well, well . . ."

"Two and a half."

"You've been taking it easy, I see. Putting on a little weight?"

"I can still buckle the same belt around my waist," Rosie protested. "With a struggle." As they shook hands, and kept shaking hands (Duclos was much impressed by this Anglo-American display of real affection), Rosenfeld was studying Holland's face. He was thinner, with a little more gray sprinkled through his neatly cut well-brushed hair. His skin, over the even, pleasant but unremarkable features, was now less tanned. Some lines had been added, too, around the grayish-brown eyes. But he still had that same amused look in them, that same quiet smile. "And how are the savage and licentious soldiery? Made you a colonel, yet?"

"Half-colonel," Holland murmured.

Not bad, not bad at all, thought Rosenfeld: British Intelligence didn't hand out promotions like *petits fours* with the ice cream. It must be some really big piece of news that had brought Holland to Paris, something that concerned the Americans and French as well as the British. And his feeling of urgency was increased as the other visitor from Berlin stepped forward and Holland introduced him, "Here is Partridge. We've been doing a little work together recently." Michael James Partridge, American, thirty-seven; Korea; then counterintelligence training at Fort Holabird in Maryland; became a civilian, moved to Berlin; past five years there spent in putting his education at the Army Intelligence School to very practical use. A good man, on his way up.

"I've heard of you," Rosenfeld said as he shook hands with the American. He looked at the light sandy hair, the gray eyes behind the thin-framed glasses, the lean face with its high brow, the shy smile, the casual clothes that increased the college-teacher look. So here, thought Rosenfeld, is my replacement. Once I get him squared away, show him the files, explain matters pending, instruct him in the local difficulties, this man will take over here when I go back to Washington. He smiled amiably. "Planning to stay long?" he asked casually.

"That depends." Partridge was equally casual. "Chris is going back to Berlin in a few days. We thought it better if we met you here, very quietly. After that Venetian affair—" He didn't end the sentence, just smiled pleasantly and led the way back to the four chairs grouped behind the screen around a small table.

Duclos looked enquiringly at Rosenfeld, who explained, "The last time Chris and I met was in Venice."

"September, 1961," Chris said smoothly. "That was a nice little job of co-operation."

Duclos caught on. "Ah—the plot to assassinate De Gaulle which you uncovered?" He relaxed and asked no more questions.

"And so," continued Chris, "Rosie and I must not even *seem* to meet again. We might alarm some more conspirators, and we don't want to warn them, do we? Really, by this time"—he was looking at Rosie, now—"I thought the cold war might actually have melted." He sighed. "They never give up, do they?"

"Some always keep trying. What is it now?"

"We have quite a story to tell you. Take place, as we say in Berlin." So they all sat down around the table. "This is highly classified information, old boy. Jim, have you got that damned gadget working?"

"It's working," Partridge said. Acquaintances making an effort to seem close to him would call him "Mike." His real friends knew better. Now, he pointed to the small box that lay beside his ash tray. "Present for you," he told Rosie. "Just something our engineers were fooling around with. It scrambles the sound waves within a twenty-foot radius."

"That's going to ease a lot of headaches. Sure it works? Okay, okay . . . And thanks." Rosenfeld was relaxing visibly. But he was still trying to guess what news from Berlin was so important that Holland had decided to bring it himself. "Don't you trust even a coded message any more?" he asked jokingly.

Chris Holland threw him a sharp look. Partridge's eyebrows went up for a split second. "Not at the moment," Chris said very evenly. "Because it happens to be a very special code that starts my story. A Russian code, only used since last November. A real puzzler." He smiled happily. "Fortunately, we had a warning about its importance along with information about its peculiar difficulties."

So, thought Rosie as he translated from Holland's understatement into more exact language, the British have a Soviet code clerk working for them, a defector in place. He knew better than to ask Holland the where or the how of the situation, far less the defector's name. But as he nodded approvingly and murmured "Congratulations," his mind went into high speed. A code as difficult and special as this one must have been would be used for high-priority messages from Moscow Central. And if it had come to Holland's attention, then the messages were being sent to Berlin; that was obvious. Possibly to the Soviet intelligence establishment there, the highly secret Rezidentura, with a senior intelligence agent in charge. "Sounds very high-level, indeed," Rosie said. But how, he wondered, did a Soviet code clerk manage to hear about such a special code? The master spy in charge of the Rezidentura would have memorized it, received all its messages himself. Unless, of course, the code had been so difficult that he had used the code clerk to help him break out the message—a violation of security regulations, certainly, but that had happened before.

Holland had been watching Rosie. The slight frown combined with the inflection in Rosie's voice when he had used the words "high level" were enough for Holland's own quick mind. "Our information was reliable," he said quietly. "So we found out."

"You managed to catch some of those coded messages coming into Berlin? That was a hell of a job. The directors of spy networks get three or four every week, don't they?"

"It was quite a job of work," Holland conceded. He glanced at Partridge. "We had some excellent co-operation, too. But even if it was difficult, it's still easier than catching the master spy with his little receiver. I wish, just once, that I could walk right in at the moment he was listening to Moscow."

Rosenfeld and Duclos both nodded. The director of a network, always a Russian, had several receiving sets in different parts of the foreign city in which he worked; he would even use a car for mobility, so that he couldn't be tracked down to one spot. And, because he had entered that foreign country illegally—on a false passport and with a carefully invented personal history—and then used various names and identities once he had established himself, he was difficult to uncover. Especially when none of the groups he organized ever knew who he was. To them, he was only one of his code names. Not even the leaders of those groups knew him, far less the exemplary citizens they had recruited as "sources" of information. He, and possibly the two other Russians who were his assistants (they had come into the country legally, as diplomats or trade representatives or newsmen for a Russian paper), knew the extent of the network that spread out from him. He alone knew all its members. And just as none knew him, so also none understood the real purpose of all the small bits and pieces of information they were instructed to collect, of the small actions they were called upon to perform. Theirs but to do, and protest their innocence when arrested. Or catch the public's tender emotions with a plea of blackmail or duress. It was, thought Rosenfeld, a sad, sad world.

Holland was saying, "At the very beginning of January, we noticed that this special code was being used in a strange way. It would appear, for one sentence, right in the middle of a message being sent in a quite different code."

"And these messages," Partridge explained quickly, "were on the steady three-a-week basis beamed at Berlin. They varied, naturally. But that one sentence, in its own special code, remained constant."

"A general directive to all areas of Berlin?" Duclos asked, frowning.

"We found it was going out to certain other areas in West Germany, too. So we checked quietly with our friends, and we pooled all our discoveries. But—" Partridge looked at Holland, becoming conscious of his silence—"that's your story. Sorry," he finished lamely. And don't let your excitement carry you away again, he told himself; you keep quiet, junior!

Holland resumed. "The sentence was very simple. It repeated the same warning and the same question, three times a week for three weeks running."

"It said?" Rosenfeld, about to light his cigarette, paused. This had to be really important.

"UTMOST CAUTION: IS THERE ANY TALK OF HEINRICH BERG?"

Rosenfeld took the unlit cigarette out of his mouth, staring at Holland.

Holland said quickly, "Oh no, Rosie, no! Blast you, man! Here I make this bloody journey to Paris, and you know all about Heinrich Berg." He threw up his hands, exchanged a wry smile with Partridge. Duclos was puzzled but gloomy; if Rosie knows, he was thinking, then he hasn't been co-operating fully with us. And I liked him, I really liked and trusted him. He looked reprovingly at Rosie.

Rosenfeld said quietly, "I don't. I only heard his name mentioned tonight at the Meurice party."

"By whom?" Duclos wanted to know. He was relieved, though.

"By a young American, John Craig. He didn't say much. And perhaps that was just as well. He's intelligent, I think—" Rosenfeld was frowning. He put the cigarette back between his lips and lit it. He decided to wait. "Go ahead, Chris. You have the real story. All I have is a small piece of conversation. It can be added later, as an interesting footnote."

Holland nodded, said briskly, "We all went to work to find out who Heinrich Berg was. You can imagine the files we examined, the search through old Nazi documents and newspapers, correspondence, everything. We put a silent team to work." A smile showed in his eyes, touched his lips briefly. "We, too, were using the utmost caution. There was no need to tip our hand and show we were intensely interested in Heinrich Berg. We found out, in short, that he had joined the Nazi party in 1934 after graduating from Munich University. He was a bright lad, took an advanced degree in psychology. He got into the brain-power group of the Nazis, and was attached in a seemingly minor capacity to the German Embassy in Moscow for four years. In 1941, he was back in Berlin, working unobtrusively under Himmler. Then he invented a special job for himself, in 1944, got Himmler's full approval, and—as a remarkably self-effacing officer in the Security Police—he made inspection tours of the concentration camps where political prisoners might be found and he would make a list of names of those whom he considered dangerous to the future of the Reich. That is, men who could be future leaders of anti-Nazi movements or regimes."

"1944 . . ." Rosenfeld said thoughtfully. "He was foreseeing a possible Nazi defeat, then?"

"Now, Rosie," Holland said with amusement, "you're jumping ahead of me and stealing some of Jim's thunder. He did a great deal of work on this. All I'm stating is that Heinrich Berg was removing all possible future opposition. The men he selected were sent to an extermination camp. But some, strangely enough, never arrived there at all. They seemingly managed to escape, and their escape was always expertly concealed, usually listed as 'dead in transit.' That is where Jim discovered something very interesting. But"—he looked at the younger man with a grin—"that's your story, isn't it?"

Partridge said, "The men who escaped turned out to be very much alive. After the war was over, they appeared in their own countries—

mostly Eastern European—where they helped establish Communist governments. That was what they were, Communists. And that was what Berg was really doing in 1944-45: getting rid of the democrats, keeping alive the Communists. Clever fellow?"

"A double agent," Rosenfeld said slowly.

"No. A Communist agent who had thoroughly infiltrated the Nazis. Another Richard Sorge, in fact. I began to get a glimmer of something like that when I puzzled over the lists of the politicals he had marked for extermination. So we began to dig deeply into his early life. We unearthed some secrets. He had become a member of the Communist party in 1931, recruited at Munich University. Spent three summers abroad, ostensibly to study psychology in Vienna, but I think he learned more Pavlov than Freud. He made at least two side trips into Russia—one to Moscow, one to Minsk. Ready to infiltrate by 1934, anyway."

Holland laughed softly. "A clever fellow, that's definite at least. He was registered as dead, April, 1945, and buried in Berlin. So we had a special squad dig up his grave one night and smuggle his coffin out where the experts could examine the remains of Heinrich Berg. The bone structure made the corpse some three inches taller than ever Berg had been. Also, Berg had a couple of molars missing—so his dentist's records said. The corpse had a full set, top and bottom. Careless? No. I'd imagine that in the holocaust raging around him when he was selecting a corpse for his coffin, he hadn't time to examine its teeth or measure it from tip of heel to crown of head. The remnants of an S.D. uniform, correct rank, had been thrown around the body. He was in a bit of a hurry."

"So where do you think he is now?" Rosenfeld asked too innocently.

Holland studied him. Partridge, who didn't know him so well, plunged right ahead. "Well, with that record, it was pretty obvious he slipped into the Russian lines and headed east. But we have uncovered surer proof than that. He had a wife and two children. They stayed behind, in the French zone—she got a job as a cleaning woman in a canteen. Then about three years later, in 1948, she suddenly packed up and left with the children. The French didn't quite like the way her departure was so secret, so well arranged. Cleaning women don't have that kind of influence. So they opened a file on her. It didn't collect much. Just one postcard to her mother from Minsk, saying she would write when her new address was settled, and then nothing for several years until one letter slipped through to the West, asking for warm clothing. The letter came from Yakutsk, in Siberia, and she asked that no German name be used, but gave a new one: Insarov."

"She said nothing about her husband?"

"Nothing. But we did find out that in 1956, among various people returning to Moscow from different parts of Siberia, there was an Igor Insarov, who was once more very much in favor. He has become important, no doubt of that. He is back with Intelligence again. Security, we think. We hear he heads a special unit on psychological control. That fits, all right. Insarov could be Berg."

"You got all that information in three and a half months? See what co-operation can do?" Rosenfeld smiled for Duclos.

"Three and a half months were one hundred and six days and one hundred and six nights," Partridge said wearily. "We knew we were working against time."

"Because," Holland explained, "in February, that special code was used in the same way, again. But this time the message was longer. IF FILES CONTAINING ANY IMPORTANT REFERENCE TO HEINRICH BERG STILL EXIST, REMOVE PERTINENT DATA AND DESTROY. REPORT ON FINDINGS AND ACTION TAKEN, BY REGULAR CHANNELS. Fortunately, we were in a position to make very quick copies of those references, and replace them in time. We didn't even arrest the agents who were suddenly interested in those files. Some of them had been totally unsuspected, but now—although they don't know it—they are helping us. That's quite a nice little bonus."

"So Berg was trying to blot out his identity?" Rosenfeld asked. In that case he could very well risk coming to Paris.

"Someone was. And why? I think the answer is in a report we had from one of our best sources in Moscow. At the beginning of this month, Igor Insarov left Moscow for Prague under the name of a Russian doctor. From Prague, we learned that a Soviet medical official had arrived and left the same day for Zürich, traveling now as an Austrian businessman. And from Zürich—well, we are still evaluating some of the reports that have come from there. One was much too definite, too quick. It came from a man we suspect is the kind of double agent who plays both sides for cash. He reported that the Austrian businessman had left for Rome. But we heard, two days ago, from one of our own men who has infiltrated a Soviet spy network in the Zürich area and works in its passport bureau. He says that the passport for an Austrian businessman had been turned in, and replaced by all the necessary papers for entry and residence in France." He smiled at Duclos. "You'll have your work cut out, I think."

"Very difficult," Duclos agreed worriedly. "If he has taken over the name and history and papers of a real French citizen—possibly of Alsatian origin, to account for any slight accent—then that is hard to trace. And if the French citizen has disappeared or died a long time ago, behind the Iron Curtain? Almost impossible to trace." He paused. "You really believe that Insarov is in France?"

"Frankly, we don't know. We only think he might be. We are checking in Rome, too. But one thing *is* certain. He is on the loose. And he wouldn't have come out so secretly if he wasn't up to something very big."

"What?"

"That's what all of us had better find out."

"And you really believe," Duclos insisted in his practical way, "that Berg and Insarov are the same man?"

"Again, we don't know. We only deduce from the facts we found that he could very well be."

"Did Berg's wife follow him to Moscow from Yakutsk?"

"No. She has vanished, and the two daughters as well. Insarov—as far as anyone knows—is unmarried."

"What about photographs?"

"None of Insarov. He is a most self-effacing and careful man. Perhaps his exile in Siberia taught him to be that. Of Heinrich Berg, we have two photographs: one when he attended a Nürnberg rally with Hitler, Goebbels and Himmler—but that black Security Police cap made Himmler's boys all look the same grim-faced type; the other was taken when he joined the Nazi party in 1934."

Rosenfeld waited. The silence continued. "Finished?" he asked Holland and Partridge. They nodded. "Then here is my footnote to your obstreperous ghost." And now it was making some real sense, Rosenfeld thought. "Heinrich Berg was seen yesterday in Paris. He was identified by a Professor Sussman, who had been a prisoner in Auschwitz. Sussman could have made a mistake, of course, but I'll check. I'll do that through John Craig. I think I can arrange to meet him tactfully. I'll start finding out what Sussman is doing here. If he is a French citizen, I'll get Yves to help me. You two"—he looked at Holland and Partridge, who were still staring at him in amazement—"can concentrate on Insarov. We'll concentrate on Berg."

"Fair enough," Holland agreed. "And we'll keep in close touch. Usual channels. I'll be leaving in a couple of days. Too bad we can't have a nice, relaxed dinner together."

"That's what comes from being a notorious character. You shouldn't have arrested a Communist agent right in the middle of the Piazza San Marco." Rosenfeld turned to Partridge. "You'll be around for some time?" I bet you will, he thought.

"He's unsullied, simon-pure," Holland said with a bright smile. "He has been just as self-effacing as Colonel Insarov."

"Then let's keep him that way. Don't contact me at my office." And then, as Partridge looked surprised—no doubt he had already worked out a nice role as a visiting salesman—Rosenfeld added, "Just a small premonition. Let's play this very carefully. Which reminds me—"

"Don't worry," Yves Duclos said, "I'll get them safely into the van by five-thirty, before young Androuet comes down into the garage at six and opens the doors."

Rosenfeld glanced at his watch, and got to his feet. "You have four hours for sleep. I'd better climb home. I've just invited myself to breakfast at the Meurice. I have to see the Farradays anyway." And now he looked grim and tired. "We think we may have an American on our hands who is devoted to Russian ideals," he said very quietly.

Holland looked at him with real sympathy. "Any clue?" So that was the reason that Rosie's usual jokes had been missing tonight.

Rosenfeld shook his head. "Well, good luck with everything."

Christopher Holland shook hands warmly. "Here's to our next meeting, Rosie." And let's hope it is one of those happy post-mortems, with all friends intact.

Perhaps Rosie had the same thoughts. He nodded, turned away without speaking. To Partridge, he said as he buttoned up his black raincoat, "I'll phone you tomorrow at noon. Where?"

Partridge gave him a number. He was certainly efficient, well prepared.

"Thanks, Jim," Rosenfeld said, and won a startled smile. Could he have been scared of me? Rosenfeld wondered in amazement. He looked almost natural, there. Scared of *me?* My God, I must be getting old.

Yves came out into the hall with him, turned on the light as he climbed toward the door in the roof. He paused as he unlocked it, signaled for the light to switch off before he opened the little panel of solid wood and stepped out on the roof. Now for all that locking, unlocking. Some months ago, when he had organized this route of arrival and departure, he had been inclined to laugh at his overcaution. Tonight, he blessed it. He blessed the soft clouds, too, that had covered the sky again with broken patterns of silvered fluff, casting vague shadows over the rooftops. The street was asleep, its windows shaded and quiet, strange contrast with the glow from the far-off boulevards, with the sound of traffic from the avenue.

It had all been a very cosy setup, a neat arrangement, he thought as he reached his own bedroom. Too bad he would have to stop visiting the studio for a while. He cursed Androuet's quick eye for a fast franc; and then laughed softly. Perhaps he ought to be thanking Androuet and his garage; they had supplied the first small warning signal. And for that, he was always grateful.

The smart girl-show had opened two months ago near the Rue d'Amsterdam. It was part of the new wave in small night clubs, rolling west and away from the clichés of Montmartre toward the unlikely surroundings of the Gare Saint-Lazare. Here, on a narrow, workaday street climbing the cobblestoned hill above the busy station, the club had taken over a cheap bar along with a neighboring cheese-and-sausage shop, converted them into one building, and used their rabbit-warren back premises for dressing rooms and offices.

Its patrons were a mixture of the restless rich and the pseudo avant-garde. It captured their trade with a room, subdued in décor and lighting, where the dance floor was twelve feet square and the music was both insistent and sour. Scotch was the correct drink at the crowded tables. Conversation was in French, Italian and English, with many references to the past season at Arosa, or the imminent trek to Sardinia and Elba (Saint-Moritz and Ischia were now definitely out), or *the* film festival (Venice was out, too), or the New York galleries, or the Dalmatian beaches. And occasionally, with correct unconcern, eyes would turn to watch the small stage, backed by black velvet, where the amusing revival of a real girl-show was now in progress. The girls were pale pink and white, no sun tan allowed, buttocks and bosoms thinned out into a streamlined contour so that the addition of surrealist items on the long lank bodies would have richest effect. Abruptly, unexpectedly, there would be a highly inventive interruption to their fertility-cult vibrations and rhythmical spasms: a moment of intellectual excitement combined with mental shock; an occurrence with content; a serious comment on the absurdity of life. It was to this interruption-moment-occurrence-comment that the club owed its newest name: Le Happening.

In the small entrance lobby, near the coatroom, a young woman was waiting for an escort who was ungallant enough to be late. (By arrangement. The number of late minutes was part of the recognition signal.) She was expensively dressed in simple black, a small green satin bag clutched in white-gloved hand, no jewels except for earrings. And they were very much in the atmosphere of the club. The right ear wore a ruby, the left ear an emerald, both encircled with pearls. Her face, pretty and cool, was deeply tanned; her eye shadow was green, her lips the palest pink. She slid her small watch back into the handbag. It was almost time: fifteen minutes after midnight. Quickly, she looked at the man who had just entered. Raincoat belted but *not* buttoned, thick-framed glasses, newspaper under one arm, new pigskin gloves, and a book with a red-and-white jacket. Yes, this must be he. Thank heavens he was presentable. He was eying her, too, looking at the red and green earrings, at her green bag and long white gloves.

"Sorry I'm late," he said, glancing at his watch. "Four minutes."

"Seven minutes, darling."

They both relaxed, smiling. "Then I'm *very* sorry." He jammed book and gloves into his coat pocket and handed it over, his face averted, to the elderly woman who looked after the coatroom. The folded newspaper, its Greek type clearly shown in the part of headline visible, was replaced under his left arm. "The train was late," he said. He was so sure that this was Erica that he had started leading her toward the curtained door even as she murmured correctly, "Next time, you must take a plane." Foolish but necessary, he supposed, like his car parked on the Rue Liége, where he had waited a full ten minutes for this entrance.

A table had been reserved for them near the door, but tucked protectingly against a wall. A "happening" was in progress, all eyes intent on the stage. Their entry, expertly guided by one of the owners of the place, who had glanced at the newspaper and the bright little green bag, then welcomed them with a nod, was unnoticed. They sat down in the semidarkness with some feeling of safety. Even when the muted blue illumination colored the room again, it was dim enough to keep their table nicely shadowed. Drinks came quietly. They didn't need to make a pretense of animated conversation. For no one seemed to be paying them the slightest attention. They looked, this well-dressed man and this elegant young woman, like many of the other couples who were watching the silvered square of dance floor with tolerant amusement.

So this was Alex, she thought, as he lit her cigarette. And can he be nervous, when he talks so little? Or is he trying to gauge me? After all, it is the first time we have made contact. But it won't be the last, so let's hope he loses some of this stiff manner. Would he have preferred to work with a man? Instinctively, she opened her bag, drew out her mirror, pretended to add some lipstick to her perfectly colored lips. She was reassured by what she saw. In the soft light, her face seemed luminous, as pretty as she remembered it: pale gold hair was perfect, slightly negligent, yet carefully in place; triangle of green shadow on each eyelid made the eyes look truly green. He was studying her profile. Now that was much better. She hoped he liked tiptilted noses and long lashes. One might as well enjoy one's work.

But, when he spoke, his voice was businesslike. His elbow was on the table, his chin resting in his cupped hand so that his lips were shielded. "Keep your bag open," he told her. "I have to leave soon."

"What a pity," she said. And I'm just a necessary nuisance, she thought angrily. She smiled brightly.

"That's better," he told her, glancing at his watch. "You were much too solemn."

She had to laugh. Alex was only anxious about his own private timetable. Where did he live? What did he do for a living? She would never know. He was an American, that was all she could guess; his French was fluent enough, but the accent was unmistakable. He knew how to dress, have his hair cut, hold himself. He was good-looking but in an inconspicuous way. For that, she was grateful. If one had to make a public appearance, perhaps run into friends, there would be no need to explain her companion. He would fit in perfectly. Even his age—the late thirties—was right; he would have money to spend. "When?" she asked, as the lights dimmed for another girl-show and the dancers started pushing their way through the tables to their own chairs. "Now?"

He nodded, relieved that he did not have to prompt her. He dropped his arm, straightened his sleeve, pulled his cuff into place. "Now."

Her lipstick fell from her fingers. He bent to pick it up, left it lying under the black shadow of the table, brought up his closed fist as if he held it safely retrieved. She showed only a fleeting astonishment as her hand felt the strange shape of the cuff link he had pressed into it. Quietly, she dropped it into the small zipper compartment in her bag, replaced her mirror, snapped everything secure. So, she thought, he had come prepared to meet Bruno, he was annoyed that he hadn't a lipstick to replace mine; idiot, did he imagine that I'd exclaim and open my hand and have a look at his cuff link? Does he think that a woman has to be plain, dowdy and intense before she can have brains? He was one of those very security-minded people, who liked things to go as planned. He would be frowning now, instead of smiling with relief, if he could know her guesses: he had got a message this evening, probably around six, when she had been given her emergency instructions, telling him to cancel Bruno and substitute her. She almost said, "Don't worry about how I get home. Someone is waiting for me in a car nearby. I'll see he gets your cuff link." But she resisted the impulse. She would only set him on edge again, at all this extra caution which spelled danger. Sources of information never liked the feeling of danger; couriers, like herself, were accustomed to it. She, for one, enjoyed it.

"Like to leave?" she asked, her hand lying lightly over her green bag. From now until she delivered the cuff link, that bag was part of her body. "I'll go first. That looks better. Shall I make my exit directly, or head for the ladies' room?"

"Directly." He wanted her out of this place before his visit backstage. That was another operation altogether, and it was its combination with this meeting with Erica that really had annoyed him. Much too dangerous, he felt, even if some crisis had caused it. But instructions were instructions, and you did not make a protest over a telephone.

"Then," she said with a pretty pout, "we are having a small quarrel. And I take my leave with a woman's last word." She tucked the bag under her arm, holding it securely with her hand. At least, he thought, she intends to keep it safe, but what if someone in French Counterintelligence arrested her on her way to deliver the gold cuff link? What if her purse was searched? Such an unlikely object would be at once examined; it wouldn't take long for trained men to find the way the heavy design lifted off, like a cap, and exposed the small flat square of microfilm. Blown up, it would make four full pages of concise information. He had found out all the answers to the questions in last week's pencil stub—a dangerous, worrying job. And now a woman, still in her twenties, enjoying every minute of her little play-acting, was holding his possible death warrant in her green satin purse. She was rising, saying clearly, "Thank you for a miserable evening. And don't call me tomorrow. Or the next day, either." She walked out as the lights dimmed completely, and all eyes turned to watch the stage.

He gave her five minutes to get her wrap and leave. Even if no one had been listening at all, she still would have played her exit lines perfectly. She was as exhibitionist as the girl-show. It wasn't difficult for him to look depressed as he paid and left the room, the folded newspaper in his hand. He had his handkerchief out as he entered the lobby, up at his face as if he were battling an attack of sneezing.

He collected his coat, for he wouldn't leave by the front entrance, and, as a seeming afterthought, made his way to the men's lavatory. With the show in progress, there was no one standing around the narrow corridors, and it was a simple matter to leave one and enter another that led behind the stage. A couple of men, watching the girls from the wings, paid him no attention—special friends dropped in to the dressing rooms frequently. A man fussed over lights, an elderly dresser argued quietly with the make-up artist, who practiced his technique too obviously on himself. He disliked this place the more he visited it; what had seemed intelligently amusing at first did not stand up to repetition, and was now preciously erotic and pretentiously boring. The nonsense world, he reflected, the supply and demand of decadence. It was comic, though, that the secret backers of this night club should find it so easy to stimulate the neurotic among their enemies and make them still more incompetent to deal with the real world.

The last corridor reached along the back of the night club. It contained four unused dressing rooms, two doors marked "Supplies, electrical," and the back entrance from the old delivery yard. It was poorly lit, its walls were peeling and cracked in the best Italian movie style, and it smelled faintly of cheese and sausage. A fair-haired young man in worn overalls and soiled undershirt was sitting on a crate near the entrance. He rose as he saw Alex, came toward him, his eyes checking the folded Greek newspaper, and knocked five times in rapid succession on a dressing-room door. It opened. A man's voice said quietly, "Come in!" It wasn't the voice that Alex had been expecting. Yet it held a familiar note as "Come in!" was repeated. Makarov—could it be Makarov?

And it was Konstantin Makarov who was sitting behind the door, keeping out of sight from the corridor. He closed the door swiftly, pointed to the chair that faced the looking glass on one wall, took the remaining chair (it was in the corner of the small empty room, beyond the stretch of light from the bulb that hung high over Alex's head), and lit another long cigarette. There were two stubs at his feet. Other stubs lay in the dust near Alex's feet. Whoever had been sitting here had retreated to the next dressing room through the connecting door that lay between Makarov's chair and the mirror.

Makarov glanced at his watch. "Well timed. Congratulations. You have been doing well in everything."

This was Makarov's old manner—cool, but pleasant, and completely professional. There was no reference to the fact that he had not seen Alex since he had recruited him in Moscow. Was he now stationed in Paris, perhaps as assistant to the director of the network which controlled Alex? The director, himself, might very well be the man watching this room from next door. The mirror was certainly a one-way arrangement, letting Alex be seen as clearly as through a window, while he stared blankly at its chipped frame and then let his eyes wander back to Makarov. He had no objection to being watched and studied. A director must have a definite curiosity about those who worked for him. He would be a Russian, of course, and, like Makarov, a highly trained intelligence agent. This meeting, thought Alex with rising excitement and pleasure, must be important if Makarov and his superior are taking a personal interest in it. But I can't even show that I'm honored he trusts me this much. He is merely the man I met in Moscow at many literary parties, under a name which was probably just as invented as the names he used in Washington and at the United Nations. Does he remember the night we got drunk together and he talked about his visits to America?

Makarov's cold gray eyes held a small smile, as if this meeting was a nice little joke to be shared between old friends. He was a short man, solid, square-faced, snub-nosed. Thinning red hair receded from a massive brow. He spoke English fluently, with a husky rasp in his voice—he always seemed to be on the point of clearing his throat—and his manner was that of a dependable and pleasant-tempered man. Suddenly, the joke was gone from his eyes. Briskly he said, "You will know me as Peter."

Alex nodded. That was definite: the past was wiped out; Makarov was dead, Peter lived.

"First," said Peter, "you made the delivery to Erica?"

"Yes."

"What did you think of her?"

"A pretty girl," Alex said coldly.

"And a clever one. Don't underestimate her, my friend. You did not like her? In one way, that has a big advantage. You will be able to keep your mind on business when you work with her. Oh, yes, you may have to see more of Erica. Bruno is out."

Alex asked, in quick alarm, "Something happened?"

"He was followed into the Bois, yesterday morning. The drop was intercepted—no, no, don't look so worried. We took quick action. Regrettable, of course. We would prefer not to be forced to defend ourselves in that way. But results justified our decision. Bruno has been saved from his carelessness and is now away from Paris, and you have been saved from discovery. You were in very great danger, my friend."

Alex was still too close to panic. He could say nothing.

"You will understand now why we advised you, on your six o'clock call to us, not to ask Antonini any direct questions at Farraday's party. We had hoped that by getting an invitation, you could talk closely with Antonini. But because of the interception of our orders to you, we decided that no suspicion must be aroused. We were forced to rely on what you could pick up in general conversation. Which leads me to our second point of business: what did Antonini say about the discovery of the microphones in the American Embassy in Moscow? Give me an exact report while the words are still fresh in your mind."

Alex told him, quickly, concisely.

"Was that all?" Peter hid his disappointment well.

"He said he was the wrong man to be asked any questions."

"Meaning that there was someone else who could tell more? Or was that just a feint, to save himself from further trouble, to pretend he is of less importance than he actually is?" The questions were rhetorical, for Peter was lost in thought. "Did the man Rosenfeld talk privately with Antonini? With any of the others? No?" Again there was only the hint of disappointment. "Well, then, anything else?"

"The usual stories about Moscow," Alex said. "And one story about a dead Nazi who may be alive." He smiled, allowing himself some credit for having waited, as a matter of tact and protocol, for the end of Peter's important questions before he presented his one small triumph. "The name was Heinrich Berg."

Peter said nothing. He did not move a muscle. He was watching and waiting.

Alex explained quickly, "I noted that name, late in February, when I was asked to check any files where Berg might be mentioned. I found nothing. I reported that back to headquarters, in March."

"Who was speaking of Berg?"

"Mrs. Farraday brought the subject up. Her brother, John Craig, had heard the story from one of his professors whom he met in Paris yesterday."

"And Craig believed this story?"

"No. But the professor—his name is Sussman—I think he should be questioned. If he did see Berg, then—"

"Berg is of no interest to us."

Isn't he? He certainly was last February. Alex remembered the chances he had taken to try to find out about Berg. And the extreme care to protect himself. Utmost caution, his instructions had read. Utmost danger of self-revelation, they should have been labeled.

"What kind of man is this John Craig?"

"Quiet, disinterested; perhaps stupid outside of his own subject; the type of intellectual who doesn't have much interest in what is going on. Politically immature. The talk, which was frank, seemed to shock him. Perhaps he did not want to believe what he heard. In that case, he might be useful to us. Physically, he is personable. Pleasant, easy manners. An economic historian, I believe."

"Why is he in Paris?"

"He is only passing through on his way to the Greek Islands—

Crete and Rhodes, places like that. So his sister told me. He is writing a book about trade routes. She told me that, too."

"Did he himself see this Heinrich Berg?"

Alex hid his surprise at the reintroduction of Berg, who was of no interest to anyone. "No. Craig only gave Sussman a drink to cheer him up—I'm quoting him—and then Sussman left. Craig was embarrassed at the story being spread around by his sister—he didn't believe it himself, as far as I could judge." And I don't make many mistakes, as Peter must well know if he has read any of my reports, and I think he has. "Craig is staying at the Saint-Honoré. Do you want me to see him soon?"

"No. Forget Berg. Forget this fantastic story. We have something more important to occupy your mind." Peter paused for emphasis. "Can you arrange for yourself to be assigned to Smyrna?"

"No."

"But there is a very large American installation near there! With their wives and children, the Americans have established—"

"I know. It is quite a civilian colony. Even so, I would need a very good excuse even to visit it. People would want to know why I was going to that part of Turkey."

"You have friends stationed there?"

You know I have, Alex thought; you've read my dossier. You've got all my possible sources of information around the world. He nodded.

"When do you go on vacation?"

"Actually, I've been planning to go to Spain for a few weeks."

"Have you talked about Spain?"

"Not yet . . ." Alex was embarrassed. "It's purely a private affair, not a business trip this time." It was a delicate reference to the fact that he hadn't had a real holiday in three years.

"Then you will cancel your idea of Spain. And you will spend your little holiday in visiting your friends around Smyrna. That is a good excuse, isn't it? Ephesus is near by, and many excursions you'll enjoy. You can also hire a boat in Smyrna and sail around some of the Greek Islands—even as far as the island of Mykonos. Yes, that would be a pleasant way to come back to Paris. On Mykonos, you could hand your information to Erica, herself. You wouldn't have to worry about meeting a stranger—no more tiresome identifications necessary.

Your work would be done, you would know you had delivered it into safe hands, you could forget about it and even have a few days of real vacation."

Alex had to smile at Peter's almost authentic enthusiasm. Smyrna should be pleasant at this time of year; the Greek Islands would be heaven. Too bad that he had business as well as pleasure on this vacation. Still, he could have been sent to Lille or Marseilles; that kind of "vacation" had happened before.

"And now you must leave," Peter said, rising to his feet, smiling regretfully. "You will hear from me. Then you will know the details of your assignment. Meanwhile, there will be no more visits to the Bois de Boulogne, no more meetings here. Not for you, my friend." He shook hands very formally. "We value you, comrade."

Alex flushed with pleasure. "I'll do my best."

"And that will be excellent."

Alex left quickly, ignoring the young man who let him out by the delivery entrance. I've been promoted, he was thinking: it is something big, and I've been picked for the job. He didn't even mind the devious journey back to his parked car, or the careful maneuverings before he could hit the right road. Even the dull drive back to his rooms, after this long day in Paris, didn't worry him tonight.

The man who now called himself Peter opened the connecting door between the dressing rooms. "What did you think of him?"

Insarov rose from his chair, switched off the translucent mirror. His usually calm face was frowning. He smoothed his dark hair, touched with gray at the temples, as he always did when he was making up his mind about a rather evasive problem. "Impression, favorable. He is intelligent. I could almost feel him making guesses about you, about me sitting in this room. But that is why you recruited him in the first place." Insarov's bright blue eyes looked very directly at Peter. "You say he is right for this job. I accept that." And I hold you responsible, the steady gaze said.

"He has never failed us yet. When something is impossible, he says so frankly. His judgment is good. He is cautious. He is punctual. He does not do this for the money. He is dedicated, completely."

"Yes, yes, I know that. Pity, though, that we haven't something to hold him—if necessary. Weren't there photographs?"

"We have some, taken at a Moscow party," Peter said nervously. "But we have never needed to use them." And we never will, he hoped. His own contributions to that party still made him sweat cold. He repressed a shiver, and smiled.

"Then good." Insarov stopped smoothing his hair; the frown vanished. "We needed an American with the right connections for this job. We have one." He pulled on his coat. "Make sure the corridor is safe."

Peter moved to the door, then, with his hand on the key, paused to ask, "That other American—Craig—I think we should keep an eye on him."

"Just normal surveillance until you are satisfied." Insarov did not seem too worried by that problem.

"But does Craig really disbelieve Sussman's story?" Peter asked, frowning. "Berg is important to us, isn't he?"

Insarov's handsome face was bland. "I really don't know," he said, and shrugged. "Now I'll say good night. Or is it good morning? I shall be in touch," he promised. As he signed to Peter to open the door, he smiled at his understatement. In the next ten days, he would keep Peter very busy indeed. But had he been noncommittal enough about Berg? Uninterested enough in Craig so as not to stress any personal connection with Berg? As for Craig—he would be watched, his background checked, more thoroughly than Peter was planning to do. Fate took care of those who take care of themselves, and Insarov was one who took most excellent care. Even his wildest risks were calculated. Methodical Peter would shudder at them, but that was why he would always stay second in command. Without risk, there was no victory. "Good night, Comrade Makarov," he murmured as he stepped into the silent corridor.

Peter stared after him. So he knows about that, too? Peter's rising terror needed all of the ten minutes of waiting, while Insarov walked through the dark streets, before it was repressed. He might think he had mastered it, but it would never leave him. It would ensure complete obedience, a nicely conditioned devotion. He would be praised for his loyalty to Insarov, and he would be flattered by such a public image, even come to believe it himself and maintain it wholeheartedly.

A strenuous day, thought Insarov as he entered the waiting car. He said nothing to the driver, who knew his business. In silence, they

headed south toward the Seine, crossed it, and turned east to the laby-
rinth of the Left Bank. A successful day, he thought, as they reached
the Saint-Germain district once more. At the intersection of two
small, scarcely lighted streets, he got out, waited in a doorway for the
car to speed away, and then strolled back to his rented apartment.

5

John Craig had slept too well, but that left him with such a feeling of energy and general cheerfulness that he had no qualms over the small margin he had given himself to reach the Meurice. He shaved, showered and dressed in twelve minutes. He was putting the last things into his pockets, searching for a small map of Paris to make sure he wandered in the right directions once he had said good-bye to Sue and George, congratulating himself on having made it as he picked up his key, when the telephone rang. There were two gentlemen downstairs who wanted to see him most urgently. "Sorry," he told the desk clerk, it would have to be some other time; he was leaving for breakfast. "They are already on their way, monsieur," the clerk said and hung up. Like hell they are, Craig thought, and locked his door.

They came out of the elevator just as he was starting along the corridor. They were mild-looking men, who appraised him with sad thoughtful eyes. "I'm sorry," he said, "I have an engagement at nine o'clock."

"We shall not detain you long, Monsieur Craig," the younger one said in good English. He gestured to his friend. "This is Detective Galland of the *Sixième Arrondissement*—the Sixth District, you would say? I am Tillier, also of that *arrondissement*. Perhaps we should go to the shelter of your room? Just a few questions, only formalities. We visited your hotel last evening, about ten o'clock, but we were told you were out for the evening." Carrying a bottle of champagne, he remembered. Who said the police of Paris were tactless? "We thought you might not be returning until very, very late. And so we must catch you at this hour. Because we should like to have your opinion of Professor Sussman."

Craig, who hadn't budged an inch toward his door, looked at them sharply, then moved back toward his room. So Sussman went to the police, he thought; he must really be desperate. "Come in," he said. "I know that Professor Sussman's problem isn't actually in your line, but I hope you'll help him and perhaps even get in touch with the right people who could—"

"Monsieur Craig," Tillier said gently, "the professor is dead."

Craig stared at Tillier, then at Galland. "What?"

"A suicide. Yesterday evening."

Craig sat down on his bed. Galland talked in quick French to Tillier, who nodded. The American's shock was very real, he decided. No need to waste too much time here. "If you could just explain this?" He pointed to the envelope that Galland drew out of his pocket. It was the one on which Sussman had written down Craig's address.

"He was going to send me some names of his friends in Rome and Athens—I'll be traveling in that direction soon—and I gave him that address when we had a drink together yesterday."

"When and where?"

Craig answered the questions briefly. Tillier was making notes.

"Was he depressed when you saw him?"

"At first, yes."

"He stopped being depressed?"

"Not exactly. He was—" Grim, determined, shocked; but also confident, hopeful, looking forward to his return to California and his family. "Suicide?" asked Craig angrily. "I don't believe it. He wasn't the type—"

"But he was depressed. You said so. And that verifies what his wife's relatives in Paris have told us. He was very morose, gloomy."

"He disliked them. No wonder he felt morose when he had to visit them."

Tillier nodded, but hesitated in entering that in his notebook. "Have you met them? Are they disagreeable?"

"Never seen them. Look, I'm not a close friend of Sussman. I only met him by accident yesterday. But I do know—at least I feel sure—that he didn't commit—"

"It would have been impossible for his death to be caused by an accident, Monsieur Craig."

"How did he die?"

The two policemen exchanged glances. "He fell from his window," Tillier said. "And it was of such a nature, I assure you, that he could not have overbalanced and fallen. There is a railing, as high as my waist, outside of his window, and I am taller than he was. And much heavier. No, even if he stumbled at his window, he would not have fallen over into the courtyard of his hotel. Have you visited him there? Then perhaps you remember—"

"I don't even know the name of his hotel."

"You did not expect to meet him again?"

Craig shook his head. "He was leaving today for America."

The telephone rang. "That's my breakfast engagement," Craig said, and picked up the telephone before Galland could reach it. It was Sue. He wasn't forgetting; no, far from it, he reassured her: it was just that two policemen were here asking him about Sussman, yes, Sussman; they said he had committed suicide and he was telling them that he couldn't believe it. Then he stopped as he heard some mumbling, an exclamation, at the other end of the line. Galland was looking at him with tight lips. "Sue . . . Sue—are you there?" he asked.

A man's voice took over. "Look, Craig, I want to make sure that these two guys are policemen. Put one of them on the line."

"They say they're from the sixth *arrondissement*." And what's the additional fuss about? he wondered.

"Put one of them on the line."

Craig gave the receiver to Galland, who was standing at his elbow. He took it, answered curtly, speaking in French. Yes, of the Sixth District . . . the Twenty-fourth Precinct, Saint-Germain-des-Prés . . . Fourteen Rue de l'Abbaye . . . Yes, of course . . . He quite understood. . . . But yes, certainly . . . And he was politely at ease again as he handed the receiver back to Craig.

The man's voice—was it Rosenfeld's?—told Craig briskly, "Just say good-bye and get over here. Don't argue the toss with them. Or else you'll spend the next eight weeks hanging round Paris while they investigate. Got it?"

Not quite. But I'll catch on, Craig thought. He said, "I'll be over in five minutes."

Galland had been talking quickly to Tillier. "Just one thing," Tillier suggested, as Craig turned away from the telephone, "if it was not suicide, if it could not be an accident, then what? Murder?"

Craig began to catch on, all right. "I just don't know," he said. And that was true enough. He had no proof of anything, just a lot of vague suspicions running wild; it would take more than eight weeks to check them out, if they could be checked. The police would end by thinking he was crazy, just as he had thought Sussman was a little crazy. "If it is, I hope you catch him," he added grimly.

"Well, that's about all." Tillier closed his notebook quickly, and followed Galland to the door. "We regret we made you late for the farewell breakfast party with your sister."

Rosenfeld really had pulled sentiment, Craig thought. "That couldn't be helped."

"Your brother-in-law has our address. If we have any more questions, he assures us that you will be delighted to pay us a visit."

Craig nodded. Brother-in-law, he was thinking. "Yes, of course," he said.

In the blue-and-gold sitting room, Sue was pouring coffee at the table near the opened window, George was busy looking through a newspaper with a quick and practiced eye, Rosenfeld was finishing his third croissant as he listened. "I tell you," Craig said, ending his brief recital of the detectives' visit, "I don't believe that Sussman committed suicide."

George folded the newspaper quickly, pointed to a small corner tucked away on the back page. "Just a moment! Here it is: Professor Jacob Sussman, et cetera, et cetera, suicide, by throwing himself from his hotel-room window. Estimated time of death, between seven and eight-thirty, when the body was discovered. Had been suffering from severe depression. Hotel owner says he behaved oddly when he returned to his room about seven. American Consulate is taking charge of arrangements, et cetera, et cetera." He handed the paper over to Rosenfeld's outstretched hand, then glanced at his watch and shook his head. "I'll have to run. Got meetings of one sort or another till late this afternoon. Rosie, you take charge here. Tell John to relax and leave police business to policemen. Especially when he's a foreigner."

But Rosenfeld was getting to his feet. "I'd better move out, too."

And again avoid the front lobby, he thought. No use having Sue and George identified with this visit of his to the Meurice. Keep them out of trouble; they've had enough of their own in the last few weeks. He had managed to pick up the information he had come here to find; it solved nothing. Still, it did narrow the field, and that was always a small step in the right direction. The three guests who had called off from last night's party were no longer interesting. Two were French reporters who had been sent to Marseilles yesterday morning in order to cover the heroin-factory story. The third man was a Canadian, but he had eliminated himself by falling in his bathtub a couple of days ago and was in the hospital at the time the stranger in the Bois de Boulogne had been collecting that chewed-up pencil stub. As for the guest who had practically invited himself to the party, there were two candidates for that distinction, one of them slightly more emphatic than the other. Wilshot had telephoned to say he was coming to welcome the Farradays that evening. Bradley was more diplomatic: he had called to ask when he'd have a chance of seeing them, and been invited. And their height? Around average, no more than a couple of inches' difference between them. They both could qualify. So did every other man at that party, last night, except Craig and the Australian. Rosenfeld looked at Craig's set face, now, and hesitated. Better spend a few more minutes here, he thought, and keep Craig out of trouble, too. He's in a dangerous mood. George's advice has riled him. Rosenfeld said gently, "George is right, you know. But so are you, possibly."

Craig looked at him with renewed interest.

"Judging by that newspaper report," Rosenfeld went on, "I shouldn't wonder if the police agree with you. Why else should they let that item be published and still go on checking every lead?"

"You mean the report is a smoke screen?"

Rosenfeld waited until George and Sue, comparing their timetables for today, had drawn out of earshot. "It could be. They never would have bothered visiting you this morning if they were quite sure it was suicide. So you just leave it to them. They are very good. Don't worry about that."

But Craig's worry was about something else. "I ought to have stayed and talked. If they are thinking about murder—perhaps they would have listened to me after all."

"Talk about what?" Rosenfeld was instantly alert. "About Berg being seen? About Sussman's suspicion?"

"About the man I saw leaving the café in such a damned hurry. He was right on Sussman's heels. At the time—well, I thought I was starting to imagine things, like Sussman."

"How old was this man?"

"He was young. Fair hair, wet raincoat . . ." Craig paused, looked at Rosenfeld speculatively. "Berg was much older, about fifty, I'd guess."

Rosenfeld's face went completely blank with the shock. His voice dropped. "You *saw* Berg? Craig—" He gestured to two chairs in a quiet corner of the room.

But George Farraday, his last-minute instructions to Sue now ended, came over to join them for a hearty but hurried good-bye to Craig. "Aren't you coming?" he asked Rosenfeld.

"Shortly."

"That's too late for me. I'm already ten minutes behind schedule. What about meeting me for lunch, along with Sutherland and three fellows from the—"

"No. In fact, George, you haven't met me today at all."

George Farraday half smiled. "I haven't? Okay. Anything else I haven't done?"

"You haven't heard that your brother-in-law was visited by the police this morning. And you haven't heard him say Sussman wasn't a suicide. You only know what he told you last night. And that goes for Sue, too. Right?"

Farraday said, "There dies another good story. Surprising how many of them, nowadays, have got to be smothered." He seemed to be joking, but his eyes were thoughtful.

"That keeps it a lot safer for everyone." Rosie looked pointedly at Craig. "Good-bye, George. And take off the pack. I'll handle this."

That reassured George. A last kiss for Sue, a wave to Craig, a nod to Rosie, and he was out of the room. She wasn't so easily persuaded. Perhaps she didn't know Rosie as well as she thought she did. "You mean there could be danger for John in all this business? Good heavens, Rosie, he only gave the poor man a drink!"

"Oh, not any real danger. Just publicity in newspapers, delays in getting away from Paris, complications . . . *You* know, Sue. Now, I want to hear from John everything he can tell me about Sussman's career. So why don't you start changing into street clothes, and pack your overnight things, and make a list of all that shopping you want to get done?"

Sue went toward the bedroom, even if a little reluctantly. She had a busy day ahead of her, that was true. "I had some things to discuss with John," she protested faintly. "Don't be too long, Rosie. I have a hairdresser's appointment at half past ten. And don't tell me my hair looks fine as it is!" She closed the bedroom door with a firm little bang.

"Craig—" Rosenfeld was beginning exactly where he had been interrupted. "Let's sit over here. Tell me what happened yesterday when you met Sussman, from the very first minute you saw him until the last. Anything could be important, even a seemingly stupid detail. It's all fresh in your memory, isn't it?" For Craig still hesitated, as if he were weighing him up. "Why am I so damned curious, is that what you're thinking? Well, it's obvious that this could have been a political murder, an assassination. Right? In that case, I wouldn't advise you to take your story to the sixth *arrondissement*. It isn't in their line of business. You need something like the Sûreté for this. I have made some friends in Paris who have certain contacts, even some influence, there. They are the kind of people you should be getting in touch with. You give me the facts and I'll see they get them. Today."

Craig was watching him, with amusement showing in his cool gray eyes.

"Well, what?"

"I was just wondering how many refrigerators you do sell."

"Refrigeration. Not refrigerators." Rosenfeld grinned, inclined his head. "I like your caution, anyway." He lit a cigarette, sat back, did no more persuading. A man like Craig made up his own mind. It would be easy to enlist Craig's help by explaining a number of facts about Heinrich Berg; it was also impossible. He thought, perhaps—if he won't talk now—I'll have to get Bernard at the Sûreté to send a couple of men and pick Craig up at his hotel. He wouldn't like that. Nor would I. It could put him in danger, bring his name into the open. And much might be lost: time, surprise, Berg himself. Rosenfeld drew a deep, silent breath.

And Craig was thinking, I'll have to trust him. George does, that's evident. And who else is there, anyway? "Sussman's death is more than a French problem. Is that it, Rosie?" he asked quietly.

Rosie looked at him in amazement. "That's it, exactly." By God, he thought, this man is no fool.

"All right," said Craig, and began his story. "I met him by accident. . . ."

The story ended. Rosie, his face expressionless, was silent. Craig rose, poured himself a glass of water. It was a relief to get rid of all those facts; it was strange, too, when he had been forced to produce them in sequence, how they began to explain each other. "One thing I do know about you, Rosie," he said with a smile. "You're a good listener."

Rosie had looked up quickly, and then relaxed. "I was just giving thanks," he said and rose, too. "It is really a pleasure to watch an accurate memory at work. Is that what they teach you in history?"

And what does that small joke mean? That he doesn't really believe Sussman's story? He is letting me down lightly? "Isn't it possible," Craig tried, "that Berg stopped at our table to point out Sussman to the man in the raincoat? The more I think of the sequence of events— the way Berg waited across the street until his man arrived, as if he had sent for him or—"

"Don't," said Rosie gently, "don't think about them any more." Pretty good, he thought of Craig's remarks, pretty good at that.

"You didn't believe—" Craig began sharply.

"I believe everything you said. I am asking you to forget it. Let me do the remembering. I will." Rosie was thinking, Berg and Insarov. . . . Yes, that seemed more and more likely. Better get in touch with Partridge and Duclos, as soon as possible. Let them contact Holland and Bernard at the Sûreté.

"Forget it? That's a steep order."

"It's just practical advice. Berg isn't alone. I can see the mark of an organization, a well-disciplined and powerful group."

"An organization?" Craig didn't like the sound of that word in the way Rosie had spoken it: it carried a threat. Was Rosie trying to warn him, without giving too much away? "He could have been acting alone, you know—with a friend or paid thug to help him."

"If he were alone and wanted to escape arrest as a Nazi war criminal, he only had to pick up and run, hide somewhere else, adopt a new name, a new life. There's plenty of space in this world for clever fugitives. But he wanted to stay here, unmolested. Why? A mission to perform, perhaps? Then he isn't alone. He didn't kill Sussman, but he ordered the killing. If he has done that once, he can do it again. And for the same reason: protection of his mission. Dedicated men, you know, have a brutal logic. To them, people like Sussman are just specks of dust in the machinery—to be wiped off, and forgotten."

"I get the message," Craig said abruptly. "I don't talk about Berg."

"And you follow your own routine exactly, as if yesterday had never happened."

"You think they'll be interested in me even if I keep my mouth shut?"

"Very interested—until they are convinced they don't have to reckon with you. So play it safe, Craig. Play it very safe."

Craig took a deep breath. He walked over to the window and looked out over the busy street. Beyond it were the Tuileries Gardens, neat paths and flower beds and carefully arranged trees. Children playing, people walking, sitting, talking, thinking. About what? Families and illness and holidays; bills to be paid, a dress to be bought, a new car, a television set; marriages and love affairs, business and pleasure . . . Nice, normal world, whose worries and alarms now seemed very simple. "And only yesterday morning," he said with a wry smile, "I was a reasonably happy man."

"So was I," said Rosie.

Craig looked back at him. I ought to be thanking him for his warning, he thought, instead of feeling sorry for myself. "When will I see you again? And where? I'd like to know how the action goes. I'll breathe a little easier when I hear that Berg is arrested." Now did I say something simple-minded, there? he wondered, as he noticed the amusement showing briefly in Rosie's eyes.

Rosie came over to stand beside him. "I'll miss this city when I have to leave it," he said, looking across the Tuileries to the Seine. "Possibly the next time we'll meet will be in New York in the fall."

"I'd like to know sooner than that."

"I'll telephone you, keep you posted. But no meetings here. No visible contact."

"Are you sure they won't tap my phone at the hotel?" Craig asked, half joking, half annoyed.

"They might at that. If I can't risk telephoning, then I'll have to send someone with a message."

Disguises are coming off, thought Craig: Rosie trusts me a little, at least. And that restored something of his good humor. Distrust, when it wasn't earned, had a savage bite.

"He will know you," Rosie went on. "He'll make contact quite easily."

"You disappoint me, Rosie. No high-signs?"

"Oh, he will shake hands, and leave a nickel in your palm."

"I'll end up rich if you send me enough contacts."

Rosie laughed, clapped his shoulder. "See you in New York, Craig, and you can tell me all about Troy. That's one place I really want to visit. I'd like to stand on the walls, look out over the plain down to the sea where the Argive fleet—" He laughed at the expression on the younger man's face. "Do you know what I once thought I was going to be? An archaeologist." He moved, still shaking his head, to the bedroom door. "All clear, Sue. Do I rate a farewell kiss, or aren't you talking to me any more?" His good-bye was easy and affectionate, and remarkably quick. Craig, watching it from the window, had to admire the tact with which Rosie could fend off questions and yet give acceptable answers. In two minutes, Sue, who thought she was being considerably enlightened, had learned exactly nothing.

"But how nice," she said as the door to the sitting room closed, and they were left alone, "how nice that Rosie knows someone at the police station who can really keep your name out of the papers. I want to see Sussman's murderer caught, but I don't want to see you mixed up in it. These Nazis can be so vindictive, you know."

"Suicide. *Not* murder. And I'll be careful," he promised. "Now what about your hair appointment? I'll walk you there, and we can talk about Father. I'm more anxious about him than I admitted last night."

"What?" she said, her worries flowing into new channels.

And how's that for a brief imitation of Rosie? he asked himself as they set out together. It worked, too. It was family, family, all the way, until the last kiss and parting hug.

71

"Follow your own routine," Rosie had told him, and that was exactly what John Craig did for the next five days.

He admired some of the pictures at the Louvre and most of the sculpture, preferred Sainte-Chapelle to Notre-Dame, took refuge from Sacré-Cœur in Saint-Pierre-de-Montmartre, spent an afternoon in Versailles, a day at Chartres, wandered through Les Halles (and ate one of the best luncheons he had in Paris in the packed company of solid merchants and stall-holders testing the meat and cheese they had sold that morning), explored the various little *quartiers,* looked at Paris from all sides of the Eiffel Tower, loitered at the bookstalls when he meant to be walking through more museums, got some al-most-exercise in the parks, took in a couple of night clubs and three movies, tried several restaurants with stars before their names (he balanced this expenditure with *bistros* and Left Bank *brasseries*), and blessed the prevalence of the French café as pleasant easement for tired feet.

And no one followed him. Or perhaps he was trying not to notice, and succeeding remarkably well. There was, he decided, no use worrying over something beyond his control. He was a traveler on his first voyage of discovery to Europe, something he had begun to plan as far back as his Korean days, when his one ambition was to get as far away from the Pacific as possible and leave the mysterious East to newcomers who didn't remember foxholes. And the plans had lain at the back of his mind during the years at college, during the postgraduate grind, and the extra jobs, and the teaching, and all the damned budgeting for pleasures and weekends that disrupted his time but were a hell of a lot of fun, too, and the articles and reviews that had led gradually, slowly but surely, to this visit to Europe. It was more than a bit of travel: it was the cumulation of hopes and despairs, of dreams and decisions, twelve years in the making and now actually his.

Or was it?

He might not have noticed anyone trailing behind him trying to play the invisible man, but strange encounters were not so easily ignored. There had been several of them, most of them either definitely or possibly innocent; but two were more serious (although if Rosie hadn't planted a warning in his mind, he might have just classified them under odd coincidence, the kind of thing that added a little spice to life), and one took his breath away. Fortunately, no one was testing his pulse at that moment.

Under definitely innocent came the old lady who had lost the right Métro; the young Dutch couple who wanted their photograph taken against the gargoyles of Notre-Dame (they had set the focus; all he was asked to do was to push the button of their camera); an American who was looking for a restaurant where prices were reasonable and the waiter might say thank you for his tip.

Under possibly innocent came the two English girls who attached themselves to him as a useful translator and then proceeded to give him a history lesson through the corridors of Versailles, ending with a shy invitation to a nice spot of tea somewhere in the little town before they all caught the bus back to Paris; and the Algerian student, of an age that indicated he was one of the chronics—the perpetual undergraduates who followed a policy of drift and never took a degree in anything. He shared Craig's lunch table in an overcrowded *brasserie,* talked volubly about universities and politics, expressed the wish to visit the United States and, in between scathing denunciations of imperialism in Cuba and Viet Nam, wondered what American scholarships or grants he could get to keep him at a college there. He ended with a handsome invitation for the evening: he would act as Craig's guide to the more recherché night clubs in Montmartre. He seemed disconsolate over Craig's smiling but definite refusal, the end of a most promising friendship as well as a free night out on the town.

But two encounters were more serious, definitely disturbing. Their skill and effrontery might have been amusing if they hadn't left Craig with the feeling that he was skirting disaster. The first was with a man possibly in his late twenties, nice clean-cut American-boy type, who bumped into him in the lobby of his own hotel, late Saturday afternoon.

"Pardon me," the stranger said, and then grinned widely as he caught Craig's arm. "Hi! Remember me? I'm Willis Jordan, Columbia 'fifty-nine. Now let me see, you're—yes, you're Craig. How's that for memory?"

It was pretty good, Craig thought. He hadn't the smallest recollection of Jordan. Not that that proved anything. Columbia University was a big place. He shook hands, half expecting to feel a nickel crushed into his palm, but there was nothing. "Frankly, I don't remember you at all," he said, keeping his voice friendly. After all, he had just shaken hands.

"Why should you? I was just one of the College boys trying to crash an advanced course on ancient history. You were one of the regulars, a graduate student no less. You didn't think much of us, did you? Quite right. We didn't last more than three lectures. Way beyond me, that stuff. But it made us feel good at the time. Big deal. Between you and me, did you ever learn much from old Sussman? He was the worst lecturer I ever heard, couldn't make out what he was saying most of the time. Or was that just because I was stupid? Could be." He laughed very generously at himself. "Come on and have a drink, just one, and give me all the news on Columbia. Haven't seen it in years."

And how do you know that I have? Craig wondered, and let that slip pass. The rest was so very good; simple and friendly, a little overconfident, like the undergraduate who had crashed Professor Sussman's course. He resisted the impulse to say good-bye and clear out, but that would look as if the name of Sussman had scared him off. "Fine," he said, and led the way into the hotel bar. It was small, square in shape, discreetly lit from the shaded brackets on its walls, a pleasant little place whose nineteenth-century elegance was fading into something cosy and comfortable. There were a few tables, thoughtfully spaced, and green velvet armchairs to match the antique green walls. Everything was old, a little worn, but clean and welcoming. Rather like the solitary bartender, behind his small mahogany counter with its three stools, stirring a dry Martini for a quietly dressed American with light sandy hair, a high forehead and thin-framed glasses. Craig had seen him around on other evenings, so he was a guest here, too. He could have been a young college professor, only his interests—judging from the magazines he always seemed to be reading—lay in auctions and antiques. "No luck at all, today," he was answering the barman, as Craig and his hail-fellow came to stand beside him. "Nothing but junk, Jules, nothing but trash held together by some glue."

Jules shook his head over the temerity of the furniture market, poured the Martini carefully, said, "You should try the Loire Valley, Monsieur Partreege. There are fine things to be discovered there."

"Perhaps I shall. Thank you, Jules." The American took his glass, tasted the Martini, nodded his approval, and left the bar for the one table still free, where he could study his catalogue in peace.

Mr. Jordan seemed relieved that the other American had gone. "Now we'll have room for our elbows," he said, grinning widely. "What's yours, Craig? Scotch? I'll try one of Jules' Martinis." Jules hardly flickered an eyebrow even if his first name was reserved for guests who came steadily. Jordan was too busy to notice. He was studying Craig, his smile still in place, trying to get back onto the subject of Sussman. "And what are you doing here?"

"Seeing Paris."

"For how long?"

"Another few days."

"Thinking of going skiing?"

Craig stared. "It's a bit late in the year for that."

"You know, funny thing, that's how I remembered your face. I'll never forget you hobbling on crutches around the campus—broke a leg, didn't you? Made a big impression on me. Here's someone who goes skiing and can understand Sussman, too!"

And here's someone who has been reading through the old class yearbooks, thought Craig. Then he had a stab of guilt. Perhaps he was being too unkind to Mr. Jordan, perhaps the man had really been around Columbia from 1955 to 1959. "It's easy enough to go skiing if you do tutoring on the weekends and your pupil has an uncle who owns a ski lodge."

But Jordan twisted back to the real subject. "And how is old Sussman? Still teaching away?"

Craig looked at the smiling face and took a deep breath. Then he said, very quietly, "He's dead."

"When?" The smile faded perfectly.

"Three days ago. In Paris. It was in all the papers. Suicide." And that, thought Craig grimly, will save unnecessary questions.

"Now what could have caused it, d'you suppose?" Jordan's sympathy was even harder to take than his genial curiosity. Craig shrugged. "Tough," said Jordan. "You always liked him. When did you last see him?"

"We had a drink together on the day he died."

"How was he then? I mean—it's a really terrible thing, suicide. Didn't you feel something was wrong?"

"No. Or I wouldn't have said good-bye to him and let him walk away."

"You mean, he was quite normal—just sat talking about nothing, passing the time of day?"

"I hope not. He asked me about my work, gave me some advice, a lot of encouragement."

"I can see why you feel so bad, talking about yourself and all the time he must have been worrying about something else."

"Now, look here, Jordan—" Craig began in real anger, and stopped. Don't be goaded, he reminded himself. "How the hell do I know what *you're* thinking? You might be planning suicide right now. How does a man read another's thoughts? Sussman was depressed, yes: he had just been giving testimony at Frankfurt. I thought some talk about his own subject would get his mind off those trials, make him forget. I was wrong. So—"

"Hold on, hold on, I didn't mean it that way. Of course you couldn't guess. But something must have been troubling him badly. Now you'd think, wouldn't you, that he had a fine chance to tell you his problems when he met you, and get rid of them? You knew him well—"

"I guess I didn't know him well enough," Craig said sadly, honestly. He frowned at his drink. I used to laugh at movies where one guy at a bar hit out at another guy, but I swear if Jordan doesn't take that sympathetic voice out of my hearing in the next three minutes, he isn't going to have much voice left. One sharp blow across his throat with the back of my hand—yes, just the way I used to practice it in Korea for night-patrol work. *Karate in Saint-Honoré bar.* A nice headline.

"Now that's an interesting thought, whatever it is," Jordan said, watching his face.

"Who knows anyone well enough?" Craig finished his drink. "What about another? You haven't told me yet what you're doing in Europe. Business or pleasure?"

Jordan looked at his watch. "It's past six. Got to get going. I have to meet a lawyer tonight; I'm publicity man for Eurasia Films, and we're running into trouble over distribution of a movie about the French Army."

"Business on a Saturday night? That's working you hard."

"Has to be, has to be . . . I'm back in Brussels tomorrow. That's the way it goes. Well, good to see you again. Here, Jules, keep the change." He pushed some ready francs across the counter, patted Craig's shoulder, and left.

"Another Scotch, Mr. Craig?"

Craig nodded. If ever a man needed grog it was John Craig, standing in a quiet and pleasant little bar, with the gentle hum of innocent voices rising from the tables behind him.

"And what about you, Mr. Partreege?" Jules asked of the thin-faced American, who had come back to the bar.

"No, thanks. Just put the rest on the bill." He dropped an extra tip near Jules, glanced at Craig, almost spoke, hesitated, then said, "Sorry, I thought I had met you before. My mistake." He looked enquiringly at Jules with a touch of perplexity mixed with amusement over his small error.

Jules said quickly, "This is Mr. Craig, who is a guest here, too."

Partridge, pausing as he was about to turn away, said, "You really look very much like a man I knew in Japan about ten years ago."

"I've been there, but I don't think we ever met." Is this another try? They're keeping me busy, Craig thought.

"My name's Jim Partridge." The stranger put out his hand. Craig took it. Pressed into his palm, he felt a small round object. "Perhaps we can have a drink together some evening?"

"No reason why we shouldn't."

Partridge said very quietly, "You handled him well. No slips." And turned away definitely, this time.

Craig finished his drink slowly. The tension was gone. So was that very unpleasant feeling of actual fear, when the man who called himself Jordan had patted his shoulder and left. He had stood there, waiting for the second drink, wondering what mistakes he had made.

Thank God for Jim Partridge. "No slips," he had said. But how had he known? Had he been able to listen to the conversation? It was a fantastic thought. Possible? Gadgets, nowadays, were ingenious. Perhaps I'll learn when we do have that drink together. At least one thing I do know now: I'm not alone.

That was a good feeling. He could even look back on the encounter with Jordan and study it with cool amusement.

Then there was, two days later, the second encounter. It began, in contrast to the Jordan incident, very quietly indeed. And ended with no amusement at all.

It was late on Monday afternoon. Craig had been searching for old maps of ancient Greece and the eastern Mediterranean, the kind of thing that he might possibly discover in the secondhand bookshops around the Beaux-Arts district. That was also the district where the girl lived, the girl with the dark hair and blue eyes who had walked away from his taxi five nights ago, name unknown, address unknown, swallowed up in the maze of streets, vanishing into the shadows. And although he produced a reasonable excuse each day to get him over to the Left Bank and keep an eye open for that smooth dark head, he had no luck at all. He had the fanciful idea that if he only kept thinking hard enough about her, she might walk out of that baker's shop, or down the street, or be standing in this bookstore like the hundred other students who did much of their pleasure reading there. But like all fanciful ideas, it was high in expectations and low in results. He never saw her. Perhaps she had left Paris, perhaps she wasn't a student. And probably she had forgotten all about him by this time. Why, he wondered with considerable irritation, why the hell didn't he forget her?

His search for maps and ancient charts had led him along the Rue de Seine toward the Boulevard Saint-Germain. He saw a possible bookshop, entered it, and found so much to interest him that he was there for half an hour or more. There were a dozen people around, picking up books, flipping over pages, putting the books down, choosing others, reading. The shelves were crowded to the ceiling, the stacks were so close together that the alleys between them allowed only one-way passage. Craig was in such an alley when a polite French voice said, "Pardon, monsieur." Craig looked up and saw a middle-aged man with kindly eyes in a likable face. Craig closed the book he had been reading and stuffed it back quickly on its shelf. "Sorry," he said, "I'm in your way."

The stranger broke into English. "Not at all. I don't think I'm going to find what I'm looking for, either." Then he laughed. "Are you following me? We are becoming good acquaintances, this afternoon. Didn't I hear you asking for maps down on the Rue Bonaparte? No luck? I, too, have had no success." His English was very passable, and saved Craig groping around for a few polite phrases in return.

"I'm giving up the search," Craig said, coming out of the book-lined passage. "It's all yours." He stood aside to let the Frenchman enter. The man's eyes were studying the shelves. He shook his head. "Not here," he said resignedly. "Just let me ask the owner. Perhaps he can tell us of another bookshop that might have your maps and my Leonardo da Vinci illustrations. One moment, monsieur!" He pressed his way through the groups of students and elderly men, reached the owner behind his table stacked high with dusty books. There was a quick outflow of fine French phrases. Craig made his way to the door, hesitated, started slowly toward the Boulevard Saint-Germain. Helpful people were pleasant, but generally useless. And yet he didn't want to be rude in return for some politeness (heaven knew it was scarce enough in Paris, nowadays, where foreigners were considered a necessary nuisance), and so he halted to wait for the stranger and at least say thank you.

"You are going in the right direction," his mentor told him cheerfully. "There is a shop, very big, very new, you might not think it of any help; but there is a back room, I am told, with all kinds of amazing curiosities. Let me show you. It is on the boulevard itself." He fell into step beside Craig, mentioning his name (Ardouin), his profession ("an engineer for aeroplanes"), his hobby (collecting illustrations of old inventions for warfare such as da Vinci's designs). There was such a bookstore, but the back room had been cleared for new stock.

Ardouin, in his own words, was desolated. This extra journey for nothing! Craig must have a drink with him, and they could finish their talk about ancient cartographers who guessed so much and were sometimes almost right.

Craig, ready to call it the end of an acquaintanceship yet still unwilling to cut it short rudely, walked along with the little Frenchman, trying to think of a chance for disengagement. And suddenly, against the friendly chatter at his elbow, against the background of cheerful street noise and bustle, there was a grim and warning note. They were walking along the same part of the boulevard where he had met Sussman. They were passing two cafés where they could have had that drink. "No, no," said his new friend, "not here! There is a much more interesting place quite near. When I was a student in Paris, it was where the amusing people met. Just down here, around this corner!"

Craig kept his steady pace, didn't let himself hesitate. He even managed to hold back the quick flash of anger that surged through his body. You'll have to go through with it, he told himself, go through with it to the end. "But of course," he heard himself say in a natural voice, answering a question about New York. "There are fashions in cafés everywhere, I guess." He looked at the faded little awning they were now reaching, the few tables on the narrow sidewalk. "Why," he said, "I know this place! I was here only a few nights ago. There's a Buddha inside, and a picture of Socrates. Right?"

Again Ardouin was desolated. "And I thought I would show you something new, something different," he said. "Shall we sit outside?" And he was choosing the table where Craig had sat before, selecting Sussman's chair for himself. He fell very silent.

"Yes," said Craig, "this is even the same table. I hope you aren't superstitious."

Ardouin blinked a little. "Engineers are not usually superstitious," he said with a smile.

"You've taken the same chair where my friend sat. And he is now dead."

"But I am sorry! Does that worry you?"

"I don't find it exactly cheerful."

"A drink is what we need," Ardouin said quickly, and signaled the waiter—he was new but he looked just as sad and slow as the other one, five nights ago. "All Americans drink Scotch, no?"

"It isn't very good Scotch, here. I'll try Cinzano. I must say—" he looked around, noticing a car parked nearby with its driver reading a newspaper—"this café is really on the losing end of this street." It was almost as woebegone in sunshine as it had been in the rain. Few people walked here, and those were in a hurry, as if they were using it only as a short cut to some place more important.

"Then we shall talk about pleasant things. Last time, perhaps you were listening to depressing talk?"

From the doorway farther down the curving street, on its opposite side, a man in a black overcoat stepped out and came walking slowly toward the café. For a moment, Craig had no answer. He looked away from the walking man, found a cigarette and his lighter, was relieved to see that his hands were steadier than he felt. "I spent more time looking than listening," he said. Good God, he was thinking, is Heinrich Berg going to walk up *here?*

"Looking?" The Frenchman was alert. "And what was so interesting on this street?"

"A girl. She was sitting over there, behind your chair. And having a very bad time." Quickly, he gave a brief description of the quarrel.

"How extraordinary," Ardouin said with complete indifference.

"It was. I mean, what could have caused such a long quarrel as that? I keep thinking about it." Yes, Heinrich Berg was sitting down at the very same table he had occupied last Wednesday. "Or, rather, I keep wondering what her man would have thought if he could have sat here, where I am, and watched his own performance. Or would he have needed a stranger's eyes, too, to see what he was throwing away?"

"I don't understand why you should be so concerned," began Ardouin impatiently, and then corrected his tone of voice to something more natural. "Unless, of course, she was very pretty."

"But naturally! That is what was so extraordinary." Craig looked in astonishment at Ardouin. "Haven't you noticed a considerable decline in pretty girls in the last few years? What's gone wrong? A cult of ugliness? Or it might be that this is a base form of democracy—let everyone look equally unappetizing, destroy the beauties, turn all girls into the same type with the same hair styles, the same grotesque eyes, the same vapid lips? Now I'm assuming that as a Frenchman you have certain standards for the chic and the beautiful, but—looking around Paris—I'd like to ask you what has been happening." Craig rattled on, listening to himself with a mild disbelief and a touch of rising laughter. For Ardouin was taking him seriously. Ardouin was looking at him nervously, and then with annoyance, and then with complete irritation; the once kindly eyes were showing both contempt and impatience. He finished his drink quickly, glanced at his watch.

"You must go?" Craig asked. Now it's my turn to be desolated. "I think I'll wait here for a while."

"Still hoping that you will see the girl again?" Ardouin asked, shaking his head. These Americans . . .

"Why not? This place seems to have its regulars." He glanced at some new arrivals, recognizing them faintly from his last visit. "She may be one of them. Good luck with the war machines!"

That produced a startled look, and then a very quick *"Merci. Au revoir."* A nice formal bow, and Ardouin was in retreat toward the boulevard. Leaving me to pay for the drinks, thought Craig. But it had been worth it.

He did wait for a while. He let Berg pass him with only a cursory, natural glance. Just another regular, that was Craig's attitude. He noticed that the car, parked not far away, had started to leave, too. He wondered whether he might not have ended inside it if he had started to tell Ardouin to phone for the police, for anyone, to catch a man who was possibly connected with a murder. Even if that was a bit of imaginative exaggeration about the car, he was thinking how he might have behaved if Rosie hadn't given him fair warning. Rosie had only been wrong in one thing so far: he hadn't given him any telephone number to call in an emergency like this. With the right number, he could have said, "If you want Berg, then he is sitting at a table only twenty feet or so away from me." And then, annoyance fading, he knew Rosie had been right. One step toward a telephone, either before or after Berg had left, and Craig might have found out whether his crude guess about the waiting car was fantastic or not.

I suppose, he thought heavily, I'm being watched even now. So he paid and left. If he looked depressed, the enemy could assume that he had become tired of waiting for a girl. And who was the enemy? That was one question he was going to ask Rosie. He would like to know who was turning his visit to Paris into a nightmare. That was a score that needed a little settling, quite apart from the bill that had mounted high with Sussman's death.

He went back to the Saint-Honoré, with the hope that Jim Partridge would be reading quietly in the bar—the news about Berg must be passed on as quickly as possible. But Partridge was entertaining two French friends tonight, a dark-haired young man with blue eyes and ruddy cheeks, and a charming red-haired Frenchwoman. They were talking of furniture, of designs in fabrics, with occasional laughter over Partridge's brave attempts at French and their equally comic efforts in English to help him out. It was a merry little business meeting, and Craig, just two tables away, found himself believing it authentic. Partridge had only given a polite nod of recognition and a bare "Good evening" as he had entered and found a seat. It was a frustrating feeling to sit there, in possession of some real news, and to have to keep it clamped to himself. Eventually, as Partridge and his friends left, he got the silent message: we'll contact you when we are good and ready, so sit tight and keep your mouth shut. What the flaming hell, he thought; don't they want to catch Berg?

He went out searching for dinner, which he didn't enjoy and which cost far too much anyway. And that was another thing, he told himself as he went angrily to bed after a disappointing movie: you'd better clear out to the Mediterranean; another week of Paris and your budget will be so wrecked that you'll have only a few weeks left in Europe. Get back to your own world, Craig, and stay where you belong. But can there be any separate worlds? he wondered as he thought of Sussman.

7

"It was tempting," Rosie said softly. "It was very tempting to have that man followed."

"You think he might have been Berg?" Partridge asked.

"The waiter's description of him was almost a duplicate of what Craig told me at the Meurice last Thursday morning. He wore the same kind of coat, walked from the same doorway, sat down at the exact table."

"No wonder Craig was so tight-faced this evening. He came into the Saint-Honoré bar about seven when I was there with Yves Duclos and Mimi. He looked as if he had just about had it." Partridge watched Rosie prowling around the small room restlessly, checking the locked window, pulling the torn shade closer to the sill, dragging the narrow strips of curtain more together. Fortunately, the light was too dim to throw any shadows in the direction of the run-down street outside. "Not very elegant," Partridge agreed as Rosie stared at the brash cubist design on the curtains, "but this is the kind of place where everyone finds it pays to mind his own business. Balances my room over at the Saint-Honoré very nicely." Both hotels had been Partridge's own idea. He had moved into them last Thursday soon after he had arrived in Paris; a cheap bag for this room, a leather suitcase respectably labeled for the Saint-Honoré, and he was nicely set up. "Easy commuting, too."

"Very neat," agreed Rosie, and gave his full approval. He sat down once more on the only chair, and faced Partridge, who was lounging on the narrow bed.

"So Berg walked away from that café," Partridge said thoughtfully, wondering what agent had slipped up there.

"If that was a mistake, then it's mine. Berg has not only brains but intuition. Better give him no warning signals of any kind. Better wait, try to find out what his mission in Paris is. Then we can pick him up, get Insarov-Berg in one neat package. That's the way I see it anyway. I may be wrong. I've been arguing with Bernard over at the Sûreté about this. He is, naturally enough, interested in any spy networks that are working in Paris. I feel that there may be more than a network involved. If Berg *is* Insarov, that is . . ." His voice trailed away with his thoughts.

"You're beginning to believe it, too?" Partridge asked quickly, and he couldn't be more delighted.

"Yes, but not for a very satisfactory reason—that is, not satisfactory to anyone except myself. I read through the dossiers you collected on both Berg and Insarov. And it was by remembering some of the Insarov details that I—well, let's say that Berg's actions today didn't astonish me too much."

"You studied Insarov and came up with Berg?"

"That's about it. But it doesn't prove a thing. I could be wrong."

Yet he had believed it enough, himself, to persuade Bernard to have a waiter installed for the last four days in the café, Partridge thought. "No photographs possible?"

He doesn't miss much, thought Rosie, and smiled. "No. The waiter had a microfilm lighter all ready to use, but Berg didn't take out a cigarette. And he kept his back turned to the restaurant. And he waved away any attempt to take an order; managed to avert his face, too. So the waiter followed his basic orders, which were to note any middle-aged man who wasn't known as a regular customer and to report to the Sûreté at once. He did this, but Berg was already leaving. He staged his exit right past Craig's table, and then was picked up by a car that had been waiting near by." Rosie thought that over. "I didn't have anyone ready to follow him, but you know something? I feel relieved about that. If it was a mistake, I think it was a mistake in the right direction. One suspicion aroused, and the whole Berg-Insarov operation would plunge underground. When, and where, it would emerge wouldn't even be worth a guess." He made a good attempt at a smile. "Yes, you could say that I had almost as bad a day as Craig, poor devil."

Partridge nodded understandingly. They could easily lose the fingertip hold they had on this case. Then all the work Chris Holland and he had done in those intense four months would be made useless. "I think the French might be pretty riled, too, if we lost Insarov just at this time. Duclos was pretty excited about some new developments."

"Oh?"

"He gave me a few background details over dinner, asked me to pass them on to you tonight. He's missing your visits to his studio."

"Better to get his news this way," Rosie said tersely.

"Someone still interested in you?"

"Infatuated with me, damn them. But let's disappoint them, shall we?" His smile became blandly innocent. "And what's exciting the French?"

"A night club called Le Happening. And guess who gave them the break on this? Interpol."

"Interpol? What were they expecting at Le Happening—heroin or white-slave traffic?"

"Either. One of the part-owners was almost convicted twelve years ago of smuggling drugs and shipping stranded chorus girls into the slave states. So when this new club was started a few months ago with no visible backers, Interpol took a quiet interest. The Paris police cooperated and placed three of its agents as a waiter, a stagehand, and the coatroom biddy. She reported that last Wednesday night, or, rather, in the small hours of Thursday morning, a blonde girl waited for an American in the lobby. He wore dark glasses. He carried a book in a bright jacket, and displayed a pair of new gloves quite prominently. He also had a folded newspaper under his arm in a distinctive alphabet—she thought Greek. He just dumped his coat on the counter, keeping his face turned to the girl. They did not call each other by any name when they met. They only stayed a brief time. The girl left first. The American collected his coat—he had a handkerchief up at his face, blast him—and then made for the men's room. But he didn't go in. He kept on going, past the back of the stage, to the rear of the building. He never came back. Must have left by one of the old entrances to the delivery yard."

"Good for the hat-check chick!" Rosie was always delighted by efficiency.

"She's reaching sixty. One of the best operatives in the Narcotics branch. She knows a recognition signal when she sees one. Oh, yes—the girl wore odd earrings: one emerald, one ruby. Sounds charming, don't you think?"

"And what did the Narcotics Squad find next morning—I suppose they searched the back premises?"

"They certainly did. In the hours when the place is closed except for cleaners, they got one of their men to slip into the back corridor. Storage and unused dressing rooms. Nothing there in the way of cartons or containers. No sign of heroin in the dust on the floor. But there was a mirror on the wall between two rooms. A see-through mirror."

"Well, now—the clever little rascals."

"That was when Interpol and the French police decided it might be espionage, and not drug-smuggling. They handed the problem over to the Sûreté. Bernard has been working on it."

"He has, has he?"

"I think he was waiting to get some results before he told us about it," Partridge said tactfully.

"Very thoughtful of him." Rosie took a long breath. "Co-operation! Oh well, it's his country. But dammit, you'd think—" He caught hold of himself. "Perhaps I've lived too long here. I'm beginning to assume this is partly my country, too. All right, all right . . . He's working on the problem?"

"He had some of his experts install a listening device in the rooms with the connecting mirror. It wasn't too easy—no furniture worth mentioning, no lamp shades, and the electric bulbs are doubtless changed regularly." Partridge's amusement boiled over into a fit of laughter. "So they wired the mirror for sound—used its frame."

Very funny, very funny, thought Rosie, but where does this lead us?

"And it worked!" Partridge said, recovering himself. "At two a.m. on Saturday morning, there was a brief conversation between a Russian and a man who was to use the name of Jordan. Instructions were given to Jordan about meeting Craig that afternoon or evening in the Saint-Honoré lobby. Also, he learned certain information about Craig based on a telephoned report from New York about a Columbia College yearbook. Also, a photograph taken of Craig at the Eiffel Tower was examined and discussed."

Rosie relaxed. "We're in business," he said very softly. He studied the arm of his chair. It was a violent purplish red, a cheap imitation velvet worn into mauve patches. He picked at a loose thread. "You'll call me as soon as Duclos passes on any more news?" It was Rosie's way of giving an order. He rose from the abominable chair, caught sight of the giant yellow roses on the blue wallpaper, and groaned. "I hope you don't ever have to sleep here."

Partridge was picking up the soiled raincoat which had lain near him on the bed. He pulled it on, and it transformed his gray flannel suit into something less affluent and more suitable for his departure through the neglected lobby downstairs. "I'll follow you out—I want to get back to the Saint-Honoré tonight."

So Jim Partridge was worried about Craig, too. And with every reason. Rosie said regretfully, "It would be easier on him if we could explain things more."

"You'd trust him as far as that?"

"If we were forced to, I'd trust him. But let's hope it never comes to that."

"Amateurs worry me. They're too big a responsibility."

Rosie inclined his head in half-agreement. Sometimes, though, they produced the most astounding results. He thought of Venice, almost three years ago. "Bless their little hearts," he said.

"Of course, Craig seems to have the right impulses. I mean, if you trusted him with the truth, he'd probably accept it. He wouldn't start trying to prove you're an idiot or a liar just so he could dodge the real issue and still keep his conscience happy."

"You seem to know him well," Rosie murmured.

"I've been listening to you. I think you like the guy. By the way, what happened to the man who took Craig to the café?"

"Photographed and followed. He may lead us to interesting people."

"And Jordan? The same treatment?"

"Yes."

"Well, that's progress of sorts. You know, I think Berg must be staying some place very close to that café. How else could he have appeared so quickly once his man had delivered Craig to the right table? And there's the problem, too, of how that man knew that Craig was going to be wandering through bookshops."

"My guess is that he didn't know, that he was told to go to work on

Craig whenever Craig was visiting the Left Bank. And that has been quite often. He seemingly likes the place."

"The curious thing," Partridge said thoughtfully, "is the difference between the two sets of instructions. Those given Jordan were precise. Those given the second man, if you are right, were much more— imaginative. What's your hunch, Rosie? That there are two different bosses giving their own type of instructions? Or is there a split in command?"

"Jim, you know I'm always battling against hunches. They seem so damned idiotic when they don't pay off." Rosie's amused eyes studied the younger man's face. He relented. "But I wouldn't discard that guess of yours. Every small idea counts in this game. And that was a good one." Rosie paused at the door. "When you call me, add ninety minutes to the time you fix for the meeting. Where shall it be?"

"Duclos suggested Mimi's shop. Rue La Fay—"

"I've heard of it. Hand-blocked linens and upholstery satin, all for the Cadillac trade. You'd never believe it, but the last time I saw Mimi she had the Lido all tied up with her bikini." Rosie was still grinning broadly as he left. For such a solidly constructed man, his movements were surprisingly light. Partridge, standing at the door, couldn't even hear the usual creak of the faulty floor boards.

He gave Rosie six minutes before he buckled the belt of his coat, turned up its collar to hide his clean shirt, pulled on a battered hat with a dipping brim, slipped off his glasses and put them into his pocket. He only needed them for reading, but they had become a habit; made him look more responsible, he had thought, a little more serious, older, more eligible for promotion. A bad habit, he decided, breeding the type of mind that was afraid of hunches. For he was still puzzling out Insarov, the man with the imaginative instructions, the man who played it by ear as well as relying on a machine-like mind. Insarov's specialty was psychological warfare, wasn't it? So that's how Rosie guessed he would stage a confrontation scene. Damn it all, he said to himself, I made out all those reports; Rosie only read them. So why couldn't I have risked a guess at Insarov's behavior patterns? Re-enactment, disclosure through shock? Yes, it was easy to see it all now, once it had happened. A nice case of hindsight. Not good enough; not good enough, when you dealt with a man like Insarov.

Then, as he left the room, he knew one of the answers to the puzzle.

He had kept thinking of Insarov as some fantastic brain, some inexorable planner, a powerful force gathering strength to destroy his enemy. But Rosie had met that type before; Rosie knew he was human. And one thing all human beings shared in common, apart from the need to eat and drink and sleep and function as a body: each had his Achilles' heel. What was Insarov's? And what's yours, Jim? He reached the desolate lobby, pushed open the finger-smeared door, and stepped into the dark street.

Partridge's call came sooner than expected. It caught Rosie in his office, just before noon on Tuesday, the very next day. *"Ici* Basdevant,"* began Partridge crisply, and then continued in heavily accented English. "About the question of the new refrigeration unit for the Caen Sausage and Tripe Distributors' processing plant—when can you have it installed?"

"Any time. Just sign the order and we can start work on it at once."

"Good. Then I shall sign the contract at four o'clock this afternoon, if that is suitable for you."

"Most suitable," said Rosie. "We shall have everything drawn up and ready. At your convenience, Monsieur Basdevant." He could not resist adding, "The first name is Alphonse, is it not?"

"Correct. There will be no delay in installation?"

"I assure you, we have the unit available. I realize the urgency of your problem."

"With the approach of a warm spring," the Sausage and Tripe distributor said, "we must insist—"

"Have no fear, monsieur, your products will be safe with us."

Monsieur Alphonse Basdevant bade a pleasant good day.

So, Rosie thought, we meet at half past two, and don't be late. Something has developed, has it? Something big? In addition to that encouraging piece of news, he was beginning to have high hopes for Partridge. The over-serious calculating machine was showing a touch of humor. Or perhaps he had had it all along, and Rosie had smothered it. Some light relief was welcome, anyway; there was no better safety valve. It counteracted Rosie's depressing discovery of that morning. His telephone had been tapped.

He became businesslike, instructed his secretary to fill out a standard contract for a refrigeration unit, to be signed this afternoon on behalf of Caen Sausage and Tripe Distributors by their agent Alphonse Basdevant. Time and place of delivery to be added on Basdevant's instructions. She could leave it on his desk. He was now going to lunch and then to a fitting at his tailor's. About time, too, didn't she think?

Rosie approved of Mimi's shop. It was close to a Métro, a bus stop, and a taxi rank. It lay on a busy street. And it shared the same entrance with five other specialized places—a little dressmaker, a little hat designer, a little travel agency, a little boutique for Florentine handbags and Perugian sweaters, and a little man for big parties. (The adjective "little" showed how talented and expensive they all were.) There were constant comings and goings, a perpetual drift of people so intent on their highly important business that the more ordinary mortals such as Rosie were not even worth one glance.

Mimi, in person, was far from little. She was the only girl that Rosie could remember who had made a bikini look as if it had been designed for a Caryatid solemnly gazing over the Acropolis, one thigh forward ready to march in sacred procession to Athena's high altar. Her hair was now a rich ripe auburn, piled loosely over a white face and dark eyebrows. But the smoke-gray eyes still had the pure intent gaze of the Caryatid, seemingly blank, aware of everything. She opened the door, with its CLOSED ON TUESDAY sign already displayed, and locked it securely behind him. *"Cher* Rosee!" she said, giving him a soft cheek to kiss and an enveloping hug from her beautiful strong arms. Then she retired with her long slow stride to her own corner, settled before her drawing board, continued her work on a current design, and left the three men to themselves.

Duclos' eyes were a bright blue today, a sign that excitement was running through his veins. Partridge had been anxious, even tense, but with Rosie's safe arrival he relaxed. Now he was watching Duclos, impatient and curious. Rosie looked at them both, pushed aside a bolt of antique satin from the one comfortable chair over which it had been draped to entice a customer, and sat down. My news will keep, he thought, looking at the expectant faces. He put aside the memory of a hurried and horrible lunch, of the long, long journey to cover the equivalent of ten blocks between the restaurant and Mimi's. "Sorry I'm late. I'm ready, Yves. Don't disappoint me."

"Jim told you about Le Happening and the mirror we wired for sound?" Duclos began. "It works. There was a long session in the unused dressing rooms last night. We picked it up, all of it. And taped it. You can hear it in detail when you visit Bernard. Part of it is in Russian, of course. We've had that translated. Part of it is in French, when a woman was getting her instructions from someone who gave his code name as Peter. Her name is Erica. She's the same woman, the coatroom attendant assures us, who met the American in the lobby last week. His name came into Erica's conversation with Peter. It is Alex. Her instructions were to travel to Greece and take up residence on the island of Mykonos. Alex would visit her there, briefly, on his way back to Paris. He would pass her some information of the highest importance. She would deliver it within a few hours to someone on the island. She would receive further instructions about that later. In the meantime, she is to concentrate on making her journey to Mykonos seem plausible. She is borrowing a house, rented by her uncle, so that she can enjoy a summer of painting. She will invite another girl to accompany her, someone who also is an artist. Then the two of them can have many parties, meet many people. In this way, the couriers or agents who make contact with her during the summer will seem to be a natural part of the general picture. Alex will be her first visitor. She is to expect him in the early part of May."

Duclos paused to take a map out of his pocket, unfold it, stretch it flat on a small table.

"Mykonos." Rosie glanced over at Partridge, who only smiled quietly. Mykonos had appeared in Partridge's report on Heinrich Berg, a small item dealing with Berg's closest friends in Nazi Germany who were still known to be alive and free. There were only two of them left in that category: one was a woman, Berg's mistress, who had shared his politics as well as his bed, and was now rumored to be in Milan;

the other was Gerhard Ludwig, who had never been a member of the Nazi party but had left Germany in 1950. It was known that he had been living in Greece and writing travel books. Three years ago, he had left Athens for the Greek Islands. He was reported living in Mykonos.

"Yes, Mykonos!" Duclos answered. "It's the most perfect place for their purpose. It has a constant stream of visitors—writers, painters, scholars, ordinary tourists who are cruising through the Aegean. It has an art colony—quite a number of French intellectuals have rented houses. There is a harbor for small yachts, sailing boats, fishing boats. The cruise ships call there; and so do the inter-island mail boats. And then Delos—"

"Yes, it's perfect," agreed Rosie. Unlikely in its innocence; and therefore all the more perfect. He rose and went over to look at the map. Mykonos had a central position among the scattered groups of islands in the Aegean.

"But where," asked Partridge, "is Alex arriving from? Mykonos gives us no indication where he has been gathering information: it's just about halfway between Greece and Turkey." He came over to join the others at the map. "It was a simpler problem for us two years ago, when we had some worry about the islands of Lesbos and Chios which lie very close to Turkey—Chios is only a few miles, practically swimming distance, from the Turkish coast, and the quickest way to get from Greece to Smyrna."

Duclos was startled. "Just one second!" he said sharply. He looked annoyed, almost deflated. "Will you please wait until we finish with questions about Mykonos before you start talking of Smyrna, or Izmir, as the Turks call it?" Having established control, he added with a friendly smile, "You Americans—you are always blasting off in every direction."

"Okay," said Partridge with a grin. "I was heading right back to Mykonos anyway, because what worried us in Lesbos particularly was an attempt to form a base of Communist espionage operations which would gather information about the Turkish coast all the way south from Çanakkale on the Dardanelles to the American base near Smyrna using Chios as either a cutout or a handy transit station but if you look at these islands' position on the map you'll agree the project was a bit too obvious even if daring and so it failed and I'm only blasting off because Rosie says they always keep trying bless the clever little rascals and that lands me right smack on Mykonos." He paused for breath, his grin broadening. If you talked fast enough, you could still make your point at the right and proper time. "All right; over to you, Yves. Questions about Mykonos."

"I have a couple," Rosie said, repressing his own smile. "But let me ask them sitting down. I had a lot of exercise today." He led the return to their chairs, settled himself once more, avoided Partridge's quick, enquiring eyes. "First, who is the girl that Erica will invite to Mykonos? Any indications?" She could be another member of Erica's Communist group; or a sympathizer, eager to help and obey; or some innocent who hadn't the faintest idea for what purpose she was being used.

"There were two definite specifications," Duclos said. "The girl must be politically immature and emotionally unattached. There were also suggestions that she must be charming enough to attract friends on Mykonos, trusting enough so that she would not be suspicious. Perfect cover for Erica, isn't it?"

"So the girl will go in good faith. She will hear and see no political evil because she doesn't believe that people like Erica can be part of her world." Rosie shook his head; how often he had seen that pattern repeated. It never amused him.

"Exactly. Erica will choose her, herself. In fact, she had two possibilities in mind, right away, and gave their names to Peter so that he could have a check made on them for security. Her favorite candidate was—" and here Duclos cleared his throat lightly—"an American student in Paris. Erica and she have attended the same art classes, seemingly. Name: Veronica Clark. Age: twenty-five. She lives in a small hotel in the Beaux-Arts district: Hotel Beauharnais."

"Poor Veronica," Partridge said. "What art student would refuse a visit to Mykonos?"

Rosie looked at him thoughtfully. "What intelligence agent, for that matter? You seem to be the expert on the Aegean, Jim. If it isn't a rude question, how did you manage that, sitting at a desk in Germany?"

"The nucleus of the Lesbos organization was recruited from a Communist network in West Berlin. We seem to be facing the same kind of thing now, but this time they're working out of Paris. And—

this time, too—the boss-man has appeared, himself, to make sure that there will be no more failures. Could be?"

"Insarov?" Rosie nodded. That could be.

Duclos threw up his hands. "Let us finish with Erica, first," he insisted. "You had two questions about her, Rosie. You've only asked one."

"Had she anything to say about the American called Alex? Anything that could give us a lead on him?"

"She remarked that her meeting with Alex last week had troubled her; he was cautious to an extreme. But perhaps he would feel easier when he did not have to carry new gloves and a travel book on tours to Scandinavia. She was reproved for her flippancy. She was told that he had every reason to be cautious in Paris."

"Meaning he is well known? Of some importance?" Rosie asked quickly.

"He has an important job, certainly. That we learned from the Russian conversation that followed next. Shall I go on with it, now?"

"One last question about dear Erica," Partridge said, glancing at Rosie. "Did you have her followed, photographed?"

Duclos looked at Rosie, too. "We tried to play it your way," he told him. "We only followed a little. After she changed cars twice, we decided that any more following would only lead to discovery."

"We'll get her on Mykonos, anyway," Rosie said impatiently.

"If you play it carefully."

"You mean Mykonos is of no interest to you?"

"Personally, I am interested. But Bernard sees his first duty in putting the spy network in Paris quite out of business. Understandably. After all, the American base in Turkey is your affair, not ours." He was watching Partridge's astonished eyes with some amusement. "Yes, at Smyrna. It is nice to know you may be very near the truth," he agreed.

"Any proof?" Partridge asked intently.

"Only what we heard in the conversation between two Russians as soon as Erica had departed. One was Peter—his voice is deep, hoarse, identifiable. The other we could not place, but he is most certainly Peter's superior. Now, let me remember. . . ." Yves was putting his facts into the neat and logical order that he found agreeable: the free-floating ideas, the quick jumps in thinking practiced by his American friends were something that irked his sense of balance and proportion. Small details, perhaps of greatest importance, could be lost in the excitement of discovery. This report was his to give, and he was determined to give it in his way.

"Alex is going to Smyrna. Purpose not disclosed. He has important contacts there. Names not disclosed—but from Peter's remarks, we judge that these contacts do not know that Alex is a Communist agent. After that, he proceeds to Mykonos. His mission accomplished, he returns to Paris. So much for Alex, except that reference was made by Peter to the Farraday party, *which Alex attended.* So he is the American you are looking for, Rosie."

Rosie, grimly silent, nodded.

"Next, there was talk of John Craig. They are no longer interested in him. They know, now, his purpose for traveling abroad; they checked thoroughly on his credentials as a historian. Peter had some reservations. What if Craig were to extend his visit to Troy down as far as Ephesus, which is close to Smyrna? What if he were to meet Alex by chance? There, the other Russian was much more casual and confident. Overcaution, he said, was another name for timidity. Alex would meet several people who knew him, no doubt. That was why he would use his real name in Smyrna and have an innocent excuse for his travels. No one would question him unless he seemed evasive. If he was not good enough to stand up to a meeting with Craig or anyone else who knew him, he was of no use for this mission. Peter made a hasty retraction. Alex, it seems, had been his choice."

"So Craig is off their list," Partridge said reflectively, and caught Rosie's speculative eye on him, and shrugged apologetically. Still, he thought, that wasn't a bad idea of mine; Craig's a natural for this job.

"It was just then," Duclos continued, his voice quickening, rising, "at the point where Peter was flustered, and as annoyed as he dared to be, that he made a slip. He said, 'In spite of what you think, I did not select Alex because of any personal interest. You will find, Comrade Insarov, that he *is* the man for this mission.' There followed a very definite silence. As now." Duclos smiled at Partridge. "That guess of yours was certainly right. Insarov must be Berg—why else would he be interested in Craig, whose only claim to notice is that he has seen Berg?"

"There was more than guessing involved," said Rosie, giving Partridge his full due.

"And more than one man involved, too," Partridge reminded them. How many agents had been alerted, each producing a small fraction of information, and some of it useless, all risking their lives? How many analysts breaking down those fractions? How many evaluators fitting them together in different ways? "You know, when I started work in Intelligence, I had a vision of Partridge, out there all by himself, keeping the peace with his little pistol and brilliant action, a life of fast cars and beautiful women and expense accounts that didn't have to be rendered." He allowed himself a laugh then, covering his own elation with a touch of self-ridicule.

"And lastly"—Duclos insisted on giving the report in full, in logical order—"they may be closing down Le Happening. Its uses are over, I suppose."

"Or have they noticed your interest in the club? These things do get around," Rosie said. That had been one of his chief problems, all along.

"Fortunately," Duclos assured him, "I think our interest in Le Happening will be blamed on Interpol. Bernard is adding a little proof of that: he is getting the police to raid the club for narcotics tonight. I thought I might drop around—" He looked at Rosie, who had glanced up sharply and raised an eyebrow. But Rosie made no other comment. And that, thought Duclos, saves a useless argument. He went on, "As for Insarov, he is leaving Paris this afternoon. He mentioned business in Milan next week. If everything goes well, Peter is to set their plan in motion. From Paris? We couldn't fathom that. Our experts are working over that part of the transcript, phrase by phrase."

"Poor old bloody experts," Partridge said cheerfully, "and they never get a trip to Mykonos, either." He choked back some of his jubilation. "I hope you're planning to send me along, Rosie. Are you going, Yves?"

Duclos grinned widely. "I'm doing my best on that, right now. Erica is possibly a French national, and she is certainly part of a Paris network. She would be a good catch for us. And she knows Peter, who is obviously the director, or one of the aides to the director, of that network. So—" Duclos spread his hands, and beamed. "It seems as if you'll get one of your old dreams, Jim: she's very pretty, this Erica, and with style. Bernard had a good picture of her made for his files, drawn from a precise description by the coatroom attendant. Blond, nose retroussé, green eyes, excellent figure, good clothes. But naturally—she must fit the circles in which she seems to move."

Rosie was not listening. He didn't even respond with the joke that Yves had expected. He said, "Jim, I'm turning this operation over to you. From today. The best thing I can do is to retire into the background."

Partridge and Duclos stared at him, at each other. "But—" Partridge began.

"Let them think I haven't one suspicion that something big is shaping up. Relax their nerves for them, shall we? Yes, Jim, that's the way it has to be. They don't know you at all. But apparently they know me."

"So you *were* followed today," Partridge said. He wished his guess about Rosie's delay in arriving here hadn't been so right.

"Very intently. I shook them off, I think. They'll only allow me one success like that. Just one more, and they'll know I'm on guard, expecting something. Which is proof I know something." He studied his hands. "Damn their eyes and ears, they've even tapped my telephone," he said in rising anger.

"They've really drawn a bead on you," Partridge said slowly.

Duclos was perturbed. "But Rosie, how could that be? You're careful, you're—"

"They are only testing me, so far. But I'd like to know who gave them the clue that I was the man to watch," Rosie said softly, dangerously. "It's someone in security, that's for sure. Or someone who is in contact with him."

"I don't think the leak came from us," Duclos said quickly. "After all, there is only Bernard and I who know—"

"It didn't come from you, Yves," Rosie said heavily. "It came from someone who has connections or trusting friends in a branch of our own security. And that's one thing I'm going to find out, even if I'm sitting on the side lines. By God, I'll find that out." He glared around the room. Then he relaxed, forcing a smile. "Now I had better make an involved exit from this place. Said I would be back at the office by four. Which reminds me, Jim, there's a contract waiting on my desk for you to sign." And how will he handle that? Rosie wondered.

Partridge rose and went over to the telephone beside Mimi. He was the Caen Distributor once more, telling Rosie's secretary that he wanted to speak with Monsieur Rosenfeld. Not yet returned? Then let him be most kindly informed that it was unfortunately impossible to sign the agreement today; another offer at a much better price was under consideration. With regrets and distinguished salutations . . .

He'll do all right, Rosie admitted to himself. He knows as much as you do about this project, perhaps even more in some of the details he gathered during the last four months. He knows the support we can give him, and where to get it. He can cope with Greek and Turkish Intelligence—he must have worked closely with them on the Lesbos-Izmir affair. He's the eventual replacement for you, anyway, so shut up. But all these admissions didn't comfort Rosie. This was one operation that he would have liked to see through, all the way to the very end. Oh, well, there was no use in delaying his exit. He shook hands with Yves. "That was an excellent report you made, a good piece of work by everyone concerned. My congratulations to Bernard. Tell him I'll be at the golf club on Sunday. I'll thank him, then, myself."

"And just when the overhead route to my studio was working so perfectly," Duclos said with real regret. "Never mind, Rosie. You'll be using it again by August. Want to bet?"

To Partridge, Rosie said, "Don't let the blue skies of Mykonos deceive you. This will be no picnic."

"I could use your advice—"

"You don't need it." He knows the ropes, he knows where to get help and how to use it. "Except," Rosie added lightly, "I think you'd better pack that little pistol, too."

Partridge grinned. "I still need your advice. Can I contact you?"

"Not in person. Through channels. I'll always be available even if I'm in the background. And I'll send you all new information I turn up on Wilshot and Bradley." His voice had been kept low. Then, more naturally, "Oh, and Jim—"

"Yes?"

"Go easy on Craig."

Partridge's grin widened. "He's a natural."

"I know. That's our big temptation, isn't it?" Rosie clapped Partridge's shoulder as he turned away to cross the room to Mimi. She was working happily at her desk, and had turned on her radio to keep her company; perhaps also to show she was much too busy listening to *Les Sylphides* to have heard any of their long discussion. She was a woman of infinite tact. Rosie slipped his arm around the strong waist as they walked in close step to the door. "Take care of yourself, Mimi."

"But I always do, Rosee!" She gave him a generous hug, a kiss on both cheeks. He left without looking back at the watching faces. "Was that good-bye?" she asked as she locked the door and was startled by an afterthought.

"A temporary one," Jim Partridge said. He actually meant that, which startled him, too. His promotion was exhilarating, he might as well admit it. But he hadn't wanted it, not quite this way. He wondered if he'd have the good sense and the guts to step aside like that, let a younger man who could be a competitor take over? Then the weight of the new responsibility hit him, full force. He walked over to the small table, pulled a stool beside it, and sat down to look at the map.

Duclos was still thinking about Rosie. "Perhaps he was too quick, there. He knows enough dodges to cover up his moves. He didn't need to—"

"Didn't he? I'll quote you, Yves: 'If everything goes well, Peter is to set their plan in motion.' But if they think that we are interested in them, then everything is not going well and Peter will set quite a different plan in motion." Insarov hadn't prepared so thoroughly without having some alternative to fall back on. Not Insarov. "You know what that could mean for us."

"They win; we lose," Duclos said soberly. "Are you planning to go to Mykonos yourself or are you sending someone else?"

Partridge thought of three men who could be sent. And yet, time was short. There would have to be a long briefing, a thorough preparation. "There are so many small pieces to be remembered in this damned jigsaw puzzle," he said, "and if they are not placed correctly, then—" He searched for a cigarette and lit it.

"Then," Duclos finished for him, "the main pieces won't drop naturally into place?"

Partridge nodded.

Duclos placed his finger on Smyrna. "What's their plan? To make sure of Cyprus, once the U.N. troops leave it? To play the same game on Rhodes, setting Turk against Greek, and both against the Americans? They tried that before. And when they fail, they wait a little, learn from their mistakes, try another way. Get rid of American bases, isn't that their purpose?"

Partridge looked at Duclos' finger, now tapping Smyrna impatiently. The American base there was NATO's chief installation in the eastern Mediterranean. "I didn't think you worried so much about NATO," he teased gently.

"I've criticized it," the Frenchman admitted, "and, from our point of view, with justification. But as of this moment, I prefer not to see it castrated." He relaxed into a smile. "Friends are the only people who can agree to disagree, no? Besides, Jim, it is one thing to give up a base by your own decision; quite another to be forced out of it by your enemy's skill in psychological warfare. That would only prove to the world that we are very, very stupid. It is not an agreeable label to have hung around our necks."

Partridge stubbed out his half-finished cigarette. "Self-defeating," he admitted. Duclos and I can work together, he thought, and gave thanks. "I wonder if you could handle Milan for us, try to discover where Insarov goes from there?"

"I'll talk with Bernard about that."

"That would be helpful. It's just possible that Insarov would discount any co-operation between you and us. Under present conditions," he added tactfully, not mentioning De Gaulle. "By the way, I think you'd be interested to know that we've sent Antonini to the Smyrna base. There is quite a job for him to do there, I hear."

"More listening devices—just like those he found in your Moscow Embassy?" Duclos was shocked.

"Also," Partridge went on, "Val Sutherland is following him."

Duclos stared. He inclined his head, pursed his lips. "Then he is not a journalist? And his Saigon assignment was only a cover story?"

"It still is. He is supposed to be in Viet Nam, right now, but he will make a long tour of news-gathering in and out of the front lines, which will explain any absence from Saigon. It was thought best to keep his visit to Smyrna quite incognito. You agree?"

Duclos did agree, emphatically, and with considerable relief. What he had been told was a demonstration of trust. Rosie's going would not make so much difference after all. "So Sutherland is the man the Communists ought to have tried to question, and not Antonini?" The idea amused him. That had been one small victory, at least.

"Sutherland is the head of our tear-out-the-walls-and-ceilings experts. He has quite a sense of humor in fixing the Russians' gadgets so that they don't know which to trust—or distrust. That can really foul up their calculations. They don't like to move unless they are really sure—they learned that lesson from Khrushchev's rockets in Cuba, remember? A big mistake."

"A mistake only because it failed," Duclos said. "We have information that the military will never forgive Khrushchev for that. Another excuse will be found to be used against him in the history books, of course—something more peace-like than charging him with the Cuban failure. It would never do to emphasize how important those rockets in Cuba really were."

Partridge looked at Duclos thoughtfully. Rockets in Cuba . . . rockets in Cyprus? "Do you suppose," he asked slowly, "that Alex is being sent to Smyrna to learn who Sutherland is and what he has discovered? As I said, one of Sutherland's jokes is to leave a few of their listening devices working so that we can feed bits and pieces of false information through them. He does this because we can never be sure that we've discovered all the gadgets they've installed. Yet, if they don't know what information they can trust, their next big operation may be turned into another fiasco. So they need Sutherland. They have got to have him."

"Abduction?" Duclos was startled.

"And questioning. They tried that on Antonini in Moscow, remember? How else could they get the completely full information they want? They've got to have it before they start setting any plan into operation."

"Then you'd do well to guard Sutherland. Completely. Every way." A new idea gleamed brightly in Duclos' eyes. "Insarov . . . Isn't he interested in psychology, in the art of questioning a prisoner? Would he deal with Sutherland himself, if they managed to get him?"

"Sutherland might be considered too important for subordinates to deal with," Partridge agreed. His worry grew.

"Perhaps they'll still aim for Antonini. Even I assumed he was your chief expert until you told me the facts."

"I think they may now be looking around for another man. Antonini let one small remark slip at the Farradays' party. Something about not being the guy the Russians were looking for. He said it half-jokingly, among friends. But Alex was there. He would pick it up and

103

report it. So the question is now: does Insarov believe it was a joke or the truth? I don't think we can risk anything on his answer. We'd better make sure that we have someone else in Smyrna along with Antonini and Sutherland. Someone who was in Moscow at the time they were there. Someone who was one of Antonini's friends." Partridge's voice quickened as if he already could see the man. "And now he turns up in Smyrna, is seen again with Antonini. Not constantly. Just enough. As if they were together but trying to conceal the fact. How's that for a nice red herring?"

"Thank God I don't fit the rôle," Duclos said. "Who is he? George Farraday?"

"No amateurs on this job. We want a professional who knows what he is letting himself in for. Thomas O'Malley."

"The Australian? Who is he working for—you?" And I never guessed it, Duclos thought with annoyance. He liked O'Malley, had known him for a couple of years.

"For British Intelligence. And if you don't know that, Yves, then I don't think Insarov will."

"But he might not believe, either, that an Australian could be on your team of experts."

"Except that O'Malley was born in the United States and lived there until his people took him back to Australia when he was twelve years old. Insarov will soon find that out, once he starts digging into O'Malley's history."

"But will he believe that 'Australian journalist' could be a cover for working with Americans?"

"Why not? He has been conditioned by his own experience to believe such a pattern of espionage exists—it's employed constantly by his own side. Think of the Polish journalists and the Czech diplomats who have been working for the Russians."

Duclos nodded. Yes, he had to admit, even chauffeurs attached to the Eastern European missions abroad had turned out to be radio experts or fully qualified engineers, often of far more importance in rank than the diplomats they drove around. All of them had been trained by the Russians; all of them acted on Moscow's instructions. Their own countries, Communist as they were, came second.

"Yes, O'Malley's the man for this job. He is as tough as they come," Partridge was saying. "He has such a sense of humor that he might even enjoy it."

"That depends on how far Insarov will go with his questioning, doesn't it?" Duclos asked grimly.

"We make sure," Partridge said equally grimly, "that Insarov never reaches that distance."

"It is still a cold-blooded idea—using O'Malley as a decoy."

"You inspired it. You said Insarov might deal with the questioning himself. If he thought O'Malley was the man they wanted, he would be on hand when they tried to take him. It's easier to question a man near the abduction point than to smuggle him through hostile territory, like Turkey, into Russia. If you were Insarov, where would you have your prisoner taken out from Smyrna?" Partridge pointed toward the map.

Duclos didn't even need to look at it. "Into the Aegean," he said. "But that doesn't necessarily mean Mykonos."

"No," Partridge agreed. But, he thought, it does mean some place where Insarov feels he has established a margin of safety.

"The examination of a prisoner could even be done on a boat, a small yacht," Duclos said unhappily.

"Yes," Partridge agreed again. But, he thought, that depends on the weather and Insarov's seamanship. The Aegean could make more people helpless in shorter time than any other body of water. Even the best of sailors ran for the shelter of an island when the north wind suddenly rose. "Anyway," he said, closing the topic, "it will be entirely up to O'Malley whether he wants to help us in this. I'll contact him through Chris Holland, of course."

"That should make everything quite regular," Duclos said acidly.

"We are not asking O'Malley to do anything we wouldn't be prepared to do ourselves."

"You mean you'd let yourself be abducted by Insarov to help the British?"

"If it would catch Insarov—yes. And so would you."

"I'd have to think about that. To help my own country—I'd agree. But, for the sake of the British—" He shrugged his shoulders. "I don't know," he said honestly.

"Against men like Insarov," Partridge said, "there are no French or British or Americans. Let's leave that kind of stupidity to our politicians."

Duclos was smiling. Partridge had offered him one of his own favorite arguments. *"Touché,"* he said quietly.

Partridge relaxed. "Why argue, anyway? As Rosie would say, we could all be wrong. Insarov may now be en route back to Moscow by way of Milan."

Duclos laughed briefly at some thought of his own. "Sorry. I was thinking of that innocent little party at the Meurice. Apart from the Farradays and John Craig, everyone else was Intelligence of some kind, except for Wilshot and Bradley."

"And which of those two is Alex?"

"The one who is planning to go to Smyrna."

Partridge smiled. "They are both going to Greece. Separately. Seemingly quite ignorant of each other's vacation plans. Bradley has leave coming up from his job with NATO; Wilshot has been talking of finding some sun and a story about Grivas in Athens. Take your pick, Yves. Which?"

"Then we'll have to wait and see which one travels farther east than Athens," said Duclos amiably.

"That's about it," Partridge agreed. Unless, of course, Rosie turned up some extra information: Alex seen without horn-rimmed glasses or his face averted or his handkerchief covering his nose and mouth. Too cautious, Erica had called him. But *she* was the one whose picture was filed in Bernard's office. "Erica's choice—the American girl over at the Hotel Beauharnais—what do you think we should do about her?"

"Nothing."

"Let her be played for an idiot?"

"Just that," Duclos said. "It's better than having her dead, isn't it?"

Put that way, it was. "Well, I'd better get back to the Saint-Honoré," Partridge said, glancing at his watch.

"Are you going to talk with Craig?"

"If he hasn't already packed and left Paris in disgust." Partridge could guess Craig's view of the situation: we do nothing, while Berg walks around unarrested.

"That would be a pity. As you said, he's a natural."

He is more than that now, thought Partridge. Craig is a necessity. He has met both Wilshot and Bradley; he can identify Berg at one glance. And who else have we got who can make that claim? "We'll keep in touch. By telephone. I don't think we should meet again in Paris."

"You won't drop in at Le Happening tonight? We needn't meet. But you never know who may be drifting around there. Alex, for instance? And there are a couple of other men who have been making weekly visits behind stage. They're due to turn up this evening. So the coatroom attendant tells me."

"Have you talked much with her?" Partridge asked quickly.

"No, no. Just a word in passing. Don't worry. She thinks I'm another policeman, one of her own crowd."

"You know," Partridge began, and then stopped short. He wasn't only taking over Rosie's job, it seemed; he was taking over Rosie's supercaution. Anyway, Duclos had his own job to do for Bernard, and the night club had become part of their action. "Can I plan on your help in Mykonos, or will Bernard need you here?" he asked.

"Plan on it," Duclos said with a wide grin. "I've always wanted to paint. Mimi, will you come as my model?" He caught up some opalescent silk from a display stand and draped its transparency around her shoulders. Partridge closed the door on their laughter. No picnic, Rosie had said. But Partridge was smiling as he straightened the CLOSED ON TUESDAY notice. From what he had heard, Mimi at a picnic could be as dangerous as a sidewinder.

Then he put thoughts, ideas, guesses, worries out of his mind, and concentrated on his careful journey to the Saint-Honoré.

Partridge had been right about John Craig. That afternoon he decided to leave Paris and head for Rome and points east. Possibly tomorrow, Wednesday, marking a week exactly since he had arrived here and gone strolling along the Boulevard Saint-Germain. Almost a week since Sussman had died; almost a week for Heinrich Berg to walk around the streets of Paris, a completely free man enjoying his victory. What was Rosie doing, Partridge, Messieurs Galland and Tillier of the *Sixième Arrondissement?* What the hell was anyone doing?

After an angry lunch, he tried to walk some of his bad temper away by marching at a good pace along the left bank of the Seine. He didn't stop at the bookstalls today. He didn't even slow up for the corner of the Rue Bonaparte as he usually did when he passed this way. The girl was never in sight. Around this district he had passed hundreds of pretty girls, hundreds of students, singly, in groups, but she was never one of them. By half past three his temper was less ragged. He took a bus back across the Seine toward the Avenue de l'Opéra, and walked on to the American Express office. There was sunshine above, trees were now a brighter green. Spring clothes were venturing out, faces looked happy to be breathing gentler air. April was a resurgence, a welling of plans and hopes. And all he could feel was annoyance and disappointment mixed with incredible loneliness. Why, he thought suddenly, no one has stopped to speak to me or strike up an acquaintance in the last twenty-four hours. And at that, he had to smile at himself.

He felt still better when he reached his destination and collected a nice assortment of travel folders. Rome, Brindisi, Corfu, Athens, Crete, Rhodes, Istanbul . . . Domes and towers, blue skies and minarets, sunshine and rippling water; delightful exaggeration and a highly colored come-on? Even so, this was more like it. Now for some airline details, an enjoyable hour of decision, and then back to the hotel to pack.

But, standing in the downstairs hall, studying a flight schedule for Rome, a crowd of young Americans around him opening letters they had just collected, he glanced up at a couple of long-haired jubilants pulling out their expected checks, and beyond them, now visible, now half-hidden, now visible again, he saw the girl. Or was it? Quickly he pushed his way through the various small groups, some triumphant, some downcast, clustering together as if they were afraid of being alone, and almost reached the smooth dark head, the profile that he remembered. Then he halted, amazed at his speedy reaction; embarrassed, too. It was the girl, all right, a slender outline in gray suit and white silk shirt among the sloppy Joes and straggle-headed Janes flapping around in their uniform of beatnik conformity—dirty blue jeans and drooping sweaters, straight from the Rue de la Huchette. From her thin-heeled pumps to her softly brushed hair, she was quite remarkable. Simplicity. A distinction of taste, of quiet manners, of independence.

He stood, hesitating. He could hardly go up and say, "Remember me?" He was the man who had witnessed her hurt. Watching her now, he could realize how her tears, shed in public, would be an agonizing memory. He had been the invading stranger, someone she never wanted to see again.

She was studying a list which she held in her hand, her face grave as she calculated and then relaxing a little as she came to some decision. As she slipped the piece of paper into her handbag, she glanced up as if she had actually felt him look at her. For a moment, her eyes widened. She had recognized him. Then, just as abruptly, she averted her head and turned toward the door. He let her go. And I'll never get a second chance, he thought; luck doesn't run that way. He followed slowly, giving her plenty of time to escape from an unwelcome encounter.

But as he came through the doorway into the gentle warm sunshine, she was standing there. Waiting. Looking toward him. Slightly uncertain, she took a step forward; then thought better of it. Does she think *I* don't want to meet her again? he wondered in amazement. This time, as she moved away with her head high, he caught up with her. "Hello, there!" he said, and stopped her completely. "Sorry for staring. I didn't think you'd recognize me."

"And I wasn't sure that you remembered me." She smiled. "I wanted to—I wanted to thank you."

"Then come and have a drink with me." He glanced at his watch. "Or tea, or coffee, or something." My God, he thought, where has all my conversation gone to?

"I'm meeting some people at half past four." She frowned at her own watch. "It isn't far, fortunately."

"That gives us exactly ten minutes to get to know each other. Couldn't you be late? Or send despairing messages?"

"Such as?" Her eyes were actually smiling.

"Oh, that you're coming down with measles."

She laughed, shook her head. "This is too important for me. You see, I'm running away." The laughter had vanished; her voice and eyes became expressionless.

He stared at her. "Where are you meeting your friends?"

"The Café de la Paix."

"I'll walk you there. If I may."

"Of course." She started walking slowly, and he fell into pace. She glanced at the folders in his hand. "Are you leaving Paris, too?"

"Tomorrow. At least, that was the plan."

She took the folders and looked through them. "All these places? But how wonderful!"

"I'm traveling until September. Getting material for a book."

"On what?" She was genuinely interested.

"Trade routes," he said, and waited for her comments. They weren't stupid. She didn't gush "How fascinating!" She didn't take refuge in a blank "Oh!" She said, "I think we'd need more than ten minutes to hear about that. Are you an economist?"

"Partly that, partly a historian."

"Ancient history?"

"Trying to learn something about it," he said with an attempt at diffidence.

"Rhodes," she said softly. "I've always wanted to visit it. Do you know, in June, there's a valley filled with butterflies? They rise in a cloud—" She smiled, handing him back the folders, checking her enthusiasm. "Of course, if the cloud was so thick that it blotted out everything, it might be more frightening than beautiful."

"So you're leaving Paris, too," he said, wondering where she was going. Back to America?

"For a little while." She added with painful frankness, "I think that's the best cure, don't you?"

He thought of last Wednesday evening, of that long and unhappy quarrel. So she was still vulnerable, was she? "It usually works," he said briefly.

"I'd have thought you would never run away from your emotions." She looked at him with new interest.

"I guess we all do, at times." He stopped thinking of his own defeats. "And where are you bound for?"

"Mykonos."

"That isn't so far from Rhodes. Perhaps you'll see your cloud of butterflies yet."

She shook her head. "The budget won't stretch as far as that. I can just manage the fare to Mykonos and back. I don't have to worry about hotel bills. I'm staying with a friend—a girl I know at art school here. Her uncle has lent her his house for the summer. It must be nice to have uncles like that."

"Provided they stay in the background and don't arrange your days for you."

"Oh, Maritta's uncle isn't going to be around much, if at all."

"Then it sounds perfect. How long will you actually stay with your Greek friend? I might be passing Mykonos in July—"

"Greek? Maritta is French. Her father was Flemish, I think. Her second name is Maas. Anyway, she was born in Paris. But lots of French artists and writers go to Mykonos, you know."

"You're going to paint?"

"And relax."

And forget, he thought. "How long—" he began again.

"Three weeks. I have to be back in Paris to finish my classes."

"You take them very seriously. More than your friend does."

"Maritta doesn't have to take anything very seriously," she said with a smile.

"Ah, those rich uncles again."

111

"There's only one, as far as I know. And not so rich, really. He just knows *how* to spend the money he has. That's an art in itself, isn't it?"

"Wish I could afford it," he said with a grin. He saw the Café de la Paix just ahead of them. He had passed this corner several times in the last few days, and it always reminded him of a bend in a river with several currents all jostling in perpetual motion. People rose from tables, people sat down at tables, people walked past on the narrow strip of sidewalk left to them, buses and cars poured in and out of seven tributaries to sweep around the Place de l'Opéra and gouge their way through the persistent streams of pedestrians. "This may hardly be the place," he said, raising his voice to be heard above the grinding gears and screeching brakes, "but don't you think it's time we introduced ourselves? I'm John Craig."

"And I'm Veronica Clark."

"What's your address, by the way?"

"The Hotel Beauharnais."

"Would you have—" A sad-faced woman, with a basket of posies for sale, stepped backward from a table and separated them. "Would you—"

"I see them," she said in a low voice. "Uncle Peter looks very solemn. Do you think he is wondering if I'll be a good influence on Maritta after all? How late are we?"

"Thirty-five seconds." Craig looked over the tables, caught sight of a blonde girl with her hand upraised as a welcoming sign. "Are you afraid of him?" he asked, looking now at the square-faced, blunt-nosed man who sat, Spanish grandee fashion, beside her. He was middle-aged, heavily constructed, and very well dressed. Not that that meant a thing: the first three hundred dollars that any fly-by-night operator made seemed to go on a suit nowadays. I'm doing him an injustice, Craig thought; he looks a very solid citizen, indeed.

"I don't know him. Maritta is a little nervous about him, though. He's very old-fashioned, she says." Veronica waved back to her friend.

"Let me come and apologize for you." Thirty-five seconds' worth of apology. He led her toward the table where the blonde and her tight-faced uncle waited. Maritta might be quite a handful at that, Craig decided, admiring the tiptilted nose, marking the expensively casual hair and the little black dress with its mink jacket. Green eyes, he noted, and a warmly welcoming smile. "I'm sorry," he said, ignoring introductions to prove he wasn't staying. "It's my fault. We met by accident. No, thank you"—this to Maritta, who was pointing to the chair beside her—"I'm on my way. Miss Clark and I didn't quite finish our conversation." He pulled out a chair for Veronica, said to her quietly, "Would you have dinner with me tonight?"

"I'd love to."

"Oh, dear," Maritta said, "I'm leaving tomorrow, Ronnie. I thought we'd go over—" She paused, looking at Craig with a dazzling smile of sweet apology. "I'm really so sorry."

"Then we'll lunch tomorrow, instead," he told Veronica. "I'll call you in the morning?" He shook her hand. "Good-bye," with a bow for Green Eyes. "Good-bye, sir. Sorry to intrude." And that should hold the old bastard, he thought, turning to make a quick and efficient exit, bumping into the sad-faced flower girl again. Well, he thought now, as he left the tight rows of tables and waited for the traffic to stop so that he could cross the street, it's always the way; you wander around Paris for a week and never see her, and when you do meet her you are granted ten minutes and thirty-five seconds. But even two minutes and twenty-seven seconds would have been worth it.

Perhaps he wouldn't leave tomorrow. A few more days would be pleasant. The week of tensions and loneliness dropped away from him, and he strode down the avenue with as much zest and interest as if he were setting out for his first walk through Paris.

When he came down to the hotel bar at six, showered, changed, and very much in his right mind, he found the small green room empty except for an Indian drinking orange juice and an Egyptian sipping lemonade. Jules' welcome was astoundingly warm. He rushed to mix a Scotch and soda, and his voice almost trembled as he confided that, today, two English ladies had come in demanding tea. With cake. Yesterday, there had been three American children wanting something called Cokes. Cokes, cakes and fruit drinks, Craig reflected, would convert Jules to tolerating heretics like himself who drank Scotch with ice and soda. It was not, Jules went on, that he disliked tea or those other drinks, except this room was *not* the place; it was an invasion of sacred rights, and he was not a cow to dispense milk.

Besides, it drove away the real customers. And there's the rub, thought Craig, and drank his Scotch and seemed to listen. She was a quite remarkable girl. In the middle of that tourist and expatriate crowd in the American Express building, she had been unique among beehive hair styles and haystack heads. At the Café de la Paix, she had made mink look negligible. He had known a lot of girls in the last fourteen years, some rather more than well. Two he had almost married. In every case, he had drifted into love before he had headed out, sometimes with regrets to remember, more often with frank relief. But drifted was the word; it had been a gradual thing of weeks, getting pleasanter and pleasanter until is seemed inevitable. That was love, he had thought. Love at first sight? He had never believed in it. He still didn't. . . . Impossible. At his age? It was worse than impossible; it was silly.

"Good evening, Jules," Jim Partridge said, sliding onto the stool next to Craig. "Hello, there! And how are you?"

"Feeling my age. How are you?" He looks exhausted, Craig thought. Business must have been hard today.

Partridge was studying the younger man with amusement. "Is that what's making you so happy and scared?"

"What?" Damn it all, I'm not so transparent as that. Or has Partridge got a gadget for thought-reading as well as one for listening to conversations across a room? Craig shook his head and laughed.

"Glad to see you in a better mood than I expected," Partridge said softly. "Make it a double Martini, tonight," he told Jules in a cheerful voice. "Found a couple of good chairs today, authentic Louis Fif-teenth, with some of the original tapestry still on them. A little care-ful cleaning and cautious repairs and we've really got something."

"Better mood?" Craig echoed, suddenly remembering the recrimi-nations he had worked up over lunch today. "I've a few complaints—"

"That's right," Partridge said smoothly. "Let's get the dust out of my throat, first, shall we? And what about resting our backs in a com-fortable chair?" He took a sip of his drink, gave Jules his approval, and led the way to a table against a wall. He sat down with visible relief, took off his glasses, looked ten years younger and gave a grin to match. "Are you doing anything this evening? I'm at a loose end my-self. What about dinner together, in some nice quiet little place not too far away? That will save time."

"Suits me. I've a lot to say. And the quicker, the better."

"How soon do you feel like eating?"

"Any time. I didn't have much lunch, today."

And I had none at all, thought Partridge. "Fine. We'll shock the French but we'll get a dining room to ourselves. Just let me finish this drink gratefully. Have another, won't you?"

Craig shook his head. All he wanted was a subdued corner in that quiet dining room. Still, he was going to be given at least some time with Partridge, so he might as well look cheerful meanwhile and talk politely.

Partridge didn't hurry. He smoked a cigarette as he finished his drink at normal speed, and listened to Craig. I'll have to remember, Partridge told himself, how little he knows. I'll have to try to put myself in his place, forget everything I've discussed with Rosie and Bernard and Duclos and Chris Holland in these last six days; forget everything I've read in those last months, every clue, guess, inference, deduction, fact. All he knows is that Heinrich Berg is a Nazi, the kind who would be none the worse of a hanging. All he knows is that Berg has friends who've given him a hard time this week. All he knows is that Berg walks free, and Sussman's murder is being called suicide. That is all he knows. Good God, where do I begin to talk with him? And how much could he stand? How much is safe—for him, for us?

"You've really been very patient," Partridge said, finishing his drink at last. "Look, can I borrow ten more minutes from you? I need to wash up. Came straight from the street. I'll admit I was anxious in case you had left Paris. And I wouldn't have blamed you, either." He drew out his wallet, riffled through some business cards and a snapshot of a girl in a bathing suit, found a small photograph and handed it over to Craig. "Recognize your friend?"

Craig, completely disarmed by this time, took it with the same easy smile with which it had been presented to him. It was a small study in truculence, unflattering enough to be a police photograph. The man staring back at him under the sharp lighting was young, fair-haired. He wore a belted raincoat. In the picture, the raincoat was dry. Apart from that, it was the man who had rushed from the café to follow Sussman.

"Thought that would keep you happy, meanwhile," Partridge murmured, taking the photograph back as he rose.

"Who got him?"

"Galland and Tillier, of course. Strictly police business. See you in ten minutes? I'll meet you at the corner of the street." Partridge made his way leisurely out of the bar, which was now beginning to have a few more customers. To his practiced eye, they all seemed reasonable people. No more Jordans swooping down on Craig, anyway. Once out into the lobby and past the observant porter, he increased his speed. Ten minutes weren't so long, considering he had to make his usual evening phone check with Bernard's office. Not that Bernard's man could have had many worries trailing Craig today: suspicion was off him, thank heavens. But it was wise to keep a finger on the pulse; in this line of business anything could happen.

The restaurant was about two blocks' walking distance from the Rue Saint-Honoré. It lay at the junction of several small streets lined with newly built butcher shops. Nearby was a giant, smoothly surfaced square almost filled with the solid bulk of a huge garage. As they skirted it, Partridge had looked at it without much enthusiasm. "You'd never believe it," he said, breaking his long silence, "but only four years ago this was one of the old Paris markets. Open stalls, cobblestones, sixteenth-century houses as background. It used to amuse me to find all that tucked away behind bright avenues and smart shops. Let's hope progress hasn't dolled up our restaurant with chrome and steam tables." But the restaurant had insisted on keeping its own character. And it was good. Not expensive. Just good. Craig relaxed completely.

The room, almost empty at this early hour, was pleasant and placid. The waiters, old as the furniture, knew how to retire into the background as soon as they had served the food. The corner which Partridge had chosen was lit just enough to let one see what one was eating. The leather backs on the chairs, padded and buttoned, were comfortable. This, decided Craig, was the kind of place people could talk. He waited expectantly, but Partridge again was in no hurry. He seemed contented with lighthearted quips through the main course, but Craig had the feeling that he was paying as little attention to the general gossip as he was to the excellent lamb chops and asparagus on his plate. Behind his easy words was a thoughtfulness. He had been like this ever since he had come down from his room at the Saint-Honoré and joined Craig with a nod and a searching glance. Those

116

ten minutes upstairs had produced something more than a clean shirt, a fresh tie, and neatly brushed hair. And what's wrong now? Craig wondered. "You know," he said as the coffee was served, "I hope that route we took along the Rue Saint-Honoré to get here wasn't symbolic. In the days of the Terror, it was the main drag for the tumbrils on their way to the guillotine." He dropped his light tone, let some of his rising annoyance show. "Whose neck is going to get chopped this time?" he demanded. What had happened to that trust Partridge had seemed to feel in him earlier this evening? If any reproof is in order here, thought Craig, it's mine to give, not to take.

"You can begin with my neck," Partridge said evenly. "You've got a few cutting remarks to make, I bet."

"And you'd win it. Sure, the murderer has been caught, but what about the man who gave him orders to murder? Yes, Berg. I saw him yesterday. He walked right past me. And I had no number to phone, nobody to warn. I got back to the Saint-Honoré, practically exploding with the news, and I couldn't even talk to you."

"That was just as well," Partridge said very quietly. "There was one of Berg's agents watching you, at that very minute. They've been tailing you ever since last Thursday morning. But so have we. Now, go on: you've got every right to complain. You've had it rough, and we didn't seem to be doing much, did we? It was a difficult situation, and you handled it well. I'll say that for you."

Craig could only stare. Grouches were not so easily registered when you were told they were thoroughly justified, even expected. Compliments added, too. "What's this about having me followed?"

"Protection. Just in case a car knocked you down and its passengers wanted to take you to the hospital. Or in case a man grasped your wrist, told you he had instructions to bring you to see Detectives Galland and Tillier and, when the needle in your wrist made you black out, helped you most kindly into a waiting car. Little things like that. Troublesome. So some self-effacing Frenchmen have been keeping an eye on you, ready to rush to the rescue. Now, now, don't look so startled. We think that phase is all over. In fact, this afternoon we were quite sure that Berg had no more interest in you. But one thing does puzzle me—"

"I haven't finished," Craig cut in. "You mean you knew about my second meeting with Berg?"

"We had reports on it."

"And you didn't follow him?"

"Let's say we weren't geared for that."

"Tell me one thing." Craig leaned forward on his elbows. His eyes were cold and skeptical. "Do you want to catch Berg?"

Partridge looked at the tightly pressed lips, the hard-set jaw. Craig could be a tough customer if he chose. "Yes. We'll catch him, and a lot more besides."

"Well what's being done about it? Don't you think you owe me a holding explanation at least? In return for handling certain difficult situations? I'd like a little more than some sugar-coated approval! Sweet suffering—"

"Take it easy, pal. We are allowed to have some serious after-dinner conversation in a public restaurant, but not to frighten the waiters out of their shirt fronts."

"Sorry." But there was no retreat in the quieted voice.

"You know, I agree with every word you say. Only, I do see things from a different angle, from a different set of facts."

"Of course," said Craig, coldly.

"I was prepared to give you one or two of them. I'd want to know them, if I were you. But—"

"That's right. There's always a but."

"You could clear it away."

"I?"

Partridge's light tone changed to sudden attack. "This afternoon you talked with a man at the Café de la Paix. Why?"

"Why? For Christ's sake—I just went to—" Craig stopped short. "How did you know about that? Oh, I see. One of those self-effacing Frenchmen, again?"

Partridge relaxed a little. Craig hadn't denied it, and that at least was a good start on this difficult topic. "You really had us all puzzled, and in our job it isn't really pleasant to be puzzled about friends. You see, one of our agents snapped a picture of that table just as a flower vendor ran some interference for him. It made a nice diversion."

"He took a photograph?" Craig hadn't seen even a Minox camera around. "How?"

"He lit a cigarette."

"I didn't even notice anyone doing that," Craig admitted ruefully.

"Good. You weren't meant to."

"Have you been photographing me all over Paris?" Craig was sharp-voiced again.

"Only when you met someone. You don't know how useful it has been to a friend of mine at the Sûreté who collects photographs and drawings for his file on subversives. In fact, he has the best file on Communists, French or otherwise, who have been active in France. You've added two to his collection in the last few days. And perhaps you could even help with some added information about a third—the man at the table. Yes, he's on file, too. He worked in Paris four years ago, then went back to Moscow. Now, judging from the photograph, he's returned to France. What's the name he is using, nowadays?"

Craig could only sit staring at the quiet face opposite him. "Communists . . . I begin to see why you're so damned slow to take an interest in Berg. A Nazi isn't worth bothering about when a Communist can be caught," he said bitterly. "Is that it?"

Partridge only shook his head.

"What are you trying to tell me?" Craig demanded.

"I've already told you. I said we would catch Berg—*and a lot more besides.*"

There was a pause. "A Nazi working with Communists?" Craig's disbelief was clear.

"You're getting close. I knew you would, once you started using your brain instead of your emotions. Actually, Berg never was a Nazi, except for show. And he did it very well, according to reports. He was said to be such a virulent Nazi that he embarrassed some neutralists, 1943 brand—Pétainists—who met him in Berlin; and they did not embarrass easily."

"I'm so damned stupid," Craig said softly. Berg's agents had been following him, accosting him, hadn't they? Berg's agents were being photographed for the Communist file at the Sûreté. Therefore Berg had to be a Communist or else the Sûreté was completely crazy. His face tightened. "Is the man at the Café de la Paix another of Berg's?"

"We don't know that. We only know that he is a trained GRU agent, holding the rank of colonel. That's big stuff, let me tell you. What is he pretending to be?"

"What's Veronica getting into?" Craig asked, lost in his own worries. "Good God, what's she getting into?"

"Veronica?" Partridge was remarkably still.

"Yes, the girl I was with—Veronica Clark. The dark-haired one—"

"I haven't seen the photograph, just heard about it," Partridge told him. "There was a fair-haired girl at the table, too. Who was she?"

"Maritta Maas, a friend of Veronica's. They're art students. Look, Jim—" Craig discovered he was almost desperate—"Veronica's in the clear. She can't be—"

"Who was the man?" Partridge's quiet voice insisted.

"Uncle Peter. Maritta's Uncle Peter. I didn't wait for an introduction. The only reason I was at that table, frankly, was to finish my invitation to dinner. I was asking Veronica—"

"Peter . . ." Partridge took a deep breath. "So he was looking her over," he said softly.

Craig's face hardened. "You know, I believe you *are* crazy. You and your friend at the Sûreté with his little catalogue of faces. He thinks a man at a table looks something like a man in his files! Is he positive? Why, he didn't even know the name of the man at the table, did he? Just a likeness, that's all. You're pouring an awful lot of heavy concrete on top of clay. I saw Maritta—a pretty little nitwit, gay, charming. The man *was* her uncle, too. I tell you—"

"Which uncle? The one who has the house on Mykonos?"

Craig froze.

"And let me be still crazier. Maritta has invited Veronica Clark to visit her on Mykonos?"

Craig could only stare, and nod.

"Then here's the craziest news of all. Dear, gay and charming Maritta knows very well what her uncle is. She doesn't know his real name, of course, she doesn't know who he is; but she knows what he is."

"Veronica?" Craig asked slowly.

"She knows nothing at all."

"Why did they invite her?"

"Not out of the kindness of their hearts," Partridge told him. "How well do you know the girl? And that's not a casual question. Tell me the details."

Craig, unwilling but troubled enough to take a hint, did just that.

"So you know her only casually," Partridge said when Craig had ended the brief story of their two meetings. "At least," he corrected himself, "that's how it would appear to most people." If I hadn't been watching Craig's face for the last ten minutes, I'd have called it casual, myself. "You know that they must have questioned her about you. I wish I could have seen Peter's face when she told him your name."

"How would he recognize it?" asked Craig, and brought Partridge up sharply.

"You called yourself stupid," Partridge said, covering up his mistake, "but I think you're too damned quick. Let's call it a crazy guess."

"I'm getting a little leery of that adjective," Craig admitted with a wry grin. But he wasn't going to be sidetracked. He came back to his question about Uncle Peter. "How would he—"

"Now the problem is this," Partridge ran on. "Will they believe you are just a casual acquaintance of Veronica's? Or will they think you're possibly a dangerous character after all—one of our agents, perhaps, using Veronica to trap them? No, I don't think they will. . . . You didn't exactly force yourself on them; you paid little attention to them. Good. They'll possibly still want her out there on Mykonos—she's perfect for them, from what you tell me. Why, even you accepted Maritta because Veronica was her friend. Yes, perfect. So—"

"You aren't letting Veronica go to Mykonos?" Craig interrupted. "You can't."

"I can. And must. What else?"

"Warn her."

"How?"

Craig finished his last glass of wine. It tasted as bitter as his thoughts. "I can see no way," he admitted. Expect a girl to listen to a stranger, like Partridge, telling her he was saving her from Maritta? Or to listen to me? "She'd think we were—" he half smiled, in spite of his worry—"crazy."

"You just can't warn people by telling them a little," Partridge agreed. As I've found out, he thought. What would Rosie have done? he wondered. Told Craig as much? Yet compared to what Rosie and he knew, Craig had been told very little.

"I'll go to Mykonos," Craig decided. "I'll be there, at least."

"To keep an eye on her or for your own peace of mind?"

"A little of each."

Partridge laughed. Then shook his head, and fell silent.

"What's the joke?"

"Me, you, and me again."

"Don't you want me to go to Mykonos?"

Partridge took a very long and deep breath. This evening, on his roundabout journey back from Mimi's shop, he had racked his brains for a reasonable approach to Craig on the subject of Mykonos; he had thought of every possible objection that might be made—this isn't my business, I've a book to write, I've got just so much time and money, I hadn't planned on Mykonos, why the hell do you have to drag me into this, why the hell can't you take peaceful coexistence at its face value and stop rocking the boat, a plague on both your houses, there's not much difference between You and Them, so why expect me to get excited? (It wasn't that the amateurs were so much a responsibility, as he had said to Rosie, but that they were such damned wearisome arguers with prejudgments popping up all over the place like the dragon's teeth in Colchis.) And suddenly, determinedly, no argument brooked, Craig had said, "I'll go to Mykonos." Partridge studied the tablecloth.

"Because," finished Craig, "I'm going in any case."

"Well—" Partridge hesitated, made a good effort at being uncertain.

"I have a perfectly good excuse. Old trade-routes Craig. You see, the island of Delos can only be reached from Mykonos, unless you have a private yacht and can cruise around in your own good time. Delos is a collection of ruins now; no one lives there. But once it was pretty important in the struggle for power between Persians and Greeks, Asia Minor and Rome. It was a control point for a lot of trade, believe me. So, I've added Delos to my list. And I'll have to stay in Mykonos. Simple."

"There's only one way you could do this with safety."

"How's that?"

"Let us supply some people to keep a close eye on you. There will be several Americans, perhaps a couple of French, and—of course—Greeks. It's their country, after all."

"Are you recruiting me?" And into what branch of Intelligence? Craig wondered. The FBI have liaison agents abroad, co-operating with foreign police and security departments. But this operation sounds more to me like something involving either G2 or the CIA. Or perhaps there is some new outfit I haven't even heard of. Still, Partridge is Rosie's man—there is no doubt about that. And there is no doubt, too, that Rosie is completely authentic and reliable or else I wouldn't have been commended to his charge by my most discreet and knowledgeable brother-in-law. "Are you?" Craig repeated, restraining his amusement as he watched Partridge's blank face.

"Good heavens, no. Although, of course, as well as keeping an eye on Veronica, and giving yourself some peace of mind, and studying trade routes, you perhaps possibly just could—do something for Uncle Sam? In the odd free moments, of course."

"Is that irony, sarcasm, or just smooth operation? All right. What can I do for you?"

"You are one of the few people in this world who could recognize Heinrich Berg."

Craig's joking stopped. "Will he be there?" he asked, his eyes narrowing.

"Perhaps. You'd know, anyway, wouldn't you? Certainly, his associates will be there. Maritta, for one."

"So," Craig said slowly, the light dawning at last at the end of the long dark tunnel, "Uncle Peter knows Berg, and that's how he heard my name before Veronica ever mentioned it to him. You could have told me. Why didn't you?"

"Everything in its place and proper time," Partridge said gently.

Craig smiled and wondered how much else he might have to learn in its proper place and time. "You'll keep me informed, won't you?" he asked, his smile broadening into a grin. "When it is suitable, of course."

"Of course," Partridge assured him, wide-eyed, innocent. "When do you leave Paris?"

"Any day. I thought I'd go to Italy first."

"Then avoid Milan. In fact, you could postpone Italy altogether—meanwhile. Try Athens. Stay at the Grande Bretagne; then we know where to reach you easily. By the beginning of May, be in Mykonos. Plan on two weeks there. We'll book your hotels, and leave the reservations in your name at the American Express in Athens. We'll pay for them."

"No need," Craig interjected sharply. When had Partridge thought out all this flow of instructions?

I bet there is, too, decided Partridge. "We'll book, anyway. Have to know where all our friends and helpers are in place, you know. There's some planning to do, so we'll call this a day, shall we? I'll see you tomorrow evening. In the bar, as usual. And you can tell me how Veronica couldn't lunch with you." He smiled briefly at Craig's disbelief. "Just another of those crazy notions, of course, but don't count on being allowed to meet her. That is, if her invitation to Mykonos is still valid."

"And if they have canceled her invitation—then what?"

"Then you can't go, either."

"I still could use the Delos excuse."

Partridge studied Craig: a reliable face, bright intelligence in the eyes and brow, strength in the mouth, a firm jaw line; a body kept in good condition, no flabbiness there, either. Partridge shook his head regretfully. "If they are so suspicious of you that they cancel her visit, then you're not going."

"If I'm willing to risk it—"

Partridge shook his head again. It was quite final. "Sorry," he said. And he meant it. His hand went up to summon the waiter and pay the bill. "Okay?" he asked as he prepared to rise. He had a hard evening ahead of him.

"Think I've got it all straight. And if Veronica doesn't go, then I forget everything."

"Exactly." As Partridge led the way to the door, he turned his head to say very quietly, a smile in his usually serious eyes, "And I hope you don't talk in your sleep."

10

Craig returned to the hotel alone. Partridge had pointed him in the direction of the Avenue de l'Opéra, from where he could easily strike toward home by well-known, well-lighted routes. Partridge, himself, had vanished into a dark street of closed butcher shops. It was scarcely nine o'clock. Early for Craig to go up to his room, but he was tired of the cosy little bar downstairs, of the same old faces and the same light chitchat around him. Besides, he had quite a number of thoughts to set in order. The place for that was upstairs in his dull bedroom, with no one else's clinking glass or braying laughter to catch his attention. He was far from antisocial—his life was one long struggle to get his work done in spite of friends and the new Italian movie around the corner—but there were times when people blotted out thought. Perhaps that was what was so beguiling about them: a kind of sweet forgetting about the realities, a reassurance of freedom from anxiety as long as they all gathered together and joked their troubles away.

He picked up his key and a letter from Sue at the porter's desk. There was also a verbal message from the punctilious porter, himself, delivered with his usual lugubriousness. There had been a telephone call for Craig, a lady's voice, no name. That was all. "When?" asked Craig. "Five minutes ago," the porter said and, his duty done, turned to sorting out keys for the pigeonholes behind his desk.

It couldn't have been Veronica, Craig decided, as he crossed the worn carpet and entered the gilded cage of the elevator. He hadn't had time to give her his address. So who was it? It didn't matter much, if no name had been left. He forgot about it as soon as he opened Sue's letter and was caught up in her effervescent style. Cheerful as usual, of course, hiding disquiet behind natural optimism. George was going to be in Washington for some time. News of his arrest in Moscow had been leaked, somehow, and had even reached a newspaper column, which made a new post abroad difficult—what foreign government wanted someone who had been publicly labeled as a spy to be stationed in its capital? Once a charge like that appeared in print, it became awkward to handle and difficult to ignore. It didn't matter if—in George's words—it was a god-damned lie. The lie was read, while the denial was ignored. "So," wrote Sue, "that's how a careless journalist can ruin the entire career of someone who has done more for his country than ever *he* has done with his little typewriter." However (the word was heavily underlined, as if to cheer herself up), this otherwise quiet stay in Washington might be the chance to start raising a family. She had had two miscarriages in Moscow, but the doctor now said she was absolutely fine, and so wasn't that wonderful? There had been some talk of poor Professor Sussman's suicide, too, even on the flight over the Atlantic. Such a small world, wasn't it, with so many unexpected people knowing everyone else? Father seemed much better and would visit them in June, when they hoped to have some air conditioning installed in their new Georgetown apartment. Take care and good luck. . . .

I'll need both, he thought, as he dropped the letter on top of his dresser. As he took off his jacket and tie, and undid the top button of his shirt, he was wondering how, exactly, George's story had "been leaked." Purposely, of course. Sue's phrase told him that. But by whom? He could guess the reason behind the planted rumor; George's career was being spiked. How many other Georges were there, anyway, saying nothing, swallowing their disappointments, covering up the wounds they had received in the hidden war? And Sue—strange how people could keep silent about their personal tragedies. Two miscarriages . . . Good God, he thought, and I used to tease her about the time she was taking to produce a nephew for Christmas. Yes, people were surprising in the way they could disguise their feelings; or their thoughts; or even their actions. Never, in fact, underestimate anybody. A historian shouldn't need to be reminded of that. He had three thousand years of human examples, taking his choice from any century, which could amaze—or shock. Nothing that actually happened could be called unbelievable nonsense, no matter how fantastic it appeared. I ought to have remembered that, he told himself, when I listened to Sussman.

And if Sussman had not died, would he have listened to Rosie, to Partridge?

Craig pulled the one chair closer to a small table, sat down, propped up his legs, began to go over in his mind all the facts, the hints, the suggestions that Partridge had given him. Heinrich Berg was not so astonishing once you thought about him in cold blood: a hidden Communist who openly joined the Nazi party. There had been at least one other man like Berg; now let's see, what was that guy's name— Richard Sorge? Sorge; the German-born Soviet spy who had been a trusted Nazi in the German Embassy in Tokyo during the Second World War. He had let Moscow know about Pearl Harbor in advance, too. Yes, that was something that needed remembering. . . .

There had been other men like Berg in those recent years, all shaping history in their own way. History wasn't just a record of wars and peace conferences; history was a long and bitter story of intrigue and grab, of hidden movements and determined leaders, of men who knew what they wanted manipulating men who hadn't one idea that anything was at stake: the innocent and the ignorant being used according to someone else's plan. But every now and again, the plan would fail. Because people could be surprising, too, in their resistance —once they knew what was actually happening. Once they knew. But before they knew? Then we have men like Partridge, he thought, or else we could lose.

And why did Partridge trust me? After all, I could be another Sorge, another Berg, waiting for my chance to infiltrate. How is he sure that I'm not a Soviet agent? We have our share of them in America. The British and Swedish and French varieties have been grabbing the headlines recently, but we've got them, too. And I could be one of them. A sleeper, they'd call me in the trade. Partridge isn't trusting me for my honest gray eyes; or the books I'm planning to write; or the friends I have chosen. He isn't judging me on these things, not by a long, long mile. They could be part of the myth I was busy creating for myself. Then why?

It could be—yes, it could be that he knows a little of my life, enough of it to give him a measuring gauge. The army must have done some work on putting my history together when I was cleared for codes in Korea. But there was college after that, graduate work, teaching. . . . Yet there haven't been any unexplained gaps in that span of my life which could have been used for indoctrination or training. No unaccountable visits to strange places, no disappearances from public view for a few weeks each year. No peculiar hiatus there, or a jump here; no special introductions into sensitive jobs, no help from outside sources. Whatever I've attempted, I've done on my own steam; there have been a few almost-successes, a lot of failures, but they are all my own.

Now a man like Berg cannot function alone. He gets a lot of assistance on his way up: the right recommendation to slip him into certain jobs, the right changes and promotions made with quiet help, always moving him closer to the center of power or—just as important for his purposes—to the centers of influence. And those who help the Bergs in this world to infiltrate have helped others like him, too. That's their purpose, their justification for existing. Yes, if I were in Partridge's field, I'd be interested in recommendations. Because anyone can make a mistake in recommending a man for a job, but no one can go on making recommendations that somehow always turn out to be against his own country's interests. Unless he is, of course, just that—against his own country's interests. If challenged, he will give that self-justification routine—who is to judge his country's interests? Meaning himself and his friends, no doubt. There are some who just can't resist playing God. And if you argue back that a country is a collection of people, not just him and his group, you'd be told that things weren't quite so simple as that. Simple? It's the majority that still counts *if* a country is free to decide its own interests. It may be a bad decider at times, slow and uncertain and blundering, but it does the deciding. It is in control. And *that* is the first of all its interests. None higher . . . Attack that, and you attack all of us. Including me. Simple? So are bread and water, rain and sun. The basics come first, then the elaborations. Anyway, there's the reason that I met Jim Partridge halfway tonight. And perhaps his reason for trusting me is just as simple and basic: he has to.

Of course, Partridge's trust wasn't excessive. I already knew about

Berg—as the Nazi, at least; I knew there was an organization behind him, and a hell of a time some of them gave me. I knew Veronica was going to Mykonos before he did—correction: before he told me about it. And I might as well admit that the idea of drifting into Mykonos, one pleasant morning in May, was already circling around the back of my mind. (It's no farther away from Athens than East Hampton or Stonington from New York—perhaps less; weekend distance, easily. I've even traveled more than that for a weekend of skiing.) So Partridge only entrusted me with a little more than I already knew, perhaps to keep me from guessing wildly and blundering into the kind of situation where even professionals fear to tread. Certainly there's a lot more to this picture than I am allowed to see. I may be told more when I reach Athens, more again on Mykonos. That depends on how I perform, I expect. Or, more likely, on what Jim Partridge needs of me. I have few illusions about Partridge, just as he has none about me.

Craig rose, found his map of Greece and the Aegean, spread it out on the table. In spite of his determination to look at this assignment coldly, as a student of history-in-the-making, his mind was alert and excited, his blood pressure rising. By God, he thought, I could enjoy this line of work. Then he laughed at himself.

There was a gentle rap on his door. Craig glanced at his watch; it was almost midnight. "What is it?" he called, but there was no answer, just another gentle rap. So he pushed aside the table, crossed the room in five steps, wondering why the porter's desk hadn't telephoned the message instead of sending it upstairs at this hour. He had the tip ready in his hand as he opened the door. Maritta Maas smiled at him.

"May I?" she asked, already inside the room, leaving a drift of perfume as she passed by. "Hotel corridors are so depressing. Don't you agree?" She turned to look at him, her head tilted just a little, her green eyes dancing with amusement.

He closed the door, smiling back. "I'm sure I'd agree with anything you said."

"That's very gallant."

"I can do better when I'm less surprised."

"I love to give surprises."

"Just like Santa Claus," he said, helping her off with her white silk coat. That was what she wanted, seemingly. The black dress was short, slender, sleeveless, low-necked.

"Oh?" She was puzzled for an instant. Then she laughed. "I hope I'm prettier than he is."

"I think you have the edge."

Again she frowned. "You know, if you speak that way you will have to translate for me. Why don't Americans speak English?"

"Because they aren't English, I suppose. But they usually speak American fairly well. Have this chair. It's more comfortable than it looks. Cigarette?" He was recovering himself. "Or would you like to go down to the bar and have a drink there?"

"It is much too crowded. I want to talk to you. Seriously."

"That's going to be difficult."

She had looked around the room before she sat down, noticing the half-packed suitcase, the travel folders scattered over the bed, the guidebook to Greece and the map on the small table. Her glance swept back to him. "Why?"

"Look at you," he suggested. She might start by pulling the tight skirt down over her knees, unpointing her slender shoes, uncrossing the elegantly posed legs, if she wanted any serious talk.

"Do you say such things to Ronnie, too?"

"No," he said frankly. And how cosy we are with Veronica's name, so natural and easy and amiable! Just a sweet old dependable, that was friend Maritta.

"Then am I being flattered or insulted?" She laughed to take any offense away from her words.

Playful, he thought. That's the word for Maritta. As playful as a green-eyed panther. He stared at her—the passing thought was so exactly right.

"No, no, no," she said, misreading the stare. "I am flattered. I cannot imagine you insulting anybody."

"Then let's begin all over again."

"And we should introduce ourselves properly. Maritta Geneviève Maas."

"John Craig."

"That's all?"

"All."

"You disappeared so quickly today, without waiting for any introductions—" Her voice trailed away, her hands gestured in regret.

"I only came to apologize for keeping Veronica late, and after that —well, I didn't want to intrude."

"You are so polite!"

"Americans have occasional attacks of politeness," he admitted, and had her laughing again. Did she really think that was funny, or was she trying some flattery, too?

Suddenly she was serious. "I'm a little—troubled. What did you think of Ronnie, today?"

"A charming girl."

"No, no—I mean, did you see much difference in her?"

"Difference from what?"

"From the time you used to know her. In America."

"I didn't know her in America. I don't really know her at all."

"But you asked her to dinner—like an old friend."

"On the contrary. I asked her to dinner to get to know her better."

Maritta was completely and delightfully embarrassed. "Oh, I am sorry! Ronnie spoke so much of you this evening that I thought you were old, old friends."

Somehow he was reminded of the question-and-answer game played by Jordan last Saturday. He might as well hurry the process along, give her all the information she was looking for. Veronica must have talked very little, if at all, about him; that was clear. "I wish we were. Actually, that's been one of the disappointments in Paris—no friends of any description. Funny, isn't it? I'm on the point of leaving, and so I meet someone I like. Two people, in fact: both girls, both pretty." He looked at Maritta with frank admiration, and won what could have been a real smile. "That's the way it goes, I suppose," he added regretfully.

"But how awful—to have walked around Paris all alone! No one to talk to . . . That couldn't have been very enjoyable."

"No. But very educational. Oh, there was an old lady who was looking for the right Métro, and a student who wanted a scholarship, and an American who spoke to me at the bar downstairs, and Jules the bartender, and a man in a bookshop, and a—"

"Next time you visit Paris, you must let us know when you are coming. Will you?"

"*Will* I?" he asked, and laughed.

She was very amused about something. "My uncle—I suppose Ronnie told you all about him?"

"No. We had scarcely time to talk about families. She just mentioned that an uncle had lent you a house for the summer, and she was going to spend a few weeks with you. Nice deal, if you can get it." Then he looked as if a new idea had just dawned. "Didn't she like your uncle? Is that what's bothering you about Veronica?"

"No, no, no," she said quickly, "I was only thinking that my uncle would be very shocked if he heard that Ronnie had—what do you say?—picked you up. It really is a joke, you know. She is supposed to chaperone me on Mykonos."

"I couldn't imagine you needing that," he said with a wide grin. "And anyway, it wasn't so much a matter of anyone being picked up. It was a very wet night, about a week ago. I had a taxi, she hadn't. It was a case either of giving her first rights on the cab, or of keeping my suit dry. I did both: I gave her a lift for the few blocks she had to go. Thank you and good night. That was all."

"And you didn't ask her to dinner? What were you thinking of, John?" Her eyes were wide, teasing.

"Yes," he admitted, "I slipped up there. I might have found Paris less educational. Do you know how many museums you have? Forty-nine. And how many—"

"Are you never serious?"

"As rarely as possible. But I'll make an effort. You were troubled, you said?"

"I suppose you intend to see her again?" Maritta's eyes flickered toward the map of the Aegean and then met his.

"I hope I'll see both of you. I have to visit Delos, so I'll be dropping in at Mykonos some time or other." He let her eyes hold his. And he could sense that it had been the right thing to say. Not just to speak casually of Mykonos, but to include Maritta in his hopes. She liked to play, this girl, and she would never play second lead to any other girl. In some ways, she reminded him of a few he had known back in New York.

"Then I should warn you. Be careful with Ronnie. I mean—she takes things so seriously, so intensely. She is just coming out of a very bad time as it is. I think she is still in love with him. An American. Did she tell you?"

He shook his head.

"He is one of those expatriate poets. They've been living together for almost a year. He exists on the small checks he gets from home each month. He believes in his genius. Ronnie believes in him. But he left her—just like that! He walked out of their studio one day. She hasn't seen him since. That was two weeks ago. Ronnie took a room at the Beauharnais, gave up her studio, couldn't bear it any longer. You see? Any other girl would have known this would happen. Any other girl would have left him months ago. But Ronnie—" She sighed. "I think she shouldn't take life so seriously, not for a long, long time. Do you see?"

He saw very clearly. Half-truth, half-fiction, beautifully blended. Veronica, if he came to Mykonos, was to be untouchable. Why? Making sure that she would be isolated from someone who might ask questions? Making sure that she could be properly controlled by Maritta—a very skillful, gentle surveillance? They were taking no chances with him, even if he seemed innocent enough. "Yes," he said at last, "I see."

"And you agree?"

He hadn't much other choice. "You could be right."

"I *am* right!"

"Just an Americanism," he said with a smile.

"You've no idea how upset she has been."

"It was a nice idea to ask her to Mykonos. That should help to take her mind off Paris. But are you going to warn off all the men who look at Veronica? You'll be kept busy."

"Of course not. I shan't have to warn them, unless they are very attractive and unmarried—like you. There are not so many of them." She was amused at the expression on his face. "I've embarrassed you?"

"I'd imagine that there would be quite a crowd of—"

"Oh yes, there will be men on Mykonos, but only the kind one takes lightly. They come, they go. Ships passing in the night. You are that, too, in a sense. Except Ronnie likes you. And she is *so* vulnerable at present. You know. . . ."

"I don't."

"It is a matter of—rebound. Isn't that what you call it?"

"She isn't in any danger of falling in love with me," he said, his embarrassment growing. "She doesn't know me, to begin with."

"Do you think that matters to a woman?" She watched him, half smiling, her lips softening. "It wouldn't matter to me." There was a little silence. "Of course, if you were really serious about her, I shouldn't worry."

"Didn't I tell you I was serious as rarely as possible?" he asked jokingly. That passed her scrutiny. He could feel her relax. The softness in her lips spread to her eyes. "Do I see you at all on Mykonos?"

That pleased her. She rose, laughing. "Why not? We can't have you wandering around all alone again."

"Oh, I'll have several friends there," he said easily.

"Really?"

"Of course. It isn't only painters and poets who visit Mykonos."

"Oh—historians?"

She really had done her homework, he thought. "I'll be spending most of my time on Delos, anyway."

"But there's no village, no hotel, on Delos. Just a small tourist pavilion with a few beds for—well, emergencies. You'll have to sleep on Mykonos."

He nodded, watching her. "That's right. I'll sleep on Mykonos," he said softly. He had actually managed to embarrass her, but she enjoyed it too.

She laughed again, turned away, walked slowly over to the dresser. She straightened his comb and brushes, fiddled with a pair of cuff links, picked up a small plastic jar of hair cream. "Men are so businesslike," she said. "So simple, the way they travel." She opened the jar and pretended to smell the cream. "Nice and uncomplicated," she told him. She replaced the jar neatly, examined a small leather box in which he kept studs and collar-stays. "This is from Florence, isn't it?" she asked casually, opening it, too.

"By way of Madison Avenue." He came forward. What the devil was she doing, pretending to play like this with all these small possessions? Or was it the letter from Sue, lying openly beside his hairbrush, that interested her?

She put down the leather box, seemed to notice the time on his small traveling clock. She turned to him, held out both her hands in farewell. "I must go. Yes, I must. I leave tomorrow. That's why I came to see you now, even if it is late. What else could I do? The dinner party went on and on and on."

He kept hold of her hands. "How was it? Plenty of advice?"

"A complete bore. My uncle had two of his friends from Mykonos to meet me—they have a house there, too. And they want to entertain Ronnie and me, introduce us around. You know. . . ."

"That might not be so bad."

"But they are so dull! I prefer to choose my own friends, don't you?"

"Much more satisfactory."

"Of course, an uncle who is one's only remaining relative must worry, I suppose," she said with a sigh.

Craig said with a broad smile as he looked at the clock, "How could he ever worry about you, Maritta?"

But irony was lost on her. Or she had finished with the topic of uncle. She said, "You are telephoning Ronnie tomorrow morning, aren't you?"

"I said I would."

"She won't be able to lunch with you." Maritta's voice was low, hesitant, and just the right amount sad. "Blame me. I asked her to attend to some business I hadn't time to finish."

"Well, I suppose it's kinder to let her do the refusing."

"But she will be free for dinner," Maritta said, watching him now with eyes wide and hesitant, as if she were letting him make the decision.

He couldn't feel one tremble in her cool hands, couldn't see one flickering evasion in her pleading green eyes. He waited for a few seconds, just to keep her impatience simmering behind that beautifully controlled face. "You don't want me to ask her to dinner?"

Her hands had tightened, her eyes blinked. "I thought we agreed—"

"I'll probably be on my way to Greece by dinnertime," he told her. He released her hands and turned to pick up her coat from the bed.

"You are annoyed with me, and I didn't want that. Please, John—I would never have asked you except that I didn't want to see Ronnie have her hopes all built up again and then find them come crashing down; you know what I mean."

"I know." And if he hadn't known so much, he would have believed the soft, anxious, urgent voice, and that pathetic look of the good friend who was doing everything for the best.

"I've embarrassed you again."

"Because I couldn't care less." Not about what you think or you want, my sweet-faced liar, he thought. Get her out of here, he told himself, or you might describe her in a five-letter word to her face. He held out her coat, and she slipped her soft white arms into the sleeves, turning her head to look up at him. "I'll see you on Mykonos," he said, "unless your uncle flays me alive for having you up in my room at one in the morning. How did you find me, anyway?"

"Oh, Ronnie told us," she said most innocently. "She even telephoned you just before dinner to see if you would join us. Didn't you get the message?"

"Someone called, I heard. No name left, though."

"How typical!" She shook her head. "But you know, it was Ronnie's call that decided me she really was rushing much too quickly—Sorry. I promise never to mention the subject again."

He opened the door, glanced into the deserted corridor with only its lonely pairs of dusty shoes waiting patiently outside each bedroom.

"Expecting anyone?" she asked.

"Your uncle and his posse of vigilantes."

"I beg your pardon?" Then she shrugged her shoulders, looked amused. "Oh, really! You Americans! . . . And where are *you* going?"

"To see you into the elevator."

This startled her into a laugh. Perhaps the well-dressed spy was not accustomed to being shown out at such an hour by her unsuspecting quarry. "But there is no need—" she began, and jumped as a sudden, sleepy protest came from the room they were passing: "Knock it off! Go to bed!" A tired groan followed, then a resigned sigh.

"Another American," she said in a stage whisper, and clamped her hands to her lips to stifle an outburst of real laughter. For a moment, Craig had a glimpse of a different Maritta, someone she could have been if she hadn't chosen another rôle for herself, someone young-hearted and merry, trying to smother a second attack of giggles as the signal for the elevator sounded with extra loudness through the silence of the hotel. Then, as the creaking cage began its slow and dignified ascent, she became the Maritta he knew. "Go back to your room. Please!" she whispered quickly, and gestured with her hand. He nodded understandingly, retreated obligingly. Who was he to compromise the good name of such a charming lady? He wondered whom she was supposed to be visiting. Someone who belonged to the elderly female shoes he had almost stepped upon?

He was at his door, waving a good early morning to her, as the elevator reached his floor. She stepped inside quickly, not looking back, doing nothing to attract the attendant's notice to Craig's closing door. What, he thought, not even a blown kiss? I bet she would do that really elegantly.

He closed the door, waited until the last whirr of the elevator had ground into silence, then opened his door one small crack. The voice that had advised them to knock it off and go to bed was Jim Partridge's. Craig was sure of that. But Partridge's door remained closed. All right, Craig thought, I can take a hint. He shut his door carefully, soundlessly, but left it unlocked. Why else would Partridge let him know he was on the same floor unless he planned to pay a visit?

By two o'clock, Craig decided that he had been too bright in his quick ideas. There was no sign of Partridge. So he went to bed. Not to sleep. This was not a night for the quiet, untroubled mind that would allow him to slip over the edge of consciousness and fall into soft oblivion. He lay staring at the darkened ceiling, the reading light at his bedside still turned on, the book in his hand dropped at his side. He was going over and over in his restless mind the myth that Maritta Maas had created. My God, he thought, if Jim Partridge hadn't warned me about her, I might have believed—I would probably have believed her. Yes, I could have believed it. I would scarcely have noticed the lie that undermined everything she said: Veronica could not have telephoned me or mentioned my hotel to anyone, for she did not know my address. I would scarcely have noticed that unobtrusive lie, simply because I wasn't being given much time for any real thought—just emotions. And I would have cut off the small warning signal at the back of my brain, the way we all do when we don't expect, far less suspect. That's how the confidence game was worked, was it? To the outside observer, removed and uncommitted, blessed with hindsight, he would have seemed more than naïve if he had believed Maritta's story. But involved as he had been, with all the little hints and honest-eyed explanations and the seemingly logical sequiturs—oh no, that was another proposition. Without Partridge, he would have been properly taken. Let's face it, men were flattered even if embarrassed by the idea that a girl like Veronica might be falling hard for them. Vanity, vanity, and all is flattery. Then he stopped thinking of himself, and began worrying about Veronica. He felt a surge of both pity and fear. Veronica was headed for tragedy. "I'll be damned," he said softly, "if I let that happen."

At four o'clock, his door opened and Partridge came in. Craig, almost asleep, stared at him dizzily, then raised himself quickly. Partridge gestured for silence, cutting off Craig's "Thank God you came" before it was uttered. He seemed normal, unconcerned, in spite of all the caution he was using. He had a quick nod of approval for the tightly drawn curtains and the meager light, perhaps, too, for the unlocked door which had let him enter so quietly. He pocketed a key which he hadn't needed to use as he bolted the door carefully behind him. Then, from the other pocket of his dressing gown, he pulled out a small box of some kind, set it carefully on the small table, and touched a switch. Nothing happened as far as Craig could hear or see, but Partridge was obviously pleased with it. Only then did he come forward to join Craig, who was sitting on the edge of the bed. "Who was she?" he asked, his voice held as low as possible.

"Maritta Maas."

"I nearly walked in, you know. I wanted to see you when I came back to the hotel, and got as far as your door. I heard voices. So I retreated. But boy oh boy, that was nearly a blooper."

"Would she have known you?"

Partridge shook his head. "It's better if she doesn't see me until Mykonos." If at all, he thought.

"So you'll be there." And thank heaven for that.

"Eventually." The visit to Rhodes and a talk with O'Malley came first. Some quiet, if reluctant, permission had come from Washington, but it was obvious that this was the type of operation which might need emergency, on-the-spot decisions; regular channels would only delay critical action, conventional controls could mean defeat. Christopher Holland, who considered red tape as only something to be cut, had thought Partridge's idea good. The rest would be up to O'Malley.

He's looking haggard, Craig thought. "When will—"

"What did she want?" Partridge asked crisply.

Craig poured it out. One thing about a sleepless night—it let him have the sequences of Maritta's talk quite clear in his mind. He included her movements over by his dresser, her tender curiosity about his small possessions. (That had struck him as odd. If he had wanted to learn about a man, he would have looked at the books propped up against the mirror.)

Partridge heard him without interruption, and then sat in silence when he had ended.

Craig said, "The only bit of real truth in all that was the fact that Veronica was in love and got ditched. The rest is invention or manipulation of the facts." He paused, but Partridge still frowned down at the rug as if its faded arabesques fascinated him. Craig tried again. "Can't we give Veronica some protection?"

Partridge nodded. "We can try. There's a girl I know who might strike up a friendship with her on Mykonos. That would be the best angle, I think. We mustn't lose contact with her. But we can't warn her, either; we've already discussed all that. It still stands."

"I'm keeping an eye on her," Craig said grimly.

"Don't stir up Maritta's jealousy," Partridge warned him. "There's something personal there, too, not just her job—"

"She'd be that way with any man. She may not want him, but no one near her is going to get him."

Partridge rose and crossed over to the dresser. He examined everything there, quickly, methodically, even running his fingers around the protruding edge of the wooden top. "Just seeing if she left any presents for you such as some gadget to bug this room. Did you express your opinion about her, for instance, when you came back in here?" The question was offhand, slightly joking, but Partridge was waiting for the answer.

"By transference. I needed a drink and got my flask and dropped a tumbler—it broke over there by the bathroom door. So I cursed it heavily for the full minute it took me to get the pieces gathered together." Craig's voice was still grim, as if he couldn't relax even over a comic incident.

Partridge glanced at Sue's letter as he turned away. Whatever he had been able to read, as Maritta must have seen it, gave him no cause for alarm. He studied Craig's tense face. This won't do, he thought. Nonchalantly, he said, "I guess she was really making a little test to see if you were a courier of some kind. Her friends go in for false lids on jars and boxes, hollow cuff links, all that stuff. They're like the inquisitive carpenter who unscrewed his navel and his bottom fell off." He searched in his breast pocket and said, "In fact, here's one example I brought along for you tonight. The police found it on the man charged with Sussman's murder. It proves he had more connection with Soviet espionage than a criminal usually has." He held out a tie clip. "Go on, open it. I filled it to let you see the kind of thing you might expect to find inside."

Craig took the tie clip. It was thicker than most, but of the usual length and decoration. He examined it, felt he was now wrestling with a Chinese puzzle, pressed and pulled and cajoled the small strip of imitation gold without any effect. He could see no join, no seam in the heavy bar of the clip.

"This way," Partridge said, taking it from him, sliding the top apart. In the lower section, there nestled a small strip of microfilm protected by an equally small strip of tissue paper. "When that's developed, you could fill twenty full-sized sheets of typing paper—perhaps even more—with the information it holds. Some of their couriers, the smart dressers, object to wearing a clip as bulky as this. They prefer cuff links. Their women use the lids of compacts, metal frames of handbags, lipsticks, watches with the works removed. . . . And then there are the flashlight batteries, hollowed out; and the special spaces inside tubes of artists' colors; toothpaste ditto. Et cetera, et cetera . . . You name them, we've found them. So have the British, the French, the Italians, and all the rest of our allies. You think I'm exaggerating? Inventing? Next time you visit Washington, I'll ask my friend at FBI headquarters to show you some of the Soviet gadgets they've discovered right in the old U.S.A. It's quite a collection, believe me. And then we meet some jovial type at dinner who tells us that we have a fixation about Soviet espionage, and couldn't we just forget the whole thing, relax the way he does, live and let live?" Partridge's quiet voice broke into a brief but genuine laugh.

Craig said nothing. But he really concentrated on the tie clip this time, his lips tight. He succeeded in opening it. He grinned as he handed the two pieces back to Partridge.

"You fix it," Partridge told him. "Their cuff links work on the same idea. Ingenious bastards, aren't they?"

"One thing's certain," Craig said, completing the small operation successfully. "They don't trust the mail, these boys."

That's better, thought Partridge, watching Craig's face, listening to the tone of his voice. "Another thing's certain," he said as he pocketed the tie clip. "They've given you just about enough basic training for my taste. I want you to pack and leave. Oh yes, telephone Veronica, but be damned casual. Play it Maritta's way and keep the Clark girl safe. Yes, safe." He paused to let that sink in. "And a lot more will stay safe, too. We are in too good a position to throw the game away now. I don't think they have any real suspicions about what we actually know. Sure they were suspicious of you, but they're suspicious of everyone, including each other. They don't know, for instance, that we have been playing along with them to give them confidence, or that we have been reacting to every move they are taking. Oh, well—perhaps not every move; that's a counterespionage dream, too good to be true. Still, we are in there guessing, with some very solid facts to back up the possibilities. So when you get to Mykonos, play it very cool with Veronica. You are bound to see her—it's a small place. But let us do the worrying about her. Okay?"

"Will you have time?" Craig asked wryly.

"We'll have to make the time." Then Partridge's voice became brisk. "In Athens, we are going to play it very loose indeed. We won't make any effort to get in touch with you unless there is some real emergency."

"Meaning I'm back on their danger list again?" Craig was grinning.

"But," said Partridge as if he hadn't heard that suggestion, "if a Frenchman makes friends with you, don't resist. His name is Yves Duclos. He will keep you in touch with me. It's safer that way. Maritta's bosses don't expect the French to be co-operating with us. Let's surprise them about that, shall we?"

"It's good to hear we can surprise them sometimes."

Partridge smiled, at that. "You saw Duclos with me last Monday evening, in the bar downstairs."

"I remember. That's when I came in, raging quietly. There was a redhead with you, too, wasn't there?"

"Can you describe Duclos for me?"

"Black hair, bright blue eyes, good healthy color in his cheeks. I couldn't see his height, of course. He looked tall, sitting down."

"Just medium height when he stands—five feet eight. Around one hundred and sixty-five pounds. Think you can recognize him easily?"

"I think so. Of course, I didn't really look at him too hard."

141

"He's a Breton. And he always wears a gold signet ring with an odd twisted design. If you ask him, he will tell you it's fourteenth century from Rennes. Got that?"

Craig nodded.

Partridge was frowning at the rug again, hesitating. "Yes," he said at last, "I'd better pass on the warning. One of the men you met at your sister's party is working with Maritta. He collects information; she passes it on. We expect him to appear on Mykonos."

"What?" Craig asked sharply. He lost his breath, regained it. *"What?"*

Partridge nodded. That was as far as he would go. He was tempted, just a little, to add that the man could be one of two. But what was the point? Craig wouldn't have been made any the wiser by an exact name. No use loading him with extra information that would only be dangerous for him to carry around. Two men . . . Is one being used, like Veronica Clark, to cover up the man we want? Partridge suddenly wondered. They are both traveling in the same direction—the Aegean area. Both have good contacts, friends in sensitive jobs who'd trust them; both would make useful enemy agents. Both, again, have spent some time in Russia; both could have been recruited there; both have been living normal lives since they came to Paris.

Craig was still recovering from the shock. He asked slowly, "But you don't know his name?"

"Not yet," Partridge said. Robert Maybrick Bradley, with a security job, no less, in NATO . . . Edward Maclennan Wilshot, who has written many articles on NATO and its problems . . . Wilshot gets a free-lance assignment from a French magazine, not always friendly to NATO, to cover the eastern Mediterranean on the day that Bradley claims the leave that is due him. That's the latest report from Rosie on the subject. But who is being used to cover for whom? That's a new angle. Better get Rosie on to it right away. Unless he has thought about it, of course . . . No, this is possibly my own idea, thanks to Veronica Clark. It could, it just could solve the problem of two men with similar journeys at the same time near the same target area. "It's been a bit of a puzzle," he admitted. "Sorry I'm so vague. But after Maritta's performance tonight, I think you needed the warning, such as it is. It would be easy to assume that everyone at your sister's party was just as trustworthy as old Rosie."

"How is he?"

"Still worrying about his weight. Played bowls, last night. Golfing on Saturday." Partridge picked up the small box from the table, went over to the door, gave an easy salute and—after a careful look into the corridor—slipped outside.

See you on Mykonos, Craig thought, and went to bed. Strangely enough, this time he slept.

He awoke at ten on a bright cool morning, and before he shaved or ordered breakfast he called Veronica.

"There's this matter of lunch," he began. "When can I pick you up?"

She seemed rather taken aback by this brusque approach. "I'm terribly sorry. I can't manage lunch today. I've got some business to—"

"That's too bad."

"I should be free by four o'clock," she said shyly, "but I suppose you have plans of your own for the afternoon."

"As a matter of fact, I have. I'm just about to leave Paris."

"I'm really awfully sorry that I disappointed—"

"Don't give it a thought. That's the way things go. . . . Well, I suppose this is good-bye."

"Oh!" Then she rallied. "Have a very good trip."

"The same to you."

"Good-bye," she said, quietly and gently and—he hoped—a little sadly.

He replaced the receiver, sat staring at it for a full minute. Then he rose, thinking now of Maritta, and his eyes weren't so pleasant to see.

11

Yves Duclos arrived at the Athens airport early on Sunday afternoon. He had taken his journey from Paris in easy stages: Thursday had seen him in Milan for a quiet talk with Italian Intelligence; Friday, he had been in Florence to meet some furniture designers; Saturday, he had spent in Rome purely for pleasure. . . . Altogether, it had been an excellent trip without any alarms or tensions. And the four days ahead of him in Athens should be fairly easy, too. It was always the same—after a week of work and urgency, of meetings and plans and problems and decisions, he was now in the waiting period. But it was not often that the waiting could be done in a place as beautiful as Athens.

The flight had brought him right over the city, with the Acropolis in full view beneath him. Like most of his fellow passengers, he was still vibrating from that spectacular approach: a precipice rising out of city roofs, golden-white columns growing out of rocky crags, and—within seconds—a landing by a bay of blue rippling water. Not so far out there, south and eastward, lay Mykonos. . . . But that, he thought as he walked briskly into the low-roofed hall where the Customs officers waited, would come later. He had four days, meanwhile, to enjoy Athens. He might manage a visit to Delphi, too; it was the French archaeologists, after all, who had dug the place out of its rubble and put the pieces together. His first visit to Greece certainly ought to include Delphi. "Nothing to declare," he told the Greek who had checked his two cases. Nothing except good intentions and high expectations.

Duclos picked up his luggage and started toward the wall of glass windows which lay at the end of the small Customs Hall, separating it from a corridor packed with waiting people. Across the corridor, he could see more windows and wide-open doors with the bright sunshine pouring in from a wide square or plaza. No doubt the buses and taxis were out there. In half an hour, he would be reaching Athens itself.

From the crowd of people pressed close to the corridor's glass windows, a pleasant voice said, "Monsieur Duclos?" It was a small, light-boned man in a pale gray suit, his hat in his hand, a smile on his face, his dark eyes questioning politely. He was middle-aged, sallow in complexion, dark in hair and mustache. Greek, decided Duclos, as he listened to the halting French, bravely tried. "Monsieur Duclos! At your service. I am from the office of Colonel Zafiris." He showed a small identification card, tactfully, briefly. "There is one of your countrymen who has been waiting to meet you. He came yesterday from Paris, from Inspector Galland. There is some new development about a prisoner of the inspector's which could be of importance—but here he is, himself." He pointed to a younger man, about the same height and weight as Duclos, fair-haired, blue-eyed, who waited with hands plunged in the pockets of his light coat, a cigarette between his lips, a bored expression on his handsome face. "I am Tillier," the Frenchman said, coming to life as he looked at Duclos. "I did not have the pleasure of meeting you on your visit to Galland last Tuesday morning. I only saw you very briefly as you left. Yes, the murderer of Professor Sussman has talked a little since you interviewed him. But we shall leave that to discuss in your hotel. We could not find where you are staying, so we had to meet you here. Let me help you." He made a gesture toward one of Duclos' suitcases.

"I can manage, thank you," Duclos said. He went through the nearest door and found himself on the crowded sidewalk filled with noise and bustle and bright sunshine. Tillier was the detective who had been assisting Galland in the Sussman case, that he knew. And this man—possibly a Norman by coloring and accent—was definitely French. What was more, if Sussman's murderer had given any information at all, then that could be of great importance. It might mean a change, perhaps subtle, perhaps bold, in the plan that Duclos and Partridge had agreed upon for Mykonos. Colonel Zafiris was Greek Counterintelligence, that Duclos also knew. Yet why this tie-in between Greek Intelligence and Paris police? Unless the Sûreté itself had telescoped action, decided that the Greeks should learn along with Duclos whatever Galland had discovered. Certainly there wasn't much time now for last-minute conferences. And yet, and yet— Duclos looked around at the family groups, at the mixture of rich and poor, of nationalities, happy faces, worried faces, no one giving one good English goddamn about anyone else except his own problems. He looked at Tillier, who was standing beside him, and tried to measure him. The face was vaguely familiar: he could have seen it last Tuesday as he left Galland's office. Yes, he had seen it. Last Tuesday? He said, "There's too much crowd here. Better if we separate. I'll go by bus. You can follow me in your car. You'll find me at the King George Hotel. I'll expect you at five o'clock. Does that suit you?" By then, he thought, I'll have checked with Zafiris as well as Paris.

"Of course. My only worry is that I must return to Paris this evening."

The little Greek said, "But Colonel Zafiris has sent his car to save time! It is over there!" He pointed to a space filled with cars and waiting taxis. A small car, dark brownish-green in color, was already making a wide turn to reach them. Its driver was in khaki uniform.

This may be the way things are done in Greece, thought Duclos, but I don't want any part of it. It is too official. He smiled genially as he moved off. "See you at the hotel," he said quietly.

"Fine," Tillier said. "If you prefer it that way—" He shrugged, walking beside Duclos. "Just one thing," he added, "have you got a room definitely at the King George? That's where I am and it's crowded. If you can't get it there, where can we meet you?" He halted as he stepped in front of Duclos, blocking his way. "Or perhaps you'd leave word at the desk for me where you've found a room? I must make tonight's flight back to Paris. I'm a day late as it is."

It was reasonable. It was time-consuming, just enough moments spent to let the official-looking car drive right up to the curb where they stood. "Oh, why not take this and save all trouble?" Tillier asked now, as the Greek opened the car door. He reached for the nearer suitcase most helpfully.

"No need," began Duclos, ready to crash through the crowd pressing around them—there was a terrace, a restaurant, just beyond the thick stream of people. But Tillier's hand switched from the suitcase to the wrist that held it. Duclos felt a sharp and painful bite as a needle pressed deep into his flesh. His voice came in a desperate gasp. "Help me, help, in the name of God, help—" But the foreigners' faces only stared blankly, briefly, as his words trailed into a drunken blur. His eyes, turned toward two children and their grandmother who had halted near him, closed. His legs buckled as his head dropped on his breast and Tillier's arms pushed him into the car.

Tillier propped up Duclos against the seat, held his weight in position with his own body. "Quick!" he told the Greek, who was handing in the suitcases.

"Not too quickly," the Greek said softly, slipping into the seat, closing the door.

The small boy tugged at the black skirt of his grandmother. "Was that man sick?" he asked.

"What man?" She pulled the skirt free from his hand, took a larger grip on the paper parcel she carried. "Stop looking at strangers," she said, her voice harsh with her own worries, "and watch out for your mother. She said she would meet us here. Where is she? Keep hold of your sister, now!"

The small boy did as he was told. He only let his eyes wander once back to the car but it was already moving away. It went so quietly, so smoothly. Not like his uncle's truck on the farm.

The car left the low cluster of airport buildings, continued its steady pace down toward the highway. It swept slowly past flower beds and fluttering flags, past tourist police and flocks of airline hostesses; past people arriving, departing, enjoying a Sunday outing; past parked cars and waiting buses, until it reached the main road that skirted the bay of blue water. It turned left and gathered speed at last. It was traveling away from Athens.

The man who had called himself Tillier took a deep breath, pushed Duclos farther into the corner. "Soon now—just past the fish restaurant and the filling station. We'll change cars there," he told the driver, "and you can get rid of that uniform." He removed his revolver from his pocket as he pulled his coat off and dropped it at his feet. "Don't forget the suitcases," he warned the Greek. "I need them."

The Greek nodded, glanced at his watch. "Four and a half minutes from here to there, all told," he said with considerable satisfaction. He looked at Duclos. "How long will he sleep?"

"Until we reach Cape Sunion."

"I would not advise taking the new shore road—too crowded on Sunday. Better strike inland a little—come round by Lávrion—"

"I know, I know," the Frenchman said impatiently. He sat forward, watching the stream of cars on the road ahead, all out on their Sunday picnics. "There's the restaurant! Get ready—" He tapped the driver on the shoulder. "Now!"

Duclos came out of his stupor as they skirted the mining town of Lávrion. He had enough returning sense to keep slumped in his corner, changing neither balance nor position. He listened to the Greek and Frenchman arguing, a faint jangle of phrases at first, then words becoming clearer as his own mind began working. All he could see through the carefully opened slits of his eyes was a desolate hillside, a few rows of workmen's houses, low and strung out over grassless earth. Where was this? Greece? The hideous smell, constant, persistent, made him think of Hades. But it wasn't sulphur—was it manganese, lead?

"Those filthy slag heaps!" the Frenchman said, and reached angrily past Duclos to shut the window. Duclos jolted forward, but was caught and held, and propped back into his corner. He had had time, though, to see the hilltops on his right where chimney stacks were perched.

"You should smell them during the week," the Greek was saying, "when the smoke belches out. That's why they're built up there, to keep people from being poisoned. They say they get lead and silver out of that slag. It's a French company that started working the mines —they take the profits and leave us with the stink."

"You know everything. Could you stop that yapping just for the last ten minutes?" the Frenchman asked sharply.

The driver laughed softly, taking no sides. He was a man who enjoyed other people's bickering.

A happy trio, thought Duclos, and wondered if there could be any dividend for him in that. He felt sick and tired, perhaps with the drug that had been pumped into him, perhaps with his own stupidity; he had expected nothing and that was the greatest of all stupidities. Now, he lay seemingly helpless in his corner while he let his brain start functioning again.

The rows of houses were gone, replaced by moorland. No sign of people here. The ground was too open to risk anything. Ahead of him he saw the beginning of trees. Perhaps there he could quickly get the door unlocked and jump and run for shelter. But the hope was too optimistic. He still felt weak; the Frenchman was holding a revolver on his lap; and when they reached the trees they were thin, giving way to more moorland. Then more trees, thicker trees, came into sight. Snatch the revolver first, he told himself, before you open the door.

The Greek was pointing to a large villa, boarded and shuttered, explaining that it was the first of many country places along this road where the rich from Athens came for the summer and shot doves in August. "He should have been a schoolmaster, this one," the Frenchman was telling the driver when Duclos reached for the revolver. But his body was slower than he had thought. It was only a vague, uncoordinated movement that came from his arm. The Frenchman cursed and hit him a crashing blow over the head with the revolver butt.

"You've killed him!" the Greek said in alarm.

"Not him. Bretons' heads are made of teak."

"The orders were not to injure him, to keep him well until—"

"He'll be well enough to answer our questions."

"He may take a little persuasion," the Greek said, with a spreading smile. "I remember in 'forty-five—"

"Keep your eyes open!" the Frenchman told the driver. "Just as you catch first sight of the pillars at Cape Sunion, there's a big house and two cottages on your left toward the sea. Stop at the second cottage. Got it?" He looked at the Greek beside him, wondering why he had to have this kind of guy along. Always talking of the civil war, he must have been only a kid of eighteen when he left villages in flames and snatched the children and carved up the men with his knife. You'd have thought he might have forgotten those things in those years in Bulgaria, but no, here he was back, looking like a bank clerk but still nursing his dreams of glory. "Keep your mouth shut when the boss arrives. We've changed our methods, didn't you know?"

"We nearly won," the Greek protested angrily. "We were closer to winning than you ever were."

"And what happened to your leaders? Heads cut off by the peasants and displayed in the market place! Signs still painted on the barns all over Thessaly calling us murderers! You 'nearly won' brilliantly." And that will shut up this know-all for the next hour at least, the

Frenchman thought. I'm in charge here and he'd better understand that. If it had not been for me, who could have identified Duclos at the airport so quickly, so quietly?

"There's the sea," the driver said. And far off, there was a glimpse of a ruined Greek temple on its high headland in stark silhouette against the western sun. Mission accomplished, the Frenchman thought with considerable satisfaction. We got him here, and there's no escape for him now.

It was dusk when Duclos regained consciousness. The room was square and small, half filled by the low wooden platform on which he had been thrown. The walls were of rough stone, once whitewashed, now gray-streaked in the fading light. There was a small window high above his head, unglassed, barred. The one low, narrow door looked solid and heavy. He put his feet on the hard-packed earth floor, carefully, testing his balance. He could stand. And walk. He made his way slowly across to the door. Yes, it was as strong as it had looked. And he could hear nothing through it.

Yet the room was not quiet. Through the window came the distant fall and surge of the sea. The air smelled clean, and it felt cool, almost cold. He crossed the room again and stood on the low platform—a communal bed, he guessed, there would be space for four rough mattresses on it—and reached for the bars. He could grasp their lower edge. Painfully, he pulled himself up to let his chin reach the stone sill, held on with his arm muscles tearing, and looked out. A bare, rocky field sloping downward to cliffs, beyond that a flat stretch of dark gray water reaching to a dark gray sky. No houses, no lights; nothing except the steady beat of waves. He dropped back onto the wooden bed, his arms trembling with the strain. He was still weak, much weaker than he had thought.

He sat on the bed, his back propped up against the heavy stone wall, and considered his position. They had taken away his tie, his belt, his shoes. They had taken his jacket and emptied his trouser pockets. They had taken his watch and his ring. From the papers in his passport-wallet, they would know that he had reservations for the Grande Bretagne. What would they do—have someone placed there to watch for any person asking about Yves Duclos, for anyone leaving a message for him? They wouldn't get much, that way. Mimi was staying at the Hilton and wasn't even going to get in touch with him until they sailed on the same boat for Mykonos on Thursday. Four days away. . . . Then he froze: his tickets for the steamer, his cabin reservation, would be left for him at his hotel. It had been necessary to book ahead to get a cabin and have Mimi in the one next door.

But how in the first place had they known where to pick him up? An informant? Or had they followed him to Rome, and, learning his destination there, jumped ahead of him to Athens? But why wait until then? They could have made an attempt on him in Milan or Florence or Rome itself. Perhaps they wanted to make sure he was heading for Greece before they moved. Yes, that could be it. Greece was the danger signal to them. But that could also show, perhaps, that they did not know too much about his mission or else they would never have waited to act until today. And so they want me for information, he thought somberly. That's why I'm still alive. Information to fill in the gaps in their suspicions. And I could give them a lot. . . . He had no illusions about human capacity to withstand physical persuasion. In the last extreme they'd use torture, that unpleasant word which so many pleasant people discarded as fantastic nonsense.

I'll have to play this carefully, he thought. When they question me reasonably, I'll have to be ready with answers that will give them no lead to Mykonos and the rest of us there. But when that type of questioning is over, then— He felt inside the waistband of his trousers, and pulled off one of the suspender buttons. He cracked it open with his fingers, and took out a small flat pellet wrapped in its thin saliva-proof coating. He clicked the two pieces of button together again, and threw it under the bed. The pellet, he placed in the breast pocket of his shirt. At the first sound of the door opening, he'd transfer it to his mouth. It could lie quite unobtrusively, he had heard, against his cheek. He would have to trust the waterproof coating—better that than finding his arms held or his hands tied when he needed that capsule. *If* he needed it, he added with a determined attempt at optimism.

It was dark now, and the wind must have risen, for the surge of sea had a heavier rhythm. Cold, too, in here. And he was thirsty. Not hungry—some of the awakening nausea still clung to his throat. He tried to forget his thirst by thinking about the Frenchman who had used the name of Tillier. That was the man who had placed him, he was convinced. What could the Frenchman know, and how much? He had seen that face, briefly, and only once. Where? Not on his visit to police headquarters, of that he was sure now. Not on Tuesday morning, then, but very close to that time. Tuesday afternoon had been the meeting at Mimi's, with Rosie and Jim Partridge. No, later than that, but still around Tuesday. . . . The evening, the late evening—at the club called Le Happening? Stagehands, waiters, doorman . . . and the man who had come from the rear of the building, when the narcotics raid started—a janitor of some kind, fair-haired, wearing torn overalls over a dirty undershirt. Yes, that was the man. He had mixed into the crowd of employees being gathered together backstage. I was just leaving, Duclos remembered. If he had quick-enough eyes to note my face and a good-enough memory to report it once the raid was over and he was freed, then one thing is sure—he was no ordinary janitor.

My God, he thought, how could one small thing like that trip me up? There must have been something else to add to it. Where did I make another mistake? Or was it chance?

He had plenty of time to try to think his way through that puzzle. For most of the night in the cold black room, he sat hunched over his thoughts. Now and again he would break away from them, rise, walk around, bend and stretch to get the chill out of his bones. Twice he lifted himself up to window level, but there was nothing to see; no lights, not even a night animal. He couldn't even guess where he was.

He must have dozed off. He awoke in bright daylight to find that a hunk of brown bread and a paper cup of coffee had been left on the floor just inside the door. It was the closing of the door that had wakened him. He ate some of the bread—it tasted sour—and drank the lukewarm coffee, heavy with its fine grounds. Still, it was liquid of a kind. His thirst was half quenched. But in five minutes he slumped into sleep. The drug lasted twenty-four hours. When he awoke, he saw the same bright sunshine coming through the small barred window. At first, he thought he had been asleep for an hour or so, perhaps less, and that it was still Monday morning. Then he had his doubts; he had slept too deeply. He felt too exhausted.

Outside, there was nothing but the lonely field, a few sea gulls wheeling with their harsh cries over the edge of the land, and far offshore two ships and a fishing boat. They disappeared out of his view as he clung to the strong bars, and then there was nothing on the shimmering blue water. Greece could be as lonely as Brittany, he thought, as he lowered himself back onto the wooden bed. Lonelier, he added grimly. There was no escape from this room. His one chance might come when they took him out for questioning, or when that door was opened again. He sat down facing it, to wait and get some strength back into his body.

In the late afternoon, when the sun had left the room but still struck sidewise across the field and the sea, the door opened just enough to let food and drink be set on the floor. Duclos jumped for the handle, tried to force the door farther open but it was chained from the outside. He heard the Greek call out a warning, "André! André!" The Frenchman answered angrily as he rushed to help pull the door shut. So they were both on guard, still bickering with each other, and the Frenchman was called André. That was all he had achieved, Duclos thought, that and the spilling of the coffee.

The dark liquid lay thick and puddled at his feet. He knelt, dipped a finger in the mudlike grounds and tasted gingerly. Yes, something had been added to the coffee, something to scatter his brains still more. There was a lump of goat cheese on the bread, this time. It smelled so sour that it could disguise anything, so he threw it out the window. The bread—was it also doctored? They might leave one thing uncontaminated, just to entice him to trust everything. But hungry as he was, he didn't risk it. He threw the bread out, too, and ended all temptation. The only weapon he had was his brains. He had better keep them working.

He had guessed right about the prepared supper, for when the sun had set and the dusk was darkening into night they came to get him. As the door was unlocked and the chain rattled, he had time to slip the pellet carefully into the side of his mouth between the cheek and the lower gum. It was comfortable enough, hardly noticeable even to him. The Greek came into the room, nodded as if he had expected to find Duclos inert and helpless, pulled the Frenchman to his feet. This is how I will play it, Duclos thought. He staggered, let himself be supported unresisting to the door.

He entered another room only slightly bigger than his own. It was lit by candles on the table; shadows were deep in its corners, its two small windows were covered with heavy sacks, its massive front door was probably locked and certainly bolted. The Greek thrust him into the one chair at the table and then went to wait under a window.

André was standing just behind the chair. A third man was seated in the darkest corner, not the man who had driven the car, someone more important, someone before whom both the Greek and André kept silent.

The voice from the corner was speaking French, quite accurately, almost fluently. The underlying accent hinted at German, with a strange overtone of Russian. He wasn't a Frenchman, certainly. Or English. Or Italian or Spanish or Scandinavian. German mostly; Russian inflections added. Duclos felt his pulse quicken, but he stared dully at the table in front of him as if he were half drugged, wholly stupefied. "Monsieur Duclos," the voice was saying, "let us not waste time. We know a great deal. We only want a small explanation from you. Why are you in Greece?"

"I am on holiday," Duclos said slowly, thickly.

"You can do better than that. Why are you in Greece?"

"On holiday. Some business, too." He was pausing between the phrases, just enough to give the impression of exhaustion, of scattered wits.

"What business?"

"Designs—I am interested in design. Greek revival—nineteenth century."

"Why did you visit Galland?"

"Burglary, burglary in my studio."

"Nonsense! Why did you visit Galland? We know you interviewed a man, accused of murder, in Galland's private office. Why?"

"Burglar. No murder, just burglary." Stick with that, Duclos told himself. You were called to the police station to identify a possible thief, arrested on another charge. You don't know the other charge. You only know there was a burglary in your studio. You had wakened to see the man escape; not the man at the police station; no identification made. Stick with that . . .

"Why did you visit that man?" the voice went on. And on. Duclos gave the same answers, again, and again, and again.

Suddenly a power flashlight switched on. The Greek directed its strong flood into Duclos' face. He closed his eyes. "Open them!" André said at his elbow, and struck him smartly on the side of the head. Just as quickly, he coiled a rope around Duclos, tying his arms to his sides and his back against the wooden chair, and knotted it securely.

"Why were you at Le Happening?" the voice asked now.

Duclos blinked in the strong light. "I go often."

"You were there when it was raided."

"I didn't know—"

"You spoke to the coatroom attendant. You spoke with her twice. You asked her about two men, didn't you? Didn't you?"

Duclos shook his head, tried to get his eyes out of the light, as he thought around this question.

"You are saying no?"

"The light—it hurts my eyes." He shook his head again.

"Closer!" André told the Greek. The beam came nearer.

"What two men?" the quiet voice went on.

"Friends—I was looking for my friends."

"Stop lying! We have a record of everything the attendant said over her counter that night. We were suspicious of her, with good reason. We know what you said. Tell us, now, in your own words."

Duclos thought, nothing I said could have identified those two men as having any connection with Comrade Peter. Nothing I said to the attendant gave that away. Only two men, two men, that was all I asked about. . . . "I hoped to meet them at the club. They never came. I asked if they had come earlier, and left."

"Your studio lies next to the building where Frank Rosenfeld lives. Does he visit you each week?"

Duclos looked stupidly at the dark corner. "Closer!" André said to the Greek. He twisted Duclos' face to meet the savage beam of light. The power lamp now rested on the table.

"Frank Rosenfeld," the voice said. "We know he is an American agent. We know that. We know everything. Give up and save yourself. He has saved himself. He isn't here. You are. Why should you suffer for an American? Give up." The light was switched off, and Duclos almost groaned with the relief of darkness. "It would be pleasant to give up, wouldn't it? Tell me how he came to see you over the roof, down the ladder into your studio. That's how he came. There is a ladder, there. The door to the roof opens easily. That's how he came. Tell us about him."

Duclos said, "The burglar came that way. He used the ladder. He came over the roof."

The light switched on, came still nearer, burning.

"It is Rosenfeld who sends you to Mykonos. Why?"

155

Duclos shook his head. "Rosenfeld? I have no client called Rosenfeld. Rosenblum, yes. Rosenblum . . . But he didn't send me to Greece."

"Why are you going to Mykonos?"

Duclos was sagging under the heat of the lamp. "To Mykonos, and Rhodes, and the islands—Syros and Tinos, and Lindos on Rhodes and Delos near Mykonos, and—" He let his voice trail away.

"I could make him talk," the Greek said. "I could—"

"No," the voice said, "not yet. He is stubborn, but he will be more helpful when he knows how hopeless it all is. It amuses me to ask him questions and to hear his quick lies."

And that, thought Duclos, is a lie in itself. They have only been trying to connect my visit at the club, the police station, the ladder, the roof, Rosie next door, the reservation for Mykonos. They sense something, know nothing. Stay stupid and ignorant, Duclos; it may be hopeless for you but not for your friends. They don't even know your connection with the Sûreté, or they would not try to make you confess you were an American agent. He said, "You're crazy men, all crazy. Why are you doing this to me? Why? I step off a plane and you—"

"Why did you visit Milan?"

So there was that, too, was there? Duclos sighed. "Business there. And business in Florence."

"Business in Milan with Italian Intelligence?"

Duclos stared, groaned as his eyeballs seemed to be singed with fire. "With an art dealer."

"In Milan you met an Italian agent."

"An art dealer," Duclos repeated.

"An agent of the Italian government," the quiet voice insisted. "Rosenfeld sent you."

Duclos shook his head. "An art dealer," he kept on. "He comes to Paris—he sees me. I go to Milan—I see him. A friend. Art dealer." He closed his eyes. André opened them with a dash of hot wax from the candle he had shaken over Duclos' face.

"You can't be so tired as that," the voice said from the corner. "I have only begun my questions. They will last until dawn, until noon, until tomorrow evening if necessary." There was a pause. The light was switched off. "Why not tell me what you know, in your own words? It would be so easy to talk with me. I know a great deal about you. I know too much about you. Tell me about your friends. Why should you face this unpleasantness for them? You are alone. They did not protect you. They left you. You are alone. Helpless. And hopeless. That need not be. Isn't it silly to argue with me like this? There is so little difference between us—no difference at all. We both want the same things in life, don't we? Peace. Peace, and pleasures, and peace. But the Americans have not let you see that. They would have you destroy me, wouldn't they? They have betrayed you and attacked us. Why don't we make friends? We could work together. And have peace. There is no difference to divide us, except the lies that the Americans have told you. Listen to me. And talk with me. Meet me halfway. Talk. That's all. And I shall tell André to loosen the rope and make Demetrios remove the lamp. I don't want to use such things. Believe me. . . ."

Again there was silence. The rope was loosened a little, not enough to free him, just enough to relieve the pain in his arms. By the soft candlelight, he saw the gleam of a revolver in André's hand. Someone forgot to tell him there was no difference between us, Duclos thought and half smiled in spite of his real exhaustion. He was faking nothing now, except stupefied ignorance.

"Begin at the beginning, tell me everything. You will be glad you did this, tomorrow."

Tomorrow, even if I talked, I would be dead, thought Duclos as he looked at the knife that the Greek had whipped out when the rope had been slackened. Demetrios might be the type of barbarian who enjoyed using a knife. He would be efficient with an ax, too. Cold metal, that was Demetrios.

"Tell me about your friends. First, the ones in Paris. When did you meet Rosenfeld?"

I have said all I dare say, Duclos thought now. Any more talk, any elaborations, and I will be tripped up. He knows no more than he did when he started his persuasion. Perhaps less. I have given him explanations that he had not expected, and he is stuck with them. He cannot move forward, find firmer footing, unless I provide the steps. So I stay silent, now. I'm weak with lack of food and water, weak with the drugs they managed to put into my body, weaker perhaps than I realize. By dawn, or noon tomorrow, I would even begin to forget the things I did tell them, change them a little, become confused. So now I don't talk at all, not at all. There is no choice really, between life and death; he would never have spoken the names of André and Demetrios if he meant to let me leave here alive. Duclos looked at André's revolver, at the Greek knife. I'll choose André, he thought. And above all, I must choose the right moment.

"When did you meet him first?" the casual voice asked as if this were a harmless conversation about a common friend.

Duclos was thinking, I must choose carefully and well. They must not learn that death comes from a small pellet broken between my teeth. How could a man on holiday, a man interested in antique design, possess such a thing as the pellet? If they learn about that, they learn that their suspicions are right. It would be stupid to give them that consolation. But how do I choose the right moment? Even make it a last attempt to escape? Would there be any chance of success? With luck, wild luck? He knew better. Only in the storybooks and adventure films did you have Duclos, with one bound, going free.

"Do I amuse you?" the voice asked quickly.

Duclos allowed himself one last sentence. "You have kidnapped the wrong man—I have no money for any ransom."

"Duclos, we know who you are. Stop this! We know. Now, in your own words—"

Duclos shook his head slowly. The rope would soon be tightened again, the squat power lamp with its beam directed at his eyes would be turned on. Questions and questions, hour after hour. No food, no drink, no rest, no sleep. I am to fear André and Demetrios, the hidden threats of violence. I am to trust the quiet voice of the unseen man, his offers of help, his touches of sympathy, his suggestions which will seem more reasonable as I grow weaker, tireder. And after that, if I haven't broken, then the real work on me will start. But I will not die as a whimpering animal, he told himself in rising anger. I am a man.

He lunged forward at the table, the rope around his body running loose, and managed to tilt it. The two candles toppled and rolled, the lamp slid onto the floor with a crash. Behind him, André caught a loop of the rope, pulled him back, raised the butt of the revolver. Duclos bit down hard on the pellet between his teeth as André struck. He let himself fall sideways, taking the chair with him. The guttering candles dripped their smoking wax on the floor beside him, flickered faintly. The room darkened. The shouts, commands, confusion were moving farther and farther away, a blur of sound fading softly into nothing. Nothing.

The Greek found the lamp and switched it on. André picked up the candles, placed them back on the table, tried to light them. But the wicks were smothered in wax. "Get fresh candles," he told Demetrios, "then give me a hand with him." He looked at Duclos lying half tied to the chair on the dark floor.

"Is he faking?" the voice from the corner asked.

"No. He's out all right." André pulled the loosened rope as tight as it would go and tied the ends into a firm knot at the back of the chair. "He's out for a good ten minutes." He stood back, waiting for Demetrios, and lit a cigarette.

Insarov rose, came out of the black shadows. "He's secure?"

"Like a trussed chicken."

"Then we'll get some air." And talk. A little talk is certainly needed. I begin to think that the alarm flashed through Peter in Paris brought me here on a futile mission. Unnecessary exposure is always disastrous. "Tell the Greek to call out if Duclos makes one sound, one small move. We'll be near at hand." He lit a cigarette as André unlocked and unbolted the heavy door, then stepped out into the cold darkness. The man on guard by the stone wall swung round with his shotgun held at the ready. "Check with my driver," Insarov told him, and sent the man stumbling along the rough path toward the road, past the second of the two small stone houses tightly shuttered, closed, empty. He disappeared into the mass of wild bushes and scrub trees near the sheltered spot, off the road, where Insarov had left his car. Insarov shook his head at the man's clumsiness. Too eager. Fortunately, this whole area was deserted during the week at this time of year. Still— He half turned to look at André, who had approached silently enough to please him. "Keep that cigarette shaded," he said sharply. "Did it take so long to make the Greek understand my orders?"

"Oh, well—you know the Greeks." André was always a little nervous with Insarov. In Paris he had only seen him vaguely, fleetingly, either when he passed through the back corridor of Le Happening or when André had been called in to the dressing room for instructions from Peter. He had never expected to see him here, hadn't even known he was in Athens. Athens? No. The car had been driven only an hour, so the driver had let slip to Demetrios—those Greeks, always imagining that you couldn't understand their language!

"You don't like them?"

"They think they are the only people with brains and courage."

Insarov smiled acidly. "And do you think your Frenchman has brains and courage? Or is he just stupid and innocent?"

André stared in surprise. "But he listened to me at the airport—he went along with me, then. That's some kind of proof, isn't it? He can't be what he pretends he is." And I saw him at the club, André thought indignantly, I saw him wandering round the back of the stage, talking with the coatroom woman, and we know now what she was. Comrade Peter took me seriously enough, trusted me. . . .

"Did he really go along with you at the airport? He might only have been humoring you to gain time to call a policeman. He directed you to a wrong hotel, didn't he? That proves he wasn't believing what you said. Did he make any reference to Zafiris?"

"No."

"He made no remark we could use against him?"

André thought back to the airport meeting. Apart from refusals to be helped with his luggage, and an attempt to leave, Duclos had made only one blunder. "He said it would be better to travel separately to Athens, better to meet at the King George. That implied something, didn't it?"

"That implies he was trying to get rid of you."

"Then who is he?"

"Perhaps working for Interpol—narcotics."

"But the connection with Rosenfeld—"

"There is no actual connection we have been able to discover. I was only trying to see if there might be one."

"And I believed—" André began in amazement, and then laughed softly.

Insarov wasn't even flattered. He looked at the Frenchman contemptuously. Did he really think this was a proper interrogation? "If you had questioned the coatroom attendant thoroughly, for several days, we might have had one piece of information to rely on. Or if you had fully investigated the report you had from your Paris sources about Duclos' visit to the police station, you could have given me more facts about any supposed burglary. We've been working only on coincidences."

"There was so little time. We gathered what we could." And it had been gathered well. Until this minute he had thought of it as a triumph that would leave even a Russian speechless. The risks had been incredible. Nervously, he smoothed his well-brushed hair; and as he felt its new coarse texture, he saw himself on Sunday night, walking into the Grande Bretagne with Duclos' luggage and passport, hair dyed dark brown, cheeks pinked up like a damned woman, wearing Duclos' jacket and hat and his watch and his ring, scrawling a signature at the reservation desk, asking for his mail, going up to the right room, staying there thirty-six hours, keeping out of sight, waiting for telephone calls. "Well, we did pick up his tickets for Mykonos," André said, still angry.

"That boat also stops at Syros and Tinos. And goes on to Rhodes. You heard him."

"You don't think he is important to us?"

"I would need two weeks of preparation, at least; another two weeks for questioning; perhaps four weeks of letting him wait in solitary confinement; more questioning. And only after all that, we might begin to know, not guess, his importance."

"Why go on, now? Why not turn him over to Demetrios?"

"Torture can be a great stupidity. If used too early, it is a self-defeating process. A weak man will agree to any story to please the torturer. I do not want agreement. I want the truth. Who *is* Duclos? Where is he going? Why? Once we learn all that, we can see what further questions must be asked. Then, and only then, has Demetrios something to work on."

"But do you expect him to answer your questions—"

"I never expect. I listen. And in his evasions, he will answer more than my questions." Insarov smiled, watching André, who was another type who thought that only he had brains and courage. "Clever men can never resist talking even to show they can outwit you. In another hour of questioning he will begin to think he has beaten me. The hour after that, all I do is to pick his story to pieces. He will be goaded to talk more, change his story, forget what he said hours before. And then, we have him."

"So you do think he is important?" André insisted, and some of his pride surged back. He had caught Duclos. Of course there were others, too, who had helped. But he had started the chase, he had followed it through.

"I hear our heavy-footed friend returning," Insarov answered, as the man came plodding back through the dark bushes. "Better tell him that silence can be of more importance than speed," he said acidly. "Better still, send him back to Bulgaria. He won't always find a place as desolate as this." He turned away before the man started reporting that all was well, no one was on the road, there had been no traffic for the last three hours.

André caught up with Insarov at the door. Insarov was looking down toward the sea, a molten mass of metal under the night sky. His mood had changed again. "It should be an interesting week," he said softly, his eyes still watching the Aegean. Then, as André swung the door open for him, he strode into the room, smiling and confident, and made for his corner. "Get him up!" He pointed to Duclos, tied to the fallen chair.

Demetrios had been sitting on the corner of the table. He reported, with his thin smile, "Never made one sound. He's still out."

"Then throw a bucket of water over him."

André had secured the door. He looked puzzled, and crossed so quickly to the fallen chair that Insarov came forward, too. "I didn't hit him as hard as all that," André said. "He ought to be—"

Insarov pushed both men aside and knelt by the chair. "He's dead," he said very quietly. And stood up, looking at André.

"But I didn't—" André protested. He turned on Demetrios. "What did you do to him?"

"Nothing. Nothing! You hit him once too often. I told you you'd kill him."

Insarov walked to the door. "You know what to do about the body. Follow my instructions exactly. No deviations from my orders. Not this time." He looked at André. "When you finish here, drive back to the Grande Bretagne, stay in your room, collect all mail and messages for Duclos. That's important. On Thursday morning, pay the bill, take his luggage, and get on board the ship for Mykonos. You will get off before you reach Mykonos, at Syros, wearing your own clothes, leaving his luggage and passport in his cabin. Hire a fishing boat, make your way to Athens. Then to Paris. Report to Peter, there."

Back to Paris? André stared in disbelief. He doesn't trust me to go on with the job. He's disciplining me. Even those detailed instructions are a proof of distrust, of censure.

"Have you got that?"

"Yes. I understand, Comrade Colonel."

"Your trouble is," Insarov said coldly, "that you have been seeing too many American movies. In future, use your brains; not your gun." He left.

André avoided the Greek's mocking smile. He looked down at the white face of Duclos, the fixed stare of the blue eyes. Even in death, losing their brightness, they seemed to be laughing at him.

"Too bad," Demetrios said, and sheathed his knife regretfully. His smile broadened. "So our methods have changed? You think you can hit a man and as long as he doesn't die, you are his kind friend? You treat this kind of vermin as if he were a naughty child. The Russian uses drugs and lies, you use your fists, and you both think you're subtle." Demetrios laughed openly and patted the knife inside his jacket with his long slender fingers. "Here is subtlety. Here is something that can ask questions all night long, and get the answers." Demetrios pushed at the body with his foot. "He knew that. And you will know it, too, Frenchman, if ever *you* are tied to a chair."

Duclos had known that? André stared at the Greek's mocking eyes, bent down beside the body, looked at its lips, sniffed like a dog. Demetrios watched him, and went into a fit of laughter. Those simpleminded foreigners, thinking they knew everything . . . Instead of treating him like a servant, talking together where he couldn't hear them, they ought to have tested the dead man's mouth. In the first few minutes they might have smelled the truth. But now the slight, bitter scent was gone.

"There's nothing there," André said angrily, getting to his feet. All he had done was to make a fool of himself for the Greek.

"How could there be? It was you who insisted on searching him when we brought him here. You wouldn't let anything slip past you. Of course not—"

"He was of no importance anyway," André said, tight-faced.

"That's what I thought all along," Demetrios said softly. So why report his suspicion and take Comrade André off the hook? "What was at stake?"

"Nothing."

"Nothing? A wasted weekend for nothing?"

"Nothing for you to worry about," André said coldly.

Then I worry about nothing, thought Demetrios, and smiled again.

"Untie the body, get the Bulgarian in here to help you carry it to the fishing boat before daylight, drop it well out to sea near Syros—"

"And not before Thursday," Demetrios cut in. "I know, I know." He took out his knife, slashed the ropes lightly and deftly. "See how fast and easy it would have been," he said, looking up at André for some small tribute to his dexterity. But the Frenchman had left. "Come on, come on," he told the Bulgarian, who was hesitating at the door. "We haven't much time."

"They left in a hurry. Anything wrong?"

"Everything according to plan," Demetrios assured him, and laughed contemptuously. He was beginning to feel very, very good, indeed. Quickly—and it was a pleasure to speak in Greek again—he rattled off the orders for the disposal of the body.

"But aren't you coming?"

"You can manage it. The fishermen will help you. I'm no sailor." No garbage remover, either.

"They've had their instructions?"

"And their money. Remember one thing—not before Thursday."

The Bulgarian hoisted Duclos over his broad back. "I'll remember," he promised. "So their scythe struck a stone?" he asked with a grin as he shifted the body's weight more evenly. "I wondered why they went off so quickly."

Yes, thought Demetrios, leaving us to clean up here. Now if the Russian had been really comradely, he could have taken the body in his fast car back to Vouliagmeni, from where he could easily reach the yacht his driver had mentioned—there were several anchorages all along that coast. But no. Swift in, swift out, that was the Russian. Dropping a body from his yacht at sea would be too much of a danger for him. Too much for Comrade André, too. Couldn't he have waited, at least, until Demetrios was ready to leave and give him a lift back to Athens? Oh no, no, no . . . "If you don't move off quickly," he told the Bulgarian, "you'll have more problems than a body over your shoulder."

"See you in Athens, comrade," the Bulgarian said cheerfully and left.

It may be back to Sofia for both of us, Demetrios thought as he picked up the lamp to take with him. The rest of the mess could stay as it was. If the rich had so many houses that they didn't need them except for a couple of months each summer, they deserved thieves to break in and leave a place filthy. He wasn't going to risk staying here any longer than he had to. He looked around the desolate room, remembering the voices. A wasted effort.

He pinched out the candles. Blue eyes brought a curse, the old wives said. He spat solemnly on the threshold, and closed the door.

12

Thursday was going to be a pleasant day, early-morning sun and blue sky promising good sailing to Mykonos. It was also a pleasant end to a very pleasant week in Athens. John Craig had his last cup of coffee out on his small balcony, watching the white-skirted Evzones on guard at the Parliament sentry boxes across the square. He was packed, ready to leave. He felt healthy and rested. There had been enough exercise in the constant walking through the Plaka or over the Acropolis or up to the American School to keep him happy. His one dislike of most cities was the way they forced you to take a bus or a subway, feel heavy with food and soft with unused muscles. But here, over the low-storied houses, the sun could bathe a street and fill it with light and entice you to walk. He had developed his first tan of the season, even if he had worked each morning in the School's library on the days he had actually spent in Athens. His own private conscience was at rest; no guilt about lazing around, or about the nights off with his friends from the School. As for his public conscience—play it loose, Partridge had said. There had been no alarms, no threats, no tensions. He had had a very pleasant week, indeed.

Time to go. If Paul and Pam Mortimer were coming to see him off—though he doubted it—they might be waiting downstairs even now. He had his last look at the streets surrounding the square—people, people, exploding everywhere. If we all keep crowding to the cities, he thought as he remembered the long stretches of lonely empty country, the villages left to sleep away the twentieth century that he had seen in the Peloponnese, perhaps that will be the real time bomb we ought to be worried about. Everyone wants the bright lights and running water, hot and cold. Everyone wants the theaters and cafés and the girls in high heels, the museums and concerts, the newspapers fresh off the press. That is one thing that Athens shares with New York (and Moscow, Rome, Paris and London, too); just name the big cities of the world and you see the same wenlike growth—the more and, if not the merrier, certainly the busier. It makes politicians' eyes bulge in delight as they count heads and think of next election's votes. It keeps a businessman beaming as he hears the music of ringing cash registers. Bigger and better . . . But what does a historian think of? Or, rather, what does he try not to think of? One of the main reasons for the fall of the Roman Empire. People. Just people, bless their happy hearts and their congregating feet.

Indeed time to go. A balcony does funny things to a man. Either he wants to make speeches, have every face upturned, shouts from every throat to prove how right, how gloriously right, he is; or he looks down over the black dots of heads carried along on the two little matchstick legs, and he thinks where do all the people come from? Where are they going? How many more can crowd onto a city sidewalk before the imbalance sets off the population bomb?

I've been too deep in history for this last week, he thought with a smile at himself as he telephoned the desk to get his bill ready. (Yes, he was checking out. On his way, right now.) I've been seeing too many remains of past glories; I can't even look at a row of overpowering columns in a ruined temple without thinking of the men who built them and walked there. And of their great-great and not so great grandsons who let them be destroyed. Let them be destroyed? What else, when you counted the years of acquiescence and drift before the actual destruction began? Yes, you looked at the temples, at the nobility of man's taste, and you remembered the art and the law and the philosophy and the knowledge that had gone with them; and then you thought, unhappily, angrily, why did those men let all that pass out of their hands into alien control? They had something worth keeping and they let it slip away. At what point could they have saved it? The point just before they started to be afraid of dying? Better barbarians than death—had that been their comfort? And the beginning of their end?

Not such pleasing thoughts on a pleasant morning . . . But as he stepped out of the elevator into the enormous lobby with its bustle of people intent on enjoying themselves, he slipped into a cheerier mood. He couldn't see any sign of the Mortimers, but the international circus was in full swing in ten different languages with ten different ways of dressing, from tight trousers to flowing robes. There were loose groups of straying Americans (pity their poor guides), tight families of French, pairs of English, solitary Arabs, explorers from Africa, Hindu saris in flocks, quiet clusters of thin diplomats, a solidity of foreign generals with high-peaked caps over brown faces and pigeon chests weighed down by medals (could one man's lifetime win so many victories?); and of course the ordinary men like Craig, in tweed jackets bulging with passports and tickets, who were wondering whether they'd make that boat or plane if the three lines at the accountants' desk didn't move along more quickly.

The Frenchman in front of Craig finished checking his bill, item by item, paid in hard cash, and waited impatiently for his change. His hands were outstretched on the counter, squarely keeping his place. His fingers tapped, as if each second of waiting was added annoyance. He wore a very handsome signet ring of gold with a strange design. Craig noticed that first. Then he noticed the man's black hair. And his height was about five feet eight, his weight not far from one hundred and sixty-five pounds. Duclos.

So he has been staying here, thought Craig, and is now checking out. Strange that I haven't seen him around, in the restaurant or lobby or bar. Still, the Grande Bretagne in its recently expanded state was a lot of space, and people had to search for each other at the crowded hours. Duclos was counting his change—he must have a rigorous expense account, to be so exact—as he turned away from the desk. The first move comes from him, Craig reminded himself, tactfully avoided looking at Duclos, and stepped forward to say to the hotel clerk, "John Craig, Room 308. *To logariasmo, parakalo.*" That always raised a smile on both sides: the clerk's, because he liked the compliment of a foreigner trying to speak his language; Craig's, because he enjoyed having to ask for his logarithm—it would have to be the Greeks who'd call your bill just that. Anyway, he had spoken his name clearly enough, and if Duclos ignored this chance meeting then Craig could stop worrying about what might have been going on during this last week of sheer enjoyment. In the early mornings after the late nights on the town, Craig had even begun to wonder, as he went to bed, if all the tensions and hidden dangers of his week in Paris hadn't been—well, not exactly unreal; Sussman was dead, wasn't he? —perhaps, just a little, exaggerated. Yet Partridge was not exactly an exaggerating type. He wasn't the kind of man who scratched his hand and yelled that his arm was wounded. He didn't ham things up. Neither did Rosie. Offhand jokers, that was what they seemed in retrospect. Craig waited now for Duclos to drop some money on the floor so that he could help pick it up, pass the time of day as a kind of introduction to a further meeting on the boat to Mykonos. It certainly looked as if Duclos must be taking the same little inter-island ship that Craig was booked for.

But either Craig's idea about how to make a subtle contact in a big hotel lobby was too corny or Duclos had no need to speak to him. For the Frenchman moved away from the line at the accountants' desk, not even glancing in Craig's direction. Everything must be normal, Craig thought as he paid his logarithm; no alarms or special messages, no advice or counsel to be heeded. So relax, Craig, and laugh at yourself a little. You'd have thought you were a prize retriever, the way your instincts pointed at that ring the minute you saw it.

As he turned away from the desk, he saw Duclos' trim figure walking briskly toward the entrance. He followed leisurely, saying goodbye with the right tips for the pecking order in their brass-buttoned jackets, and left the indirect lighting of the lobby for the brilliant, cutting light of Athens' skies. He stood on the steps, waiting, getting his eyesight back into focus after the sun's bright glare. His suitcases were in charge of a bellhop, one of several with many suitcases. Adonis, the porter-in-charge, was gesturing up taxis as firmly as any New York cop directing traffic. But there was a small crowd of travelers down there on the sidewalk, so he might as well enjoy the scene until his turn came. Duclos was less patient, which surprised him—the Frenchman was even trying to thwart Adonis and take the nearest cab as his. And now, too, he could see Duclos' face. It was about twenty feet away, as against ten feet in the Saint-Honoré bar, but it added to his surprise. Hair and coloring were the same; but surely the jaw line had retreated. Or was he seeing it from another perspective, looking down the slope of sidewalk instead of from across a level room? He lit a cigarette as Duclos, politely but definitely put in place, cabless, paced up and down, drifting nearer.

Craig glanced casually back at the man. It was either the same gray tweed jacket that Duclos had worn that Monday evening or something very close to its color and cut. But the profile wasn't quite the same. Near enough, but not exact. Damn it all, thought Craig, if there's one small pride I enjoy, it's my memory for faces; I remember them better than I do names. At that moment, Duclos, halting by the steps, looked in his direction, and he could see the man's eyes. They were blue, certainly; but even under the bright sky that intensified all blue eyes, they hadn't the remarkably clear color that Craig recalled. Duclos turned at the steps and paced downhill toward the diminishing queue.

Craig drew a deep slow breath, his first in the last ten seconds. His cigarette was out. He threw it away. And what do we do now? He looked quickly at the people standing near him outside the entrance to the hotel, and wondered if they had noted his brief confusion. He thought not. He felt a mask settle over his face automatically, a kind of instinctive self-protection. Then a vintage Chrysler came moving slowly up the street and, as it approached him, an arm waved wildly and he heard Pam Mortimer's voice calling. Paul was driving. And was that Clothilde and Bannerman in the back seat? So these crazy characters actually have come to see me off, he thought, and ran down the steps toward them.

"Hi!" Pam said, talking across her husband, "where's your luggage, we've come to take you to the pier, didn't you expect us?"

"Any promise given at one in the morning in a *bouzoukia* joint is not meant to be held against you," Craig said, but he was delighted.

"Tim roused us out of bed. Said you ought to have *someone* to wave at!"

"Let me get my luggage away from Adonis, and I'll be with you."

"And in a hurry," said Paul. "I'll have to keep the car running." He was holding it expertly with the clutch on the incline of the street. "The traffic cops around here would have New Yorkers screaming."

"I'll get out," said Clothilde, and she did, "and I'll put one foot on the sidewalk and another in the car and that should establish our claim to this patch of pavement for at least two minutes." She was also pleased, thought Craig smiling, to show her early-tanned legs and her black patent sandals. She noticed his glance, for she laughed and told him, "All dressed up to wave good-bye. Hurree, hurree . . ."

He turned and headed down the street for the luggage. Duclos was getting into a cab now, suitcases and all. Duclos? Very close, but not Duclos, Craig decided. And what do I do? Just travel with my amiable maniacs down to the Piraeus and get onto the boat there as if nothing had happened? He felt the same frustrated anger that had attacked him in Paris, on the evening he had seen Heinrich Berg for the second time without being able to do anything about it. Unless, of course, he thought hopefully as he tipped everyone in sight (it always felt like that, anyway), there was someone around keeping an eye on thee and me, someone who really knew Duclos and could spot the difference. One of the bellhops was now hurrying up to the car with his two bags. Craig, still stumbling over his problem, followed more slowly. He found it was hard to smile and make the necessary jokes as he climbed in beside Clothilde and Bannerman.

Clothilde said, "Don't look so worried, John, you really were very quick. Besides, Paul enjoys holding a car on a hill—it reminds him of San Francisco."

"And that reminds me of something else again," Paul said, now quite serious. "Did you hear that Sussman was dead?"

"Yes. The Paris papers said suicide." There had been no public mention, as far as Craig had seen, of the arrest for murder.

"That's too bad. They tried to entice him to Stanford, but Berkeley got him first. Wonder who'll succeed him there?" Paul talked on for a bit about university gossip, about visiting archaeologists, about the new discoveries in Crete.

"Oh, Paul," said his wife, flinching nervously as they skimmed past lumbering cement trucks on the Piraeus highway, "please don't talk while you drive—it always makes you forget to look at the speedometer."

Mortimer laughed and slackened speed slightly. The old car handled well, could pass anything on the road, and that was all he cared about.

"Put him in Crete," Pam went on, her tone kept light to show she intended no public snub, "and he's the most cautious archaeologist, everything dug up with a teaspoon. Put him behind a wheel, and he's a fiend."

"Have I ever had one accident?" Paul asked.

"Let's not break that record on the day you're shipping John out to Mykonos." The car slowed still more, and everyone stopped sitting so tensely. Wives, thought Craig, were really useful at times.

Clothilde said, "We're all going to come and visit you for a weekend, John. At least, I'm trying to round up a group of us. We'll hire a caïque and come sailing in like a bird on the wing." There was still much of the wandering minstrel in Clothilde, even if she had been spending the last five years of her life putting fragments of ancient vases together. She was the kind of woman, Craig thought, who'd always be split right down the middle between her intellect and her emotions. A pretty girl with brains had a hard life, almost as hard as a historian being caught up in power politics. But a girl could always solve that split by getting married and forgetting that her brains and training were the equal of any man's. Of course, only a man would think of that. It was his world, all right, and it was a neat solution for him, too, to see the pretty invader repulsed from serious competition and invited to join his bed and board instead. Yes, thought Craig, men had it every which way. He smiled and shook his head.

Clothilde said quickly, "You don't like a caïque, John? But it's wonderful, so—so—"

"Watch out, Craig," said Bannerman, speaking at last, "or she'll have you bobbing around the Mediterranean in one of those walnut shells following the course of Odysseus or some damn Homeric hero."

"Now you enjoyed it," Clothilde told Bannerman, "you know you did. Look at the photographs you took, and the article you wrote for *Horizon*—"

"Which got turned down. I guess it made them as seasick as I was."

"Then you can use it for a chapter in your new book." And thinking of books in progress, she looked at Craig, was about to say something and then didn't. Everyone who was writing a book had his hours of gloom, she thought.

"Yes?" he asked her.

"Don't fret," she said understandingly. "On Mykonos, you'll have the most *wonderful* sense of peace. You'll be able to write there—I couldn't imagine anything more soothing."

Craig gave her soft brown eyes a special smile of thanks, patted her knee, and then looked quickly at Bannerman in case he had overstepped. It was possibly Clothilde who kept Tim Bannerman hovering around Athens. He was one of those humorous types, dark-haired, dark-eyed, fairly tall, with good shoulders and a well-disciplined waist, that seemed to get along with women and men for very different reasons. He fitted into a variety of circles, too, American and Greek, everything from scholars and journalists to poets and peasants. Bannerman didn't lift an eyebrow, one of his favorite comments; he was looking at Craig blankly, as if his mind were very far away from the back seat of this car. "As long as the sea stays nice and flat, I won't worry about anything," Craig told Clothilde. "Hey, Pam, what do you think the prospects are today?"

That set the women talking, with interjections from Paul to keep them right: anyone who lived in Greece always seemed to become a specialist on winds and weather. So in a general sweep of conversation, with Craig's relapse into silence nicely covered, they arrived in the busy streets of Piraeus. Paul threaded his way through them skillfully to reach the broad confusion of the water front. Everyone was now giving directions, except Craig. The inter-island boats were that way, not over here, this was where the liners docked and there the freighters; aim left now, go beyond the wharves, those ones—see?

"I know the way," said Paul and made a wrong turning. "I swear they keep moving these crazy wharves around," he said, as he got back onto the right route.

It would have been easier on the nerves, Craig thought as they avoided loaded carts rushing in all directions, to have taken a taxi, but not so good for the liver. They bumped their way over the rough pavement, skidded on some inset rail lines, swerved around a pyramid of baskets almost twenty feet high, and saw three small ships in various stages of loading at a long quay. "I knew they were around here somewhere," Paul said, chose the ship where the most frenetic efforts were being made, and eased the car as near as possible to the mixture of objects and people spread around the dock in utmost confusion. There were wardrobes and bedsteads, sacks of sugar, crates of oranges, goats and chickens, ancient trunks roped round, battered cases and brown-paper packages, women in shapeless cotton dresses and draggled cardigans, women in smart suits with high heels and swollen hair styles, men in rough caps and wide-lapeled jackets that never matched the trousers, pale students with bulging rucksacks and thin beards, red-faced young soldiers on leave, men in snap-brims and natty double-breasters, children bundled tightly in heavy clothing for the big ocean journey.

"Oh dear," Pam said as she stepped out and looked at the smallest of the ships, "I hope you have an outside cabin, John. Here, better take these Dramamine. I brought them just in case." And wouldn't you know it, she thought, the new boat for the Mykonos-Rhodes run had to be laid off today. Poor John . . .

Craig burst out laughing in spite of his worry.

Bannerman grinned. "I'd take them if I were you." He added quietly, "And that's the first laugh you've given today. Feeling okay?"

"Sure. Just wondering how we're all going to get packed in. We're sailing in ten minutes."

"The farther east from Gibraltar, the longer the minute," Paul said, and became very businesslike. "First thing is to find a steward and get him to take your cases down to your cabin. That makes sure of your space, too. Then you can wander around and join the fun. Like some help with the language?"

"You take charge," Craig said with relief. The only English being spoken around him was by two American middle-aged women with sensible shoes and guidebooks. Everything else was in a torrent of Greek, except for a trickle here and there of French. Even the laughter, harsh and strong, sounded foreign.

"You couldn't have pleased Paul more," Pam said, watching her husband walking over to the gangway. "He adores being demotic in Greek. Come on, let's investigate the baskets. Whoever piled them so high and so neatly?" Clothilde was already halfway to the pyramid. That kind of mystery delighted her. It was obviously done by a nimble-handed gnome in a state of weightlessness, she called back over her shoulder.

"I'll see about the luggage, first," said Craig, and began hauling his bags out of the trunk. Bannerman helped, politely, not too energetically. He was looking at Craig with some deepening speculation all his own. Just then, a taxi drew up and the imitation Duclos stepped out. Craig saw him, froze for a moment, reached back into the car for his raincoat. "That's everything, I think." His words felt as tight as his face. He avoided glancing in the man's direction.

Bannerman said, "Hey, you dropped something!" He bent quickly and picked it up, pressed it securely into Craig's hand. "I've been wondering how to get it there for the last five minutes," he admitted with a short laugh. Craig glanced at the coin in his palm: it was a nickel, all right. Bannerman was saying quietly, "I know, I know. Contact only in an emergency. My feeling is you've got one on your hands. What's been troubling you?"

"Duclos." The Frenchman was now carrying his suitcases on board. His head was bent, eyes on the steep gangway. He looked to neither right nor left. He was a man who didn't want to be noticed.

"Didn't he make contact with you at the Grande Bretagne?"

Craig shook his head. "Do you know him?"

"By description and photograph. He is just getting on board, now."

"Not Duclos. That's someone else."

Bannerman actually stared. "Are you sure?"

"Almost sure. Enough to worry about it."

"Look—why don't you join Paul? Stick close to him. I have a couple of Greek friends I'd better talk with. Yes, they're going to Mykonos, too. Perhaps—" he paused again, and smiled—"yes, we'll let the Greeks handle this little business. They're very resourceful." He stepped away, seemingly to avoid a cart being pushed along, piled high with mattresses.

Craig lit a cigarette, threw his coat over his shoulder, picked up his two bags, and set out for Paul and the steward he had collected. "Now," said Paul, once the formalities of documents and tip were over, "we can stroll around and watch what's going on. Wouldn't miss this for anything. It's a slice of real life."

"How long do we have?" Craig's eyes were looking around the dock. Bannerman had disappeared. Or was hidden by the crowd. There was no sign of the man who was pretending to be Duclos—he must have settled in his cabin. He certainly wasn't among those who hung over the ship's rail and yelled last messages down to the people on the dock. No transatlantic sailing had more enthusiasm.

"Oh, about fifteen minutes—yes, when they are really good and ready to sail, they'll whisk all this stuff off the dock. You'll be amazed how quickly they'll do it. Now, where are Pam and Clothilde? And where's Bannerman?"

Fifteen minutes turned to twenty. "Where's Bannerman?" Paul was still asking.

"He met that architect friend of his—" Pam said. "What's his name? Elias something or other. Look, there they are!"

Bannerman was coming forward with a small dark-haired man, dressed neatly in gray, who carried a suitcase. They were talking casually, cheerfully, in English. "Elias is also going to Mykonos," Bannerman announced as he completed the introductions. "He's studying the ground for a new hotel."

Craig shook hands and felt he was being quietly studied, too. But pleasantly. Elias had an easy smile, brightly intelligent brown eyes, a thin dark mustache stretched over sensuous red lips, and gleaming white teeth. Shirt, suit and tie were restrained and elegant. A successful young man, you'd say, and a happy one. No worries, no strain on that thin, handsome face. "I think we go on the boat," Elias said. "It is time."

"Wish I were coming with you," Bannerman said, enthusiasm for travel apparently breaking loose. "What do you say, Clothilde, shall we go?"

Clothilde looked willing. She always was. But Pam said quickly, "Timmy, don't be silly. She hasn't even a coat to keep her warm."

"Well, don't be surprised if you see me tomorrow or the next day," Bannerman told Elias and Craig, still keeping a joke in his voice. "Better get on board, now."

"Can't imagine why they are so late," said Paul. The cargo, both things and people, was mostly loaded. He looked up at the crowded railings of the ship and saw a redhead. "Now isn't that something? Was that what caught your eye, Bannerman?"

Craig looked up, too, and recognized the girl. He was sure of her: she had sat at the same table in the Saint-Honoré bar with Partridge and Duclos. She wasn't laughing, today. She was grave-faced as her eyes searched the dock. Pam was saying, "French. You always can tell." And Clothilde, studying the simple gray wool dress and the high-brushed hair, said nothing at all.

"On board!" Bannerman said briskly, ending Craig's good-byes and thanks, pushing him firmly toward the gangway. Elias was already stepping onto the deck. What's the big hurry? Craig wondered, but he smiled all around and waved as he followed the Greek. And just as he reached the deck and was searching for a free space at the rails, he began to understand. Two olive-green cars, neat and businesslike, were drawing up quietly on the dock. Three men, neat and businesslike, too, moved with precision and speed toward the ship. They boarded her easily, with no questions. The purser was there to welcome them, as serious and silent as they were. They disappeared down the narrow staircase into the section where the first-class cabins lay. Few people noticed; most were still concentrating on calling last-minute messages to their friends on the pier. The crew were standing by the lines, ready to cast off. The narrow planks aft were already being removed. Only the first-class gangway still waited.

Four minutes passed by Craig's count. It was now twelve-fifteen. On shore, Bannerman was pointing out something interesting at the ship's stern to Clothilde and Pam Mortimer while Paul stayed by his car, looking at his watch, no doubt wondering about that one o'clock lunch party he was scheduled to give for two visiting scholars. Beside Craig, two men who had been talking quietly together in an incomprehensible language—they were northerners, definitely, judging from their heavy blunt features, white faces, fairish hair: Balts or Poles, perhaps Czechs?—fell totally silent. The bogus Duclos and the three imperturbable Greeks were leaving the ship in close formation, complete with his luggage.

Before their tight group had even reached the dock, one of the men near Craig went into action. He headed for the gangway, got one foot on it, began explaining in a mixture of inadequate Greek and useless French that he had left a suitcase behind—he must get it—it was impossible to sail without it. He ended the argument abruptly by pulling free from a restraining hand, made a dangerous dash down the half-free gangway, jumped onto firm ground. He stood there only for a few seconds as he recovered breath and dignity, then stalked off in high dudgeon. To the nearest telephone? His report would be a shocker, Craig thought, watching the dwindling figure of the hurrying man, watching the two official cars speed away with their prisoner. Now there's a slice of real life for Paul to observe. . . . But Paul had barely noticed, if at all. And the others? They were gathered around Paul, laughing at one of Bannerman's quips as he pointed to the ship, arms circling high, Clothilde's long green scarf fluttering.

That reminded Craig to start waving, too. Paul, still glancing at his watch, was ready to drive off. Bannerman gave one last salute as he stepped into the car. Craig returned it, with a broad grin. Bannerman certainly had the most resourceful of Greek friends.

As they sailed out of the enormous port, siren-blasting their way between fishing boats, freighters flying every imaginable flag, two destroyers making for the naval dockyards on the opposite shore, an Italian liner, a Greek cruise ship, launches, more fishing boats, Elias halted nonchalantly beside Craig. "It's going to be quite a pleasant trip," he said, smiling brightly.

"Slow in starting. What was all that commotion on the dock?"

"The purser tells me there was a smuggler on board. Narcotics."

"Really?"

"Yes. A Frenchman named Duclos, the purser said. One of the detectives told him the man had been chased all across Europe." Elias shook his head over such an extraordinary world. "I think I will make a constitutional before lunch. Would you care to join me?"

"I had better get below and check on my suitcases. See you later."

They went their separate ways. At the railing, the light-haired man gripped the rails and stared straight ahead. Strange, thought Craig in amusement, to show so little concern for the traveling companion who was left behind, to stand so tensely when Duclos was named as a wanted man. His amusement ended when he thought of Duclos —surely that was really taking a lot of liberty with a name, to tie it up with narcotics, even in rumor. Why? And where was the real Duclos, anyway?

He went down the narrow companionway to the next deck. Here were about twenty cabins along a narrow passage. The first one was empty, its door swinging to the rhythm of the boat. They were coming into more open sea, now. The next one had its door open, too. There was a woman inside—the French girl with the superlative figure in the simple gray dress. She was standing, holding onto the narrow bunk, her head bent. She raised her face as she heard his footsteps halt. She had been crying.

"Can I help?" he asked awkwardly.

She shook her head, picked up her coat and bag from the bunk, brushed past him, her face now calm, determined. Head erect, she climbed the steps, vanished out of sight.

13

They came to Mykonos in a blaze of pink and vermilion sky, with feathered sweeps of cirrus clouds so high that they had already shaded into gray, leaving the last golden glow to the threatening mass of cumulus on the north horizon. The island was a spreading slope of hard rock molded into small hills, barely green, its contours carved so near the bone that the occasional farm scattered over the rising land must have its richest harvest in stones. Down below was a curve of bay, with the little town at one side—flat-roofed houses of brilliant white, their square outlines broken by blue- or red-domed churches, clustering in a tight mass at the water's edge—and there the long jetty formed a breakwater to harbor small craft, fishing boats, masted caïques. Across the bay, at the other tip of its crescent, there was a mooring quay in the shelter of a rocky headland for a few yachts. Anything larger had to anchor outside.

Craig stood on the rising and falling ship with the rest of the passengers who were going ashore, looking over the rail at the motorboats and light launches coming out from the shelter of the breakwater, dipping and rolling as they met the heavy waves of the rising sea. There was a marked silence around him, ship friendships forgotten, the rough squalls that had sent them all retreating to their cabins or huddling in joint misery in the bar now merely minor interludes. A loose gangway had been rigged against the side of the ship. "You just grip hard, and don't look down," one of the American women began telling her companion. "I remember arriving here from Rhodes at one

179

in the morning during a *real* storm—" Yes, thought Craig, that kind of traveler was always remembering, and bringing less comfort than she intended. He waved down to the upturned brown faces, far below, of the thin agile Greeks who were maneuvering their small boats near the bottom step of the gangway, calculating pitch and toss with expectant grins. Now, *there* are people who are really enjoying themselves. If that fat lady falls into the water, they'll have the best laugh of the week.

The French redhead was a practical woman, Craig noted. She had tied her head securely in a large scarf, bundled herself against wind and spray in a tightly belted coat, put her high-heeled shoes into her pockets, and was leading the way down the swaying stairs in her nylons as if she had been doing this every morning for setting-up exercises. He followed her, carrying the fat lady's handbag, with Elias steadily coaxing them onward from the rear. The operation, from something a little tricky and outside of most experience, turned into a comedy routine. Craig, safe in the steadily swaying launch, waited for it to be filled—to the gunwales, naturally; Greeks never did things by half—and found he was watching the slow procession downward with a relaxed smile. It was all a matter of perspective. From here, the gangway looked solid, the ship enormous, and only the hesitant feet were dangerous. The Greeks laughed, pushed, pulled, and yelled encouragements. The confusion was complete and yet under control.

"I think," said the French girl, as she put on her shoes and stood up beside him, "that the worst is yet to come." She looked at the darkening stretch of open sea between them and the breakwater. "You are John Craig? Yes, Jim told me. . . . I am Marie Aubernon. Mimi for short. I am staying at the Leto, around the bay. And you?"

"At the Triton—it's in the town itself." Could she hear that, he wondered, with all those shouts around us?

She nodded, looked away, studied the little boat alongside that was being loaded with luggage. "Yves Duclos was to have introduced us," she said very quietly. "But—" She shrugged her shoulders, her face impassive, only her eyes troubled. "What happened to him?"

"I don't know."

She bent her head, tightened the belt of her coat. "We'll meet on shore," she said, moving away to the shelter of the small cabin.

The boat was packed, at last, and started its homeward voyage.

Mimi had been right about the stretch of rough sea, but once they were inside the breakwater the violence of wave and wind abruptly ended. Dusk had fallen and the lights of the front-street cafés welcomed the passengers as they began their long walk up the jetty. "Tomorrow night," Elias said cheerfully at Craig's elbow, "we'll be sitting at one of those tables, watching the new arrivals. We'll meet, of course. Everyone meets in Mykonos."

"Any sign of the man whose friend left him in such a hurry?" Craig asked quietly.

"Got off the boat at Syros, more than three hours ago."

"Good. That's one less to worry about."

Elias only smiled. He increased his pace, drew well ahead, and was lost among the straggle of arrivals.

Craig followed the porter who had picked up his bags and taken the lead. As they reached the front street, he pulled off his raincoat—it was now too warm, away from the sea wind—and began to relax completely. Everyone meets on Mykonos, Elias had said. At this hour, certainly, it looked as if the entire population of three thousand-odd had flocked to the water front for the main event of the day. The broad street ran level with the shore, was in fact part of it. On one side were beached rowboats and fishing nets, on the other arcades and café tables. Brown faces everywhere, bare arms, bare legs, sun-bleached hair, and curious eyes. Ahead of him, Craig saw Mimi with her coat and scarf over her arm. Judging from the prolonged, swivel-headed stares that followed her slow, even stride, Mimi was going to be quite a success on Mykonos.

Purposely, he had avoided returning the cool appraisal from the café tables. This was a night to slip into Mykonos quietly, not a time to be noticeably curious. Besides, he preferred watching Mimi and her triumphal progress: her skirt was just tight enough to give it full advantage. Then he heard his name clearly called, and was forced to look to his right. It was Maritta Maas, waving gaily. Beside her was Veronica Clark. He ignored the two handsome long-haired types in mock fishermen's jerseys and tight red pants who sat with them. Nor did he stop. He called back laughingly, pointed to the porter waiting now at the corner of a small street, waved, and went on his way. He was glad to get out of sight, worrying now whether he had sounded natural enough, whether he had hurried too much, whether he had succeeded in seeming just a casual kind of character; and he couldn't even remember what he had called to them, not exactly—but thank heavens they had found it funny. At least, he had left Veronica laughing.

You'll have to get used to this, he told himself as he followed the porter along the narrow twisting street, so narrow that he could touch the whitewashed walls of the houses on either side. And all the little wandering streets were the same, their paving stones whitewashed to match the houses with their balconies and narrow stone staircases that led to the upper floors. You'll have to get used to coming around a corner and meeting Veronica face to face. You won't even see her until she's twenty feet away from you. And the hell of it is, your heart will leap every time you catch sight of her, just as it did back there.

In a few minutes, they had walked through five of those quiet crisscrossing streets, the porter always a little ahead, for there was no room for two to walk abreast in comfort unless closely arm in arm. A town with possibilities, thought Craig. No worry about getting lost, either. You only had to head toward the sea breeze and you'd be back at the bay. The street-lighting system was simple, too: single bulbs in brackets attached to house walls; not too many, just enough to show the way through the white maze. By moonlight, street lights wouldn't even be necessary.

The porter halted and looked back, a sign perhaps that they had reached the hotel. It was at the end of this fifth small street, on the edge of what seemed to be a wider stretch of flagstones. In fact it was a square, a miniature one, with a very small church and a couple of dark spiky trees—cypress? cedar? something like that—and two other narrow streets leading out of it.

"The Triton?" Craig asked. The place looked like any of the larger houses around the square.

His guide nodded, spread a white smile over his wrinkled brown face, and pointed to the stone staircase that hugged the side wall. Craig climbed up its steps, narrow and high, avoiding the pots of flowers on each tread, and stood on the entrance balcony under a pergola of vine leaves. From here, he could see part of the street along which he had come, half of the ghostlike square, and about ten yards into the streets on its other side. Where was everyone? Down at the bay, or eating supper, or already in bed? Suddenly, he heard footsteps; two men walking into the square, crossing it. One was speaking in German, a quiet continuous stream of words. He was small and fat, wearing shorts and a bulky sweater. The other, tall and powerfully built, dressed in white trousers and dark blue blazer with a scarf folded at his neck, looked up instinctively at the open belfry of the church as if something there had caught his eye—a gentle swing of the bell's tongue, perhaps, or the stirring of a bird. It was Heinrich Berg.

Craig moved against the wall, out of the lighted threshold, stood motionless. But Berg had heard Craig's brief, careful step. Quickly, his eyes glanced up at the hotel balcony and saw the Greek porter standing in the doorway. His friend was pointing at the vine on the pergola—it seemed, for a moment, to Craig that the finger was aimed straight at him—and then burst into explanation. In the autumn, that vine was covered with huge clusters of grapes, unbelievable, most useful as well as decorative, the wine in Mykonos was quite passable. . . . The footsteps passed on, the voice died into a murmur, a door somewhere around the corner—in the square, perhaps, or in one of the small streets leading off from that corner—closed heavily, and there was silence again.

The porter was gesticulating politely. Enter, he was saying, and welcome, and there are the bags which I have carried with the greatest care and brought safely to your destination. Craig couldn't understand a word of the dialect, but he offered the man his choice of money from a handful of coins in his hand. It was a system that worked well. The man clattered down the steps happily, with more good wishes for a long and healthful stay, and Craig stepped into the small low-ceilinged room that had been turned into a reception lobby. There was a gray-haired woman, brisk and formidable, waiting behind a desk; a smiling but silent young man in a very correct dark suit, who came hurrying at the clang of Madame's bell; two young maids, with shining cheeks and nervous giggles, to seize the luggage and bear it away down a small dark corridor. Reservation, passport . . . It was the usual routine. Madame made it protocol. He floundered through a Greek phrase, trying to ease the extreme formality, and was corrected firmly. So he fell silent.

She studied him as he signed the register. "You admired our view," she told him severely in halting but determined English, which might be another way of reminding him that he had kept her waiting for at least five minutes before deigning to put a foot across her threshold. Or was she curious about what he had seen out there? She was frowning heavily, gathering strength for another attack on the English language. "It is beautiful?"

"Beautiful," he assured her. "The flowers are beautiful also," he added most politely. Now can I leave? he wondered.

She bowed in agreement rather than dismissal. Her voice became less harsh, although it would never be called mellifluous. "Herr Ludwig admires the vine. He always admires the vine."

Craig decided not to leave, not quite so hurriedly at least. "Herr Ludwig?"

"You hear his words tonight? He admires very much."

"Perhaps Herr Ludwig would like to have a few bottles of its wine." But he had gone too quickly for her, there, so he slowed down and said, "Herr Ludwig also admires the wine."

There was a bright gleam of laughter in her sharp brown eyes. "For three years, he admires. He does not get."

"Poor Herr Ludwig," he said, and friend of Heinrich Berg at that. But this wasn't the time for any direct questions; better to follow the silent man who was waiting for him at the door. Ludwig was a three-year-old institution here, at least; and Heinrich Berg was visiting him, judging by the guided tour he had been given through the square.

"Dinner is nine o'clock," Madame called after him. He bowed again, smiled amiably, but his thoughts on Berg were now passing into light shock. Berg—here, on Mykonos? It was Berg, all right. The black hair was the same, although the gray at the temples hadn't been noticeable—either it was a trick of the lighting in the square or it had been darkened. And the handsome face was Berg's, too. So was its calm, almost benign look. Even when he had glanced upward, alert, watchful, Berg had not dropped that expression. By God, thought Craig, I'd like to be around when he loses that mask.

When did he get here anyway?

The yacht *Stefanie* had arrived with the sunset at Mykonos and moored under the headland on the quiet end of the bay. She was one of the newer craft that were being built to capture the tourist trade, a hundred and fifty tons of compact pleasure for five passengers and three crew—one to steer and chart, one to fuss around, one to cook and clean up. She had two 120 h.p. diesels capable of driving her along at twelve knots, and two masts mostly for decoration or romantic moods, although—when necessary—they could be rigged for silent approaches and departures. They were rigged now, as if the *Stefanie* was just a pleasure schooner with no real power within her neat white hull.

The *Stefanie* was slightly different in other ways from the usual yachts hired to sail through the Aegean. The crew had been replaced by three excellent sailors who were not Greek. This had happened when the yacht had begun its present charter, in Corfu, an Ionian island just a short haul from the Albanian coast. There was rather an original turn in the chartering, too. An attractive woman of fifty, no less, with a French passport in the name of Jeanne Saverne, a slight hint of German in her accent, residence in Milan, had paid a handsome fee to have the *Stefanie* delivered to her at Corfu. Not to her, exactly. To some friends who would use the yacht until she was able, later in May, to enjoy the Greek Islands herself. (Bless all insurance companies, Jim Partridge had thought, when he came across this piece of information in the careful records of the agent who was responsible for the *Stefanie*'s safe handling. The insurance agent had only made one mistake: he had assumed, since the yacht had been sent especially to Corfu, that the "Greek Islands" would be those in the Ionian Sea. But after a quick call at Brindisi, the *Stefanie* had quietly abandoned the Ionian and headed for the waters around Athens. Which was, after all, halfway to the Aegean.)

It was such a neat operation, beautifully calculated, simple and innocent in appearance and yet—once questions started being asked— as complicated and peculiar as an artichoke being peeled leaf by leaf, that Partridge and his friends would have felt considerable satisfaction if they had seen the small red boat that drifted gently over the bay when the *Stefanie* sailed into the harbor. And they deserved some congratulations. Partridge had raised the first questions. (If Insarov is renting a house on Mykonos, what will he need for transportation— something safe, discreet, nonremarkable? The usual Greek yacht? What yachts have been chartered this season? Where? By whom?) His friends went out searching for the answers. Within one week they had peeled the artichoke nicely. The four previous months helped, too, of course. Four months of facts dredged up, examined, correlated, remembered—even such small details as the various names used by Heinrich Berg's mistress of twenty-five years ago. Jeanne Saverne, there it was, the name she adopted along with a new identity when she had slipped into France after the war; the name she was still using in Milan, where she had been living for the last few months, quietly, discreetly, with no overt political connections whatsoever but enough spending money to charter a yacht. So Partridge had hired a fishing boat. Or, rather, he had suggested his idea to Elias (in charge of the Greek end of this counteroperation), who had the right contacts on Mykonos. And there, floating around so innocently, were the small red boat and a couple of thin-faced Greeks with dark eyes and black mustaches, caps tilted over their tanned foreheads, patched trousers and work-stained jerseys. It had been very simple, indeed, once the *Stefanie* had been noted in Phaleron Bay last Tuesday, to track her by each port of call, arrival and departure, as she sailed nearer and nearer Mykonos.

"Here she comes," said one of the fishermen, and rearranged the fish they hadn't caught in the bottom of their boat. "She made good time from Paros. I can count three passengers." Taking it easy, they were, lounging on deck chairs, looking back at the sunset.

"Three," agreed the man at the oars. He dipped them slowly, gently. "Shall we draw closer?"

"We're near enough. They are using binoculars."

"Admiring the town across the bay?" The rower had that Greek sardonic smile on his intelligent face.

"But of course. Just normal tourists . . ." The fish-arranger looked over the side of the small boat and studied the water. "Better ease us in toward the shore, near the Leto. That's a good halfway point between the town and them." And the road to town passed that way, too, if anyone should set off from the *Stefanie* on foot. Most people would use the dinghies from their yachts to ferry them across the bay; but these strangers might plan the opposite—the road at this time of day was deserted. "They've timed their arrival well. There's the mail boat from Athens, standing in." Everyone would be gathering on the front street to watch the new arrivals. Dusk would soon be here, too. "Start rowing. Stand up and face the way you're going. I'll keep watch on the yacht now." He began playing around with the folded net coiled in the prow of the boat, his back to the land, as if he were trying to straighten some tangle. The yacht was moored by one rope only. She had dropped anchor, too, to prevent swinging. She was secure, yet not so tied up that departure would be complicated.

"There's a storm coming up." Even inside the bay, there was a difference in the bobbing waves, still small but now sharply chopped, with even a few miniature whitecaps beginning to show. "I'm going closer to the shore."

"Don't get me out of sight of the yacht, that's all. Take it easy, easy. Not too fast. That's fine. You look like a real Mykoniot."

I wish I felt like one, the other thought, as the strain on his thighs and shoulders increased. This wasn't as easy as it looked. Next time, he told himself, I'll let someone else do the rowing. I can't even look around and see what's happening. "What's going on?"

"Nothing."

That was always the way . . . nothing, and waiting, and nothing, watching and waiting, nothing.

"Two men leaving the yacht, taking the path to the road."

"Then what?"

"They've turned right. They're walking briskly. Very clever. It's dusk, but the street lights aren't yet switched on. They could reach town before that happens." There was a long pause. "Yes, they are coming around the bay. Get to the shore."

They were pulling their boat up over the narrow stretch of beach when the two yachtsmen came walking past, only separated from the fishermen by the low stone wall that edged the deserted road. In the fading light, the two strangers looked very similar, both in clothes and in height. They walked straight on, in silence, barely glancing at one fisherman now unloading his catch while the other balanced the oars over his shoulders, and didn't slacken pace until they reached the part of the road where it turned away from the shore as it reached the outskirts of the town, to swing around some buildings at the water's edge. And there an odd thing happened. A third man had been waiting for them near the buildings, a small, fat man in shorts with a bulky sweater pulled over a flowered shirt. He shook hands solemnly with one of the men and fell into step beside him, while the other simply turned on his heel and retraced his steps at the same brisk pace. He passed the two fishermen on their way into town and gave them a sharp glance. But they were too busy discussing the possible price they could ask for their catch at the Triton to pay him any attention.

They had other reasons, too: the man hurrying back to the yacht anchorage was obviously of less importance; he had only been escorting his companion safely to the meeting place. "Protection?" murmured one of the fishermen. "Or is it to confuse anyone who might be watching the *Stefanie?* And who is the fat friend who is now doing convoy duty?"

The other fisherman shook his head. "We're in trouble," he said worriedly, looking for a place to ditch the oars and the fish. For the two men ahead of them had disappeared down the narrow lane, just beyond the group of buildings, which would lead them into the big main square which lay at this end of the town. "They're not going to parade along the front street, you may be sure of that. They'll use the square to branch off on a road right around the back of the town."

He increased his pace as he spoke, but even so, when they reached the wide, deserted square, all they saw of the stranger from the yacht and his solid guide was their backs as they vanished up one of the small streets on its other side. "You follow, if you can. Don't let them get suspicious, though. A safe distance, these were the instructions." He took the fish from his companion's hand and watched him hurry across the square. Here's a town, he thought angrily as he looked down the full stretch of the front street with its café lights welcoming the procession of travelers from the Athens boat, here's a town where you can walk its length or breadth in five minutes, and where you lose a man in three seconds flat. The dusk was deepening, more lights were coming on, here by the water front. He watched a red-haired beauty, following her porter and luggage, strolling toward him; French, he guessed by her clothes, and probably going to the Leto—she was entering the dark lane now to reach the shore road around the bay. That's right, he told himself bitterly, you know everything except where that man from the yacht was going.

There were several small pieces of comfort, though. The man had been seen. The man had been followed into town, and not to one of the houses scattered on the hills around the town. The man would never have put a foot off his yacht, never even have anchored, if he had any suspicion at all. The man's friend could be identified with a little work and care; he was either a tourist or a foreign resident—certainly not a self-respecting Mykoniot in that ridiculous clothing. So these were the crumbs of comfort. Now we shall wait on that road around the bay, and wait, and wait, until the man returns to the *Stefanie*. A clever man, certainly. Who is he?

The lights went on in the little streets and lanes. Perhaps in time to let us catch up with him after all? Always keeping, of course, at a safe distance; these were the American instructions. The fisherman laughed silently. Whoever gave these directions had never seen Mykonos.

14.

Dinner at nine meant nine-thirty. It ended almost at eleven. This was due partly to the amount of food divided into many courses, and partly to the valiant attempts of the young smiling fishergirls, decked up in spotless aprons, to serve from the left and pour from the right and remember all the funny ways of foreigners. It was a generous and comic meal, actually the best of combinations. Nor did Craig have to do much talking. The other guests were either French or English, and both groups showed something of the new nationalism in Europe by disliking to speak in anything but their own language.

When he stood once more in his small, low-ceilinged room that overlooked the little square, his plans for the rest of the evening—to wander around the town for an hour, find his bearings—were now quite discouraged. Everyone here was already in bed, it seemed; Mykonos had closed down for the night. There wasn't a movement or sound from the lanes around the church square; windows were shuttered, lights were out. This was a place of sea air and heavy slumber, and probably of early rising. He might as well call it a day, catch up on his own sleep (twenty-four hours short after his week of *tavernas* in Athens) and face Mykonos tomorrow. There were also two immediate problems: how to be able to avoid Veronica Clark nonchalantly; how to avoid Heinrich Berg completely. He could solve them for tonight, at least, by going to bed.

He had been right about sea air and heavy sleep, but he didn't get down to breakfast until almost ten. The rest of the guests in this rambling hotel (three houses joined together by Madame's will power and run on her indomitable energy, with scurrying maids dropping spoons or unrestrained giggles as light relief to complete obedience) had already left for bathing beaches or high-minded excursions to Delos. He had the small enclosed garden all to himself. It was really only an alcove formed by the jut of the hotel's second house into the church square, shut off from the two sides of public view by a thick high wall, whitewashed like the flagstones and every other stretch of stone in sight. It contained three tables, seven pots of flowers (the softer side of Madame the Terrible), vines growing around the second-floor windows overhead (they might even bloom as hibiscus once summer was here), and three oleander bushes to break the hard line of the eight-foot wall. Everything, except the rampant vines, was miniature in scale. It was therefore also excessively private. It was a corner of complete peace—the good-natured shrieks from the kitchen were a long way off—and, what seemed even more important, of reasonable security. No one from the outside, not even the houses around the square, could look into this patch of garden. Comrade Berg, if he were studying his neighbors this fine blue-skied morning, would need something stronger than binoculars to pierce the Triton's high, thick wall.

Madame came to supervise for a few minutes. He admired everything, he assured her. Yes, he was most comfortable, the coffee was excellent. He would sit a little longer, look at some guidebooks, study some maps, and might he have another cup of coffee?

And after that? he wondered. Out. Out to meet Veronica with Maritta smiling in the background? As for Berg—well, it was more than possible that he would not do much walking through Mykonos by this excessively clear and bright daylight. Yes, morning, and breakfast, changed one's perspective on problems, thought Craig.

"May I have some coffee, too, Madame Iphigenia?" an American voice asked from the dining room's doorway, and Jim Partridge stepped out onto the terrace. He was tanned and smiling, a little leaner, a little more gaunt under the cheekbones. He was dressed, like Craig, in a dark cotton shirt and gray slacks. He was adding a few phrases in atrocious Greek to please Madame and send her beaming toward the kitchen; perhaps to help Craig, too. For there had been a moment of blank astonishment, and then—as Madame's attention was diverted—time for recovery. "Do you mind if I join you?" Partridge asked in a normal tone of voice. He glanced around the enclosed terrace. "It would be difficult to sit in lonely state in a place this size."

"There are some guests at this hotel who could manage it very well," Craig said with a grin, remembering last night's deep freeze. "Delighted. Sit down. My name's Craig."

"I'm Partridge."

They shook hands solemnly and sat down, and looked at each other. "Thank God you're here," Craig said in a low voice. He glanced briefly at the hotel's two second-floor windows that overlooked the terrace.

"Anyone up there?"

"Just a couple of maids. And the silent young man."

"Then we'll talk about the weather and skin-diving until coffee arrives." Partridge tilted his chair comfortably, lit a cigarette, stretched his shoulders. "That was quite a storm last night. I was on one of those cruise ships—five glorious days on five famous islands; you know the routine—and bucked a north wind all the way from Crete to here. So when I stepped on land this morning, I decided I'd stay awhile and let the cruise do without me."

Now, come on, thought Craig as he listened with a broadening smile. Partridge on a cruise—that would be the day! Still, it all sounded authentic, and just the usual routine of new arrivals: my storm was bigger than yours. He will end by persuading me he has done nothing but pleasure-hop all around these islands since I last saw him in Paris.

The coffee arrived with one of Madame's laughing handmaidens, and they could drop the light chitchat. Upstairs, the beds had been made, the rooms tidied, and there was no more rustling at the windows, no more whispered comments on the two men sitting so lazily in the garden. The silent young man had left for some errands in town; Madame's instructions to him floated out in all their detail, and would keep him busy for a full hour. "A grand old girl," Partridge said softly.

"Carved in granite. The Mount Rushmore type."

"And a heart of—well, let's say solid silver. You can trust her."

"She knows what?"

"Nothing at all. But Elias—you came over on the boat with him yesterday, didn't you?—well, he's the nephew of her sister's husband. That makes him family."

"Very special?"

"Special enough on these islands. His friends are her friends. He brought me here, this morning."

"Didn't she expect him to stay, too?"

"And occupy a room that earns five dollars a day? Elias has tact. That is why she thinks so highly of him."

"Well, that's nice to know. What about the silent young man? Last night he stared too much, for my comfort."

"Probably he was just admiring the cut of your jacket. I bet he intends to have his next suit built exactly like that." As Craig relaxed and laughed, Partridge added, "Tourists are just like lions in cages— a kind of zoo for the local inhabitants. Don't let a few stares worry you. If a Greek looks at you at all he is paying you a compliment. How about the windows upstairs? Are we still being complimented?"

"They're empty."

"All right, then. Let's talk. But keep your voice down as low as possible. Tell me all about the Duclos incident. Where did you first spot him?"

Craig gave the brief account as crisply as he could. "Have they found the real Duclos?" he asked. Partridge shook his head. "What happened to him?"

"He arrived at the Athens airport last Sunday. That, we do know. Later, a stolen car was found abandoned a few miles away, along with a stolen uniform." He paused. Then he added grimly, "The man who impersonated Duclos may have been one of the kidnappers. The Greek police will get more out of him yet. They know how to handle that type, but it takes time. So far, he is saying nothing at all, not even with Duclos' ring and passport confronting him. Once a man starts inventing a story, it's easy enough to let his own quick wits trap him. It's a kind of mental jujitsu. You lead him on, let him think he is superior mentally to you. And then he outwits himself." Partridge had lost his taste for coffee; he pushed his cup away, stubbed out his cigarette. "So if ever you find yourself questioned, throw away your pride and play stupid. Name, rank and serial number—the last two being as misleading as possible. That's the safe way, perhaps not for you, but certainly for your friends."

"Did Duclos play it safe, like that?" Not for himself, but for Mimi and Partridge and all the rest. For me, too, Craig suddenly realized.

"If he had a chance to give a false rank and serial number, he'd keep them simple. And stay with them."

If he had a chance . . . "I suppose everyone breaks under torture."

Partridge nodded. "Either that," he said at last, "or he killed himself to prevent it. He would size up his captors, know how far they'd go. He was a very levelheaded man, and a brave one."

"You think he is dead?"

"I think so." There was emphasis on the pronoun.

"The others don't?"

"Division of opinion. The usual flap. Suggestions that we even get the Greek police to move in on Maritta Maas right now, while the French pick up Uncle Peter back in Paris. Better those two than nothing at all, that's the feeling. And that's why I'm here, actually. I wanted to see for myself if there were any storm signals around you. If there are, then I'm wrong about Duclos and he did talk. In which case, I'd better get you out of here as quickly as possible."

"I think you are right about Duclos," Craig said very quietly. "For two reasons. The first one is the minor one—me. Remember what I told you about the man with the high cheekbones and blunt nose who left the boat hurriedly at the Piraeus dock? Well, he had a friend with him on board. At first I thought the two of them might have been tailing me. But the one who sailed didn't come to Mykonos. He got off at Syros. Now, if Duclos had given my name to his—his examiners, would that man have got off at Syros? Paid no attention to me? He didn't even know who I was. He was on that boat, I now think, simply to keep an eye on the fake Duclos. They knew it was a tricky business, that impersonation, and if anything went wrong they wanted to learn who had recognized the fake. That could be the reason why they were sailing with him." He paused. Partridge was looking at him with an odd expression in his light gray eyes. "Could be?" Craig asked, wondering if he had been too blatantly stupid.

"Could very well be," Partridge murmured. "And if that's your minor reason, I'd like to hear what you think is more important."

"Heinrich Berg is here."

Partridge was really startled, and didn't even hide it. "Here—on Mykonos?"

"I saw him last night," Craig began, and gave a quick account of the whole incident, from his view of the square to Herr Ludwig's taste for wine. "Do you think Berg would have appeared on Mykonos if Duclos had told him we were all gathering here?" he ended. "So that's the second reason why I think you're right. Duclos didn't talk."

Partridge sat very still. "Then," he said, "we now have three people who can actually identify Insar—can identify Berg, right on this very island. You, and two of Elias' agents who were pretending to be fishermen yesterday when a yacht came into the harbor. They saw one of its passengers being met by a small stout man in shorts, a flowered shirt, and a large sweater." Wouldn't you know it, he thought, two rather minor agents and a complete amateur? "Three who can identify," he repeated, a smile beginning to break. "We're really getting ahead in this game, aren't we?" His smile faded and he was back to some anxious thinking again.

"I can manage to dodge Berg," Craig said, misreading the frown on Partridge's face. "He won't risk walking about in daylight; you notice he came into town in the dusk, when the streets were mostly empty. So if I avoid the small square, show no interest in the Ludwig house, arouse no suspicion that I know he is here, I can wander around the rest of Mykonos quite normally. Of course, there is just one thing. He may not be in Ludwig's house. He may be right back on the yacht. In that case, I'll keep away from that side of the bay. Okay?"

"The yacht sailed at six this morning. But he wasn't on board."

"And that worries you?" Craig asked, watching Partridge's tense eyes.

"Now that I know that it's Berg himself who is in Mykonos—yes." Partridge hesitated, then added, "I'll have to leave, right away. As soon as I can get transportation out."

And here I'm stuck again, just guessing, just wondering what the whole thing is the hell about. Craig said, "I wish I didn't feel I were punching my way into a sack of cotton wool." He tried his coffee, but it was cold. Madame would be shocked at such waste, such casual treatment of her time and coffee beans. He picked up both their cups, rose, and emptied them into a pot of flowers.

Partridge had been studying him as if he were deciding something. Suddenly, he made up his mind. "What worries me is simply this. Everything is moving far too quickly. I've miscalculated. I thought from the information we had that there was a week ahead of us, at least a few more days, to get everything set up here, and wait. But if Insarov has already arrived—yes, Insarov is the name that Berg has used for nineteen years—then he must expect the information from our base near Smyrna to be delivered very, very soon."

Craig stared at him. "So that's your real problem," he said slowly. Heinrich Berg and Sussman's murder had led all the way to Smyrna. . . . "How soon?" he asked bluntly. "Perhaps even now—by radio transmission?"

Partridge shook his head. "He'll use the *Stefanie*—the yacht that brought him here. It has twin diesels. Say around twelve knots. We're about eighty miles at most from that part of the Turkish coast. The *Stefanie* could make it in six to eight hours of straight sailing."

"Then she could be back here tonight."

"No, she'll wait for darkness off the Turkish coast before she can risk her pickup. And she will need darkness here, again, to deliver it. If she can't reach Mykonos before dawn, and I doubt that, then she'll have to wait and sail in at sunset tomorrow. Yes, sunset tomorrow is the more likely hour."

"That seems a pretty complicated maneuver for a Soviet agent to deliver a strip of microfilm."

"Not just microfilm. It has to be something more than that. Two houses and a yacht are hardly necessary for passing information, disguised in a lipstick or cuff link, over a café table on the water front. No, this information is more important than any microfilmed report could be. That's how we reason it."

Craig thought that over. What would be the most important kind of information that could be discovered? It would have to be as full as possible, quantity as well as quality, rich in details, completely authentic. And that, he thought with a shake of his head and a wry smile, would be any foreign agent's dream. To get all that and get it quickly—not just in one stolen document here, a report there, and weeks of fitting all the fragments of information together . . . "So they are going to abduct an expert, are they?" he asked quietly. He had startled Partridge, but it wasn't such a brash assumption. It had happened before, or almost. The American expert on electronics whom he had met at the Meurice party—Antonini, wasn't it?—had nearly been kidnapped right into a hospital bed in Moscow.

"That's what they think," Partridge said, recovering.

196

"Then you'd better guard your expert."

"We have. For the last ten days we have been doing our best to steer their attention onto the wrong man. Let's hope we have succeeded."

"And all this is going on at the base near Smyrna?"

Partridge nodded.

Craig whistled softly. "Not something to do with electronics again?" He had meant it as light relief, but Partridge's narrowed eyes looked at him sharply. "I did meet Antonini," Craig reminded him.

Partridge relaxed. "You're too damn quick," he said. And you're forcing my hand, he thought. One could tell a stupid man very little, and not worry about his safety. But one couldn't stop an intelligent man from thinking his way through a puzzle. The trouble was, even a man with bright brains could go off on a tangent if he weren't given some basic facts. Tangents could be dangerous. "You were right," he said, weighing his words. "It's that old devil electronics again. The Communists never give up, do they? It's obvious that our real expert would be invaluable to them. As well as the recent alterations he has been making in their wiring system at our H.Q., he also remembers the alterations he made in our Moscow Embassy. You see—" he was about to explain carefully.

"Yes, I remember thinking in Paris—on my first night there, at my sister's party—just how important it would be for the Russians to know which of their listening gadgets were still functioning reliably." He looked at Partridge's blank face. Possibly he wasn't accustomed to being interrupted. "Sorry," Craig said. "Perhaps I'm jumping off on the wrong foot."

A smile flickered at the back of Partridge's eyes. "You've saved me a lot of time," he said blandly. "Any further ideas?"

"Just one question. Back in Paris, you told me an American was bringing information to Maritta. Is he involved in *this?*" Craig's voice was a mixture of distaste and doubt. The man was a traitor, but would he aid and abet a political abduction that could only mean torture and eventual murder?

"He could very well be."

"You aren't sure?"

"You can't be sure of anything, not at this stage. But I do know one thing. He couldn't refuse, or else he'd be ditched. He's ambitious as well as dedicated. That type can persuade himself into accepting any order. He may not enjoy this extension of his duties. But he is being tested by this additional assignment, and he knows that."

"You mean they chose him just to test him?"

"If you work for men like Insarov, there's always a test of complete obedience. But also—he happens to be one man who could entice our expert, or his stand-in, on board the *Stefanie*. You see, he is a friend of both of them."

Craig drew a deep, slow breath. His lips tightened. "Who is he?"

"If we knew that, it would simplify everything. We still only know him as Alex." Partridge hesitated briefly. Better warn him, he decided. Something may go wrong. Alex may slip through our fingers, turn up here. "We do know one thing about him. Alex is one of two men. He could be either Bradley or Wilshot."

"Then both Bradley and Wilshot are in the Smyrna area?"

Partridge nodded. "One of them is being used, obviously, to cover the other. A very clever and cautious man is Alex. He will go far, if he succeeds in this assignment."

If he succeeds . . . "You are putting your substitute expert in a pretty nasty position," Craig said frankly, and didn't disguise his aversion. He didn't like the idea one bit. Was Partridge only one of those damned calculating machines after all?

"Not if he follows instructions. We don't intend to have him abducted. We only want him to discover who Alex is. Whoever invites him for a quick and pleasant trip on the *Stefanie*—that's the American we're looking for. We'll have Alex quietly arrested, right then and there, in Smyrna. And we'll pick up the rest of his friends, simultaneously, here and in Athens and in Milan and in Paris. That's how we've planned it."

"And if it doesn't work that way?"

"We'll board the *Stefanie* the minute she docks in Mykonos," Partridge said grimly. His worry was deep and real.

"Why not before then?"

"At sea, they might have time to send a radio warning to Insarov when they saw us approaching. They could even kill our agent, and dump him overboard. But—" Partridge took a deep breath—"we won't have any of those problems if he follows instructions."

That's the second time Partridge had said that. He's worried about it, really worried, thought Craig. "Is your man one of these heroic types who thinks he can solve everything by himself?"

Partridge shook his head.

"Perhaps you haven't told him enough."

Partridge raised an eyebrow.

"Then, he might not realize how important your instructions were. Knowledge is sobering. A kind of restraint on bright impulses."

"You make me relieved that I've told you too much," Partridge said dryly.

"Much safer," Craig assured him. Although, he thought with amusement, he didn't go as far as telling me the name of either the real or substitute expert. There's a lot he hasn't told me, probably never will. All he has done, really, is to give me full warning on what's at stake. "Much safer for everyone. I'll keep my head down, well down."

"And if they were to start questioning you?"

"You thought about that before you even started talking with me. When they are on the point of hooking the really big fish, you know they aren't going to waste time or run any unnecessary risks with a minnow."

"I wouldn't rate you quite as small as a minnow," Partridge said with a smile.

"It's how *they* rate me that's important. And to them I'm just an annoying coincidence, perhaps not even that." Craig paused. "What do you want me to do?"

"As little as possible."

"I ought to make some contact with Maritta, find out quietly when she is expecting new guests. That's what you brought me here for, wasn't it? To identify this Alex if he slips through to Mykonos in spite of your plan. You know—I have a feeling that he has become just as important to you as Berg."

"He is as important, now, as Berg was twenty years ago."

"You think he could become another Insarov?"

Partridge nodded. "And for that reason, he *is* one of our main targets in this counteroperation. Because, in terms of the future, we're responsible. When we deal with men like Alex, we are really like doctors practicing preventive medicine. In twenty years, even less, Alex could become the most dangerous man in America." Alex, tested by this assignment, adopted by Insarov as his bright young man, trained and guided, pushed and helped . . . "He is trusted now, by a lot of reliable people. He has their confidence. He could infiltrate higher and higher. He could go very far, indeed."

Craig said nothing.

Partridge, looking at his watch, had his own grim thoughts. How did he get back to Smyrna? There was no ship arriving here until the evening, and it was traveling in the wrong direction. So, now that he had given Craig an over-all warning, he had better start sending a message to Smyrna. Relay it through Athens, utmost urgency. Tell them to double the watch on O'Malley. Even more important, make sure he follows his instructions to the very last letter—and no more.

For that was the real joker in the pack, thought Partridge. O'Malley and Duclos were friends. At least, they met in Berlin two years ago, and liked each other. And O'Malley has heard about Duclos by this time. He might just have one of those wild attacks of stubborn Australian courage, decide to go all the way with Alex in order to make sure of leading us to Insarov. Because he doesn't know we've found Insarov, that we've got him if only we keep our heads and don't spread that piece of news around. But how do I get this information through to O'Malley without warning Insarov? For he has his ear close to the ground, that's certain. How else could he have heard, except through some leak in security, that our chief expert's part of the job in Smyrna was just about ending? He must have several agents around; Alex, alone, couldn't find that out. Let's hope to God that Insarov hasn't discovered the real expert is Val Sutherland. Let's hope Insarov isn't having a very big laugh right now, over O'Malley.

"You look," said Craig, "like a man on a high wire working without safety nets."

"That's how I feel," agreed Partridge, and tried to smile. No, he couldn't risk getting news through to Smyrna that Insarov was actually here. All he could do was to warn O'Malley to stick with his instructions, to do no more than that on any account. If only he could have seen O'Malley, spoken with him— He looked at his watch again. "Involved, isn't it, getting in and out of this island?"

"Hire a submarine," said Craig with a wide smile.

"Damned if I wouldn't—if there wasn't so much daylight around. That sea out there seems lonely until you start counting the fishing boats or the caïques. And there's one thing about sailors, they have long eyesight. No, I think I had best start sending messages to Aunt Matilda in Athens." He rose, and then stopped as if a new idea had struck him. He considered it for a full half-minute. "Look, if Madame Iphigenia wonders why I don't turn up for dinner this evening, tell her I went over to Delos this afternoon and probably am staying at the tourist pavilion over there for the night. Will you?"

Craig nodded. Had Partridge really thought of a way to get back to Smyrna? But why the rush? "Half a second!" he said, reaching for the map in his guidebook. "Just where," he asked very quietly, "is Maritta's house?"

Partridge hesitated.

"I'll do nothing rash," Craig said irritably.

"It stands by itself on the hillside above the bay. Here, in this direction." Partridge pointed to the map. "Don't mark it. Memorize. But that's not much of a map, is it? I can get you a better one. I'll leave it in one of your suitcases. Or are they locked?"

"No."

Partridge seemed amused by that. He was about to add something more, but decided footsteps were marching through the dining room. He only said, "Give me five minutes. Then look. *And* lock." He signaled good-bye, and left, almost bumping into Madame at the dining-room door. "Just leaving," he told her cheerfully. "Your nephew is going to take me out to Megali Ammos for a swim."

"Such a nice man," Madame Iphigenia told Craig, looking at Partridge's retreating back. "So gentle. So well behaved." She looked now, severely, at the tray of dirty breakfast dishes.

Craig repressed a smile, gathered his map and books as Madame picked up the tray to remove such an eyesore from her garden. He rose to open the dining-room door still more for Madame's widespread elbows.

"You swim also?" she asked. "Our visitors admire our beaches."

"I think I'll walk around the town and admire the windmills."

That mollified her slightly. He wasn't just someone who sat around a garden all day, dirtying dishes. "There is much to do in Mykonos," she assured him, and hurried on.

"Let me help," he suggested, but she resisted. So he crossed the dining room and opened that door for her, too. It led into a winding corridor which made communication with the kitchen, a full-throated shout away, a fine example of modern labor-saving ingenuity.

"You admire this house?" she asked.

"Very much." Sharp eyes, had Madame Iphigenia. He had been looking for any outside doors—surely a wandering place like this must have more than one entrance. "I'm interested in architecture," he added to excuse his curiosity. That was true enough, anyway.

"Americans admire old houses?" she asked now, in obvious un-belief.

"Why, yes." Where had Madame got her ideas about Americans?

Madame stared, shouted toward the kitchen, brought a maid running along the corridor, delivered over the tray with a burst of instructions, and then looked at Craig. "Come!" she told him, and led the way.

It was a quick and complete tour through corridors, under arches that supported ceilings, up and down narrow staircases, past corners of rooms jutting at odd angles. It left Craig a little dazed, almost breathless. But he did discover he had been right in his guess. There were three separate exits to the hotel, one of them on the church square. That was the one to be avoided.

Before he set out for his stroll through the town, he went up to his room. Partridge had already been there. In the smaller bag, under his camera, there was a neat pistol. Loaded. There was also the promised map, binoculars, and a pocketknife which, startlingly, turned into a switchblade. He decided to carry it. And the map. He put the binocu-lars into his camera case and decided to carry that, too. He buried the pistol inside a pair of socks, replaced them in the bag. He locked it securely, shoved it on the top shelf of the wardrobe.

Two weeks ago, he thought, I'd have been laughing fit to crack my ribs, making bright remarks about what the best-dressed agent is wearing this season; yesterday, I might have produced a grin, felt a touch of embarrassment when I next met Partridge. But today? Well, I've learned about Duclos; about a lot of things. The more you know, the less you scoff. . . . If I came to Europe to fill in some gaps in my education, I've certainly succeeded.

He picked up his sunglasses—he'd need them for that strong light and those brilliant walls—combed his hair roughly to give him the right tourist look. From a distance, he wouldn't appear much like the man in the neatly tailored jacket, correct collar and tie, who had stepped on shore last night. He slung the camera case over his shoulder, checked map and knife in his pocket, and left. Much to do on Mykonos, Madame had said. She could be right, but not in the way she meant it.

15

In half an hour, Craig had walked through and around the town. It was a place of patterns, imposed, interposed. Cubes, arches, horizontals of steps, vertical balustrades, curves of domed churches, cylindrical windmills each with twelve triangular sails in clocklike precision. Bright sunlight cast black sharp-edged shadow. Houses, stairways, pavement were a blazing white. Color was left to the domes, to the fishing boats drawn up along the front street, to the potted flowers on the stone staircases, to the twisted dark green trees with their sculptural trunks, to the carved doors, to the inside shutters of the windows that stared out in bare rectangles from their whitewashed walls. People had their patterns, too: slender girls, stout women, headcloths and cotton dresses gathered around the wells; thin boys on small mules; men in caps, with creased brown faces and dark mustaches, some working in bare feet with trousers rolled up modestly only to mid-leg, others already gathered around their own tables at their special cafés; and the tourists—those who kept themselves covered like the Mykoniots, those who bared thigh and arm as much as possible—wandering aimlessly.

But among all those faces, all those walkers and talkers, there was no one he recognized. And then, just as he was looking at some of the arts and crafts in a shop window on one of the narrow streets, Mimi came strolling along in green trousers and a white silk shirt patterned to match.

"I followed you for three streets," she said in triumph. Her face was pale, there were deep shadows under her dark gray eyes as she lifted her sunglasses to look at him more clearly, but her voice sounded normal and she was even producing a small smile. A girl who hadn't slept much, he decided, but who was determined to face the day.

"I never even saw you," he admitted, annoyed with himself.

"You weren't meant to."

"Not even in those tight pants?"

"That makes it a greater triumph." She looked down at her thighs. "Too tight?"

"Not on you, Mimi."

"Now look at that darling little horrible skirt in the window, and we shall pretend to be discussing its hideous stripes."

"A skirt? I thought it was a tent."

"Keep looking at the window as we talk. Your friend is in that little shop just three houses away. She is alone."

Veronica? "Thank you for the warning."

"But it isn't a warning. I want to meet her. Shall we go and look at its window?"

"Look, Mimi—I don't think this is a good idea."

"It is. I want to make friends with her as quickly as possible." She smiled again. "I bumped into her once, this morning, but she did not stay to talk. Is she shy or proud? Or frightened?"

"Is something wrong?" he asked sharply. Mimi started walking toward the other shop. He had to follow her, even if he didn't want to go near the place, to get her answer. "Look, I don't think we should go in there."

"Why not? The sooner I meet her the better."

"Don't girls ever talk to each other quite naturally?" he asked in exasperation.

"If she sees we are friends, she will trust me much more."

"You know, Mimi, this is not an easy situation."

"I know. Jim told me all about it."

"He did, did he?"

"He also told me to take care of Veronica."

Craig halted at the shop window, looked at a death mask of Agamemnon, several models of windmills, fishermen's striped shirts that owed more to the Riviera than the Mykonos harbor, guidebooks, glossy oils of storm-lashed rocks, replicas of the Parthenon, hand-loomed cloth that was at least authentic. Was Mimi's interest in Veronica only a short cut to Maritta Maas? The French were chiefly interested in her, he remembered.

Mimi was watching him with a small sad smile, as if she guessed his doubts. "I won't draw her into danger, John," she said very softly. "Let me worry about her. Meanwhile. You can't."

"All right," he said, and stood aside to let her enter.

Mimi was saying over her shoulder, her voice now bright and clear, "You know, these materials are really beautiful. Magnificent texture —and look at this design!" She pointed to the hand-loomed cloth displayed against the walls of the small room and took off her sunglasses to study its patterns and colors.

But he was looking at Veronica, barely six feet away from him. She glanced up from some notes she had been making at a table where the shopkeeper had cleared a space for her. Beside her was a slightly battered book, almost like a ledger, with handwritten paragraphs in Greek and French and English. As he came up to her, he caught a glimpse of one heading: Room for rent. She closed the ledger quickly, dropped her pencil and notebook into a large straw bag, and faced him—confused and startled and yet, he felt, delighted. She wore a simple dress of blue linen, the color of the sky over Mykonos. Her arms and legs were bare and tanned; her dark hair was brushed smooth, falling to one side of her forehead; her lips, parted in that wonderfully real and spontaneous smile, were colored a soft but glowing pink. Then, as he stood there, looking at her, saying nothing, the welcome in her face died away, first in the blue eyes, then in the lips. The smile became a formality, her face guarded.

"Hello," he said casually, "I thought you'd have been swimming this morning. Or painting. How's the work going?"

"Too many distractions, I'm afraid." She gathered up her bag from the table, seemed to be leaving. Yet she hesitated. Something *is* wrong, he thought; Mimi was right. Something is troubling Veronica. But what?

Craig looked at Mimi, who had wandered back to him. "Here's someone else from Paris. Mam'selle Marie Aubernon—Miss Veronica Clark."

"From Monterey, actually," Veronica said as she shook hands with

Mimi. Large blue eyes met large gray eyes. They seemed to like what they saw, or felt. "I'm only on a prolonged visit to Paris. I'm studying art there."

"But so did I! And then I stayed on. I came from the Auvergne originally. Do you know it?"

"No, but I've always wanted to visit it."

"Mountains and mists. And rain."

"And folk songs."

"You like music, too? But of course—" Mimi addressed Craig, "Now, don't laugh at me—I often do my best work with a stack of records playing beside me."

"Perhaps that's what you need," he told Veronica, "to get inspiration started." Well, he thought thankfully, the two of them seem to have hit it off. Mimi's warmth was real enough when she let it rise above that cool, detached exterior. It was time for him to move on. The small room was becoming crowded with the three new customers who were strolling in. Two were English, a quiet couple. The third was by himself, middle-aged, broad in face and shoulders, dressed in shorts and a striped shirt hanging loosely over his solid waistline, still wearing his sunglasses so that Craig couldn't be sure of the direction of his eyes. I saw that man, Craig remembered, strolling up and down outside this shop, as if he were waiting for someone. And as that thought struck him, Craig noticed how still Veronica was standing, her eyes on the man's back. Automatically, he asked, "Where is Maritta?"

"Somewhere in town, seeing friends. I—I had some shopping to do." Veronica glanced again at the stranger, who was interested now in model windmills.

"So have I," Mimi said quickly. "But I'm completely bewildered. The shops are so—so separated. Some don't even *look* like shops! I need sun-tan lotion, film for my camera. And can you tell me where these materials are woven? You see, that's my business now—I'm a decorator, and fabrics are my special thing. Do you know where the looms are? On this island itself?"

"Right in town."

"You know the street? Would you show me?"

"Of course. When would you like to—"

"Now. Why not? Or have you some engagement for lunch?"

Veronica shook her head.

"Then will you lunch with me? Unless, of course, Mr. Craig—"

Craig smiled for Mimi. I could wring your pretty little neck, most lovingly, right here and now. "I've had enough shopping for one day," he told them. "See you around." He paid the smiling woman, who kept shop with such hopeful patience, for the half-dozen postcards he had picked up; someone ought to buy something, he had thought, as the English couple left without finding anything they wanted and the man in the striped shirt still poked and touched and handled and wasted time. Craig moved to the door. Then we'll see whether that man is interested in me, he thought; or is this Maritta's idea of how to keep watch on Veronica when she strays alone into town? He stepped into the narrow street, put on his sunglasses, began walking slowly toward the bay. But he hadn't drawn off the man in the striped shirt. The man was still staying near Veronica.

It was just after noon. At once, the streets were deserted, all work stopped, everyone indoors. Only a few bemused visitors still wandered around, trying for camera angles in the white silence. Now's the time, thought Craig, and left the big square at the end of the front street, choosing the steep road which would lead him up onto the hillside. Above the town there were groupings of houses and dovecotes, small white cubes set down on harsh gray earth, with long walls of rough gray stones forming terraces to hold whatever soil there was from slipping into the bay. He sat down with his back to one of those walls in order to get off the sky line—the hillside was as bare as that. There must be other ways to Maritta's house. Certainly, he couldn't dare approach it in daylight. Still, this was the time to get his bearings. And admire the view. It was magnificent: deep blue sea, other islands, high blue sky, white clouds.

He had only walked for ten minutes, but he was far enough up on the hill to see all the houses, sparsely scattered, that stretched along its wide flank. Some of the houses followed the curve of Mykonos' small bay; others climbed high above it. He got out Partridge's map and compared it with his own. Just there, Partridge had pointed. That was the area high above the north end of the bay where the yachts sheltered. He could see five or six houses in that direction, spread over the steep slopes of barren ground. But which house? Partridge had been deliberately vague, just to keep him out of trouble, no doubt.

Partridge's map was good, well detailed. But houses were only indicated by dots, and the house which Maritta's dear kind Uncle Peter had rented could be one of five, at least.

He took out the binoculars and brought them all up amazingly close. Too close. What he could be doing to someone, someone could be doing to him. So he swung around in the other direction, facing southward—more bare hills and the road leading to the beaches; and then he looked directly ahead of him, over the town, westward. But he was still keeping the pattern of the view to the north end of the bay in his mind. There were two houses, well separated from each and any other, that had paths leading down to the road around the bay. For that reason alone they were his likeliest candidates. One of them had some kind of small building on its far side—perhaps a cottage or one of the ubiquitous dovecotes. Otherwise, from this distance, they were much the same. They even had brave attempts at gardens—he had seen rounded tops of trees inside their white walls. By contrast, the rest of the houses above the bay stood bare, open. If I were someone like dear Uncle Peter, he thought, what would I rent? Protecting walls, shading trees, and a road however rough and rugged right down toward the yacht anchorage. He put away the glasses and his maps; lit a cigarette, lounged against the gray buttress at his back, and watched the drifting clouds sending their shadows chasing over sea and islands. Then he rose, dusted off his trousers and shirt, walked down to the town. The small excursion had taken only half an hour altogether. A wasted half hour? No, he decided. He hadn't found what he wanted, but he had learned that by night he could easily find his way on those ribbon paths that followed the stone terraces right across the length of hillside. And he had seen a view.

He found a quiet *taverna* on the shady side of the big square where a few of the local men, regulars obviously, were grouped around a couple of tables. They looked at him gravely, accepted him with a nod when he made his good day with *"Kali mera sas,"* and returned to their discussion. The talk was always in a low steady murmur, he noticed, just as the drink before them was always a glass of water with an occasional small cup of coffee. There were a couple of fishermen, some men from the harbor, a carpenter, a few old men, and possibly the driver of the taxi that stood on the other side of the square beside three small carriages with bonneted horses. Or mules. The ears twitching through the holes in their straw hats looked very pronounced, even from this distance. It was a peaceful scene: sunlight viewed from shadow, men's voices harshly droning, horses dozing, a taxi waiting for an afternoon hire to the beach; and dominating it all, from the center of the deserted square, was the bust of a strong-faced woman who stared defiantly out to sea, much in the way she must have rallied the fishermen of Mykonos, back in 1822, to sail out and fight the Turks. Craig settled in his corner, behind the screen of talking men, and looked out to sea, too. From here, he had a view not only of the front street right down to the breakwater, but of the several exits from this square. Opposite him, toward the shore, was the beginning of the road that led away from the town around the rest of the bay. That was the way that Veronica must take to meet the path up to the house on the hill. That was the way that Mimi would follow to reach her hotel.

He ordered lunch from a small boy in a large apron—rice and chopped veal wrapped inside vine leaves, served cold—and ate it slowly, studied his map, kept an eye ready for any movement along the front street or into the square, and finished a glass of resinated wine, amber in color, revolting at first but at least liquid and cool. If you drank it long enough, he thought, you'd probably begin to think this was the way wine should taste. Like those inland ranchers in Argentina who imported fish for Fridays from the coast, and before refrigeration was in use came to believe that bad fish was a delicacy. Like the grouse-eaters, too, in London, who had accustomed themselves to high game because once there was no other way to eat it.

There was still no sign of Mimi.

He made his half-cup of coffee last almost as long as the natives could. They were drifting away now. Only four men still sat around. And no sign of Mimi. I've guessed wrong, he thought. She must have cut lunch in town and gone back to her hotel. But if that had happened in the thirty minutes he had taken to explore the hillside up above the square, then it looked as if Veronica and she hadn't got on so well together after all. Which meant, in turn, that Veronica was still more isolated than ever. Damn it, he thought, his worry now churning into anger, I'll have to think of some plan of my own. If Mimi has failed, I'll have to take some action. And what is Partridge going to say to that? *Do as little as possible*, that was his firm advice this morning. But since then, there has been a slight change in the situation here. If Veronica is searching for a room in town, what's the reason behind it?

Calm down, calm down, he told himself irritably. Give Mimi another half hour. Once you've talked with her, you'll have something to go on. Then you can start thinking about some plan of action—if that's necessary. You know the dangers; you know what's at stake. . . . He reached for a cigarette, lit it slowly, stared gloomily at the empty square.

Suddenly, he was aware of someone standing in the shadowed doorway beside him. He turned his head sharply, saw Elias. And how long has he been there? Craig wondered, both startled and annoyed.

Elias was surveying the peaceful harbor, as if he had just enjoyed a lengthy meal indoors and was speculating on how to spend the rest of a sleepy afternoon. But unless he had been sitting behind the stone arch that held up the small dining room's ceiling, or had been in the kitchen itself, Craig was positive that Elias had not been there when he had taken this outside table. Elias was speaking to the four men—friendly, desultory talk that lasted a few minutes. This politeness over, Elias looked at Craig, nodded. "Did you have a pleasant walk?" He pulled a chair up to Craig's table, sat down and accepted a cigarette. "Very quiet," he went on, glancing around the square.

"Too quiet," Craig said, recovering his breath. Who told him I went for a walk, this morning? The same person who told him I was here?

Elias was now studying Craig. "Was it wise to climb up the hillside?" he asked gently, but there was sharp reproof in his eyes.

"Just normal tourist behavior," Craig tried. "Wanted to photograph the dovecotes and windmills."

"You were not using a camera," Elias said, looking pointedly at its case. He added magnanimously, if coldly, "You were very careful, that I must say."

"Keeping an eye on me?" Craig asked with a grin.

"I'm in charge of you. For the time being." Elias was not smiling.

"Oh?" Craig glanced across at the other men.

"They don't understand English. Besides, they saw us arriving from Athens last night on the same ship. It is natural that we talk for a little."

"Were you telling me that Partridge has left?" Craig asked very

211

quietly. So he did find a way off the island, and more quickly than I expected.

"Almost," Elias said. Even if his friends at the other table did not speak English, he seemed a little shocked by the direct question. "And you—how do you like Mykonos?"

"I'd like to be able to rent a house here some day." If he doesn't like it straight, I'll give it to him sideways, thought Craig. And I'm not going to waste time either. Once he finishes that cigarette, he'll rise, talk to the others and then drift off. "I saw two, with a fine view, up above the north end of the bay. They had trees, looked cool." He watched the small smile spreading under Elias' dark mustache. "Are they ever offered for rent?"

"One was rented this summer."

"Oh?"

"But very expensive, I hear."

"Well, you always have to pay for privacy."

Elias was studying him, head slightly held to one side, fine dark eyes gleaming in amusement. He only nodded.

"Which one?" Craig insisted. "Oh, of course I shan't do anything about it, this year. But some time in the future—"

"I wouldn't recommend it unless you like the sound of doves."

So, thought Craig, the house had a dovecote. "Noisy?"

"In the early morning—impossible. Unless you like to be wakened with the dawn, of course." He turned his head to see what had so quickly caught the American's attention. Down along the water front there was a group of visitors easily remarked by their fancy dress. The two young men—the bearded one was an English novelist, he had heard; the other, with the long shock of hair, was a French painter— wore yellow and red linen shorts, respectively. The three young women wore blue, green, and flaming pink: the American girl, Mimi, and Maritta Maas, in that order. At least the American girl had the taste to wear a dress in public. Oh, well, bright colors made one's job easier. Elias rose, paused with a frown as he noticed the baffled look on Craig's face. Trust Maritta, Craig was thinking as he stared at the blonde girl in the pink trousers, trust her to complicate his simple plan. How did he manage to talk to Mimi, now? How long, in any case, had she managed to be alone with Veronica before Maritta had joined them? Long enough to get any information about what was going on, up in that house on the hill? Something was wrong, somewhere. He usually could shake off his premonitions, but this one had stuck with him ever since the meeting with Veronica. It was raising its nagging little voice again, even as he watched the group sauntering nearer and nearer, listened to the talk and laughter beginning to invade the square.

Elias shrugged, sat down beside the other men, and observed as they did, with a mixture of amusement and irritation, the strange behavior patterns of those foreigners: the women wore trousers, the men wore little-boy clothes. If they came here saying that life was absurd, it was because they made it so. The only one he would worry about was the woman called Maas, but at present she seemed positively harmless in her gaiety and charm. She was giving the little boys some last-minute instructions as they halted to say good-bye. "Not a minute later than five o'clock," she called over her shoulder as she walked on toward the taxi. "We mustn't miss the sunset!" She halted to wait for the American girl in the blue dress whose hand was still held by the bearded Englishman. Ah, thought Elias, I can guess what is troubling Craig. He glanced at Craig's table, and was confounded.

For Craig had seized the chance when Maritta's back was turned to rise and wave to Mimi. The quick movement caught her eye. She stared across the wide square at the *taverna,* then walked slowly on. Craig stepped into the safety of the room behind him, called for his bill.

Most unorthodox, Elias thought, but even if crude it had produced the required result. Maritta Maas was now on her way to the taxi, looking over at the *taverna,* only seeing the group of five men around a table. The taxi driver was on his feet, pulling on his jacket, shouting that he was coming. Mimi was searching her handbag, exclaiming in dismay. She had left something—her sun-tan lotion—where? Had it fallen out in the café, or in a shop? The American girl was trying to remember.

Maritta Maas cut the discussion short. There was no time to go back to search, she was late, she had so much to do, there was only one taxi left, she couldn't risk losing it, and where was the other taxi anyway? (Ah, thought Elias, she would notice that; she would ask that question.) But the driver's answer was accepted. It had taken a sick man over to the monastery at Tourliani. It wouldn't be back for another hour, perhaps two. Mimi was insisting she had to have that lotion; she was starting to burn with the sun and sea air. There was no female argument against that, it seemed. Mimi set off toward a small street, Maritta calling directions to the nearest shop. And the American girl, who had been watching the battle of wills in silence, said very sharply, "Oh, stop being such an idiot, Maritta; she won't get lost. Why are you bossing everyone around nowadays?" That subdued Maritta completely. She got into the waiting car with only a small laugh of protest. They drove off.

Yes, thought Elias as he glanced with unexpected approval at Craig standing within the shadows of the doorway, the unorthodox maneuver had been very effective. But that was the way. . . . Sometimes you planned carefully, found nothing. Sometimes you acted on impulse, discovered much. The small scene in the square had revealed enough to rouse his curiosity. The Maas woman wanted everyone under her eye, her control. The Maas woman was in a very great hurry. The Maas woman was under considerable tension. Now, why? On a placid day like this, with no action yet expected, with only patient waiting ahead of them all, why should a well-trained agent like Maritta Maas have such seemingly small and stupid anxieties?

Quickly Elias spoke to one of the fishermen sitting beside him and sent him walking after Mimi. Then he rose, too, and joined Craig. "There's a lavatory near the kitchen, beside the back entrance. I'll meet you on the lane outside. In two minutes." He smiled and added, "That was interesting, wasn't it?" His good humor was completely restored.

Most interesting, Craig thought. Veronica is on the point of complete revolt. But why? He nodded and moved to the upholding arch which framed, inside the alcove it formed at the back of the room, shelves of bottles in neat rows. There was a counter, with glasses, in front of them; and the small boy watching water boil on a small stove to one side. This was the kitchen, Craig decided and pointed to the only door he saw. *"To meros?"* he asked and headed through. He found himself on a narrow street, an outhouse door built under the usual flight of stone stairs to the second floor. He slowed his pace, put on his sunglasses against the white glare, lit a cigarette, consulted his guidebook, stepped aside for a girl riding sidesaddle on a small mule, nodded to two old men holding up the side of a house, and put in the required two minutes without much trouble. "Just across the next street," Elias said behind him, and fell into step.

"Mimi?"

"I have arranged it."

That was all. But the tone was amicable, a return to yesterday's pleasant interchanges on the journey here. He has decided to forget my climb onto the hillside, Craig thought, and smiled. Greeks, he was discovering, might tolerate fools, but not gladly. And yet who had been foolish? he couldn't help wondering. Elias probably knew every inch of that hillside for a three-mile stretch on either side of the town. But had he forgotten how it might feel to be a stranger, dumped down in the middle of strange terrain, strange voices? Or does he think my job is over, now that I've placed Berg right here on Mykonos? In that case, he'll have to do some rethinking. I am in, for the duration. Whatever is going to happen, I'm staying in.

16

Mimi was sitting with her back to the window in the barely furnished room, watching the door as if she weren't quite sure whom to expect. The fisherman was standing near her, studying her with interest, from her slenderly tapered trouser legs to the hand she kept hidden inside her large bag. When she saw Elias and Craig, she relaxed. The hand slipped out of the bag, and she laughed for the fisherman, who was just about to leave. He grinned back, saluted her, and, with a few remarks for Elias, left.

"The language difficulty was extreme," Mimi said. "I was beginning to wonder if I had made a mistake."

"But surely he gave the password," Elias said.

Mimi nodded. "I was beginning to wonder if I had mistaken that, too. Pear tree. That is a very strange password."

"All the better," Elias said.

"Who chose it?" Craig asked, beginning to smile. "Partridge?"

Mimi shook her head. "He doesn't like it, either. No, he said some —joker in Paris chose it. Operation Pear Tree."

"An American joker, at that." I can hear Rosie's voice, thought Craig, and smiled widely.

"A password may seem foolish," Elias said severely, "but in this operation with so many foreigners working together, there are times when we must know quickly who is to be trusted. Such as that moment," he added for Mimi's benefit, "after you left the square." He went over to the window, stood carefully at its side, looked out. "Begin!" his back seemed to say to Craig.

Craig glanced at the view outside as he pulled a chair over to Mimi. He could see clear across the small bay to the yacht anchorage under its sheltering headland. This room—or, rather, this office, for there was nothing here but a couple of chairs, a wooden table and a telephone— must lie right over one of the arcades along the front street. At least he knew where he was. In his quick journey here, Elias had really bewildered him. A very cautious man, Elias. Craig sat down, and asked bluntly, "What's worrying Veronica?"

Elias stirred restlessly, frowned at the harbor. Surely it wasn't some personal matter that had brought Craig hurrying here? Sometimes Americans were really—then he was listening intently as Mimi began to talk. For her voice was urgent, serious.

"For the first few days after Veronica and Maritta got here, everything was normal. Very pleasant. Just the two girls alone in the house, and two servants."

Elias broke in, still watching the harbor. "They were brought especially from Paris, two weeks ago, well in advance. Does Miss Clark realize that?"

"No. She said they were the disagreeable type—nothing but glum silence. She was astonished that there were any servants at all just for Maritta and herself. But extra guests have appeared. Two men. One came three nights ago. The other came the following night. Friends of Uncle Peter. Maritta said it was most annoying, but what could she do—tell them to go away? Everyone wants a free bed on Mykonos. That is the trouble with renting a house."

"Plausible," agreed Craig. "But haven't they started arriving a little early?" He looked over at Elias.

Elias' lips tightened. Yes, it was early; too early. But something else annoyed him. "We have had expert observation on that house for almost a week. Two days ago, when extra food was ordered for this weekend, we checked. We had reports that friends of Miss Clark were expected for a short vacation."

"Friends of Veronica?" Craig exchanged a glance with Mimi.

"That is what the delivery men were told. So far, these visitors have not been seen. No one knows that they have arrived." He looked at Mimi almost angrily.

Mimi shrugged her shoulders as much as to say, "Well, it isn't my fault." Then she smiled gently. "They don't come into town. They seem to stay around the garden, in the shade of the trees or on the porch, which is well covered. And there is a wall around that garden. I know. I've tried to see inside, too, from a back window of my hotel. Quite useless."

Elias was still brooding bitterly about the unseen arrival of the two men. "They must have come from the north, from another part of the island. They did not arrive by Mykonos itself."

Craig nodded. Silent sympathy, not criticism, was what was needed at this point. Besides, remembering the map he had been studying, there were plenty of coves and inlets around the island's broken coast line. The small bay that formed the harbor of the town itself was really only part of a large desolate bay that stretched north far beyond the headland sheltering the yacht anchorage. That's one route, he thought, noticing Elias' face, that will be watched with extra care from here in.

Elias' anger was suppressed. But his voice was still acid with annoyance. "Miss Clark does not seem to be so stupid as the Maas woman judged. Yet did she not find it very strange that the two visitors made no effort to go out?"

"Yes. But Maritta said one had been ill, and the other did not care for too much sun."

"What do they talk about? What language do they use?"

"French, mostly, although they speak it with a foreign accent. But Veronica does not meet them much. Maritta has been taking her to lunch and dinner in town. In fact, Maritta always seemed to be with her in those last two days. This has irritated Veronica. Then last night, she was awakened by the doves. Something had disturbed them. She could see no one from her window, but she was sure she heard voices from the direction of the dovecote. She tried to warn Maritta, only—she could not leave her room. Its door was locked. And that made her angry, my friends."

"And that was why she decided to find a place in town," Craig said thoughtfully. He was pleased, too; Veronica was not the simple little fool that Maritta had taken her for. Thank God for that. The perpetual innocent was a compulsive loser. "Well, good for her! If she can get away with it," he added more soberly.

"She will never be allowed to leave," Elias cut in, "not at this critical stage of their plans."

"Did she tell Maritta at breakfast that she was going to look for a room?" Craig asked quickly.

218

"Yes. Maritta just laughed, rushed off to an appointment in town, said they could talk about that later. Veronica went for a walk in the garden to try to think what she should do: wait to discuss it with Maritta or go straight into town herself? And then, as she passed the dovecote, she noticed a great silence. And no movement. The doves had been taken away. She tried to go in, but one of the servants stopped her, said the doves were diseased and had to be removed." Mimi paused, watching Craig's face. Even Elias had turned around to stare at her. "Somehow, that troubled her." And I've troubled you, too, she thought, looking with surprise at the men's faces.

Craig was remembering the usual shape of a Mykonos dovecote: a square, squat tower with decorative ventilations on top and solid blank walls beneath. "Are they preparing to house a prisoner?" he asked softly. Elias only shrugged, pursed his lips. He turned back, grave-faced, to look out of the window. Craig said to Mimi, "So Veronica came right into town? And found that she wasn't alone, even then. That man in the striped shirt was keeping an eye on her, wasn't he?"

"Yes. She became really frightened then. But he did it so openly and seemed so ordinary that by the time we went to the café on the *quai* for lunch, she could even laugh at him. He didn't stay. He went to report, no doubt." Mimi was smiling. "Because, before we had finished lunch, Maritta arrived with Tony and Michel."

"The Beard and Flowing Locks?"

Mimi didn't quite follow, but she caught Craig's sharp tone. "But they are such nice boys," she murmured. "Really very sweet."

Boys . . . "They are older than you are, baby."

"They are children," she said gently. "Maritta is using them—as she has used Veronica. That is all."

"Have you anything on them?" he called over to Elias.

Elias shook his head. He stood very still, and then pointed to the sky. "There it goes!" he said softly.

Both Mimi and Craig rose to look. There were shouts from the street below. The fishermen, spreading russet nets to dry in the sun, were watching, too. "That's a very small plane," Craig began, and then stopped. Where could any aircraft land on this rocky island? "It's a helicopter!" he said, watching the nose-tipping black dot as it circled widely toward the northwest as if it were headed for Athens. "When did it get here? I heard nothing."

"It came in by the south," Elias said smoothly. "It landed about fifteen minutes ago near the monastery of Tourliani in the center of the island to pick up a man who is very sick—he needs an immediate operation. It took off for Athens at once. As you see." He turned away from the window. He said to Mimi, "I had some questions about the Maas woman, but I think you have already answered them. Except one: why was she in such haste to get back to her house? Why couldn't she wait five minutes, ten minutes, and give you a lift to your hotel? It is on her way."

"That," Mimi said firmly, "is my last piece of news. Are there any other questions before it? John—" For Craig was still watching the vanishing dot. He came away from the window, sat down again. Plenty of questions, he was thinking as he looked at Elias. Why Tourliani? He remembered his guidebook's photograph; a very small village, a few houses around a long, wide, and open square—good landing ground, certainly, and ten miles from nowhere. And once that helicopter is out of any telescope's sight, will it stop heading northwest and swing east? "You boys really amuse me," he told Elias with a wide grin. So Partridge was on his way to Smyrna.

"Boys?" picked up Mimi. "I thought you didn't like—"

"Boys in red and yellow shorts with shirts open to their navels. Okay, okay. They're sweet, bare feet and all." Then he relented: Mimi's English was almost perfect, but her sense of joshing was still undeveloped. He became serious again. "Did Veronica read her declaration of independence to Maritta over your lunch table? Did she say she was absolutely decided about finding a room of her own?"

"She tried. But Maritta's technique was brilliant. She was full of understanding. She started telling me, and Tony and Michel, what a miserable place her uncle's house had become with his friends—they were so dull and stupid. She said no wonder poor Veronica wanted to leave. She wanted to move out, too. Why, she couldn't give any more amusing parties, couldn't feel free to enjoy herself! She had become a housekeeper, worrying about their food and drinks and what they liked and did not like. She was going to ask them to leave. She had been cabling her Uncle Peter that morning, begging him to stop giving out invitations, she hadn't come to Mykonos as a housekeeper."

"You used that word twice. Did she?"

"She used it several times. She was implanting her reason, you see, for being in such a hurry to return to the house." Mimi smiled for

Elias. "There is your answer," she told him. "She was rushing home to arrange a very special dinner for them, tonight, in order to put them in a good mood when she asked them to leave tomorrow."

"Po, po, po!" Elias said. "Did she expect anyone to believe that? She will have to find a better excuse to cover her real business. She spent much time, this morning, in the house of Mr. Gerhard Ludwig."

"It was only half of her excuse," Mimi said. "The other half made it very plausible, indeed."

"And what was the rest of her excuse?"

"She is giving a party—on the island of Delos. Yes, she has already reserved the rooms at the tourist pavilion there—it is a simple place, so she will take food and extra blankets, and she is hiring a boat to take us across. All *we* have to worry about is our coats and toothbrushes. She is arranging everything. We sail at five o'clock." Mimi laughed softly. "And it is a heavenly idea. She made it so—so—inspired. She woke this morning, remembered it was May Day—a time for parties—saw the sea was calm, thought of Delos, imagined how peaceful it would be at night when all the tourists had gone, how wonderful the ruined temples would look under moonlight." Mimi looked at Elias with amused eyes. "Oh no, everyone believed she had much to arrange for us before five o'clock, except me, and I had to pretend to believe her more than anyone."

"Surely Veronica didn't forget all her fears so—" Craig began.

"I accepted for us both, before she could make any objections," said Mimi calmly. "*And* kicked her leg gently under the table."

"Is this wise?"

"I think it is very wise to follow Maritta's wishes."

Elias nodded. "So there are five of you going."

"Eight—that fills the little pavilion, doesn't it? There will be two of Tony's friends, whom Veronica likes. And you."

"Me?" Craig was incredulous. "That's the last thing that Maritta wants. She has done everything to keep me from talking to Veronica. No, Mimi, she isn't going to risk any confidences between Veronica and me."

"She is going to call your hotel and invite you herself."

"She doesn't know my hotel."

"How many are there in Mykonos? Five, six at the most. She can try them all in a few minutes."

Craig looked quickly at Elias. "She will, too," he said grimly. "Better give Madame Iphigenia instructions how to deal with that call."

"You are not going?" Elias asked as he moved slowly to the telephone on the table. He stood frowning at it, not touching it.

Mimi had risen and was on her way to the door. She had given all her news; it was time to leave. She halted, looking at Craig in wonder. "John—surely you can't refuse a night on Delos! Think—"

"I've thought of it," he said bitterly. Marble shimmering in the moonlight, a mile of ancient columns and temples, a silver sea around them. "An island all to ourselves. I can even set it to music."

Mimi shrugged. "I think it's wise to follow Maritta's wishes," she said again. "She does nothing without a purpose. Well—make up your mind. I'm leaving. The same way as I came in?" she asked Elias.

"Do you remember it?"

"I hope so. I spent a lot of energy memorizing it."

"And my congratulations," Elias said unexpectedly. "You have been most helpful."

"My thanks, too," Craig said, and gave her a warm smile. "You'd terrify Maritta if she knew how much you learned from Veronica in a couple of hours. That was one thing she never intended to happen."

Mimi laughed, delighted with both their words and that idea. "Oh, I knew how to steer the conversation, that was all. And Veronica needed to talk. But I would have learned much less, I think, if it had not been for you." Her dark gray eyes looked at Craig, and turned most serious. "I did tell one fib. I said I had known your sister when she lived in Paris, was devoted to her, so I felt I knew you well, too. And I thought you were someone Veronica could trust, quite apart from being two Americans in a foreign land. Then she said that she had wanted to speak to you, this morning, but—just couldn't; you might be embarrassed, you weren't really interested in her or her troubles. 'Tell me what they are,' I said. 'I'll talk with John Craig. He is a very casual type. But he will listen, I'm sure.' And that decided her. You had helped her once before, she said." Mimi's eyes were studying him thoughtfully. "Whatever you did, then, certainly had results this morning." She opened the door carefully, glanced out into the empty corridor. "All peaceful," she said softly. "How very nice . . ." She closed the door soundlessly behind her.

Elias was looking at the telephone again. "Do I call my aunt and tell her that you were only staying at the Triton for one night until you found a room to rent? That is quite usual, you know. Most people rent rooms; much cheaper. And there are so many hundreds of them, here on Mykonos, that even Maas might take a week to find you." He paused, then added casually, as if he had only just thought of it, "Of course, you could accept her invitation—meanwhile."

"Is that what you want me to do?" Craig asked bluntly.

"I am not in charge of you." Elias was slightly amused. "Certainly not for the last ten minutes or so." He glanced at his watch.

"But who else? Partridge is halfway to Smyrna." Craig was unexpectedly depressed about that fact. It left him feeling isolated, uncertain. "Who is the new man in charge here?"

"In charge of the Americans?" Elias' emphasis was polite but decided. "Why not Bannerman? I think our friend is now walking toward the Triton Hotel. He should have arrived in the taxi that returned from Tourliani some ten minutes ago."

"He stepped out of the helicopter as Partridge stepped on?" Craig found the vision amused him, even lightened part of his depression.

Elias nodded. His fingers touched the telephone. "Do I call the Triton and block that invitation?"

"I'll take your advice and keep Maritta happy."

"That is always the clever thing to do."

"Meanwhile," added Craig.

He had left Elias and taken a circuitous route back to the hotel. He needed the walk, he needed a fifteen-minute delay before he met Tim Bannerman. There were a number of things he had to sort out in his mind. Craig always found that his brain worked best if he brought himself right up against his problems, examined their variables, and then established the precedence of their importance. Nice comforting procrastinations, a general wait-and-see feeling, were not for him. On the one hand but on the other hand—no thank you. He liked to catch the facts by the scruff of their necks, pull them face up and have a good look at them, however unpleasant. And if he couldn't catch them all—for he was the amateur wading in very deep waters—he could at least see their shape if he thought hard enough about what he had actually glimpsed.

So . . .

The Smyrna area was Partridge's first concern. He had only visited

Mykonos to make sure that the situation had not been endangered by any information that might have been tortured out of Duclos. Even Insarov's arrival here had not shifted Partridge's concern. Rather, it had intensified it. It was clear warning that the climax was approaching. Hence the haste in which Partridge had returned to Smyrna. For that was where he intended this whole counteroperation to be completed successfully. It was in Smyrna that the dangerous rôle, played by one of his agents, could be safely ended along with the career of an American called Alex. From Smyrna, too, would come the instructions to pick up Insarov and all his friends.

The Mykonos area was therefore of secondary importance, so far. It was only a kind of safety net, carefully rigged to save Partridge's agent and catch Alex if the plans at Smyrna swung out of control.

But that was all from Partridge's point of view, thought Craig. From Insarov's? In his calculations, Mykonos was to be the successful climax of all this operation. He had geared everything to that. Therefore, any instructions followed by Maritta Maas were geared to that, too. Therefore, even such a small thing as this invitation to Delos was to be examined from every side. Nothing that Maritta was told to do could be considered as whim or charming fancy.

Maritta and this bright idea for a party . . . What had she said back in his hotel room in Paris about Delos? Yes, in Paris Maritta had already known about the small tourist pavilion on Delos. For emergencies, she had said. Emergencies. Were the emergencies on Delos tonight—or here on Mykonos? Certainly, Maritta had made sure her uncle's friends would have the house on the hillside, emptied dovecote and all, very much to themselves. She had also made sure that Veronica and the people she liked, the people to whom she might have talked, were all safely off this island. Tonight. And if these inferences seemed a little farfetched, he had only to remind himself that nothing Maritta did could be considered whim or fancy.

Yet, one thing puzzled him. He was remembering Paris again; this time Partridge talking to him about the man at his sister's party—the man called Alex—who was coming to Mykonos, where he would hand over to Maritta the information he had collected. (But now it seemed that the information to be delivered was the source itself—an abducted expert.) Maritta and Alex had worked together before. Therefore they could identify each other quickly, and Alex's delivery would be safely made with neither doubt nor delay. But that meant

Maritta had to be here when Alex arrived. She, alone, was Alex's contact. In that case, she would never have arranged to go to Delos if the *Stefanie* were expected tonight. Craig, he told himself sadly, you just got carried away in your deductions: a hell of a historian you'll make.

And then his thoughts leaped. If Alex was sailing on the *Stefanie,* why should he need anyone to identify him? Or why should he have to come here, at all, if the *Stefanie* brought in its prize? His job was over in Smyrna when he enticed that man aboard. Or wasn't it?

Craig smothered his rising excitement. Once more, he went over the facts he knew about Alex, few as they were. Yes, Alex was a courier, passing on information to a safe contact whom he definitely knew. Now what was it Partridge had said in the Triton's little garden? Something—oh dammit, it was a phrase, a simple but revealing phrase. About Alex and his duties. No, it had slipped to the back of Craig's mind, was hovering there, tantalizing, elusive. Relax; don't strain it, he told himself. If the phrase was important, it would turn up in its own good time.

He headed for the little street where the Triton stood. There were a lot of people around now. Shops had opened again. Trade was brisk. Life was normal. "I tell you," one white-haired Englishwoman was saying to her exhausted friend, as Craig stood aside to let them pass, "there *are* three hundred and sixty-five churches, and we've only found two hundred and ninety-three."

Madame Iphigenia was at her post in the Triton's small lobby. "There was a telephone call," she announced. "A woman's voice."

"Did she leave any number?"

"She refused to give it," Madame Iphigenia said with annoyance.

Then that was Maritta. "She will call again. I'll be in my room."

"We change your room." Madame had dropped her voice to a conspiratorial whisper. "My nephew Elias advises that. It has not such a pleasant view, but no one knows you are now there except myself and one maid. My nephew also advises you leave most of your luggage in your old room. Come. I show you."

"Just let me get my toothbrush."

"It is already provided."

"Well, just let me get my camera. Right?"

So they made the quick and familiar journey, and he managed to get

Partridge's automatic safely into his pocket in a matter of seconds while Madame Iphigenia played watchdog at the door. He changed into a fresh shirt, picked up his raincoat and a sweater for tonight's journey. It would be a cool trip across the strait to Delos. He almost forgot razor and toothbrush. A man spending a night on Delos would certainly take these. Now let anyone check on this place, he thought, as he slipped them into his coat pocket.

"You remember this way?" Madame whispered as she led him along a twisting corridor. Indeed, he did. That morning, it had been part of their tour of inspection. The rooms were unused in this wing of the house, under change and construction for the summer season. "I am sorry," she said with real anguish as she showed him into his new quarters, still smelling of paint. "The workmen will not be back until Monday. No one comes up here. It is all right?"

"It's very much all right. Thank you for helping me. What did Elias expect?" A secret search, or some unexpected visit?

She hesitated. "I do not know what this trouble is. I do know my nephew." And with that, she left him. As she disappeared around a corner, he heard a distant voice calling her back to the front desk. He dumped his coat, camera and sweater, and after a last glance at the makeshift arrangements he made his way down by the back stairs to the enclosed garden. It would be better that he be found easily when that telephone call came for him. There was also the matter of Bannerman.

The telephone call came first. "I thought I wasn't going to find you," Maritta began.

"And I've been looking for you all day."

"Have you heard about my party on Delos?"

"Are you turning archaeologist?"

"No, no. It's a moonlight party. Tonight. Will you come?"

"Yes. But how? Do we swim?"

"Five o'clock at the harbor. Bring a coat. And a bright smile."

"When do we get back?"

"Oh, we'll stay overnight. There are eight of us. Veronica included. I'm glad you accepted before you heard she was coming."

"There's only one thing. I'm expecting some of my friends from Athens to arrive tomorrow evening."

"Oh, we'll be back before that. I've arranged for our boat to pick us up at three tomorrow. It's only an hour's journey from Delos."

"Weather permitting."

"We are in luck, I think. The water has scarcely one ripple. At five o'clock, then?"

"At five. Coat, smile and camera."

"Tomorrow morning you can take some heavenly pictures by the dawn's early light." She laughed, rang off.

He replaced the receiver, stood frowning down at it. He had managed that all right, but he felt no sense of achievement. Without Partridge's warnings, he thought, where would I have been with a girl like that? Neatly wrapped up in a package labeled *Fool*. I wouldn't have been the first, and certainly not the last. And she could fool me yet, he thought somberly.

Madame Iphigenia cleared her throat tactfully. He swung out of his thoughts, looked up and saw Bannerman, as natty a tourist as ever dawdled along the cafés on the water front. Faded red shorts and a pink linen shirt, no less. Behind him, the silent young assistant manager was absolutely slain with admiration.

"Hello, John!" Bannerman said. "Told you I'd join you for some *bouzoukia*. Found any places, yet, where they haven't heard of 'Never on Sunday'?"

So we continue Athens, thought Craig, and gave a smile of relief. "How's Clothilde? And the Mortimers? Still in Athens?"

"They'll be here this weekend. Clothilde really means to arrive in a caïque. She always seems to find one that hauls coal. So I backed out of that. What about a drink?"

"Fine. I'm on my way to Delos at five, so we'll have one for the road."

"Any room for me on that trip?" Bannerman asked with a grin as he clattered downstairs to the dining room and bar.

"Not unless you like sleeping on the cold hard ground."

The silent young man was on their heels, ready to see that they were served, no doubt. He took their order, relayed it to the kitchen, busied himself in the dining room as they went into the small garden. "Hell," Bannerman said softly. But he didn't have to worry long about continuing their light conversation, for Madame's stern voice sent her assistant back upstairs to take charge of the desk, and they were free to talk.

"Partridge thought he was just curious," Craig said quietly as the young man left the dining room with a last backward glance.

"Well, people are innocent until they give cause for suspicion. Can't go around thinking everyone is part of a nasty plot," Bannerman said lightly. "But that little guy isn't local. Elias has been checking. He came in as a replacement only three days ago—from Athens. Highly recommended. Madame Iphigenia is about to blow a fuse. She's kept him so busy running errands all day that he's worn out. Didn't even have the energy, or time, to check on your luggage." Bannerman's broad smile was reassuring. "They've planted an eye in every hotel, of course, just in case someone recognizable—like Rosie —suddenly turned up as Mr. Smith." He studied Craig's face. "Nothing to worry about. Elias has good eyes of his own."

Madame Iphigenia was making sure of that. She had installed herself in the dining room and was checking linen and silver.

"Both houses are being watched?" Craig was still uneasy. There had been a slip-up three nights ago, when Maritta's guests began arriving. But that, of course, had been before Elias had appeared.

"Closely. He has men on the square next door as well as up on the hillside, too. Believe me—"

"I do." Craig had to smile. Now he could see why Elias had taken such a dim view of his own stroll up there today.

"He has a man up on the headland above the yacht anchorage, just to see what's sailing in from the north. He has a man in touch with the harbor master who checks every vessel in and out. He has even made sure that the launch taking you to Delos is manned by the usual local men. You can leave all the details dealing with geography to Elias. He knows how."

"And what's your job?" Craig asked, some of his anxiety leaving him. "Looking after me?"

"And myself, and a couple of other Americans who are wandering around looking like poet and painter. Also, we are keeping our own lines of communication open. Co-operation doesn't go as far as letting the other fellow handle your own particular business." Bannerman grinned cheerfully. "The English have sent at least one man here, too. They have a certain interest." He sounded vague about that. "Then the French—well, they'll be breathing hard on Elias' neck."

"I take it, when you didn't mention him, that there is no word of Duclos?"

"None." Bannerman watched Craig's face. Quietly, he added,

"That's the second good man the French have lost in this operation. The first was in Paris on the morning you arrived there—they killed him to protect Alex, we think. Yes, you could say that the French are hopping mad. They won't let one escape, you can be sure of that. So ease up."

"Alex—" began Craig, and stopped. Suddenly the lost phrase had decided to stop playing coy and came right to the front of Craig's mind. "Extension of his duties," Partridge had said, talking of Alex and the attempt at abduction. Yes, an extension of his duties . . . And there was something else too: Alex's special mission had been an "additional assignment."

"Come on now. Share that one," Bannerman said with amusement.

"Haven't thought it out yet," Craig admitted. "It may mean nothing. He's a careful, supercautious man, isn't he?"

"Alex? As cagey as they come."

In that case, would he arrive here on the *Stefanie?* Craig's mind was racing now. "Suppose he had his usual job to do, as well. Wouldn't that explain why he had to come to Mykonos at all? Otherwise—why should he endanger himself by appearing here? The additional assignment—" Craig paused to make sure that Bannerman had caught his meaning—"was completed when he trapped our expert. Or a reasonable facsimile thereof."

"Go on."

"He would probably balk at traveling in the same yacht as the man he helped to capture, wouldn't he? He might be the type who would complete his special assignment, and then want to forget he had anything to do with it. The supercautious wash their hands of everything as quickly as possible."

"They do." A small smile glimmered at the back of Bannerman's intelligent eyes. "And I'm not stealing any of your thunder if I tell you we had some similar thoughts. Why else did we want you on Mykonos? But there's one thing—we don't intend to let that son of a bitch get out of Turkey. That's why Partridge is there." He looked at his watch. "He's there, all right."

Craig was silent.

"Now what?" Bannerman asked sharply. "Do you agree with Elias?"

"Elias? I wouldn't know. I keep trying to guess what Elias is thinking and come up with the wrong answers."

"You froze when I mentioned Partridge and Smyrna. Why?" As Craig still hesitated, Bannerman added with one of his old friendly smiles, "I really want to hear what you think, John. Come on, give!"

"Well—" He decided to risk it. "I feel that the kidnapping may be completed. Partridge could have reached Smyrna too late to prevent it." He hesitated, but Bannerman was listening seriously, waiting for Craig's reasons, face and eyes now intent. Craig said, "There has been too much happening under the surface today, too many preparations right here on Mykonos. That house on the hill is ready and waiting. Maritta spent the morning at the Gerhard Ludwig place in town—so Elias' men reported. She wouldn't go there except under orders, and they wouldn't be given her unless something important had developed. So important that it was time to give her final and detailed instructions? They're so confident of success that they may actually know they have succeeded." He hesitated, decided he had said more than enough. "And that—for what it's worth—is how I see it. I hope I'm wrong."

"Elias didn't discuss this with you?"

"No."

"Two separate opinions," Bannerman said slowly, thoughtfully. And from two very different points of view. Both added up to the same thing. Mimi's report on the Clark girl had turned out to be a depth charge. "If Elias and you are right, we have real trouble ahead." But he did not sound overpessimistic at the prospect. Perhaps he enjoyed the idea that, instead of being assigned to a place of secondary importance, he had stepped right into the critical area. He tried to check his rising excitement. "*If* you are right," he repeated. "Poor old Partridge," he added with some real sympathy, "he will be even madder than the French." Strange how things break, he thought; Partridge has worked for four solid months, day and night, on the Berg-Insarov puzzle. "This is really his show, you know. We wouldn't be here, any of us, if he hadn't seen one small glimmer of light in a purposely thick fog."

"Operation Pear Tree," Craig said. He was feeling slightly better now that Elias was expecting anything to happen, any time. At least, he thought, we won't come in for a landing with the wheels up.

"Did he tell you?" Bannerman asked in surprise.

"No. Mimi dropped the word. It's puzzling our allies, I think."

"Then it should puzzle the opposition still more. I don't expect many of them know 'The Twelve Days of Christmas.' Do you remember the tune? Good. When you've got something to tell me, or vice versa, and there's a crowd around or something, whistle a few bars, will you? Keep it just for emergencies." He rose, clapped Craig on the shoulder. "I may come to wave you off to Delos. We'll see. . . ." He raised his voice to normal as he reached the dining room. "I'll wire Clothilde in Athens and tell her that the Triton is keeping a couple of rooms for her and the Mortimers."

"When do they get here?" Craig called back. "I was thinking they'd arrive tomorrow evening."

"Sunday. Perhaps even Monday. They may find themselves unloading coal or sugar all around the Aegean. Clothilde has a special knack of picking the slowest caïque." Bannerman, taking the steps two at a time, clattered his way up into the lobby. Madame Iphigenia had reached it just ahead of him: she knew when to take her cue. The very correct and silent young man was at the desk. He was a little flustered, as if he had just made it there before Madame had started up the staircase. "I have a wire to send to Athens," Bannerman confided earnestly. "How do I go about it?" There wasn't even a small smile showing on his face.

"Markos will translate it for you and send it," Madame said, staring fixedly at her assistant. She looked exactly like that statue on the main square, as if she were facing the Turkish fleet, her chin out, jaw set, eyes steeled, and a two-thousand-year-old Greek curse right there on her lips.

17

It was almost five o'clock, and the strong western sun shone straight into the harbor of Mykonos. Even as Craig walked along the water front, raincoat over his shoulder, sweater and camera case in one hand, he could easily distinguish the launch Maritta had hired from the other boats moored all along the wharf. It was the one with the crowd of people around it. Either the party had grown or the send-off was to be an event. Strange how the news had spread—there must be at least thirty of Mykonos' younger set grouped together on the break-water. Or quay. Or jetty. Or mole. Or wharf. He never could make up his mind what to call it. It served all these purposes. It was a bulwark of heavy stones rising less than five feet above sea level, with a flat top of cement, twelve feet or so wide, on which crates and sacks and men and mules could all find space. On its left was the open sea, if not wine-colored in the evening glow then certainly dark blue tinged with cop-per, and a protecting waist-high wall to discourage the spray. On its right was the still water of the harbor, and an array of small craft roped to their moorings on the wharf.

He passed two caïques still unloading crates of fruit and boxes of soft drinks, several fishing boats now being scoured clean, rowing boats, another caïque, and reached the crowd—a merry one, as he had guessed by the drift of voices over the calm water. French, Eng-lish, American. No wonder the German, Swedish and Dutch tourists had looked a little sourly at the breakwater from their café tables under the arcades. It was a fine evening for a sail across a few miles of rippling sea to Delos. And this *was* a wonderful idea for a party, he thought as his eyes looked over the bronzed faces and bright clothes for someone he could recognize; if only, he added to that, Maritta had not been instructed to invent it. For a moment he envied all these innocents, hooting and hollering around, who took it at face value.

And there was Veronica. With Tony and Michel in attendance. They were grouped in front of the launch. He hoped she wasn't looking so relaxed and happy because of them. They couldn't be as witty as all that, dammit, he thought as he heard her laugh.

"Yes, she's beautiful," Mimi's voice said at his elbow. She pulled him gently over to the sea wall, with a smile of apology to three girls with swinging hair and pink-white lips who were just about to surround him. "They want to go, too," she murmured. "You looked a very pleasing prospect." She leaned against the wall, stared out to the open sea, and pointed to a far-off island. "Maritta is not coming," she said softly.

He studied the island.

"The blankets and food arrived with one of the servants in charge. Don't look around, John! He's standing over at the other side of the mole. The caïque is just behind him."

"Checking us on board?" He forced a smile, tried to look as if they were talking about something pleasant. He swung himself up to sit on the wall, which let him have a quick glance at the man standing by the edge of the quay. Thin expressionless face, watchful eyes. From where he stood, he could keep easy count of everyone who stepped on board the launch. "What excuse did Maritta send? I bet it was a beauty."

Mimi nodded. "Better get the details from Veronica. We've been talking long enough together. I'll start making the rounds—just the girl who wants to meet everyone. One thing: I told her I had let you know about her problems. I said you would help her. I had to, John! Why else did I listen to her this morning if I was not going to tell you? That was my story, remember!" She looked toward the north and pointed again. "Look! Fishing boats! Where did *they* come from?" She was including two young Frenchmen in her question. Craig jumped down and left them speculating about their cameras. The tantalizations of photography (it sounded all right in French) were the perfect pictures always presented when the light was too yellow, the sun too glaring and direct.

Craig moved through the crowd, and then halted, avoiding the interested glance of one of the girls with the pink-white lips so very pale against her tanned skin. He stood for an agonizing minute, looking toward the north headland, staring at the three red fishing boats and the cabin cruiser that was following them in to the smooth waters of the harbor. Then his mind began to work. He calculated quickly and waited. His timing must be exact. The cruiser was drawing toward the yacht anchorage. The three boats were gliding around to find a space somewhere along the quay, their sails now flapping idly. Okay, he told himself, okay. He walked straight over to Veronica.

"Hello!" he said with a wide smile. "And when do we shove off?" He gave Tony and Michel a friendly nod.

"Five o'clock always means five-thirty in this part of the world," Michel announced. "That is one of its charms."

"We seem to have some extra company," Craig said, looking at two men with sleeping bags and a girl carrying a blanket.

"Why, it's Josie!" Michel exclaimed, and turned to welcome her.

Craig looked at Veronica. "What's this I hear about Maritta?"

Tony said, "One of those impossible guests fell down some stairs and broke his leg. Maritta is staying with him until the doctor arrives. Really bad luck."

"Yes. Pity he didn't break his neck."

Tony laughed before he looked shocked. Then laughed again.

"Don't you think someone should start loading people onto the boat? It would be a pity to miss the sunset on Delos."

"But they all want to come," Tony said in mock despair.

"Then let them. They can sail over there and back, anyway. The launch will hold about thirty, tightly packed. In this sea there's no danger." The launch was an odd contraption, definitely one of those mad Greek inventions, with a flat-topped hatch rising out of the deck and taking up most of it. On either side of this protuberance there were long shelves, acting as benches, facing out to sea, backed by ropes for the seated to grasp. The railing in front of their legs was another lightly strung rope. The captain and his mate were aft, along with a high smell of kerosene. Their smiles were cheerful.

"It can take forty, even in a storm," Tony told him, in the tone of an old-timer. "Never lost a passenger yet. It bobs like a cork, even up the highest wave."

"That must be fun," Craig observed and half turned from Tony, edging him out. "And when did the broken leg take place?"

Veronica's smile widened as Tony drifted away to start organizing. "He will never manage it under twenty minutes," she warned Craig.

"That's a pity. I was counting on ten." He was watching the three fishing boats. Soon they would be very close, blotting this part of the quay from any watcher on the hillside. If Maritta or her friends had a telescope trained on the launch, their view was about to be ruined. Perhaps permanently. The three boats, barely fifteen feet long, had stopped moving. It looked as if they were waiting for the launch to leave and give them space to tie up. There was a good deal of raucous shouting, anyway, between its captain and the fishermen.

Veronica studied his face. She said, "It really was an accident. I saw it. But his leg isn't broken. Only a twisted ankle, I think. He complained a lot, though."

"And it happened just before you left?"

"Why, yes."

"Veronica," he asked quickly, "will you help me?" He looked deep into her blue eyes. "I mean that. Will you?"

"Of course," she said slowly, trying to hide her growing astonishment. But I thought I was the one who needed help. Is he in some kind of trouble, too? "What's wrong?"

"Trust me. Please! And cover up for me, will you? I'm not going to Delos."

The soft smile was wiped off her face.

"No, no," he said urgently, "keep smiling as we talk. Please. The monster is watching us."

Her eyes flickered over toward the man Maritta had sent. He was staring at her, in that grim and sullen way which she disliked so much. She forced a smile as she looked back at Craig. "I won't notice your absence until we reach Delos. And then I'll laugh it off. Is that what you want?"

"Yes. Say that I probably stayed behind to keep Maritta company, cheer her up."

She dropped her eyes. She was half believing that herself. Her smile vanished.

He grasped her hands. "Please!" he said again.

She nodded.

His grip on her hands tightened. "That's my girl," he said softly as he released her. She looked at him, wide-eyed. If the monster hadn't been watching them, he would have kissed her, right there and then.

Instead, he backed away, seemingly still continuing their conversation. "I'll give Tony a hand," he called to her. "It's time we were leaving. Save a seat for me!" He kept on backing to the edge of the quay, then turned very quickly as he reached the haggard-faced man, bumping heavily into him, saying "Sorry!" as his hands went out as if to save the man from toppling back into the water. He seemed to lose his own balance. His shoulder crashed against the swaying figure. The man fell, too astonished to shout, and landed with a splash between the launch's stern and the high prow of the caïque.

There were screams, yells, and a rush of excitement. "Throw a life preserver!" Craig told Tony. "I'll get a small boat to pick him up." He left, making his way through the jam of people. The shouts had given way to laughter, loud advice, raucous comment. There was a mixed stream of Mykoniots and visitors beginning to run up the quay. Craig bundled his coat tightly around the camera case, looked for the likeliest small boy. He found one, trying to edge his way into the steadily growing crowd.

Craig caught his arm gently, smiled, bent down to reach the right eye level, held out thirty drachmas (a round dollar in any man's money) and offered the bundle. "Triton," he said, pointing to the bundle, then back over his shoulder in the direction of the town. "Triton?" The boy nodded. He was about eleven or twelve years old, large brown eyes in a thin intelligent face. Craig tapped the bundle again. "Triton. Madame Iphigenia." No, that was the wrong word. "Kiria Iphigenia. Triton."

I know, I know, the boy's eyes seemed to say impatiently. He took the thirty drachmas, tucked the bundle under his arm, looked in the direction of the excitement around the launch. A cheer was being raised.

"It's all over," Craig said. "Get going, buster!" He gestured down the jetty, quietly, urgently. The boy folded the bill safely into his pocket. He tapped his narrow chest. "Petros," he told Craig solemnly. Craig shook hands formally. That seemed to seal the bargain.

"Triton. Kiria Iphigenia," the boy assured him, as if he were addressing a very small child.

Craig nodded, put a finger briefly up to his lips. Let's hope, he thought, that the gesture translates itself properly into Greek.

It must have. The boy's eyes opened wide, bright with a new excitement. He grinned widely, tapped the side of his nose, pushed his way through the fringes of the crowd, headed for town.

Craig straightened his legs, pulling on his sweater. It was too hot for this time of evening, but its dark blue color disguised the striped shirt he had worn for the trip to Delos. Now all he had to do was to find a straggle of tourists. He chose a clump of people, fishermen and visitors combined, and filtered into its center. The trek along the breakwater became short and simple. Alone, he would have felt every step under sharp-eyed scrutiny from either the front-street arcades or the house on the hillside. He kept his head down, his hands in his pockets, and stayed with the crowd.

Far behind him, now, he heard the launch let off a high tenor blast. He didn't look around, kept on walking, and was still in the shelter of the group as he reached real land. He passed three fishermen leaning against the wall of a chapel as he made the sharp left turn into the front street. He was almost certain that the youngest was the man Elias had sent chasing after Mimi, today, but he had only time for one quick glance and one returned stare. He walked on nonchalantly, chose the first café he saw, and slipped out of the cluster of tourists to find a small table at the very back of its deep awning. The trouble was that those Greeks, to foreign eyes, seemed very much alike, with their grave faces and dark hair and heavy mustaches. The fishermen had noticed him certainly. If he was Elias' man, then all Craig had to do was to sit here and get some thoughts back into order. Also, he'd like to watch a little.

He edged his chair around just enough to let him have clear sight past the screen of men at the front-row tables. Now he had a good but protected view of the long breakwater. To his surprise and pleasure, the launch had already moved away from its moorings. Quick work after all, he thought gratefully. Tony must have got them all on board in record time once the man was pulled out of the harbor. There was a small close group on the deck of the caïque, as if that was where he had been deposited. No doubt they were getting him to cough up a surfeit of water, and telling him never to stand again at the edge of a wharf crowded with young maniacs. Certainly there was no sight of the man on the jetty itself. It was rapidly emptying, returning to its usual placid routine.

Craig watched the launch move into the harbor, sweep around

widely to port, pass the end of the breakwater and out to sea. It gave three short and cheerful blasts of farewell. In a similar mood, he ordered ouzo and coffee. Well, there I go, he thought, bound for Delos. Not even the waterlogged man in the dark suit, now climbing onto the jetty from the deck of the caïque, would guess otherwise.

It was forty minutes later, almost six o'clock, before Bannerman strolled in. He looked around the few tables that were occupied—this was a fisherman's haunt; later in the evening it would be crowded with them—and said, "You've got good taste in cafés." He sat down facing Craig, his back turned to the street.

"It was the first place I could duck into and stay out of sight."

"Sorry I missed the fun on the dock. But there was an emergency. I came here as soon as possible."

Judging from Bannerman's face, his news was bad. Craig said, "Well I'm glad our communications system is working, anyway. That was Elias' man I saw?"

Bannerman nodded. "What made you bug out?"

"Because Maritta did."

"Oh!" said Bannerman, a new light dawning. Quickly he asked, "And they think you've left?"

"I tried raising a little fuss, enough to cover my retreat back into town, I hope."

"I heard about that." Bannerman almost smiled. "Veronica Clark was a great help, too. Got them on board and the launch moving before anyone could count who was sailing. What did you tell her?"

Craig was still staring. Veronica had done that?

"What did you tell her to get her co-operation?"

"Nothing. Just that I wasn't going. Just that I needed her to cover for me. That's all."

"She certainly did." Bannerman sounded relieved. "Didn't waste a second. Good girl. If I felt in a better mood, I'd be laughing out loud." He leaned both elbows on the table, cupped his chin in his hands so that his lips were guarded. "Bad news from Smyrna. You and Elias guessed right."

Craig bent his head over his cup of coffee, studying the heavy mass of thick muddy grounds. "They got our man?"

"This morning."

This morning, thought Craig in dismay. If only I had known where to report, last night, that Heinrich Berg was walking through Mykonos—if only I had tried to get hold of Elias—if only I had telephoned Bannerman in Athens. There would have been time to warn Smyrna, to have all precautions doubled. But I didn't think, I didn't know what was at stake. There I was, imagining that I was becoming ridiculous, taking too many precautions, having too many suspicions. And the truth was I didn't have enough. He remembered Rosie telling him that the smallest things could be of the greatest importance. . . . Do we always have to remember, too late? he wondered. "If only," he said, "I had got in touch with you last night."

"You didn't know—" began Bannerman.

"I didn't have to know. I ought to have reported one small fact, and let others do the evaluating."

"Look—it's over. Over, and nothing can change it. Stop those 'if only's.' Don't you think we each carry a pack of them around on our breaking backs?"

"Okay." Craig drew a deep breath. "So they got him this morning."

"And the news wasn't known until late this afternoon. They used timing as part of their plan. It's always a winner."

"Who was he?"

"A volunteer. Only three people know his name, and I'm not one of them. There was a fourth, but he's dead." Bannerman's lips tightened as he thought of Duclos. Yes, only three now: Rosie, the Englishman Christopher Holland, and Partridge. "The fewer the better, of course. Or else Insarov might have learned he was abducting someone who didn't know one thing about microphones and similar gadgets."

"Then he won't get much out of your man."

"Nothing that is of any use to him. I suppose we could say that's one success we had," Bannerman said gloomily.

And a grim one, thought Craig. "What now?"

Bannerman dropped his hands, looked casually over his shoulder, glanced at the breakwater, surveyed the water front. "I'd like you to keep out of sight, until it's worth while showing yourself. Never spoil a surprise." Only the front-row tables had their groups of men so far, all friends, all knowing each other. That was a safeguard in itself. No unaccountable fisherman, no inquisitive tourist. "We're out of the main drag here. We might as well relax and have some coffee."

"We could move inside—it's empty. Or is that more noticeable than sitting here like two normal people?"

Bannerman nodded. "Besides, I want you to keep your eyes on the breakwater. I'll watch the street. I don't think pretty little Maritta stayed home from Delos just to play pinochle with her abominable house guests. What excuse did she give?" He signed to the waiter for coffee and angled his chair to look along the water front.

Craig told him and raised the first smile of the evening. "Maritta as Florence Nightingale," Bannerman said. "So far, there have been no reports that any doctor was sent for. But you didn't expect that, did you?" He shook his head. "What *will* she think up next?"

"That's what I'm waiting to see. If she weren't so dangerous, she'd be my choice for Comedy Queen."

The coffee came, and Bannerman began giving the rest of his news. "The yacht *Stefanie* never entered Turkish waters," he said quietly, his left hand holding a cigarette close to his lips. "Nor did she visit Chios, which is the Greek island nearest Smyrna—there's even a small ferryboat that runs between Chios and Smyrna. So Chios seemed the logical place, but it wasn't planned that way. Instead, she docked at the island of Samos, farther to the south."

"That's the closest Greek island to the Turkish coast. It's less than two miles across the strait, there."

"You know your geography."

Craig smiled. "Blame it on history. The ruins of Ephesus are near that strait."

"Yes," said Bannerman very softly, "and Ephesus is just about fifty miles south from Smyrna. . . . Get it?"

So that was the route of operation: Smyrna, to Ephesus, to the coast, to Samos. And the *Stefanie*. "Alex made up a party for Ephesus," Craig said thoughtfully. Clever bastard . . . It was a popular trip; anyone visiting Smyrna usually made it. He had been warned, back in New York, that if he ever went there he could expect busloads of tourists from the cruise ships docking at Smyrna. A man could easily go unnoticed in a polyglot crowd surrounded by miles of ruins. Ephesus was big. And yet— "Surely," Craig added irritably, "our man was being guarded?"

Bannerman nodded. "There was one of our agents with him constantly—pretended he was some kind of assistant and close friend.

We couldn't have a phalanx of guards around the pseudo expert; that would have looked too obvious, as if we were expecting trouble. We had plenty of checks on his movements around Smyrna, though. He had his instructions to stay there. He should never have accepted the idea for a jaunt to Ephesus—I don't know what got into him." Bannerman sighed deeply, frowning. "Seven people made up that party. Two cars. That was the way the kidnapping was worked."

"How?" pressed Craig. He could scarcely believe that two trained and experienced men could have been so easily trapped.

"The group scattered, spent a couple of hours wandering around Ephesus. They planned to meet at the cars at a fixed time—they were returning to Smyrna for lunch. But one of the cars drove off just ahead of the other. Those who gathered at the second car found they were two short—the 'expert' and his assistant—but assumed they had got tired waiting and taken the first car."

"And those in the first car took it for granted that the two men were returning in the second car?"

"So they say."

"But if they reached Smyrna by one o'clock or so, why didn't Partridge get the news here before he left? Someone must have been dragging his feet."

Bannerman shook his head. "The first car decided to make a detour, visit a nomad encampment." He looked at Craig. "Ever seen one? The Turks keep them well outside their towns. Black leather tents, beehive shape. Camels. Slit-eyed people. Straight Genghis Khan. Sounds good, doesn't it? Good enough to keep that first car from returning to Smyrna until almost five o'clock this afternoon. Some detour."

And only then would the disappearance have been discovered. Clever Alex. "By that time, the *Stefanie* had left Samos?"

"She left at three."

"Which means she could arrive here any time tonight," Craig said softly.

Bannerman said nothing. He was a worried man.

"At least," Craig added, "you've got Alex. He's stuck in Smyrna until everyone is questioned, and he won't have much choice in his answers, either. Which car was he in? The first, I bet."

There was a strange expression on Bannerman's face.

"Don't tell me that both Wilshot and Bradley went on that trip to Ephesus!"

Bannerman glanced up quickly. "Who gave you the names?" he asked sharply. "Partridge?"

"As a kind of afterthought this morning."

"Just as well," Bannerman said, alarm giving way to relief. Now he could talk more freely. If Craig knew as much as this, he could help. Every ounce of assistance was needed. "The situation is becoming high emergency," he admitted.

"Alex—"

"He backed out of the trip to Ephesus early this morning."

"*Both* Bradley and Wilshot backed out?"

"Both. They had a chance of a free ride on a plane to Rhodes today. They took it. Begged off Ephesus."

"They seem to be pretty close friends."

"They've become quite good friends in this last week. They reached Rhodes around nine this morning. We checked. They left before ten o'clock, hitching another ride—this time on one of those twin-diesel yachts that would give them a cruise through the Aegean en route to Athens. Bradley's leave is just about up; he is heading back to Paris. We know that. Wilshot's articles on the Turks' new attitude toward America, because of this damned Cyprus trouble, are completed. Everyone knows that, too. So everything seems perfectly regular. Even the hitchhiking. Anyone who visits this part of the world is always on the lookout for a free ride so he can see as much as possible. Just tell him he can sail with you here, or there, and his eyes start glinting. Have you noticed?"

Craig nodded. He was still thinking of Alex. Careful and cautious, Partridge had called him. "Who actually arranged that trip to Ephesus?"

"It was dreamed up, yesterday evening, at a cocktail party in Smyrna given by Bradley and Wilshot. It seemed one of those spontaneous-combustion ideas that come with the fourth Martini."

"Who first suggested it?"

"That's being investigated right now, you can bet all your traveler's checks. But does anyone remember exactly who said what and how and when at a cocktail party?" Bannerman smiled sourly. "Yes, even that was calculated."

They were silent for a full minute. Then Craig said, still puzzled, "That agent of yours—the one who was keeping an eye on your expert—did he sell out, you think?"

"No. Not he. I've worked with him."

"But how—"

"They'd deal with him first. Probably he is lying behind some ruined temple, his skull smashed in with a chunk of marble." He fell silent again, his face cold and expressionless. "Three men dead, one captured for interrogation. The cost comes high." He looked at Craig. "It may come higher. You could bow out now and no one would blame you."

"There's a matter of identifying Alex."

"Yes, I admit I'd like your help with that. I know both Wilshot and Bradley from their photographs. Never met them. And there's two of them."

"They'll come ashore together?"

"That's my guess. Alex will make sure of a cover to the very end. They'll separate, of course, when Alex is really getting down to business."

"I'll take one, you take the other. How's that?"

There was a broad smile on Bannerman's face. "Perfect."

"When do you expect them?"

"Any time, frankly."

"And meanwhile, I just keep looking across the harbor?" Craig asked, and did. "So far, no twin-diesel job is anywhere on the horizon. There's that cabin cruiser over at the anchorage, of course. It's scarcely powerful enough, though, to get from Rhodes to here by five o'clock."

"The harbor master reports it came from Delos. Before that, Tinos. Wrong direction for Rhodes, anyway. It plans to spend the weekend at Mykonos. Two men and a woman. That's the crew."

"Two men?" Craig was still hanging on to his doubts.

"Look—" Bannerman raised an eyebrow. "Elias phoned Delos, and that cabin cruiser *was* there."

And did a more powerful boat, arriving from Rhodes, touch in at Delos just before the cabin cruiser left? Craig looked at Bannerman, one of the nicest guys he had met in a long, long time, and wished Partridge were here. "I believe you. It was there all right. But damned if I wouldn't find some excuse for a visit over to that anchorage except that—" He shrugged in a good imitation of Elias.

Bannerman noticed, and smiled. "Except what?" he asked.

"Both Bradley and Wilshot would spot me and wonder why I was snooping around."

Bannerman's amusement doubled. That was the way with those amateurs, he thought, all bright-eyed and bushy-tailed. Let them have one or two small triumphs and they start teaching everyone his business. "I have a very good reason for not snooping around, too. I've got to stay here. Period. A matter of keeping in touch with the big outside world. We don't work that through the Greeks or anyone else. Stop raising your blood pressure." And then he relented. "Elias made an excuse to have their passports checked: not one name we knew."

"And their faces matched the photographs?"

"Exactly. Elias' man even went into the cabin and glanced at one of the men, who was taking a nap. Okay bud? And yes," Bannerman added emphatically, "it was all handled tactfully, sort of offhand style, to raise no suspicions that they were being checked. Does that answer all objections?"

"Meanwhile," said Craig with a grin.

At least he can take a reprimand well enough, Bannerman thought. "Now this is what we do. When that twin-diesel job arrives from Rhodes, I'm going to be heading around to that anchorage. Alex has never seen me. I'll make sure—without going through the passport routine—who is on board. That gives us the warning, right? After that, we wait until they move ashore. I don't think Alex will go up to the house on the hill to see Maritta, not right away."

Not ever, thought Craig. Alex, cautious and careful, wouldn't be seen near that house. "Do you really think he might go there?" he asked very carefully. No criticism, Tim; no criticism implied at all.

"When it's dark, perhaps. Maritta has got rid of Veronica for the night. The house will be safe enough, even for Alex."

Now that's what Bannerman would do, or I would do, if we were in Alex's shoes. But will Alex? . . . Craig frowned, looked at the placid harbor. Outside the breakwater, the sunset was starting. And not a sign of a ship coming from any direction. "Maritta may have been making the house safe for the *Stefanie*'s arrival."

"It needs darkness to unload its cargo," Bannerman said abruptly.

"And it isn't taking the direct route to Mykonos from Samos. That, we do know. They'll make very sure that all is well before they touch land."

Craig agreed with that. In the art of caution, Insarov could give Alex some twenty years.

"And it won't arrive while Alex is here. *He* will make sure of that."

Craig could agree with that, too.

"He is due first. He has to be. If he is Bradley, he has got to be back at his desk in Paris by Monday morning. If he is Wilshot, he has a final interview with Grivas near Athens on Sunday. Neither can hang around here too long."

Craig nodded again.

"We can only make some educated guesses about what Alex will do once he sails in here. We just have to be ready for anything. You stay and watch the town while I'm around near the anchorage. Any suggestions?"

"I'd like to know how the hell I get in touch with you if necessary when you're on the other side of the harbor. It's a damned loud whistle from here to there."

"Relax, relax . . . That's all set up. Why do you think I've been waiting here?" Bannerman glanced at his watch. "They should be passing any minute now."

"I hope they speak English. I know about four phrases in Greek: good day, thank you, please, where is the toilet?"

Bannerman grinned. "They know more Greek than that. I'll leave one of them with you and take the other with me. Adam is the name of the guy who will keep fairly close to you. Only get in touch—" He broke off. "See those two characters ambling down the street. The fair-haired guy with the sunburn is Adam: green sweater, medium height, round face—got him? The stocky dark-haired chap is Bill. Okay?"

The two Americans, hands in pockets, strolled slowly past the café.

"Consider yourselves introduced," said Bannerman. "Now I can leave you. Only get in touch with Adam if you really need a contact."

"Whistle a bar or two?"

"Yes. Our little theme song." Bannerman was in good humor again. He rose. "I'll be with Elias for the next half hour or so—just checking." He sighed, but not too deeply. "This is the stage that kills me. All these damned decisions . . ."

"And I stay here?"

"Why not? You can admire the sunset and keep your eye on that street." He gave an easy wave, and left.

In spite of the low, carefree voice, there had been an edge of urgency in that last instruction. Keep your eye on the street. . . . Whom did Bannerman expect to come walking down there—Maritta?

If so, Alex won't be far behind. Maritta's actions are tied to his arrival. Of that, I'm convinced. Or at least, that's what I think. Think? Or feel? Or am I wandering in outer space? I could be wrong, there's always that doubt. He looked across the harbor at the anchorage—two placid boats lying close together, painted ships on a painted bay —all peace, all innocence. I could be wrong, he thought again, the doubt growing. All right, all right, he told himself irritably, let's watch this blasted street.

18

The street was busy now, so busy that it was baffling. Faces and voices and footsteps; and no one recognizable. The cafés, too, were filling up with people who had come out to admire the sunset. Even this one, where Craig sat patiently (obedient but bored, he thought wryly), was showing life. Some of the more artistic visitors were wandering in with their girls. "This is really authentic!" one said in delight as her friends pulled two tables together and corralled every available chair. The fishermen paid little notice, but their talk paused heavily and philosophic gloom masked their faces as they stared out at the calm harbor, only seeing another refuge invaded and about to be permanently occupied. Craig's lifeline, Adam, arrived, too, bringing three friends to sit only a couple of tables away. Craig felt cheerier, ordered coffee and another ouzo to keep the waiter happy, and returned his full attention to the street.

Then he heard the steady grumble of an outboard motor, and looked quickly at the quiet waters of the harbor. A small boat was halfway across from the yacht anchorage, moving smoothly in toward the breakwater. Where had it come from? The sloop or the cabin cruiser? It was edging its way past the fishing boats and caïques, coming as far inshore as possible. There was a man and some luggage in the prow; a woman at the tiller. Craig looked quickly around the tables, but the men there didn't seem to find it strange. They were more concerned with watching to see if the woman would make a mistake in steering, for, once she had nosed the boat into an opening between two fishing boats and brought it neatly against the jetty, they lost interest and found something else to talk about.

Craig looked along the street. No one was hurrying to meet the man on the jetty, now standing there with his two suitcases at his feet, watching the boat reverse safely. The woman waved; the engine roared for the first minute and then settled into its steady beat. The boat headed right back to the yacht anchorage.

Craig glanced at Adam's table. The conversation there was hilarious, but Adam had noticed, too, in between laughs. The man was picking up his suitcases, walking smartly to the head of the quay. He stopped to speak with a group of fishermen beside the small chapel there, but seemingly found no helpful answers. Next, he spoke to an old man, was directed on to another group. Someone gave him the information he was seeking. It was, apparently, a place to leave his two suitcases: a cart, standing by itself at the end of the quay with a few bundles already waiting for shipment out on the next boat. It was a slightly offhand baggage room, but the stranger accepted it after a little hesitation. Then, with his suitcases deposited neatly, the man headed for the front street. He was walking at a medium pace, obviously interested in everything he saw, someone who was putting in time before he caught the evening boat. No one was paying him the least attention. His actions explained themselves. He had arrived too early, which—in any Mykoniot's opinion—was wiser than appearing at the last minute and expecting miracles. Such things happened constantly; foreigners neither understood boat schedules nor made allowances for weather.

The stranger had plenty of time. He stopped to look at the painted fishing boats drawn up on the beach, at the nets spread over the short stretch of sand and pebbles. An Englishman, Craig guessed. He was wearing a faded blue blazer, loosely cut dark gray flannels bagging a little from travel. He took out a pipe and pouch, began the ritual of filling and lighting as he crossed the street toward the first café. Now Craig could see a thin tanned face above a nonchalant collar and tightly knotted tie. Striped, of course. He was almost a professional Englishman, from well-brushed hair down to solid shoes. As he reached the front-row tables, he glanced at his watch, decided to have a drink. He entered casually, eyes searching for an agreeable spot.

Craig's spine stiffened. He sat staring. My God, he thought, I didn't find Bradley; he found me! For at the moment of sure recognition, Bradley's eyes had swept along the back row of tables and seen Craig. He stopped, looked again, hesitated. Then, hand outstretched, he came forward. "Craig, isn't it? Why, this is a delightful surprise!"

"Bradley!" Craig's voice was astounded enough to carry across several tables. "Sorry. I didn't recognize you at first." Which was true.

"I didn't know you were here," said Bradley, completely at ease again. "And how is your charming sister?"

"Sue and George are both fine. They're in Washington now. Sit down, why not? Have a drink."

"If there is anything drinkable." Bradley smiled, hesitated again, then sat down. He looked around, adjusted the knot of his tie, pulled at his cuffs. "I feel rather overdressed. But I'm in transit. Returning to the big city tonight—catching the boat for Athens when it does come in. Thought I'd come over and have a look at Mykonos and something to eat before we sail. That's around ten, isn't it?"

"Give or take an hour. But I expect it will be fairly punctual tonight. The weather is good. You're in luck. What will you have?"

"Nothing at present, thank you. I have to meet a friend for a last drink together. Remember Wilshot?"

Craig reflected a little. "Wasn't he at the Meurice party, too? Yes, I remember him vaguely. We didn't talk."

"We came up from Rhodes, today. One of his friends offered us a lift—if that's the right word. Nautical terms are out of my line. Anyway, it gave us a last chance to see some of the islands. Otherwise, I think it was a mistake. Wilshot was seasick from start to finish. He is looking for a room now, at a hotel. Says he is going to spend tonight on terra firma, and look up some old friends. Extraordinary chap. He seems to have friends everywhere."

"Too bad you can't stay longer, yourself."

"Yes, it looks a quaint little place. Definitely informal." He looked around again, studying the people at the tables. "And how's your book coming along?"

"By fits and starts—the way most work gets done out here. I'll be spending some time on Delos. And then I'll push on."

"You know, I was thinking of you last week. When I was in Troy."

"How was it?" Craig asked with real interest.

Bradley plunged into a quick account, mostly on the peculiarities of getting there, of traveling through the naval and military zones that fringed both sides of the Dardanelles. "Then I drove on down to Smyrna. Fantastic journey on incredible roads, camels around every corner. Don't miss Bursa, by the way, when you go to Troy. It's the old Turkish capital—before they took Constantinople. The Green Mosque there is quite remarkable. Well—" he looked around again— "it seems as if I'll have to search elsewhere for Wilshot. Say, why don't we all have dinner later tonight?"

"I'd like that. But I'm waiting for a girl."

Bradley looked at the three coffee cups and two ouzo glasses. "You've had quite a wait, I see."

"No one is very punctual around here. And it's just possible that I'm at the wrong café. I haven't really got accustomed to Mykonos yet—only arrived here last night." He glanced at his watch. "After seven," he said in amazement.

Bradley rose. "If you see Wilshot, tell him I'm around, will you? I'll have a quick look at the town and then find a likely place to eat along here somewhere." He looked vaguely at the water front. He smiled and added, "I was told that the best way to catch the boat is to sit at a café until you see it approach."

"That saves a lot of fussing and fuming," Craig agreed. "Well—I won't say good-bye. We'll probably keep bumping into each other for the rest of the evening. Everyone does in Mykonos." Adam had already risen, along with two of his friends (Greek, they were), and was leading the way out into the street, talking over his shoulder to them about Kazantzakis. The third (a Frenchman, Craig had decided) still sat at their littered table, looking at the English girls across the café with a lazy interest which might win him a very successful evening indeed.

"If your girl doesn't appear, join us for dinner," Bradley said. He nodded pleasantly and walked off.

Magnificent sunset, thought Craig, and studied it for the next two minutes. Anything to keep him from his impulse to look after Bradley. Or after the two Greeks who were tagging along at a respectable distance. Adam had left in the other direction. Do I wait for Bannerman, wondered Craig, or do I follow my own impulses and leave this damned table and go looking for Maritta? For the truth is that we'll never know who Alex is until we see him with her. Bradley or Wilshot? . . . He had thought Partridge and all his boys a little slow at deciding. And yet, he found he wouldn't make up his mind, either. You couldn't pin treason lightly on any man. And this double play, carefully calculated, was as baffling as Alex had intended it. Friendly innocent or confidence trickster, which was Bradley? No, Craig thought, the only sure way of knowing will be when Maritta makes contact with Alex.

Bannerman arrived to find Craig paying the bill. "Going some place?" he asked with a grin.

"You know damned well where I'm going."

Bannerman looked around, checked on the nearest tables, seemed reassured, sat down beside Craig, and dropped his voice to a low murmur. "Take it easy. Maritta only left the house on the hill five minutes ago. She is walking in. That means we have at least fifteen minutes more before she reaches town. What did you make of Bradley?"

Craig shook his head. "He says Wilshot is in town."

"I know. He's at the Triton now, trying to get a room."

At the Triton. "Right next door to Herr Gerhard Ludwig?" The odds were increasing on Wilshot.

"He says he was advised to go there."

"Advised or instructed?"

"You really are getting the hang of this," Bannerman said in great good humor.

"I'm getting holes in the seat of my pants from so much damned sitting."

"And what had you in mind? Take a stroll and walk right up to Erika and her dear Alex?"

"Erika?"

"Her play name."

"I'll stick with Maritta." He still couldn't get accustomed to Insarov, still called him Berg as often as not. And the man *was* Berg. Maritta *was* Maritta. The rest was smoke screen.

"Safer for you," Bannerman agreed. Names had a habit of slipping out sometimes, as he had just proven to himself. *"If* you insist on talking with her. But why? And have you a real excuse? You'll need it, or you'll be blown sky-high. And perhaps us along with you."

Craig shook his head. "Let's leave here, and I'll tell you what I have in mind. It could work." Dusk was just about to cast its first thin veil over the sky. Soon the gray hour would come, the café lights would go on. He rose and made his way out. Bannerman had to rise and follow. Craig turned to his left, avoiding the front street, talking casually about Fellini and De Sica, as if Italian films had been their discussion. Bannerman noted all that and approved. They took the first whitewashed lane away from the water front, then cut along to their left again on the next narrow street, circling around to reach its other end. The crisscrossing streets had their evening quota of women standing at their doorways, of old men here and there watching with interest. Everyone else had left for a stroll along the water front.

Craig had begun speaking very quietly from the minute they had branched up into the alley, walking closely in between its tight walls. "I won't press my luck. I'll disengage if I see it's near breaking point. Contact *has* to be made between Maritta and Alex if there is any exchange of information between them at all. Right? This isn't the kind of place where you can drop something for another agent to pick up casually—too many people, too many kids around who could pick it up first. How much chance would one of those trick pencil stubs have, for instance, if a small boy saw it? Mykoniots don't waste one inch of string. Right?"

Bannerman nodded.

"So it has to be direct contact for safety. From one hand to another, or at least within sight of each other. Could be?"

Bannerman nodded. It was an odd feeling to hear Craig arguing everything out for himself, reaching conclusions that had been made days ago in Athens.

"So you need someone to get as close to them as possible. And that's me."

"Is it?"

"Have you got anyone who could walk right up to them and join them? With a perfectly good excuse? If Alex is Wilshot, I'll tell him that Bradley has been looking for him all over the place. If Alex is Bradley, I'll take him up on his dinner invitation. How's that?"

"Tempting."

"You'll have your men all around, anyway. If I get the deep-freeze treatment and have to bow out, nothing is lost. What d'you think?"

"I like it. Especially the bit where you make them break their rules. They'll learn each other's real names from you." He laughed softly.

"They don't know—" began Craig in astonishment.

"Neither name, nor occupation. Safeguard." Bannerman laughed again. "These are real conspirators, you know. Not counterespionage agents. There's a difference; in purpose and methods. They are the masters of the double image." Then Bannerman shook his head regretfully as he came back to Craig's idea. "I like it, but I'm not going to let you do it. You've forgotten two things: yourself, and what could come afterward."

"But I'm leaving that to you," Craig said with a smile. "You've got your alternative plans all made for dealing with Alex, haven't you? How many?" he asked jokingly. "A, B, C and D?"

Bannerman looked at him impassively.

"But how are you going to deal with Maritta? If you have Elias pick her up, take her out of circulation—well, that could cause a five-alarm fire. And yet, you'd like to keep her from handing that information from Alex over to—well, who's your guess?"

Bannerman's eyebrow lifted. "Is this what I get for leaving you alone with a sunset?"

"Inspiring," Craig admitted with a grin. "Come on, you old *bouzoukia* expert, what's there to lose if I play it very, very cool?"

"And where do you propose to start this operation? You can't be in two places at once—and there are two men."

"I'll compromise. I'll stay near Maritta. And leave the hard work to all you boys."

"There aren't so many of us now," Bannerman said very quietly indeed. "Elias is putting every man available, once darkness sets in, up on the hills as lookouts around the nearest bays and coves. We figure the *Stefanie* will drop off her cargo in a quiet spot and cruise peacefully at sea until morning. Then she makes a nice innocent approach to Mykonos."

"So that leaves—"

"Adam and myself. Bill has gone with the Greeks into the hills—liaison between them and us." Bannerman barely paused as he gave a passing thought to two other Americans, cosily installed this morning with complete transmitting and receiving facilities. He wondered briefly if any further news had come in from Smyrna, or—just as important now—if the wave length for local communication between here and the hills was working out all right. "Then there is an Englishman, but he is over on Delos, tonight." Craig looked swiftly at Bannerman, who didn't elaborate but went on smoothly, "And there's Mimi, at Delos; which leaves one Frenchman here. He's a good man. But the French are so damned eager to get Maritta that they may act if they think she is slipping away from them. From their point of view, they are within their rights. But from ours—well, all we'd get out of it would be Alex."

"And another man dead," said Craig, thinking of the *Stefanie*'s prisoner. And Heinrich Berg free. "Then you need me, whether you like it or not. So let's get moving." He halted at the next corner. "This street takes me back to the water front. I know, because this is the way I arrived yesterday evening." The dusk was thickening now. The white houses were luminous ghosts. Soon the lights, here too, would be switched on. "I think I even know her favorite café—I saw her there, last night, just around this time." He started down toward the front street.

Bannerman came with him. "Why not?" Bannerman said to Craig's unasked question. "We were seen constantly in Athens together." And then, as they were almost at the water front, he asked, "What makes you think she'll meet Alex at a café? Why not in one of those quiet streets we've just been passing?" He had his own answer but he was curious to find out if Craig did have a reason. That was important— no adequate reply, or a wrong one, and he'd stop Craig even now.

"He's a complete stranger to Mykonos. So was I last night. And I couldn't have been sure of meeting anyone in the dusk, at the right time, on the right street. The water front was the only place I could have reached with any certainty."

"Good enough," Bannerman said quietly, and walked on.

"What's more, this isn't the place of big hotels and public lobbies. Strangers are noticed here if they are in places where they don't belong. And any walk up to a lonely mill, or onto the hillside, could be noted, too: this is the time of day when women have stopped work to look out of their doorways. So the safest place is the most normal place—the water front, where all visitors congregate. That raises no speculations. Right? Or wrong?"

It was right as far as Mykonos went. Bannerman nodded, glanced at his watch, increased his pace. "Let's cross the front street, walk on the beach, look at a fishing boat or two. Adam is waiting at the square; he will follow her in once she passes through it. If you are right, she should be swinging along in a few—" He did not even have to finish his sentence. He grasped Craig's arm, pulled him behind a stone staircase as Maritta Maas strolled along the water front barely thirty feet away.

"Quick reflexes," Craig said, looking with respect at Bannerman.

"And damned poor timing." Bannerman drew a deep breath, and gestured to Craig to resume walking. "We could have run smack into her. She must be pretty confident to come so quickly into town. All the better," he added with a broad smile. "She'll really be set back a mile when she sees you. Now, look, I agree to your plan, with one addition. Me."

"We're going in together?" I might have guessed that was why he listened, Craig thought wryly. He's using me to get close to Alex. "I introduce you all around?"

"That's the idea. I'll stick with Alex. You hold onto Maritta. Spend the evening with her if necessary. Keep her from delivering that information anywhere, until Adam and his French friend think up a way of getting it from her. Of course, there is another way—" He looked at Craig, reflectively.

"No thanks," Craig said sharply. "I don't tangle with any girl unless I like her. Just keep my love life out of this, will you?"

"Only a mild suggestion." They had reached the front street. Bannerman grasped Craig's arm again. "Gently does it." Adam was walking past the entrance of their lane. He noticed them, all right, but didn't stop. Something more interesting seemed to lie ahead of him. "Give him a minute," Bannerman said, and paused to light a cigarette. "Let them all get into place. Then we walk in."

"I don't think it will be as easy as that."

"Nothing ever is. But I'm counting on you to startle Maritta. Set her off balance. That's when mistakes are made."

"Alex will keep his head—"

"Let him. We've got him, whatever happens. False passport, the use of, however temporary. Elias will hold him on that."

They turned the corner carefully. Maritta had halted in front of her usual café. She was standing, her back turned to them, looking out to sea. The small launch she had hired for her party was returning from Delos, easing its way around the breakwater to come into the shelter of the harbor.

Again, Bannerman had to light his cigarette. They stood for another full minute behind a pillar of the nearest colonnade. There was no sign of Adam; he made good use of every available shadow, seemingly. Craig wondered if Maritta had not her own watchers posted along this water front. And inside the café?

"Take it easy," said Bannerman softly, and kept talking. "You know, that was a clever dodge with the fake passports." He passed over his own mistake in letting it work; he ought to have gone over to the anchorage himself, just to make sure who had arrived. "Hindsight is easy," was all he said. "It's clear now that the man sleeping below was the non-Alex. The real Alex handled the passport identification on deck while his stupefied friend didn't even know what was going on."

"Which makes his record just about perfect for the whole trip."

"They slipped something into his cocktail. Elias' man thought he was drunk." Bannerman grinned cheerfully. "So keep your glass in your hand, tonight. Useful tip when drinking with Alex."

At this moment, Craig was wondering if he would even meet Alex. Maritta might be merely taking an evening stroll. That's the way she looked from here. Casual, untroubled, innocent. Abruptly, she swung around toward the café. Hair slightly ruffled from the sea breeze, hands deep in the pockets of her belted fleece coat—a pale green that came to life as she stepped into the circle of light—she walked slowly through the rows of outside tables. She smiled to one group of acquaintances, waved to another, managed somehow to be drawn into neither. She paused at the wide entrance to the room, hesitated whether she'd go inside or sit under the colonnades at her usual table. She decided that it was perhaps turning chillier than she had expected and stepped over the threshold.

"Damn," said Bannerman softly. "It would have been so easy to watch her if she had sat outside."

"Too easy. Come on, let's go." She could be meeting Alex, right now, thought Craig worriedly.

"There's Adam," Bannerman said as they approached the café. Adam had decided on an inside table, too, tonight. The Frenchman with the bedroom eyes was drifting in, looking around with his usual lazy appraisal even if he had managed to bring along two of the English girls with him. "Technique," Bannerman said with admiration.

"If he has to leave them quickly, two are company and they won't feel so lonely." He raised his voice as they reached the first row of tables. "The trouble about these Karagöz plays is that you never can find them. You hear plenty about them—"

Craig had paused, almost imperceptibly, as he noticed the lonely American seated at one table, a man in his thirties, well-dressed in a light tweed jacket, who was watching the people stroll by. He glanced at Craig but didn't recognize him in the broken light. It was Ed Wilshot.

Craig walked on, saying, "They are pure folk art, of course, as raw as it can come. You may be able to find them in the smaller places— perhaps they'd have to be toned down for Athens."

"Until the avant-garde discovers them," Bannerman said, looking at Ed Wilshot as he passed. His face was impassive. "And that will really muck them up." Better keep Maritta in view, he decided.

They halted at the doorway, accustoming their eyes to the bright lights inside. Craig was saying, "What do you think, Tim? Outside or in here?"

"Chilly out there. It looks as if there's going to be a change in weather. Let's find a table inside." They entered casually.

19

It was a square room, with the usual massive arch framing the shelves of bottles on its back wall. The twenty tables, plastic-topped, had clusters of rush-bottomed chairs. It was simple, clean and fairly crowded. Adam was seated near the door, talking with two local men. The Frenchman and his two excellent excuses were at a table against one wall. And Maritta was there. By herself. She was staring at Craig unbelievingly.

He pretended to catch sight of her then, and waved as he started toward her. His hand almost froze in mid-air. At the next table to Maritta's, tucked into a corner behind the arch, reading a paper while he enjoyed a lonely *apéritif*, was Robert Bradley.

"Hey!" Craig said to Bannerman, who seemed to be heading for the opposite wall, "I'm going in this direction." He nodded with a grin toward Maritta. She had recovered enough to smile back. She was even primping, getting ready to welcome him; she had taken out her compact and lipstick from her deep pocket, and was studying the need for repairs in a small mirror.

Bannerman was looking at her, too, a bright smile spreading over his handsome dark face. "That's an idea!"

"I didn't ask you," Craig said, leading the way.

"I'm still accepting," Bannerman told him, following him with a laugh.

It sounded natural enough. As natural as the sudden falling of the lipstick, which landed with a light clatter near Robert Bradley's feet.

He bent to pick it up, rose to return it into Maritta's cupped hand, smiled politely at her thanks, and sat down again, adjusting his tie as he picked up his newspaper.

Bannerman's trained eye was admiring. That was one of the neatest exchanges he had seen in a long time—a double exchange. First, Bradley had substituted a fake lipstick for Maritta's; secondly, as he had placed it in her palm, he had found something there to pick up. Bradley hadn't enjoyed receiving in addition to giving. For a moment, his face was tight, the nostrils slightly dilated. The hand that had made the exchange was now slipping casually into his pocket. Then he was adjusting his tie again. Bradley really was a cool—Bradley? Alex. We've got Alex, Bannerman thought, and gave Maritta his very best smile.

She was a cool operator, too. She had taken off the cap of the lipstick she had received from Bradley, to show it was apparently authentic. Quickly, she colored her lips, closed the lipstick, and dropped both it and her compact back into her coat's deep pocket. She tilted her head and looked at Craig.

Craig was concentrating on Maritta, not even noticing Bradley. That lipstick is a stronger pink than she usually wears, he noted as he grinned like a happy idiot. "I've been searching for you everywhere, just about giving up hope. What took you so long to get into town?"

This approach startled her again. "Why—" She looked at him blankly, recovered. "And how did you get here from Delos? Swim?" There was challenge in her voice and eyes.

"But I didn't go! You didn't expect me to, did you, when you never turned up?" Craig looked incredulous. "Didn't you know I'd get your message?"

The brilliant green eyes flickered nervously at Bradley's back. "But I didn't send any—"

"Maritta," Craig said gently, "don't tell me you didn't want to see me. Without benefit of the usual rabble." He looked with a grin at Bannerman.

Bannerman said, putting out his hand, "This oaf doesn't seem to want to introduce me. So I'll do it myself. Tim Bannerman."

She shook hands, smiled, but only said, "Why don't you sit down, Mr. Bannerman?"

No name given, Craig noted. And just what had been exchanged between Maritta and Bradley? The lipstick, probably; and anything else? It had been too quick for him. But Bannerman was in such good spirits that he must have noticed something important. Craig looked at Bradley's back, and decided to make this a really merry party. "Hello, Bradley!" he said. "I thought I saw Ed Wilshot hanging around outside. But come and meet the prettiest girl on Mykonos."

Bradley had turned around, resigned. He mustered a correct smile. He rose again, the always perfect gentleman.

"Mr. Robert Bradley, Miss Maritta Maas—" Craig clapped Bannerman's back—"and Mr. Timothy Bannerman the Fourth." Craig pulled around an extra chair. Just the life of the party, he told himself; but he was, in fact, enjoying himself immensely. "Join us, Bradley. It must be gloomy waiting for a boat all by yourself. Have you had dinner, yet? Well, join us again. I wish you'd take Bannerman off my hands, though. Maritta and I were planning to—"

"We were not!" Maritta said sharply, and looked at Bradley.

"Sorry, sorry," Craig said very quietly, "I didn't know we had to keep it a secret." Then he smiled brightly all around and signaled to the waiter. The mention of Wilshot's name, he noticed, was keeping Bradley nicely in place: it might be difficult to explain to Wilshot why he had been given wrong directions where to sit. At any rate, Bradley wasn't leaving to meet his friend outside. Or perhaps he was more interested in Maritta's connection with Craig. The more she protested, the more coldly he looked at her. Do these people have to make reports on each other? Craig wondered. Maritta was certainly ill at ease. She had even forgotten to challenge him with shouldering her servant off the dock.

But once the drinks arrived, and Bradley's attention was held by Bannerman's easy flow of talk, she made an effort and recovered herself. And she didn't disappoint Craig. "What was that story I heard," she asked coldly, "about a man falling into the water?"

"He did. It was some idiot who was standing on the edge of the quay. There was a jam of people. What did he expect, anyway?"

"And you stumbled against him?"

"Look, Maritta, he tried to pull me in," Craig said with a hint of protest in his voice. "I nearly took a high dive, myself."

She studied him. "So you didn't go to Delos. . . . Veronica will be quite upset."

"No one is going to miss me one bit. There was a mob scene on that jetty. Everything just got out of hand. Not my idea of a romantic picnic. Besides, I told you I had lost interest. Can't you get it through your pretty blond head that I only accepted the invitation because of you?"

"I thought your chief interest was in old ruins."

"In daylight. By myself. When I can keep my mind on my work." He glanced at the other two men. Bannerman was at his best in this kind of confrontation; he was talking amusingly, constantly, holding Bradley's attention in spite of his wary coldness. It was thawing a little, as if Bradley had completed the job of sizing Bannerman up and had decided that he would prefer to talk with him rather than seem to have any contact with Maritta. He ignored her completely, a man who had no interest in her whatsoever. And for once Maritta did not seem to mind such neglect. Craig said very quietly, "Maritta—what about having dinner with me?"

"I'm sorry. I have to get back to the house. I only slipped away for an hour to—to get some medicine in town. I had nothing stronger than aspirin."

"Oh, yes, I forgot. Tony or Veronica, or someone, told me your guest broke his leg. Is it serious?"

She hadn't been listening. A new idea had entered that quick little mind. She smiled brightly. "You know, John, I might stay and have dinner with you. The house is really so unbearable—like a hospital. Why do men with a small hurt always think they are dying? It's nothing serious, really. And I couldn't find anything stronger than aspirin in town, anyway."

"Then that's fine. Let's start moving out."

"Where shall we have dinner? The best food is at either the Leto or the Triton. The Triton is nearer. Why don't we go there?"

And since when did a slender figure think about the importance of good food? The Triton—with three exits, one of them right next door to the Ludwig house. It would be a simple way, with a few more excuses like washing her hands, tidying up, to make sure of delivering that lipstick. Craig smiled. "That's an idea." He glanced at Bannerman, wondering if he had heard. Craig did some quick calculations of his own. He rose, helping her pull the coat around her shoulders— she had kept it with her, all this time, instead of throwing it over a spare chair. "Good-bye," he said to Bradley. "Have a good trip."

"Give my best to Sue and George."

Craig's eyes noticed the small addition to Bradley's dress: the striped tie was now held by a clip of gold. He wasn't wearing any tie clip when I first met him today, Craig thought, I'm sure he wasn't, I'm positive. "I'll do that," he said, shaking hands.

Bradley's bow to Maritta was no more than politeness demanded. That might even be relief in his eyes, as if he were glad to be rid of her. She was equally distant. Her smile for Bannerman was enchanting.

Craig caught her arm and started leading her toward the bar at the back of the room.

"Why—" she asked, halting, looking at him.

"I've got to call the Triton and arrange for a table for two. And why don't you call home and tell them you won't be back until—" he smiled down at her—"well, let's say midnight. Then they won't start worrying about you."

"Midnight?"

"Unless you could manage to spend the night in town." He held her eyes with his.

"Just a minute, my friend, not so fast!" Bannerman was beside them, his voice clear and carrying. "Where do I join you later in the evening?"

"You don't," Craig said with a grin, "you old—" he dropped his voice as if his description of Bannerman wasn't for any lady's ears— "tie clip."

Bannerman heard it, barely, but enough. He laughed. "Okay, okay." To Maritta he said, "What about going swimming tomorrow? I'll meet you at the taxi stand at eleven."

"We'll see about that," Craig said, took Maritta's arm and led her to the telephone that sat proudly at the end of the bar.

"What did you call him?" she wanted to know, smiling.

"Oh, just a term of endearment among sailors."

She didn't know her Dr. Johnson, but she got the idea. "I think he's charming," she said. She was so much back to normal, so much enjoying herself, that she did not even notice Adam was strolling to the door or that the Frenchman was leaving his two pretty girls. Bannerman had rejoined Bradley with a joking remark, while Bradley ordered something to eat with a look of distaste for the limited menu. Maritta glanced back at their table. "And I think that other man is horrid. He never even spoke to me. I don't think he really likes women, do you? Perhaps you ought to warn your nice friend. How long have you known Mr. Bannerman?"

"Long enough not to trust him near you. He has been visiting Athens for several months—he's a writer. Now, ladies first." He handed her the telephone. "Make it nice and vague. I don't want your friends chasing into the Triton with a shotgun. Tell them they haven't a thing to worry about. You are spending the night with a friend. Right?"

She smiled. "Perhaps," she said. And then as she waited for an answer to her call, she laughed softly and said, "Perhaps that would be wise."

She did keep it vague. She did not mention the Triton. She did not even mention John Craig. No worry, she told them, everything was splendid; everything was well. They asked her one question. Her answer was a decided "Yes!" A touch of triumph was in it, too. She ended quickly, "I'll manage. Don't worry. I won't be late."

She replaced the receiver. "I have to be back by ten tomorrow," she said, not blinking one eyelash, to explain that last quick sentence. "Now it's your turn—" She followed the direction of his eyes. Sauntering into the café were Tony and Mimi. "What—" She hurried toward them. "What on earth happened?"

"We came back with the launch," Mimi said. "Oh, how nice and *warm* it is in here!"

Tony was looking around in his vague English way, nodding to various groups, noticing Bannerman and Bradley. "Everything went wrong," he told Maritta. "They swarmed ashore on Delos, all having the time of their little lives. We kept the launch waiting, tried to coax them back on board. They wouldn't go. It was, I suppose, absolutely hilarious. I'll see the joke tomorrow."

"How many stayed?"

"Hundreds."

Mimi laughed and said, "I counted eighteen. They'll freeze to death."

"Unless they bundle," Craig said with a grin. No one got the joke.

"There would have been no beds left for us," Mimi said, shaking her head. "They ran faster than we did."

"Yes," said Tony to Craig, "we were properly up a pear tree. So Veronica and Mimi and I decided we'd—"

"Veronica?" Maritta's voice was sharp. "Where is she?"

"Oh, we left her looking for the man who drives the taxi. I told her it was no use. Either he's in bed or he is at the fishermen's pub down the street dancing a mad *bouzoukia*."

"Is she going to the house?" Maritta was tense.

"I should think that was the idea. She said she was going to pack." But Maritta was already halfway to the door.

"I couldn't stop Veronica from coming back," Mimi said very quietly as she and Craig followed. "I did not want to, of course. Tony and I were glad of the excuse. I think we are needed here tonight."

"When did she decide?"

"Just as we reached Delos. She did not speak all the way across. All at once, she made up her mind—like that!" Mimi snapped her fingers. "And then Tony managed to start everyone landing. He would make a very good *agent provocateur*." She laughed for Tony, slid her arm through Craig's. "Now it is our turn, I think," she said as they all came out into the colonnade.

Maritta was standing in the middle of the street, looking toward the main square where the two taxis were parked during the day. "I can't see her," she called over her shoulder to Craig. She was frightened, really frightened. "And there is no taxi."

"Then she is walking," Craig said more calmly then he felt. "Forget it, Maritta. Let's have dinner."

"But she can't go—" Maritta bit the phrase short. She was close to complete panic.

"We can easily catch up with her, if that is what you want."

Maritta made an effort and tried to look normal. "It makes everything so awkward. Don't you see, I can't possibly stay in town if she is alone at the house? It wouldn't be—*convenable*." She looked up at him so disappointedly. "It just ruins everything, doesn't it?" She set off at a very brisk pace.

Craig called after her, "Mimi says she is packing and coming back into town—so why bother?"

Maritta pretended she hadn't heard. Her pace increased. Just ahead of her, Adam and the Frenchman were sitting on the low wall that edged the beach near the square.

"Maritta! Wait for me!" Craig shouted. But she hurried on. Adam and his friend now saw her direction. They slipped off the wall, began walking ahead of her. It looked as if she were following them.

"Oh, let her be!" Tony said loudly. He had a tight grip on Craig's arm. "Remarkable thing!" he said very quietly. "Why doesn't she want anyone near that house at such an early hour?"

Mimi was watching the two men walking ahead of Maritta. They were reaching the narrow lane that disappeared around some buildings at the water's edge. They entered it, vanished from sight. Maritta would have to take that way, too. It was the quick route to the bay road. "Time for me to leave," she said quietly. "I'll be needed, I think." There was a strange small smile on her lips. "Where did she put the information she received? In her pocket?" Then she looked at Craig's face. "Don't worry," she said. "She will be luckier than Duclos." She left them, walking swiftly, her graceful stride surviving even the broken paving stones. She waved back. "See you tomorrow," she called over her shoulder.

"I wonder if Tim needs any help," Tony said, and looked toward the café. He saw Elias and another Greek sitting quietly in the shadows outside. "No, I think not."

Craig was still watching Maritta as she reached that dark lane. She was almost running, now. Running right into it, he thought.

"She'll be all right," Tony murmured. "Just an informal arrest. A quiet detention, until it's safe to make it known." His grip on Craig's arm slackened as he drew him casually toward the deeply shadowed beach.

"I'm not worrying about her," Craig said grimly. Maritta and Alex—the hell with them. "It's Veronica."

"Yes," the Englishman agreed. "I think I'll pass the word. You'd better wait here for Bannerman." He glanced at the American's face, and then looked back at the colonnade. "Do nothing rash."

"Nothing you wouldn't do."

"I don't like the sound of that one bit," Tony said with a smile. "Meanwhile, there's a chap over at the darkest table—by the edge of the colonnade. He's the one who was trailing Veronica this morning."

"Striped shirt?" Craig resisted glancing around.

Tony nodded. "He has been trying to make up his mind whether he ought to keep an eye on Maritta, or whether he should phone in his report. I know the feeling well. . . . The telephone wins, I hope. . . . Good. He doesn't think Maritta is in any trouble. She probably gave him no signal of distress. So a report is sufficient unto the evil

265

thereof. I don't imagine we want even that, do we? Shall I deal with him? Or you?"

"I think your touch is more inspired."

"Thank you," Tony said gravely, and moved with unconcerned nonchalance toward the man who had left his table and was heading, cautiously but definitely, for the café entrance. The man halted, stood aside. Bradley and Bannerman were coming out. Bannerman was still talking his head off; Bradley was looking peeved, as if he had just about reached saturation point. But he kept his polite mask in place.

"No trouble at all," Bannerman was saying. "You'll need an extra hand with your luggage, and we may have to hurry. I think I see her lights now!" He pointed out beyond the breakwater. "These mail boats slip in so quickly. And they don't always wait. She's early to-night. Must have been good weather all the way. Come on, let's run. No one will hold it against us."

Bradley and Bannerman started at a very quick pace down the water front. Elias and his man rose and followed at a half-run, passed them, drew ahead. They, too, were apparently worried about catching that boat. Other prospective passengers were rising from their café tables; some even began to run. The power of suggestion, thought Craig, lighting a cigarette to give him time to think. Think of a plan of his own . . . No use waiting for Bannerman. Once Tony could pass on the news about the house on the hill, Bannerman's hands would be even fuller than they were now. Craig watched the distant figure of his friend running close beside Bradley. And suddenly, an extraordinary thing happened.

Perhaps it was one of the paving stones with its raised edge that had caused it, perhaps the patched shadows on the street were to blame. Bradley stumbled, pitched forward. Bannerman was helping him up, dusting him off. Then they were hurrying again down the street.

From the colonnade, came Tony's voice calling out loudly for help. "I say—someone—quick! This man seems ill!"

Craig's eyes glanced over at the café. Tony was looking in bewilderment at the stout figure he had propped into the nearest chair. Three people went forward. "Is he drunk?" someone asked.

"I don't know. He collapsed practically on top of me," Tony said. "Most peculiar, really." He stepped back, let the waiter and some fishermen take over. There was a good deal of growing excitement, various suggestions, and then a simple solution arrived at. The inert body was carried indoors and the problem deposited on the poor woman who ran the place.

Tony came back to where Craig was standing at the edge of the beach. "He will live," he said. "But he won't wake up for another six hours. Just in time to be arrested along with the rest of his friends. He was, you might say, a standing duck."

"You play rough."

"Only when I'm *very* hard pressed," Tony said in his gentlest voice. "And we don't have much time, you know." He looked across the dark waters of the harbor to the breakwater. Under its meager lights, the small crowd of travelers were carrying their luggage up to the motorboats that would take them to the ship waiting out at sea. "Good-bye Alex," he murmured.

"They'll let him get on board?"

"Of course; he must be seen to be leaving safely. But on board—well, I suppose Elias has some way of having him detained in a cabin."

A matter of false passport, thought Craig. "Look, when Bannerman gets back, tell him I'm—"

"You wait and tell him yourself. Why did he go down to the pier, anyway? Elias and his man were there."

"They didn't know about a tie clip."

"Oh?" Then Tony laughed. "So that's why old Tim clicked his heels together? That stumble, you know."

Yes, thought Craig, understanding it now, a fall and a brush-down from helping hands was a very quiet way of losing a tie clip. "Once Alex stopped being hurried, he would notice it."

"Too late, too late." Tony started to stroll down the street. "I had better meet Bannerman. Coming?"

"No, I'm going."

"I think you should wait," Tony said. He halted, frowning slightly.

"Tell him not to worry. I'm using the direct method." Craig moved off. Time to go. Maritta would have made her quiet exit. Alex had made his. Nothing would be endangered at this moment. "I'll be there in fifteen minutes," he said as Tony came after him. "I'll have Veronica back here in another twenty."

"Things are moving very rapidly," Tony said, his voice no longer vague and drifting. "You heard Maritta."

"I know. That's why we can't wait." Craig walked off rapidly toward the square. Tony watched him go. As soon as he was out of sight he'd probably start running. I would, thought Tony. And if I hadn't to stay here and pass the word that the volcano is about to go up, I'd be on his heels.

He waited patiently, smoking, wandering around the fishing boats on the dark beach, until he saw first Bannerman and then Elias returning in the very best of spirits. He crossed the street slowly, hands in pockets. "Now hear this," Tony said, very quietly, as he joined them.

Craig followed the shore road, curving around the semicircle of the small bay, until it almost reached the yacht anchorage. Just before that point, marked by a sparse grouping of meager trees, there was a rough track branching to his right up the hilly fields. This should bring him fairly close to the house he had marked on his walk that morning: the one with the dovecote, Elias had said. The track, trail, or fourth-class road should lead to the house itself.

He glanced back as he started the winding climb. All was peace. The town clustering at the other end of the bay was a spreading galaxy of lights surrounded by darkness: a string of naked bulbs along the breakwater; another on the road he had traveled around the bay; a bright glimmer from the hotel and houses spaced along the shore; riding lights on the cabin cruiser and sloop, seemingly asleep at their anchorage; and, far out beyond the breakwater, the brilliance of the inter-island boat, lit from stem to stern, like a beacon of welcome on the black water. Above him was the vast stretch of ink-blue sky over sea, some stars appearing gradually, the waning moon now five nights into its last quarter, softly silvered clouds blowing gently in from the north.

The breeze touched his cheek, cooled his brow. Down on the road, he had run as lightly, as silently as possible whenever the patches of shadows had been deep enough. Now, on the open hillside, he climbed at a steady pace. If he was being watched, he wanted to give no impression of abnormal haste.

Normal. That was to be his password.

And he was being watched. From behind him, down at the small cluster of stunted trees that marked the cutoff, came the soft cooing of a dove. It was so natural that he almost believed it, except that another dove sounded immediately, plaintively, from one of the long retaining walls that stretched along the dark hillside back toward Mykonos. He didn't alter his pace or turn his head. But the careful warnings changed the house just above him, sheltering quietly behind its high white walls, from a place of comfortable innocence to something more formidable. The downstairs windows were shuttered, giving only a few streaks of light. Upstairs, everything was in darkness except for one window that lay at the extreme end of the house. Veronica's, possibly. Certainly it overlooked the opposite side of the rough garden from where the dovecote stood.

The front gate was unlocked. The garden was a mass of shadows. He slowed his pace, marking the path that branched left to the dovecote, the clusters of bushes, the grouping of small trees, as he followed the paved walk to the house. There was a porch in front, covered with climbing vines, and then the door.

His mouth went dry. Name, rank and serial number. Or name, purpose of visit, reason for making it. And that's all, he reminded himself as he reached the three steps to the porch. Keep it simple: that's what Partridge advised you. And check your arsenal. The automatic was deep in his right-hand pocket; the knife in his left. He knocked on the door. Come on, come on, he thought irritably: you know someone is here; don't tell me you haven't radio contact between your man on the hillside and this house. The door opened.

"Is Miss Clark ready?" Craig asked, clearly but pleasantly.

The man who had opened the door, a dark silhouette against the light from the hall behind him, stood in stolid silence, unmoving. Then, "Come in," he said, drawing aside.

"That's all right. I don't want to trouble you. I can wait for Miss Clark out here on the porch."

"No trouble," the man insisted. He spoke English well. His first hesitation had not been caused by any language difficulties; perhaps he had been puzzled by Craig's direct approach or by his total lack of interest in gaining entry to the house. He had had his orders, for he now led the way directly toward a well-lighted room on the left side of the high-ceilinged hall. There was another room, opposite, and the clatter of plates being cleared. Dinner was already over. Early for Mykonos, thought Craig, glancing at the narrow staircase that began outside the dining-room door and mounted steeply to a wooden gallery under a curved arch. Veronica, he was asking her silently, didn't you hear my voice? I spoke loudly enough.

"Go in," said the man, who was dressed like a servant in a black alpaca jacket and narrow bow tie and yet seemed very much his own master. He nodded to the arched doorway of the sitting room, and Craig walked in. He halted, looking around, ready for anything; and tried to hide his sudden sense of foolishness. He had interrupted a bridge game. No more than that. The whole setup couldn't have been more suburban. Three men and a woman at a green card table in a large and handsome room, shutters cosily closed, a coffee tray in front of a large fireplace, couches covered with roses, pink silk shades on a dozen fussy lamps, too many pictures, too much bric-à-brac.

The woman rose and came forward to welcome him. She was a faded beauty but still strong and graceful in body. She had a charming smile, as soft as the low-necked lace blouse she wore with her long silk skirt. "Do come in," she said in pleasantly accented English. She was, possibly, French.

"I don't want to disturb you." Craig was keeping near the door, hanging on to his smile, which he hoped didn't seem as unnatural as it felt. "I've come to help Veronica back to town with her overnight case. Has she finished packing?"

"How very thoughtful of you, Mr.—?"

"Craig. John Craig."

"You are not disturbing us in the slightest. We were only cutting for deal."

The three men murmured their agreement but did not rise. Two were quiet-faced unknowns; but the third man, who now turned to look over his shoulder and nod across the room in greeting, froze Craig's spine. He was Heinrich Berg. Insarov.

"Do sit down, Mr. Craig," the woman was saying in her best hostess style. She had a delicately studied way of pointing, with her palm held upward, fingers relaxed.

"No, thank you. I can't stay long. The party is just about to begin in town. Would you tell Veronica I'm here?"

"A party?" asked Berg, rising, drifting slowly over to where Craig stood. His voice was politely interested, quiet and even to match the look in his eyes.

Craig was forced to look back at him. "It's to replace the one that fell flat on Delos."

"And Maritta?"

"She is staying in town overnight, too."

"Why didn't she come here for Miss Clark?" The blue eyes were disingenuous.

He is measuring me, Craig thought. He is wondering if my smile is as stupid as I hope it looks: he is like a wrestler, circling around, arms lax, muscles loose. All right, I'll be the fatuous American. "No taxis," he replied, and laughed.

They all smiled, as if they knew Maritta.

"Jeanne," said Berg, "why don't you go upstairs and tell Miss Clark that her friend is here?"

She nodded and went into the hall. If, thought Craig, I were to see her in a heavy sweater, yachting style, I might even identify her as the woman who brought Bradley so expertly across the harbor this evening.

Berg was saying, "Miss Clark is a charming girl. But she worries us. Why does she want to leave this house? We think it is rather comfortable." He smiled sadly back at his friends around the table, who nodded and agreed with an equally desolated smile. "In fact, Mr. Craig—Craig?"

"Craig."

"We were a little hurt. After all, Maritta has been very kind, everyone has tried to make Miss Clark feel at home. Now why should she want to leave? Do you know?"

Craig shook his head. "But I'd make one guess."

"Oh?" The blue eyes were blandly innocent, but the scarred eyebrow was more noticeable.

"Transportation."

"I beg your pardon?"

"If you were twenty-five, and a girl, and with all your friends living right in Mykonos, would you enjoy walking back and forth three times a day?"

Berg stared at him. And then was amused. His silent friends were amused, too. "I suppose this house might seem inconvenient if one did not enjoy walking," he agreed. "And Americans do not walk very much, do they?" He turned toward a servant who was carrying in a silver tray with bottle, snifters, and cigars. "Ah, here is the brandy. Will you join us, Mr. Craig? You know, I keep feeling we have met. Some place. Where?"

Craig looked thoughtful, polite. Then he smiled and shook his head. "I think," he said, moving toward the hall, "I hear Veronica now." He ignored the servant with the tray, although it was hard to be oblivious of someone he had shouldered off the jetty into the harbor only four hours ago. The man's cold look pierced his shoulders. And I bet that quick whisper to Berg has nothing to do with the selection of a cigar, Craig thought. Now what happens? We were so close to leaving, so damned close. He smiled up the staircase and said, "Hello, there! Everyone is gathering at Tony's place. The fun starts any minute. Come on, Veronica, we'll have to hurry." He took her small night case. Her face was too pale, he noted; her eyes were frightened, her smile taut. She took his outstretched hand. Her fingers were ice cold, their clutch desperate. "We'll get the rest of your things tomorrow, when we find a taxi. There wasn't one in sight tonight. We'll have to walk. Sorry." He looked down at her shoes and saw with relief that they were flat-heeled. "But there's some moonlight, so a walk has its compensations," he went on, still speaking rapidly, still trying to get her back to normal. Thank God she hadn't blurted out some innocent question about what was he doing here or how had he known she was leaving. "Maritta is sorry the Delos picnic turned into such a rabble. We'll have a better party right in town. You know, you should wear blue more often; it suits you."

She laughed at that. And the tight grip of his hand as he steadied her down the last few stairs was reassuring. "My trouble is I can't resist wearing it," she could joke back, and faced the men in the room with growing confidence. "Good-bye," she said, still trying to keep her voice normal, walking on to the front door. "Good-bye," she repeated to the woman, who followed them across the hall.

Will we really be allowed to leave? Craig wondered. His back was turned to the two servants, now; his hands were fully occupied with Veronica and her small case. But the door was opened and he was thanking the faded glamour girl and calling good night in general over his shoulder. The door closed behind them. We made it, he thought, we made it.

He took a deep breath as they left the porch. He kept their pace normal, although his first inclination was to run. "Talk normally," he whispered. "About anything. Laugh, too, if you can." He shifted his grip from her hand to her arm, drawing her closer to him. We made it, he thought again, as they reached the gate. But why? His story had just managed to pass, but then that blasted servant appeared to have a close look at him; and there had been some trouble with Veronica, too. She had been both scared and angry, almost reaching the fine Celtic pitch of being fighting mad. Yes, there had been bad trouble upstairs. So why had they been allowed to walk out like this, as if nothing was at stake?

The answer came to him as he closed the gate behind them. A dove cooed twice, and then twice more, from the hillside shadows; a dove answered gently from the road below. So we didn't make it, he thought. They only wanted us clear of the house, far enough away to cause it no trouble. He pulled Veronica quickly in front of him, his own back against the wall near the gate. "Just for a minute," he told her. "Put your arms around my waist. Make it look good. Someone is watching us from the trees down by the road. That's the way. Just give me a chance to see where we'll move next."

"Then there *is* danger," she said softly. She put her hands lightly around him, leaned her cheek against his breast.

"Yes." He looked over her head, down the rough track to the main road. His eyes picked out the scraps of possible cover: an outcrop of rock, a few bushes, another of those long retaining walls that terraced the hillside, the thin group of trees at the sharp turn into the road. Not much. Not much at all.

"In a way, I'm glad," Veronica was saying. "I thought I was going just a little crazy. They locked my door, you know. If you hadn't come, I'd have been kept there all night. The woman pretended it had only stuck when she came to tell me you were downstairs. But it was locked all right." But why? But why? . . . She said nothing more, waited, feeling the strong steady heartbeat against her cheek.

He said at last, "They expect us to head for town. So we take the opposite direction. We'll go halfway down this trail, walking normally. We reach the bushes, dump your case, keep low, and run like hell along the shelter of the stone wall that leads north beyond the headland. There's another bay there, a big one—" He tried to remember the details of his map. "There's a road edging it, too, part of the way at least—"

"I know the bay—it's just a continuation of this small one—or is it the other way around? I went exploring for a place to swim there."

"What's it like?" he asked quickly.

"Cliffs, caves, coves with little beaches. Stony hillside, a few scattered houses mostly closed until summer. Lonely."

"Good. Let's head that way. Find a nice comfortable wall. And sit it out until dawn comes up." He felt the fleece of her blue coat, warm and soft to his touch; she wouldn't freeze, thank heaven for that.

"Won't they still be searching for us then?" And why, she wondered again, why? . . .

"I don't think so." We may not even have to wait until dawn, he was thinking. If Maritta's panic had any meaning, the end of all waiting should be nearer than that. He remembered, too, the feeling of calm expectancy in the house on the hill: dinner over, everything cleared for action, nothing to do but play bridge until the *Stefanie* unloaded her cargo; and the dovecote, empty, ready for its prisoner. "Zero hour is too close." He turned her head gently to look downhill. "See where we are going. The bushes—the wall—and then straight north. Got it?"

"Yes."

"Once we leave this trail, move quietly. Keep your head well down. If I drop on my face, you fall flat, too. All right—here goes!" They left the garden wall and started down the rough path. He walked slowly, his arm around her waist. He looked at her. She had lost her fear; her eyes were wide, her face alert, but the strain had gone. "No questions?" he asked softly.

"Later," she said, and smiled.

She really believes I can get her out of this, he thought, and felt strangely more confident. Later . . . A very encouraging word, tonight. It implied a future.

From behind the shelter of the thin trees at the fork in the road, a man in rough clothes, as dark as the shadows around him, watched the couple leave the wall. They had stopped their love-making at last, and were now walking slowly down toward the main road. "They'll be here in five minutes at this rate," he told the man who had slipped down through the fields to join him. "What instructions? Hit and hold?"

"Eliminate. Both could be dangerous. They are on their way back to town."

"Dangerous?" They look harmless enough to me, he thought. Still, that wasn't for him to decide.

"We can take no chances with them—not at this hour. Now, let's see—the path is too open. We'll wait for them as they turn this corner to reach the harbor road." For a brief instant, he looked up the hillside. The couple, arms linked, were almost halfway down the trail. "Get in position. Let's see how the shadows lie." He led the way, carefully from tree to tree, over the rough ground. There was not much cover to work on. But he had begun their retreat just in time: the couple were still far enough away not to be warned by any movement. "We'll have to stand down there," he decided as the trees ended and the ground fell away steeply in a bank of bare rock to reach the road. "As near the corner as possible. Then they won't notice us until they come around the turn."

"They won't notice anything. They didn't even see you come down off the hill."

"I didn't intend them to see me," the other answered curtly. He slipped down onto the road. "Quiet!" he warned, as his companion's heel scraped against the rock. "No firing, remember! A shot from here could be heard clear across the harbor."

"I know, I know. Hit hard. And then?" There was no shelter here at all. The first man looked worriedly along the road to town that stretched around the harbor. No one there, *Gott sei Dank;* everyone indoors, eating.

"Hit very hard. Then we carry them. To the cliff over there. And drop them. A romantic walk—dangerous by night. What better?"

"It's a fifteen-minute haul up that headland."

"And five minutes back. That leaves us plenty of time to get into position again."

"It won't be so easy," said the man in the rough clothes. He disliked wearing them as much as taking orders from this jumped-up Czech colonel.

276

"You take the girl, then." The other was contemptuous. "These were the orders from the house. No suspicions of any kind to be directed toward it."

And that was that. *"Zu Befehl."*

"Quiet! They should soon be here."

"Pity that we had to lose sight of them."

"If we could see them, they could see us. Keep silent! Listen!"

A minute passed. Almost two. The man who had been giving the orders cursed under his breath. He moved back from the corner—he dared not risk looking around it—and scrambled quietly up the rock face of the bank, his big and powerful body moving lightly, cautiously. He advanced carefully through the trees, stood very still. He cursed aloud. The other came after him. "But where are they?" he asked, his eyes searching the empty trail up to the house.

"They have taken a short cut over the fields back to town. But it's too rough for the girl. They'll have to get down to the main road by the path behind that large hotel. Come!"

"But we can't get them there—"

"We can get them before they reach it." Quickly, he turned and jumped down the bank, started running lightly along the road in the direction of town. In two minutes, even less, he could branch up one of those straggling mule paths before he was near the hotel. He could intercept them there, near the little graveyard's wall. "We'll get them," he told the other, who was loping swiftly by his side. He believed it.

"Someone," Craig had said softly to Veronica as they came down the rough path from the house, "has just snaked down that hillside on our left. Keep looking at me. That's the way." So there would be two men down by the corner of the road, two sweet-cooing doves. "You're doing fine," he told her, and shifted his arm from her waist to let him clasp her hand. They were halfway to the road, almost at the clump of bushes he had chosen for their turnoff point. He could feel Veronica's hand tighten in his, making sure of her grip as she prepared to run. They kept the same steady pace, slow, nonchalant, for those last twenty yards.

Abruptly he pulled her off the path, dropping her case among the bushes, raced for the long stone wall and its dark band of heavy shadow. Shoulders bent, heads down, they kept on going. The earth under their feet was soft and loose, easier than he had judged. Then the field ended, and the rougher ground began. He pulled her down into the shadow of the wall. He put a finger gently to her lips. Together, unmoving, they sat with legs pulled up under them, well within the sheltering band of blackness.

Now it was the time to wait. They had only been running for a full minute, not much more. They were still too near the path for safety, yet the ground had become too difficult, too deceiving, to take at such a speed. Better to stake everything on remaining hidden from eyes that start scanning the open hillside, he thought, than on placing distance between the waiting men and us. So we wait; and we'll soon know if we managed to baffle them. They had to take cover from us down on the road. I saw a movement in the trees, and then nothing. How much time will they give us to appear around that corner? And when we don't? Well, we'll wait. And see.

He placed an arm around Veronica's shoulder and drew her close to him. They sat very still, keeping their silence. His eyes were fixed on the little group of trees down by the main road. Strange thing, this rising moonlight. It both hid and revealed unexpectedly. From a distance, roughness and smoothness could hardly be accurately judged; a dark shadow could be a hole or a sharp-edged rock. But there was one real piece of luck for them: the bay of Mykonos faced westward. So these long, retaining walls over the hillside all faced west, too. At this time of night, with the moon coming up behind them, the shadows were just right; a few hours later, the moon would be overhead, and these shadows would be gone. Luck? Heinrich Berg would share the same luck, but he would be contemptuous of that word. Why else had he chosen such and such a time, and such and such a place, if he did not make use of all the help both time and place could give him? Berg, or Insarov—there he sits peacefully in his quiet house, thought Craig, a man who likes his comfort and a game of cards with amiable friends. He has planned every move his agents make, every action. He has planned for months. And when someone unforeseen, like Sussman or Duclos, threatens the perfection of those plans, he is dealt with quickly, summarily, without benefit of hesitation.

Craig glanced at Veronica. She was watching him. Her blue eyes would be large with questions, if he could only see them clearly. He tightened his grip on her shoulders reassuringly, and looked back at the trees. Were we about to be dealt with in just that way? he wondered. As Sussman was? And Duclos? He wouldn't like to put that question to the test. Evasive action along this hillside seemed a more comfortable answer, even if the earth was cold and the stone wall hard. His back stiffened as he heard a distant voice. From the trees. A short phrase. Perhaps some kind of oath? He hadn't caught the language—perhaps it was one he couldn't understand. He thought he heard a scramble of feet over rocks. But he could see nothing. He took a deep breath. Waited. And then signed to Veronica that they were moving on, over the rough flank of hill stretching northward. Let's get as far away from that house as possible, he was thinking; as far away from that road into town, too.

He helped her rise, pushed her head down with a grin to remind her to keep as low as possible, and took the lead. They moved with caution. The need was for quietness, not haste.

Following the wall, the terraced fields falling away on their left, they passed the small headland and could see the beginning curve of the large bay. A deserted coast it seemed, with neither village nor hamlet in sight; rough and dangerous, perhaps, with cloud shadows chasing over a gun-metal sea and the far-off islands. Bare, bleak, empty.

"We've come far enough," he said, looking back. The house on the hill was no longer visible. Carefully, he selected an outcrop of rock just ahead of them that looked as if it might give better protection than any wall. "Down there," he told her, pointing. It would give them a good view of the narrow road (his map had been right) that followed the shore. At least, he thought thankfully, when the time comes to get back to Mykonos we can walk on a strip of hard-packed earth instead of scrambling over a hillside from shadow to shadow. As they drew nearer the outcrop of rock, it looked better and better. Its bulge and jut would shelter them completely from the house they had left behind them and from the rising moon.

He led her, quietly, around the prow of weathered rock, steadying her over the rough fragments underfoot. Then, suddenly, he heard a rustle. He turned to see two black shadows break off from the darkness of the wall of stone, reached for his knife, snapped it open. A strong hand gripped his wrist, a hard body turned his weight and threw him. He tried to twist free, to strike out. A knee pressed firmly down on his chest, a tight grasp was on his throat. He looked up and saw Partridge.

21

Blankly, Craig and Partridge stared at each other.

"Well," said Partridge softly, rising and letting Craig breathe again, "you do get around, don't you?"

"And where the hell did *you* come from?" Craig asked angrily, picking up the knife that had been smashed out of his grip. He rubbed his wrist, easing its numbness, and looked for Veronica. She had stopped struggling in the firm hold of a small, lean character who had caught her from behind, around waist and shoulders. Like Partridge, he was dressed in black, an invisible shadow once he drew back against the sheltering strata of rock. There was a third man, also dark-clothed, crouching over a radio set. He was now canceling the alarm he had sent out about the two prowlers who had come down the hillside.

At least, thought Craig, his anger beginning to subside into annoyance with himself at the way he had been so neatly ambushed, at least we seem to have got organized around here. And he felt better. "Are you all right?" he asked Veronica as they followed Partridge into the shelter of the outcropping rock. She took a deep breath and nodded.

"I took your advice," Partridge was saying, "and hired a submarine." He grinned and pointed to the bay beneath them. "Landed half an hour ago by way of a small rubber boat. Chris knows all about such gadgets." He nodded to the man who had held Veronica so effectively. "Colonel Holland, to be precise."

"Takes me back twenty years," Chris said, sucking the heel of his hand. "Used to pop in and out of Crete like that, right under the Nazis' guns." He spoke nostalgically, with a definite English accent. "No strain." He looked at his hand, still slightly bleeding, and then at Veronica. "And what on earth is a girl doing here?" he asked very quietly.

"I haven't the faintest idea," Veronica said with a touch of sharpness. "I just go where John pulls me."

Craig said quickly, "Veronica was being held at the house. I had to get her out before the balloon went up. They're expecting the *Stefanie* any minute now. So—well, I got her out. Our road back to town was blocked by two men. I thought it wiser to get as far away as possible from them. This seemed the safest direction."

Partridge and Holland had exchanged a long glance. Partridge asked, "And how did you get her out of that house?"

"No trouble, there. We walked out. Politely."

"Explain."

Craig explained. "Okay?" he asked worriedly as he ended.

Partridge looked at him blankly, checked a laugh. Okay? It could have been very far from that. Amateurs walked in where professionals would hesitate; and walked out, too. Politely. This one had also produced useful verification of a puzzled report: it had actually been Insarov himself who walked quite openly over the hillside to that house at dusk this evening. But if Craig had been held and questioned, if there had been time for Insarov to go to work on him? Partridge repressed his anger. "Okay," he said quietly. He looked at Veronica. "How much does she know about all this?"

"Nothing."

Holland looked disbelieving. He cleared his throat. His comment was quite clear.

"Nothing," Veronica said sharply. "I warn you I have a lot of questions. But I'll ask them when I feel sure I'll get some honest answers. In this last week, I've become very tired of lies." She drew the collar of her coat more closely around her neck, chose the flattest stone, and sat down.

Chris Holland watched her thoughtfully. This was not the time for light relief and pretty females. She was a complete nuisance on this hillside, but she knew it. He relaxed visibly. "Discreet," he admitted in frank surprise. She stared out at the dark fields falling away beneath them. He added, "You bite very nicely, too." She had to smile, then, and he could turn back to Partridge and Craig.

Partridge had been doing some very quick explaining: Elias had left Mykonos and circled widely over the hillside to join some of his men stationed along this bay, while Bannerman had been instructed to stay in Mykonos in charge of radio contacts. (Partridge did not specify, but Craig made his own guesses. There had to be direct links with the various groups on the hill as well as lines of communication with Athens, Smyrna, if not Paris.) But when it came to a report on the enemy operations, Partridge was more expansive. The *Stefanie,* lights out, had anchored briefly off a lonely stretch of shore farther north. She had unloaded two men and a large sack into a small boat, and then slipped out to sea under sail, lights beginning to show as land was left behind, a pretty picture of happy innocence. The small boat had brought its cargo safely into a cove where a man, a boy and a mule were waiting. "They have loaded the mule and left the cove. They're coming down that road," Partridge said, pointing toward the shoreline. "The boy and man are with the mule; the two men from the ship are following close behind. According to our reports, we'll sight them in ten minutes or so."

"There's the *Stefanie,*" Chris murmured, looking at the lights of a yacht some distance out at sea. "She has made a little detour, bless her sweet heart. I suppose she'll dock at Mykonos just as O'Malley is being brought to the house. Nice diversion." He noticed Craig's head turn at the mention of O'Malley. "That's why I'm here, if you wondered. O'Malley happens to be a special—friend of mine."

"I had been wondering," Craig admitted frankly. It had been easy to place the Greeks' interest in this operation, easy to understand the French participation. So O'Malley was a British agent, was he? "I've also been wondering why the hell you don't have that mule train intercepted right now. Unless, of course, you fellows like to do things the hard way."

"We would also like to catch the man behind it all," Partridge said dryly. "Before we make one move to find out what's in that sack, we had better be sure that we've picked up any of Insarov's men who may be stationed around this bay. Otherwise, there could be some warning signal, and Insarov would be gone. He's an expert in flight and concealment. He has had nineteen years of practice."

Craig looked down over the bleak flank of hillside, its shadows darkening as the clouds rolled in from the sea. "Who is picking up Insarov's men? The Greeks?" And one hell of a job that would be.

Partridge nodded, keeping his eyes on the road. He was no longer interested in the *Stefanie*. "They watched them take position an hour ago. It won't be too difficult."

"Not if Elias' men can move in as you did." Craig was still smarting from the way Partridge had pinned him down so easily. Dammit, he thought, I was supposed to know something about hand-to-hand combat at one time in my life.

"They're the experts," was all that Partridge said. "Chris, what about getting closer to the road?" He looked up at the sky. "Now's the time. In ten minutes, that cloud patch will have passed over."

"The nearer we get, the better I'll like it," Chris said grimly. Partridge moved quietly toward the man who was concentrating on the radio. There was a low mumble of voices—no doubt, thought Craig, the change in position was being given out, perhaps some new reports from Elias added to complete the picture—and then Partridge slid back to him.

"All set," Partridge said, trying to hide his growing excitement. "Elias is giving Insarov's men time to report that all is well as the mule enters the homestretch. Then he closes in. From their flank and rear. We intercept, down by that biggest group of rocks near the road. There's a mule path that branches up this hill from there, Elias tells me. That's the quickest way to the house. It's his bet that they'll take it. Ready?"

Chris nodded. He signed to the radioman to come along. "Always make sure of your communications," he told Craig. "Coming?" he added in his offhand way. "We could use you, if you felt like it."

That was obvious, thought Craig; there were a man and a boy with the mule, as well as the two men who had brought O'Malley ashore. He looked at Veronica.

She had read his thoughts. "I'm all right," she said miserably, and tried to smile. "I'd only get in the way down there." And it's no use trying to explain that I grew up fighting and wrestling with five brothers, she thought unhappily. "If I need you, I'll pretend I'm a dove." She smothered a small laugh.

"Come on," Partridge said to Craig, deciding for him. "She's well hidden here." The deep blue of her coat melted into the night. "Just stay exactly where you are," he told her.

"I won't even breathe," she assured him, and huddled still more against the rock.

"God in heaven!" Chris said softly, staring down at the white ribbon of road. Craig looked, too. The mule and a cluster of dark shadows had just appeared in view. They were still about two hundred yards away, he calculated, little black shapes slowly moving, steadily drawing nearer. Over the mule's back was a shapeless burden. It was one thing to talk of "cargo" and a sack being brought ashore; it was quite another to see it. Could O'Malley be alive? Craig looked at Chris, but the Englishman had already left, taking the most direct route to the road. Partridge had slipped away, too; so had the radio expert. Craig glanced around at Veronica.

She was watching the road. "What's the mule carrying?"

"A man."

She drew a sharp, quick breath. "Go! Please go," she told him. He moved off swiftly, making for the nearest stone wall, taking cover in every patch of available shadow. He is as good as they are at this, she thought with a touch of defensive pride; and they were very good indeed. She couldn't actually be sure that she was seeing them, now: movements here and there, yes; but what or who was moving, no. She thought she saw one black shadow reach the cluster of rocks by the road, and possibly a second. She stopped searching for them, and looked along the road, watching the mule and its sagging load.

I asked my first question, she thought, and perhaps I shan't need to ask any more. That answer was enough. She felt chilled to her spine, and it wasn't the night air that made her shudder.

22

Craig reached the boulders by the road. From above, they had looked fairly protective; down here, they seemed dangerously few, none higher than a man's shoulder. Still, this was the only real cover for a silent ambush. The drifting clouds had swept over and away, just as Partridge had predicted, and the moon was beginning to swim clear of their last seaweed-like strands. Soon, the road would be brightly lit until the next cluster of clouds came blowing across the land. But if the strengthening light made Craig uneasy, how much more would the men on the road feel exposed? They were about a hundred yards away from where Partridge and Chris waited beside him—the radioman had chosen a niche between two boulders, where he was already in contact with Elias and pleased with what he heard for his thin dark face split into a reassuring grin as Craig glanced at him curiously. And they were hurrying. Or trying to hurry. A mule took its own good time. Obviously, they were hoping to reach the path that Elias had mentioned before the moon was cleared of cloud and the road became too uncomfortable. It was possible, thought Craig, that their nerves were in a worse state than his.

How was Veronica? He looked over his shoulder, up toward where he had left her. He could see nothing except the deep band of heavy shadow under the long ledge of rock. He could stop worrying about her. It was the safest spot on all that bleak slope of hillside.

And where was Elias? Partridge had been talking in a whisper with the Greek at the radio. Now he edged back to Craig, noticed his eyes searching the hillside to the east of the road—to the west there was only a strip of land edging the restless sea—and nodded reassuringly. "They're out there," he whispered, just as Craig saw some shadows moving down the terraced fields from the north. "They've got their end well under control." He was silent for a long moment, perhaps thinking that his end had better be under control, too. One mistake, and the whole effort could be ruined. "The idea is this: as the mule reaches the boulders, Chris and I slip around them to get the two men at the rear. You step out in front of the mule and stop the other man. The Greek will deal with the boy. He says Americans are too trusting, that you might hesitate, think he is only a kid of sixteen, and then we'd be in trouble. That boy could make a quick run for it. Any warning at this stage could cripple the whole operation."

"I get it. No firing. How do I stop the man? Wave this around?" Craig drew the automatic from his pocket. It was a neat little weapon, more for close defense than any real attack. If his visit to Insarov had gone wrong, he could have found it very useful. Here, with open ground around and a chance to dodge and run, he doubted if any man was going to find it intimidating.

Partridge pulled a revolver and a silencer from a pocket, fitted them together, handed the complete weapon over, and took the automatic in exchange. "They'll be heavily armed. Our best plan is complete surprise. Don't let them have a chance to reach for a knife or a gun. All set? Remember—fast and silent, don't give him time to yell a warning. A shout could carry back to the headland." And there were two men near there, Craig remembered, guarding the approach to the house itself. Were they still searching for Veronica and him, or had they reported failure?

"All set," he told Partridge quietly, listening now to the plodding hoofs of the mule, the shuffle of quiet footsteps. Partridge and the grimly silent Chris moved past him, slowly, step by step around the boulders. Craig edged the other way, joining the Greek almost at the side of the road.

They crouched low, shoulders pressed against a curve of rock. Five seconds to wait, perhaps less . . . Craig counted them off. At two seconds to go, he heard the crack of a stick against the flank of the mule, saw its head jerking sharply, its pace quickened for an instant. Then it slowed back to its own rhythm, almost stopped. The boy was at its side, tightening a loosened rope around the shapeless sack. The man had his stick raised for another encouraging blow. Suddenly they stood still, looked back as they heard the sound of scuffling. The boy was reaching for his knife as Craig and the Greek moved in.

The man was quick, quicker than the boy. He whirled around on Craig, his stick aiming for the wrist that held the revolver, and then—as Craig side-stepped that blow—hit backhand at Craig's throat. Craig dodged, came in to strike down the stick with the butt of his revolver, struck again at the man's mouth opening in a shout. The man staggered, turned, tried to run. Craig struck for the third time, at the base of his neck. The man fell, lay motionless.

Partridge, a little out of breath, came to stand beside Craig, made a quick check. "Well," he said with cold satisfaction, "you didn't do him one bit of good, did you?" Then he went over to the mule, where Chris and the Greek were already starting to unknot the ropes.

Craig was still looking down at the man near his feet. I got mad, he thought, I got really mad there. He looked at the other two men and the boy, who were also stretched out on the road, and then at the obscene sack now being lowered gently from the mule's back. He took a deep breath. I guess we all did, he thought as he went over to help.

They carried the sack to the shelter of the boulders. In the moonlight, O'Malley's face looked like death itself.

"Alive?" Partridge asked.

Chris, listening for a heartbeat, didn't answer. Then he nodded. "Barely. Heavily drugged." He searched in one of his pockets, found small wire cutters, started snipping the cruel strands that bound O'Malley's wrists and ankles. He took off his jacket, covered O'Malley's thin shirt. "Where's Elias?" he asked irritably. "We'll need help."

"The vanguard's arriving," Partridge reassured him. Craig counted four men, then a fifth, coming down to the road. They were coming fast, caution discarded for the present in the mounting sense of triumph. But everyone seemed to know what to do. They worked quickly and silently. The unconscious men were dragged to the side of the road, their jackets and rough sweaters removed, their mouths gagged with tape, their hands and feet tied. Two of the Greeks were improvising a sling to carry O'Malley down to the beach. "A boat will pick him up there," Partridge told Craig. "Don't worry, we've got it all planned out. We hope. So far, it has worked." He pointed to the mule, then to the sack, now being partly filled with stones and spare clothing. "That's how we get close to Insarov."

"You are going to walk in?" The idea was so simple that it staggered Craig.

"Right into the dovecote. Four men, a mule, and a sack. That's how we get Insarov to open that big front door. Like to make one of the four? I'm serious. You know the way. You've seen the layout."

Craig glanced up the hill.

"She'll be all right," Partridge said, following his glance. "Elias is sending a couple of men to get her back into town. They'll soon be joining her. Sorry I can't spare any from here."

"Do they speak English?"

"That's the problem," Partridge admitted.

"Then I'll cut up the hill and tell her to expect friends. I'll join you on the mule path. Just point it out, will you?"

Partridge didn't look too pleased, but he pointed it out. "That's the one. And take care. We've a long way to go yet." He handed Craig a cap and a jacket. "You'll need these to make you look authentic."

The cap was too big, the jacket too small, but possibly that was very authentic. Craig stuck the revolver securely in his belt, and started looking for patches of shadow on the hillside again. Thank God, the clouds were thickening once more. Behind him, the constant surge of sea seemed louder, more insistent. The wind from the north had freshened. There was a salt smell to the air. He hoped that the boat picking up O'Malley would get him safe to harbor before any squall started. Poor bastard, Craig thought, he didn't even know he was with friends again.

Halfway up the hill, with only about fifty yards to go before he reached the rock strata where Veronica sheltered, he stopped in the shadow of a rough stone wall. And looked back. If he hadn't known about the activity and bustle down on the road behind those boulders, he would never have guessed just what was going on. He would have sensed something was happening, certainly. But what, exactly? It was difficult to judge. What had Veronica made of all this? She couldn't have had as clear a view as he had expected. He could imagine the questions piling up inside that beautifully shaped head with its smooth dark hair. Blue eyes and a perfect profile. Would he ever be given a chance to sit down opposite her at a harmless café table, and admire? Like a normal human being?

He had his breath back now after that wild crouching sprint up the hillside. He pulled himself up over the edge of the retaining wall, rolled over onto the next terraced field. He was thinking that some farmer was going to explode tomorrow when he saw his spring planting of barley. And at that moment, he heard a dove. It sounded again. It's one of them, he thought at first, flattening himself on the green shoots, motionless. Then he remembered. It's Veronica warning us. Veronica . . .

Veronica had been watching the road so intensely that she had not even noticed the man who had come over the hillside from the direction of the house. It was when he stopped abruptly, his feet scraping over a rough fragment of stone, that she knew he was there. And very near. She could hear his heavy breathing, as if he had been hurrying, before she caught sight of the crouching man. He was trying to find a place where he could see what was actually happening down on the road. He still wasn't sure. He half rose from his kneeling position, staring down at the boulders.

So he has just got here, she thought thankfully, once her first attack of fright and panic subsided; and there isn't so much to see down there at all, now. Five minutes earlier, and he would really have known what to worry about. He is so busy watching the road that he hasn't noticed John—I know it must be John who started up the hill toward me. But he will see him as soon as John leaves that wall. Oh stay there, stay there, forget about me, don't come! But he will come—oh, let me think, let me think. . . .

The stranger's breathing was normal now. He moved a step forward, and she could mark his profile quite clearly. He hadn't noticed her, possibly couldn't see her as long as she kept quite still within the rock's deep shadows. That was all she had to do. Keep still, stay safe. But solutions were never as simple as that. There was John, just about to come over that wall any time now. There were the men, three of them, following a loaded mule as it started forward. There were other figures, too, down there, melting away like silent ghosts. They had only been visible briefly, but that instant had been enough. She knew it, even before she glanced quickly back at the man.

He stood absolutely still, completely astonished, unbelieving, staring down at the road. Then he swung the strap of his radio free from his shoulder with savage haste, and, as he pulled out its aerial, stepped toward the shelter of the rock.

She came out of her feeling of helplessness. She called; called again.

John had heard her at least. She saw him drop to the ground as her hand searched for one of the heavier stones at her feet. She turned to face the man.

He couldn't see her clearly, even at this short distance. But he hadn't yet made his radio warning. "Boris?" he asked, took a step forward, then halted abruptly. His free hand reached into his jacket. Veronica rose and threw the stone.

It caught him sharply on his forehead, and he stumbled onto his knees, head sagging. His hand was still inside his jacket but the other arm had let the radio slip from its grasp. It lay beside him, its strap loose over his wrist. She reached for it, wrenched it free, hurled it aside. It didn't go far enough, not as far as she had hoped. "Oh!" she said in despair, and started toward it.

The man staggered erect, pulled his hand from his jacket and aimed. And in that split second between taking aim and pulling the trigger, a quick movement downhill caught his eye. He glanced instinctively to his left even as he fired. Veronica felt the breeze of the bullet kiss her cheek, heard the soft sigh of the revolver. She did not risk his aim being spoiled a second time, but dropped flat on her face. She heard another shot fired, again with that gentle sigh. This time it was the man who fell, and moaned quietly, and then lay still.

"Veronica!" It was John kneeling beside her, touching her gently, almost fearfully.

She tried to rise, to be practical, to be nonchalant, and only half succeeded. "He didn't have time to send out a warning." Her voice broke; she bit her lip.

"Veronica—"

"I'm all right. You spoiled his aim." She tried to laugh and failed in that, completely.

Craig lifted her and carried her out of the deep shadow to a softer patch of earth where he could see her more clearly. Again he knelt beside her. No, she hadn't been wounded. Bruised and shaken; but no bullet graze, no rock splinters. She was all right.

She lay back, looking at the sky. It had never looked so beautiful. I'm alive, she was thinking, I'm alive. . . . His arms went around her, drawing her up to him. She met his kiss with hers.

The ambush at the road had taken seven minutes by Partridge's watch. Seven minutes of delay; that was how Insarov would see it. He must have checked with each of his outposts as the mule had come on its hour-long journey, making sure of the time for each stage. And now there were seven minutes to be accounted for. "Keep your eyes open," Partridge told Chris Holland needlessly. "We may expect one of Insarov's men appearing on that hillside above us, just to make sure everything is all right."

Holland's high spirits had returned: his fears were over; O'Malley was alive and safe. "Ease up, old boy. All he will see is one mule, gaunt and revolting; three men prodding the poor beast along, giving a convincing imitation of real fishermen; and a very silent package being brought safely to the house. A little late, it's true, but you know what mules are. The worst part of this whole operation was getting that bloody animal to start up again. Thank God we had our Greek friend with us." He grinned widely. "A Greek-speaking mule. That's all I needed to send me to bed laughing."

"What did you expect it to speak?" Partridge was trying to take Holland's advice, but he was still on edge. Sure, everything was going well, but it was just at a time like this that something went wrong. It always did.

"You're a real worrier," Chris Holland told him cheerfully. "Craig knows how to handle himself. He will dodge any of Insarov's scouts and join us exactly where you told him to meet us. Where was it, anyway?"

"Before the path branches down to the main road again. I thought we'd better start up the trail to the house in full strength."

"Nice clusters of clouds." Chris looked approvingly at the veiled moon, and then at the rising terraces of bleak land, ridged with walls. "Sure we didn't land on the dark side of the moon?" But for all his light talk, he had his gun out first as the Greek spoke a low warning and nodded to the path just ahead of them.

"It's Craig," Partridge said with a surge of relief. Perhaps I do worry too much, he conceded to himself. Or perhaps when I've put in another ten years on operations like this one, I'll be as cool as Holland. Or perhaps I'll worry even more. Anyway, he thought, looking at Craig, so far so good. So far . . .

Craig had left the shelter of the low wall where he had been lying, and was taking his place in the procession. "Thought I had missed you. I had to wait until the two Greeks arrived."

"Didn't they arrive just when we got the mule going?" Partridge asked sharply. There had been movement up there by the rock strata. Too much damned movement, he had thought at the time.

"No. That was one of Insarov's men. He tried to send a message, but Veronica delayed him. And I got close enough to have a shot at him. Cancel that one."

"Pretty good shooting," Chris said.

"Not so good. I aimed for his knees and caught his chest." He paused. "He shot at Veronica."

"She's all right?" Partridge asked.

"Fine."

"But how did she delay—"

"Post-mortems later," Chris said, dropping his voice from its low tone into a whisper. "From now on, let our Greek friend do the talking." They had passed the small neck of headland and were almost back on the main road to Mykonos. In a few minutes they'd reach the sparse group of trees and the track that branched up to the house.

Partridge nodded, looked curiously at Craig, and wondered.

At the trees, the Greek urged the mule uphill with a couple of shoves and a flow of demotic oaths. Craig, the collar of his borrowed jacket turned up, the cap well down on his head, his face tilted as if he were watching the sack on the mule's back, must have passed unrecognized. He breathed more easily as he heard the cooing of a dove behind him, and then the answering call from the same old wall on the hillside. The rest of Elias' men, now surrounding the house, would find these two easy to pick up. The same thought must have struck the Greek, for he slowly nodded in solemn agreement as he made way for Craig to take the lead.

They came to the small clump of bushes where Veronica's case had been dropped, and then—as the mule decided to snatch a bite of spring leaves—were halted, milling around (the Greek cursing the mule's ancestry, blessing its lack of progeny, in a sibilant whisper), pulling and pushing and hauling.

Okay, okay, thought Partridge, anyone watching would think he now understood the delay of seven minutes.

Look out for that damned sack, thought Holland, and lunged at the rope as it began to slip.

That lousy mule, thought Craig, he'll nose right into Veronica's case and come up with it between those long yellow teeth.

The Greek's thoughts were totally unprintable even in the twentieth century. He vented them all in a kick where it would do the most good. The mule set off at a run uphill, one wisp of branch dangling from its mouth.

"Come on, Carmen," Craig said between his teeth as he caught up with it and grasped its rope halter. It quieted unexpectedly. The entry through the gate in the white wall was sedate, circumspect. Sweat could now break out on four brows.

Firmly, Craig turned the mule's head toward the path on his left. It was quite dark here, with bushes and shrubs growing wild. He didn't look toward the placid house, shuttered and quiet, not even when the front door swung open and a stream of light fell across the porch. A tempting target, he thought, but he did as he had been told and kept on going at the same steady pace toward the dovecote. The mule was amiable enough now, as it drew the dangling branch into its mouth inch by inch, chewing noisily. The Greek brushed lightly past him in the shadows, heading for the dovecote's door, a knife in his hand. Craig felt for his revolver. So did Partridge and Holland, close on his heels. The door of the dovecote was open. A small light burned inside.

The Greek stopped at the side of the door, motioned to the mule to hurry. Which it did not. He followed it into the stone-walled room. Someone spoke. The Greek replied. Then he must have struck, for something fell. The Greek was back at the door, beckoning them in.

"You know this character?" Partridge whispered.

Craig looked at the man on the floor beside a rough wooden table. He nodded. It was the man he had shouldered into the harbor. "One of the servants."

Holland had lifted the candle from the table and was also studying him, eyes narrowed, recalling a photograph in a secret file. Servant? Assistant chief of the secret police in Khrushchev's brutal cleanup of the Ukraine in 'forty-eight; promoted to full charge in the Hungarian investigations, possibly responsible for the betrayal and disappearance of General Maleter. The Hungarian Freedom Fighters would say a clean knifing had been too good for him. A nice little nest we've uncovered here, thought Holland, and exchanged glances with Partridge as he replaced the candle.

The Greek whispered a warning from the door. Partridge and Craig hauled the body to the side of the room, while Holland pulled the sack free from the mule's back and threw it on top of the dead man. That, he thought grim-faced, could have been O'Malley lying there.

Craig stood by one side of the mule, drawn against a wall, and kept his back turned to the doorway. Recognition was his chief danger, meanwhile. Partridge sat on the edge of the table, Chris stood in front of the sack; each had one hand nonchalantly on his hip, the other behind his back. The Greek loitered near the door, shoulders slumped, hands in the pockets of his ragged trousers.

Two men entered. Craig glanced briefly from under the peak of his cloth cap, saw one of the house guests and the other servant. Insarov was still taking his time, was he? Craig bent to rub the flank of the mule, and it kicked out gratefully.

The servant spoke sharply to him in a language he didn't understand. He nodded, keeping his head turned away, and tightened his hold on the mule. "Get it out of here!" the man repeated, now in German, then in French. He looked more closely at Craig, took a step forward. His back was turned to Partridge, giving a perfect target for the revolver butt that smashed down on his skull. Holland and the Greek moved simultaneously on the other man. The surprise was complete and effective. He went down like a wall of loose bricks.

"Never," said Chris Holland softly, as they used the ropes from the sack, along with belts and ties, to truss the two men as helpless as chickens for roasting, "did I think I'd bless that mule." He removed their weapons: an automatic and a revolver apiece, large caliber, fully loaded. Pessimists, he thought.

"We were obviously supposed to get it out of here," Partridge said, back to worrying. "But where?" We'll keep this element of surprise, he thought, if we don't step away from the pattern of their arrangements. "Did you notice any stable?"

Craig shook his head. "Let it chew its head off in the garden," he suggested, crossing quickly to the door as lookout. The Greek was more expert than he was at tying the unloosenable knot.

"And have Elias, when he arrives, think someone is waiting in ambush for him?" Partridge asked testily. No, it was too tricky having a mule blundering around the strange shapes and shadows of this garden. Dangerous, too, to keep it in here. It was restless, perhaps it had smelled the blood on the floor; if it started kicking, in one of its sudden frenzies, all hell would sound broken loose. It's always the way, he thought bitterly: at a time like this, we've got a mule on our hands.

Craig could see the upper side windows of the house, shuttered and dark. No gleam of light, either, from the direction of the porch. "They've closed the front door again," he reported. Dismay gave way to irritation, to real anxiety. It would have been better after all, he was thinking, if we had rushed the house when the door was first opened. A very solid door, he remembered; it would take a battering ram to force it open once it was locked and bolted.

"The problem is not insoluble," said the Greek quietly in excellent English and a highly educated voice. "We'll get the door open when we want it." He came over to stand beside Craig, smiled enigmatically, and looked not at the house but in the direction of the hillside to the north. He made a polite gesture for silence and settled to wait.

Wait for what? Craig wondered. He had his answer when a small blue flare, a safe distance away, shot up over the fields.

Partridge took a deep breath of relief: Elias was in position, Insarov's men had been neutralized, time to move in. At last, he thought, at last. . . . He beckoned to Chris, who had been spending those three last agonizing minutes in examining the contents of a large wooden box in the far corner of the dovecote.

Chris came forward, saying, "All their usual paraphernalia. Thorough questioners, those boys. They'd make the Inquisition look like a

Sunday-school picnic. Come on." He took Craig's arm and led him out onto the path. The Greek was ahead of them, dropping from his normal walk into a shambling slouch.

Craig looked around for Partridge.

"He's tying that damned mule to a tree," Chris whispered, and shook his head. Insarov would simply have put a silenced bullet into it.

The Greek was almost at the beginning of the path to the front door. He halted, drawing close to a tree, looking back. Chris halted, too, kept Craig with him. Partridge joined them, running silently. Partridge whispered to Craig, "You lead. Get us to the porch under the best cover you can. Okay?"

Craig nodded and started quickly up through the garden, desperately remembering the trees and clumps of bushes he had noted earlier tonight. The Greek was hurrying up the longer path to the house, quite openly, a messenger with urgent news.

Craig reached the side of the porch, hoisted himself over its wooden railing. Partridge and Holland followed silently. The Greek was almost at the steps. Someone had been watching the front path, for the door of the house opened. At the first gleam of light over the threshold, Partridge and Holland flattened themselves against the house wall. Craig was not quick enough. He stood motionless against one of the wooden uprights on the porch, and hoped its mass of encircling vine disguised his outline. He need not have worried. The Greek's wild string of sentences was holding all attention.

"What is he saying?" the woman's voice asked inside the hall.

The Greek came up the steps, speaking more slowly. "Dead," he kept repeating, "the man is dead." He gestured back in the direction of the dovecote.

"Dead?" a man's voice asked. The door opened more widely. He shouted back over his shoulder, "The American agent is dead!"

"*Achtung*—" That was Insarov's voice, clear, decisive, quick.

But the warning was too late. Partridge and the Greek lunged together, caught the man as he reached into his pocket, knocked him senseless. Holland had blocked the door, kept the woman from closing it. The front gate burst open; Elias and two men came running at full speed toward the house. The woman screamed. Holland and Partridge stepped into the hall.

As simple as that? thought Craig, and followed them. The woman had stopped screaming. She had backed away to the staircase but someone grasped her wrist and pulled her into the main room. Insarov was in there.

As simple as that, thought Craig. If he had had his way, he would have forced the house some fifteen minutes ago; and he would have failed. There would have been five men facing them, and no help from Elias possible. A little waiting was a necessary thing, it seemed. He glanced at his watch as he nodded to Elias. Fifteen minutes, all told, since they had first turned inside that front gate with a temperamental mule. Barely two hours since he had stood on this very spot and looked up that staircase, worrying about Veronica. The life and education of John Craig, he told himself wryly, and moved toward the room. At the door he hesitated, and let Elias join Partridge and Holland inside. He stood with some other men, a tight group of watchful faces, but made sure he could see Insarov. This was the moment he had promised himself: the dropping of the mask, the abandonment of that bland, benign look on the face of Heinrich Berg.

But the mask was still in place. If there had been alarm, or fear, it was under control. Berg—or Insarov—was standing at the fireplace, facing Partridge and Holland and Elias as the master of this house. Not even as he watched the handcuffs, which a Greek detective was clamping around the woman's wrists, did his expression change. Nor did Partridge's words make any impact as he pointed to the woman and said, "The French want her. Jeanne Saverne. Take her down to the house where they are holding Maritta Maas. Also the man at the front door. He is using a French passport."

"And I think," said Holland, watching the unemotional face staring so calmly at him, "you could put out the message to Athens for relay to Paris: Pear Tree is in full harvest. Then," he was smiling at the certain embarrassment on Partridge's face, but still watching Insarov, "Uncle Peter can be picked up."

"And we'll let Smyrna know," Partridge took over, watching Insarov, "that O'Malley is well, and in good hands. He is regaining consciousness in a nice soft bed. Also, we have caught Alex. His name is Robert Maybrick Bradley. We'll pass that news to Paris, too. Our agent there would be very interested in tracing his contacts at NATO."

"And I shall advise Athens," Elias said, joining in, watching Insarov, "to inform the Communist agent whom we arrested yesterday morning as he attempted to take a ship from the Piraeus that he might as well tell everything about the kidnapping and murder of Yves Duclos. Because the man responsible for Duclos' death has now been arrested." He nodded to one of his men. "Take him," he said, pointing to Insarov.

Insarov's cold glance lingered on them one by one: Elias, Holland, Partridge. I shall remember you, he seemed to be saying. He did not bother to glance at the four other men crowded near the door. They were the subordinates, only worth thinking about if he were to try to break out of this room. The time was not right for that. They were all too excited, too ready to fire their revolvers. It would be madness to reach for his. There was a suspicion of a smile on his lips, but the scarred eyebrow was markedly noticeable. "A mistake," he said ominously, watching Partridge. "Put away those silly pistols. What a ridiculous figure you cut!" Then he looked at Holland. "A man of your age, and of some experience no doubt, ought to know better than to come in here like an American gangster." And now it was Elias on whom the sharp blue eyes rested. "There will be repercussions. Very grave repercussions, indeed. You will be reduced to peddling fruit on the streets of Athens." He waved a hand, dismissing them all, and turned his back to look at the picture over the fireplace.

Elias said, "You are under arrest, Igor Insarov." He nodded to two of his men. "Search him."

Insarov tried to pull his arms away from their grip, then—as they swung him around to face Elias again—dropped all resistance. He even smiled. "Another mistake. Insarov left half an hour ago. You will find him on the *Stefanie,* now out at sea. If you can find the *Stefanie.*"

"Dear dear dear me," Holland murmured. "We did make a mistake. We forgot to tell him that the *Stefanie* and the cabin cruiser, and even that harmless sloop, were all boarded with little resistance, just ten minutes ago."

"Search him," repeated Elias.

"Take your hands off me! Diplomatic immunity!" Quickly, he repeated it in Greek.

The two detectives froze, looked at Elias.

Partridge shook his head. "Ah, that old story. Is it the best you can do, Insarov?"

"Search him," said Elias.

"My name is Pavel Ulinov, I am a citizen of the U.S.S.R. I am a special adviser to our Economic Trade Mission visiting Milan in connection with a projected contract for the sale of petroleum. I have the standing of assistant to the third secretary at our Embassy in Rome. I have full diplomatic immunity."

"He sounds almost convincing." Partridge was more interested in the revolver, the flat silver case with two bogus cork-tipped cigarettes inserted among the regular ones, the metal lighter, the heavy fountain pen, which were being taken from Insarov's well-cut blue blazer and crisply pressed gray trousers.

"He's a bloody arsenal," Holland was saying, examining the cyanide-gas pen very gingerly, and then the one-bullet lighter, and the poison cork-tips, before he laid them all out in a neat row on the card table. "I'd give this chap a body search. He's a really comic character. If he thought our pistols were stupid, God knows what he has taped under his armpit. You amuse me, Insarov."

There was the first sign of anger on Insarov's face. "My name is Pavel Ulinov. I have diplomatic immunity," he repeated, his voice harsh with controlled rage. "You will regret—"

"And now you are beginning to disappoint me," Partridge said. "You should know better than to try that gag on us. Diplomatic immunity does not extend to officials who operate outside the jurisdiction which grants that immunity. So cut out the double talk."

"I demand—"

"You demand nothing. Since when did the Soviet Union give diplomatic protection to a Nazi war criminal?"

There was complete silence.

"If you insist on claiming the protection of the Soviet Union," Partridge went on, "we shall give the full details of your Nazi career to the newspapers. In fact, there is a journalist on Mykonos, right now, who might think this was the biggest story of his career. Ed Wilshot."

"I believe you know his name at least," Holland said. His voice was becoming more and more gentle. He had been examining Insarov's revolver with respect. "Special job," he told Elias, "no expense spared." He laid it back in place on the card table to take the cuff links from one of Elias' men. "Really, my dear fellow, you fascinate me," he said to Insarov, as he found a hinge in one of the cuff links and sniffed at the powder inside. "You have a Borgia complex a mile wide."

"And once the Wilshot story was spread all over the front pages of the world," Partridge said with a grin, "what government, however much it has owed you, would even admit it knew you? No, you would be branded traitor at once, Insarov. Or should I say, Heinrich Berg?"

"I have never been a traitor. Heinrich Berg means nothing. To me, to anyone." The voice was tight, clipped; the words were spoken with dignity.

"Heinrich Berg is of no importance?" Holland asked too gently.

"None." The clever eyes were measuring the watching faces again, trying to gauge what they actually knew.

"Not even to the Israeli Vengeance Squad?" asked Holland, leaving the card table, sitting on the arm of a chair. "You know," he said almost conversationally to Partridge and Elias, "we might possibly make a telephone call right now to their man in Athens. That could be the quickest solution. It would spare the courts at Frankfurt a lot of trouble and expense."

The clever eyes flickered. The lips tightened. "I have been a trusted Communist agent for twenty-seven years. I saved many lives in the concentration camps—"

"Communists' lives. What about the others you sent to their deaths? Or don't they count?"

"There is no proof, no evidence, that such things happened. I did not look at a man's politics—"

"You didn't?" Partridge asked softly. "Professor Sussman thought otherwise. That was why you had him murdered, wasn't it?"

Berg looked at Partridge in bland astonishment. "Sussman? And who is he? I never knew anyone called Sussman. Your charges are a mockery, based on completely false assumptions. You have turned your opinions into facts. No court of law would listen to them, not even a Western court ready to believe any lies—"

Partridge signaled to Craig. "Would you step over here for a minute?" To the others beside Craig, he said, "Wait outside on the porch." Elias made certain of that by adding a quick phrase in Greek.

"Sure," said Craig, and left the doorway and came forward. "That's

Heinrich Berg. Sussman knew him. And he knew Sussman." He looked at Berg. "That is not an opinion," he told him. "That's solid fact."

Berg stared at Craig. The mask of confidence slipped. For at least ten seconds, he stared at Craig, desperately searching for an evasion, another plausible defense, a subterfuge. His lips tightened, his eyes narrowed, his voice rose. "And you are prepared to stand in court and swear to it? You are prepared to face the retribution of my comrades? You think I am the only one who pretended to serve the Nazis for the sake of a greater—" He had revealed too much. He caught his breath, forced back his anger. His voice almost returned to normal. "I say Sussman was lying. You say he is dead. I know nothing of that, either." His eyes looked vaguely around the room, noticed that the hall had indeed been cleared. The policemen beside him, now that they had searched him, were no longer holding him by force. They were waiting for further instructions, trying not to look baffled—as they must be—by the flood of foreign words they didn't understand. The older American was consulting quietly with the Greek; the Englishman was studying the ceiling with folded arms and bored insolence. Berg looked at Craig, the one man who was still watching him intently, and measured the distance to the card table as he pulled down the disarranged sleeve of his jacket. "My one mistake," he said, half to himself. The mask was back in place. "Is that how you like to imagine yourself?" He smiled tolerantly. Craig was empty-handed, his revolver stuck back in his belt.

"You made several," Craig said, trying to control his temper.

"Indeed? Name them." Berg took a few nonchalant steps away from the fireplace, clearing his path to the card table, and halted to face his accuser. The policemen had followed, but his arms were still free. "Name them," he repeated, almost conversationally, and could feel the policemen's suspicion subsiding at his quiet voice.

"Duclos."

"Duclos? And who was he?"

A man to whom I owe my life, thought Craig. He said nothing.

"Do go on, Mr. Craig. You interest me." The voice was friendly, the eyes aloof. He was thinking in quick complete jumps: the revolver, first—it's at the edge of the table; then Craig as a shield; then out of this room, into the hall; a farewell bullet for my one mistake; the door under the staircase—they haven't found it, there has been no alarm, Jeanne did not have time to use it—yes, surprise is the most powerful weapon of all. He glanced again at the Englishman's folded arms. Too casual . . . So not that way, Insarov told himself, and checked his move to the card table.

"Disappointing?" he asked the Englishman, and turned his back on the table. "You can remove that tempting revolver. I am not one of your wild Americans who shoots his way free. Why should I? I am innocent of all your charges." He addressed himself to Elias. "If you persist in this folly of having me arrested, I demand you take me at once to Athens where I can meet representatives of my government and prove my innocence. I am not, I repeat I am *not* Insarov. I am only here in this house as a guest. My real mistake, Mr. Craig—" he studied the younger American with cold eyes—"was to trust Insarov when I accepted his invitation to dinner and a game of cards. And—" he turned on Partridge now—"if I lied to protect my host—a foolish story about his escape on the *Stefanie,* I admit—it was only because he went to the dovecote and I thought I could give him a chance to escape. Or did you kill him? No doubt. Washington won't care for that, will they? They have this strange idea that a captured man will talk, give them information in exchange for a cigarette and a few kind words. I do know one thing about Insarov. He would not have been what you call a—a singing canary."

"So Insarov is dead, is he?" Holland asked softly. "And you only carry that little arsenal around with you for fun?"

"My life has been threatened twice in the last ten days. I am only protecting myself."

"Of course."

"Judging from your performance tonight, my precautions were thoroughly justified," Insarov flashed back. There, he thought, I've silenced the Englishman's sneering laugh. In better humor, he added calmly, "I know nothing of Sussman or Duclos. The men you have already arrested for their murders will not involve me in any confession you force out of them. You have no evidence against me at all."

"I have a list," Partridge said very quietly, "of three hundred and four men condemned to torture and death in a Nazi extermination camp. They were selected by Heinrich Berg."

"Fascists. Who weeps for them?"

"Fascists?" Partridge's anger came to the surface. "They never were fascists. Never! They were future leaders of a democratic Europe, men who'd oppose any totalitarian—"

"Berg was acting under orders, risking his life to defeat the Nazis. He will take his chances in a fair trial. World opinion will not judge him as you have done."

"World opinion? Or do you mean arranged demonstrations, carefully rigged picketing?"

Holland said, "I can see the placards right now. SAVE HEINRICH BERG! BERG WAS OUR ALLY, HAVE WE FORGOTTEN? BERG, SÍ; YANKEE, NO." He paused, added, "You know, Insarov, you have almost talked me into a telephone call to my Israeli friends."

"And tell them—if they abduct or kill me—they will lose *three* of their leaders! Two can play at their game!"

"Get him out of here," Partridge said tensely.

Insarov started walking slowly to the door of his own accord. "I know," he sympathized, "you must feel completely frustrated. Such a brilliant operation to end with the capture of the wrong man. What *will* Washington say?" He turned to the two Greeks, who were taking their place on either side of him. "Coming?" he asked genially. He was passing Craig now, ignoring him completely. "Are these really necessary?" he was saying to one of the Greeks, who had produced handcuffs. "I assure you I am more eager to get safely to Athens than even you are." He halted as if to let the handcuffs be snapped over his freely extended wrists. He brought his hands up in a violent blow against one Greek's throat and the other's jaw, lunged for Craig, caught him from behind with a tightly hooked left arm, reached with his right hand to pull Craig's revolver free from his belt, jabbed it against Craig's spine. "Don't shoot!" he warned. "Or Mr. Craig will regret it." He moved the revolver to the nape of Craig's neck. He felt Craig's resistance ebb. "That's wise. Now we back out. Into the hall. Steady pace." He unlocked his arm, gripped Craig's left shoulder, began his retreat to the door with Craig shielding him perfectly.

Craig took the first few steps backward, forced his body to relax. Desperately, he looked at Holland's watching eyes. One more step . . . He swung fast to the left, pivoting on the ball of his foot, dropping his weight to the floor. Christopher Holland fired from under the cover of his folded arm.

"My one worry was that I'd get you, too," Holland said to Craig as he walked over to look down at Heinrich Berg. He helped Craig to his feet. He waved aside Craig's word of thanks. "Just concentrate on getting your breath back again."

Craig looked down, too, and regretted the movement. He must have jerked his neck when he had made that quick lunge away from Berg. Partridge was saying nothing as he joined them.

Craig rubbed the nape of his neck, had three questions at least on the tip of his tongue, decided this wasn't the time. Then Elias asked one of them. "But *where* was he going?" He crossed quickly to the door, staring into the hall as if he could find his answer there. He waved impatiently to the two other Greeks to follow—one was still nursing his jaw as they clattered after him to the rear of the house.

Partridge came out of his thoughts, glanced quickly at the door. Bill and two of his friends had run in from the garden and were standing there, revolvers ready. "All over," he told them. "Bill, give Bannerman the signal to start sending. He knows what. And you can add the news: the big boy is dead. Details will follow." Once Bill and the Greeks had left, he added quietly, "I suggest that we keep Craig's name out of our reports about tonight. Much safer for him. No one heard him identify Berg, except us and the two detectives. Elias assures me they don't understand English."

"Much safer," Holland agreed.

Craig looked at them both. That answered another of his questions. "He actually has friends who'd—"

"You heard him, John," Partridge said. "That threat against you wasn't part of his bluster."

"Ex-Nazis who are Communis—" Craig began.

"Take our word for it," Holland said grimly. "They exist." He glanced at Partridge, lightened his voice. "Stop worrying about Washington. Tell them that if a dead man gives no information, he also commits no more murders. Frankly, I wouldn't have laid one shilling on his staying in jail. He would have weaseled his way out, or his friends would have pried him loose—probably just as well he forced the solution. He was a—"

Elias entered alone. "Yes, he could have managed it! He could have escaped." His face was tight with anger. "There was a door under the staircase; it has been blocked for four years, but no longer. It was made ready for use."

"Leading where?" Partridge asked sharply.

"Into a clump of bushes, planted there when the door was sealed up. The garden wall is only a few yards away at that point."

"It's still a ten-foot wall." Surely any ladder must have been discovered when the grounds were searched just after entry; not every man had crowded into the hall.

"There was a gardener's barrow filled with hard-packed earth against the wall."

"That would give him one step. He'd need at least two others."

"He had them. There were two wooden pegs, painted white, driven into the wall, one above the other. All he had to do was reach the top, roll over, drop down onto the hillside." Elias looked bitterly down at the body of Berg-Insarov. "This was the only solution, my friends." He glanced up at Craig, added somberly, "You were almost a dead man."

Which answers my third question, Craig thought.

Partridge rested his hand on Craig's shoulder. "The Greeks always have a phrase ready. All I do is tell you to get back to your hotel. There's no need for you to hang around here." He grinned and added, "Look out for the traffic, will you?"

"I'll do that." Craig glanced at Berg for the last time and left.

He came slowly out onto the porch. There were several men there, two of them bandaged, talking quietly, keeping guard over three firmly tied prisoners and a body in a sack. The woman called Saverne had already been taken away. The moon was high now, and in the cool night air there was the faint fragrance of a flowering vine. Craig took off his cap and tossed it away. There was a sympathetic laugh from the men around him; they were tired, they were hungry, they were filthy, but soon they, too, would be throwing off their rough clothes. He dropped his borrowed jacket over the mule's back, down by the gate. Someone had set it free, shooed it home, but it had just remained standing there, dozing in the moonlight.

That was the last picture he had of the house on the hill; a mule nosing in to a white wall, a torn gray jacket warming its sprung back, its ears twitching spasmodically as it dreamed of a life where there were bushes in abundance and no more burdens to be carried. Which reminded him. He stopped at the bushes and found Veronica's case.

The doves had been silenced, he noted grimly as he rounded the corner with its sparse trees and took the main road for Mykonos. The little bay seemed placid, sheltered from the rough sea by the long breakwater. The lights around the harbor were bright and welcoming. It was twenty-five minutes to twelve. In the big hotel, people had just finished dinner.

24

Craig was exhausted, but he never walked a quicker mile than the one that brought him around the bay into town. He came down the narrow ill-lit lane almost at a run, into the wide empty square with its Heroine of the Turkish Repulsion gazing out to sea from her central pedestal. Tony was lounging against her, hands in pockets, still dressed for the aborted picnic on Delos.

"Welcome back," he said, drifting over the square to join Craig. "Did you have enough exercise for one night?"

"Just about."

"We've heard the news. Don't rupture yourself trying to tell me all about it." He grinned widely. "If I sound slightly miffed, I am. And Tim Bannerman, in his own phrase, is fit to be tied. We missed out on this show completely."

"You had your share," Craig said. "You were promoted, I guess."

"Kicked upstairs to communications. I did get a little breath of salt air for a while—brought O'Malley back in a howling squall, and frankly, I was sicker than he was."

"Where is Bannerman now?"

"Still talking with Paris and points west. He's on the upper floor of that windmill just above the breakwater with a couple of other hardworking types. Don't tell him I know." He stopped, listening, his head cocked to one side. From a café along the water front came the music of a mandolin, a guitar and a zither. They were playing, in the strange half-tone scale of Greek folk songs, a brave attempt at "The Twelve Days of Christmas."

Craig halted, making sure; and mustered a smile.

"Much too good a tune to let die away unsung." Tony addressed the distant café impatiently in his low voice, "Come on, boys, come on. You finished the introduction six bars ago. Must do better than that for the party tomorrow night. That's the way!" Men's voices had begun to sing. In Greek. "I've only had time to get them as far as the sixth night," Tony said, "but we'll manage the rest tomorrow. Catchy little thing, isn't it?" He smiled delightedly as Craig began to laugh.

"Old Partridge is going to be fit to be tied, too," Craig predicted, recovering himself. But he felt better, much better, for that fit of laughter.

"See you tomorrow," Tony said vaguely, leaving Craig to cut up the little streets toward the Triton. He wandered down the front street toward the music, joining with the hoarse Greek voices in his flat tenor.

> "The sixth day of Christmas
> My true love sent to me
> Six geese a-laying,
> Five gold rings,
> Four colly birds,
> Three French hens,
> Two turtledoves, and
> A partridge in a pear tree."

Craig's pace quickened. He was still relaxed, still humming in rhythm to the flowing, ebbing tune drifting over the town from the water front. Tomorrow everyone would be singing it; by next week everyone would be dancing to it. Old Rosie, back in Paris, would never guess the influence of his brain child on the cultural patterns of an Aegean island. Craig began to laugh again, and then sobered up. He had come into the little square with its church and ghostlike houses. Other ghosts were wandering around there, too. He could see Berg stopping beside the church, looking at its small belfry; suddenly swinging around to look up at the hotel's high entrance under the heavy vine. Even now, thought Craig, I can feel the chill in my blood as I drew back, stood motionless, against that wall. The man is dead, lying in a room of rose-patterned chintz and pink lamp shades. If he were alive? I wouldn't climb these steps so confidently.

He reached the entrance under the vine. Madame Iphigenia, a

shawl around her shoulders, was there to greet him. "She is well," she whispered. "She would not eat until you came. I have kept food in the kitchen for you both. Hot food. You wash and change. In your old room. They entered. They searched. What a mess! We have cleaned it all. It is comfortable again." She fell silent, looking at him, taking the small suitcase from his hand, shook her head. "But it is good, now?"

"Very good." Then he smiled, and said, "Madame Iphigenia, I admire you very much."

He ducked under the low lintel of the door and entered the small lobby. One light burned there, casting a soft shadow. Veronica was sitting in a high-backed armchair. She had bathed, and washed her hair—it fell loose and clean over her face. She was asleep, huddled into a thick dressing gown that was twice her size.

He put his hands on the arms of the chair, bent down, kissed her gently.

She was awake at once, looking up at him with those wonderful eyes.

"I didn't mean to do that," he said softly. He kissed her gently again.

"All right?" she asked, still anxious. "Everything is—"

"All right," he told her quietly.

She looked at him. She smiled. "That will be my only question," she promised him.

"We'll have plenty of other things to talk about." He kissed her once more. "Plenty."